It was a happy scene...
The winter wastes; the igloos; cheerful, laughing, roly-poly faces —his friends, the Eskimos—the gentlest, most warm-hearted people in the world.

And they *were* cheerful, laughing, gentle, and warm-hearted.

And busy, active, playful.

In fact, when Dr. West tried to take a census, he couldn't be sure that he hadn't counted the same ones several times over.

Or *had* he?

And if not, how could they all be so very young? Where had they all come from?

But it was still a happy scene.

Then...

THE
ESKIMO
INVASION

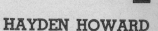

HAYDEN HOWARD

BALLANTINE BOOKS • NEW YORK

BALLANTINE BOOKS, INC.
101 Fifth Avenue, New York, New York 10003

To **Frederik Pohl**

Human enzyme for writers
Editor of GALAXY Science Fiction Magazine

Definition of an enzyme:
A complex organic substance that accelerates
(catalyzes) specific transformations of material

CONTENTS

The
Eskimo
Invasion

1.

LOVE
IS
THE
NAVEL

FEELING HIGH WITH FREEDOM, HE WAS DR. JOE WEST.

Like Icarus with aluminum wings, he thought quickly as laughter, his propjet engine singing.

Through the slanting Arctic sky, he flew the old de Havilland Turbo-Beaver as if he were the pilot. Over the ice on Franklin Strait he raced the shadow of this ski-plane.

Wryly grinning, he blinked at the glaring summer ice. Even this near the North Magnetic Pole the sea ice was breaking up like a psychedelic checkerboard. "Too late for a ski landing, too early for pontoons."

Ahead, ankle-deep in cracked ice rose the cliffs of what was supposed to be the Eskimo Cultural Sanctuary.

Welcome to Canada's living musuem, he thought sardonically, hoping the monstrous radar dome on the other side of the Boothia Peninsula was asleep. He'd been warned that what crouched beside that main Guard Station was one ancient F-111B swing-wing jet fighter on a steam catapult. *Trespassers will be violated,* Dr. West thought, his grin narrowing. *But catch me first.*

Instead of blundering north from Hudson Bay, he had chartered this bush plane from a more devious distance. Fifteen hundred miles away in Yellowknife he had begun his trip. Laughing, with his normally introverted personality turned inside out, last night in the Yellowknife airtel he'd been able to swing with his first really satisfactory sexual happening in nearly two years, and he knew why.

The world's most hopeless problem had been yanked from his shoulders in Berkeley. This month he'd been asked to resign as Director of Oriental Population Problems Research. Pushed into his sabbatical year with pay, he was trying to enjoy what he couldn't forget. Through the shrill singing of the propjet he raised his angry baritone:

> Pent-agon from whom all blessings flow,
> Praise Pentagon plans from here below.
> Praise them, all ye pro-fess-ors.
> Or lose your grants to younger whores.

He was an older thirty-four. The worst of it was, he couldn't even explain to Phyliss what was happening. *I'm hooked by the National Security Act. My mouth would be a traitor to my country.*

From the nesting cliffs rose dark-winged swarms. *Naturally these isolated generations of cormorants no longer are accustomed to planes*, he thought. But he was startled when something smacked against the aluminum wing, leaving a bloody streak.

"I'll take 'er!" the pilot shouted, violently awakening from his long forty winks.

In the bar in Yellowknife, the semilegal bush pilot had astounded Dr. West by asking a gigantic charter fee for this flight. "Me aircraft's me life! If we're arrested, I shan't mind jail for violating the Eskimo Cultural Sanctuary. It's the confiscation of me Turbo-Beaver! Ten years I've been scrimping."

A former R.A.F. ground crewman, he'd confided he left a wife and her mother in England's marmalade Newest Town ten years ago. Enjoying free transport to Canada, he'd discovered he was only another English-speaking statistic in the language race against the French-Canadians as he shivered through ten winters of commercial net fishing through the ice on Great Slave Lake. "Ten years of me life to buy this aircraft and fly."

As if fearing cormorants more than radar, the pilot lifted his pricelessly antique Turbo-Beaver high above the cliffs. "Which direction—we search—for the 'skimos?"

Peering down, Dr. West grinned with excitement. *No one's had a legal look at these people for twenty years.*

Barren hills protruded from muskeg still sparkling with snow. The Boothia Peninsula wrinkled south over the horizon. Larger than Vermont and 2,000 miles nearer the North Pole, it appeared empty of men.

As the plane banked, Dr. West saw flocks of geese rippling north. He looked north at the glint of ice still blocking Bellot Strait, that historically futile Northwest Passage. With awe, he saw these geese were flying north of the northernmost promontory of continental North America.

Beyond sprawled the hazy hump of Somerset Island, larger than New Jersey entombed in permafrost. The old buildings at Fort Ross had been removed twenty years ago when this vast Eskimo Cultural Sanctuary was voted by the Canadian Parliament. Dr. West visualized north of Somerset Island another five hundred miles of Sanctuary ice embedded with other islands of diminishing life extending into the Arctic Ocean where ancient ice curved over the world fifteen hundred miles toward the dim coast of Russia.

"Search south," Dr. West shouted through the whining of the propjet engine, "south along this west coast of Boothia."

"If any are still alive after twenty years," the pilot shouted. "Look for safer ice for us. Me aircraft needs to set down to refuel herself."

Dr. West stared down at glaring ice crisscrossed by pressure ridges. *For abrupt stops?* Against the back of his neck he imagined the hurtling fifty-five gallon drums of jet fuel. Massed behind him in the fuselage, those heavy drums of extra fuel seemed so flimsily tied. *Avalanche*, he thought. *Funeral pyre*. The reason *he* was here instead of those eager ethnologists and demographers from McGill University no longer was so laughably——.

"Big dark spot ahead," the pilot shouted, "on that rocky point."

Dr. West stared ahead at the rocky Jeffersonian profile of the point. On its chin, on the broadest ledge above the sea, he saw the dark indentation in the rock. As the aircraft approached and the ledge grew, he realized how huge it was.

"Too big for a campfire scar," the pilot shouted. "You think—something from the old days? Your government was setting up radar installations all over the North like pimples then. Maybe a supply plane crashed. But I can't see wreckage."

"No airplane would smash a pit that big in solid rock." Dr.

West imagined it was some sort of natural phenomenon, perhaps a dark extrusion of soft volcanic material which had eroded back, leaving this shallow crater. *But geology isn't my specialty.* Nor were bombs, but Dr. West visualized a tactical atomic weapon being tested here. Perhaps a meteor had blasted this oval scar in solid rock. He even imagined another huge Mars rocket rising from Russia, capitalistically malfunctioning and falling back here with a tremendous blast, and terrified Eskimos fleeing, trying to break out of the Sanctuary. "Crater's probably been here for thousands of years. Keep flying south."

South was by eyeball and gyrocompass. In the aircraft, the magnetic compass revolved and twitched. Dr. West thought the North Magnetic Pole was supposed to be in or near the Boothia Peninsula this year. To the disgust of cartographers the Magnetic Pole shifted erratically through the years as if following some mysterious drifting within the Earth's core.

The next rocky point, the next ice-choked bay, the next promontory showed no evidence of Eskimo occupancy. But dark leads of open water radiated outward from the promontory, a good place for seal hunting, Dr. West thought. In his eiderdown parka was his copy of the hurried census the McGill University ethnologists had taken twenty-one years ago while the cultural sanctuary concept was being debated in Parliament. The McGill census had counted 112 Eskimos. The next year, Hans Suxbey as first and only Director of the Eskimo Cultural Sanctuary had not permitted his former colleagues to return. For twenty years Hans Suxbey had battled to keep out all whitemen's cultural influences.

"We won't find nobody alive," the pilot shouted. "Without their Family Allowances, without kerosene or rubber boots or ammunition all those 'skimos have starved——."

"I see them! At the head of this bay on the river flats, their tents." Dr. West shouted with excitement: "Thirty or forty tents!"

This was a surprisingly dense concentration of Eskimos in one spot, he thought. Since prehistoric Eskimo hunters were able to support only a few children, probably there wouldn't be more than three children per tent, plus the man and wife, plus an occasional old person. He estimated an average of five Eskimos per tent. "At least 150 Eskimos. Perhaps they all gathered at this one river to wait for the summer run of char."

"Shore ice looks too broken for us to land—safely."

"Fly on down the coast." Dr. West thought this might be his only chance to scout the Boothia Peninsula from the air. "There may be other camps."

But the pilot circled. "Better to make me first landing attempts here—while I know I've plenty of fuel to lift her and try again."

The pilot kept circling the aircraft farther and farther from shore. "Better ice out here." He flew a downwind leg. On the base leg he lowered the flaps to 50 degrees. Turning into the wind the Turbo-Beaver sank down at eighty mph toward the ice, while Dr. West hunched forward as if he could duck all those fuel drums stacked behind him in the fuselage.

"Big crack ahead," the pilot remarked as the ice rose to meet them, and he advanced the throttle lever, making the propjet engine scream with last instant power.

Skimming above the ice, the Turbo-Beaver climbed. Scowling, the pilot attempted another landing pattern, while Dr. West tried to look nonchalant. Like a brick, the Turbo-Beaver dropped in. The skis skipped along the ice while the pilot slid the throttle lever past *idle* into *reverse*. The reversed pitch prop frantically beat the air as they slid toward the Mississippi-wide crack with the pilot shrilly cursing. Instinctively, Dr. West ducked. The Turbo-Beaver swerved alongside the open lead, momentarily tail into the wind, and spun around. Motion ceased.

"Piece of cake," the pilot laughed. "Me Turbo-Beaver may be old because her first owner bought 'er way back in '67. But twenty-two years old and she hasn't killed a pilot yet."

Dr. West was looking toward the distant shore. The tents were so far away they were specks.

"Hop out, sir. Help me work these planks under the skis. Shouldn't want to freeze her to the ice."

The wind felt sharp against Dr. West's cheeks as the pilot handed down his sleeping bag, rifle, camera and ninety-pound pack of supplies. He didn't want to sponge off Eskimos who might be starving. Staring at the shore he could see smaller specks moving among the tents.

"They'll come." Visible through the double doors of the fuselage, the pilot hurriedly was rigging a rubber hose from a fuel drum to the floor tank. "If we hear the F-111 overhead, I've lost me aircraft." Violently he began to hand-pump. "No use walking, sir. They'll come out after you."

Dr. West hoped so. Uneasily he suspected some of these Eskimos at some time must have attempted to leave the Sanctuary. They would have been turned back by the blue-and-white uniformed Guards. Logically, they might think all whitemen were their enemies. After twenty years of isolation, these Eskimos might have strange ideas about the world Outside.

"They're coming." The pilot called from his higher observation point in the doorway of the ski-plane. "Only one dogsled. Maybe a dozen 'skimos running behind."

Dr. West grinned with excitement. The McGill University crowd were so damn curious to know how Canada's Fifth Alternative for her Eskimos was turning out. But the ethnologists and demographers hadn't been curious enough to risk being arrested and losing their various research grants from the Canadian Government.

Dr. West knew the Five Alternative Program offered more varying life-possibilities to Eskimos than the U.S. offered to Indians or Anglo-Saxons. With a less cumbersome population than the United States, Canada had become more flexible in dealing with her people and economy. He hoped Canada was becoming a guide dog for the United States.

The loading doors of the Turbo-Beaver slammed shut. The cockpit window opened. "Pick you up at this camp, one week from today."

"One week?" Dr. West bleated. "We agreed one month."

"The way this ice is breaking up, in a month I'll be lucky to walk away from the crash. Impossible to land——."

"We agreed on a month. Come back with pontoons."

"Should of thought of this sooner, I should." The pilot was glancing up at the sky as if he expected to see the F-111B circling like a hawk. "Eskimos travel. Probably gossip like old ladies. Word of me aircraft will spread from this camp to the Guard Stations."

"There's supposed to be no contact."

"Those Guards are human, sir. 'skimo girls are a bit of all right, I hear. Even in a week, word about us may travel to the Guard Station, and you'll be arrested. If I come back in a month, I bloody well know I'll be flying into an ambush. Me aircraft's me life!"

Dr. West stood looking up at the pilot. What could he say?

The pilot said: "Allow me another week for engine trouble before you walk out to the Guard Station and give yourself up."

"I could survive all winter," Dr. West retorted. "I spent an entire year with the last primitive hunters in Alaska."

"I'll be back for you in a week. Be ready." The pilot started the squealing propjet, and the Turbo-Beaver taxied across the ice, its fuselage dimpled with two decades of dents. Screaming faster and faster, it lifted itself, fleeing, shrinking away to the west.

Because Dr. West had ninety pounds of concentrated foods, plus rifle, sleeping bag, camera, notebooks, binoculars and other whitemen's paraphernalia, he didn't walk to meet the sled. Discouragingly, it had halted on the ice. The specks were clustered beside it. *Are they arguing what to do about me? Theoretically, they've been segregated from whitemen for twenty years.*

He hoped they would greet him with shy grins and outstretched hands like those last Alaskan wanderers, whose daily lives resembled Canada's First Alternative for her Eskimos. They trapped a few furs and were in debt to whitemen. Seasonally pious, they hung around missions and suddenly were gone. The Canadian Eskimos of the First Alternative reappeared at Government Posts to collect their Family Allowances. With much flour and bacon, and harmonicas playing and raisins fermenting and old women dancing, they celebrated all winter. The Canadian Government still hoped the other Four Alternatives would end this alternative or at least tidy it up.

The Second Alternative encompassed the Eskimos permanently working at Government Posts or at Arctic airfields and mines or in the growing Arctic transport industry. Their children more regularly attended school.

The Third Alternative had grown from the Second. Eskimos with more education migrated to the cities. There was a Professor of Sociology at McGill who had been born in an Eskimo village. These Eskimos simply were vanishing into the Canadian melting pot. Their Eskimo cultural heritage was lost.

The Fourth Alternative was Canada's pride. Eight years ago Dr. West had lived for a year with the Co-Op Eskimos of Bylot Island and Baffinland. But the first Co-Ops had begun far back in 1958 at Ungava Bay near Labrador. During the next thirty years these Eskimo Co-Operatives had spread throughout the Northwest Territories. In spite of its ponderous bureaucratic title, the Cooperative Development Section of the Industrial Division of the Department of Northern Affairs and Natural Resources shrewdly and patiently had helped these Eskimos learn enough self-confidence to begin making their own group decisions. From carving soapstone art objects the early Co-Ops expanded to quick-freezing fish, to breeding reindeer, to shipping meat, to renting shops as sales outlets in cities. After guiding sportsmen, Eskimos cooperated to construct tourist airtels. From investing Co-Op self-help funds in new Eskimo ventures, Co-Op Eskimo groups ventured into the stock market. They owned houses, boats and ice cars and watched TV and smoked cigars. The Co-Op Eskimos had created a strong subculture, which no longer was Eskimo.

"The true Eskimos are vanishing," an Assistant Professor of Ethnology at McGill University had cried out before a Parliamentary Committee more than twenty years ago.

A Fifth Alternative for Canada's Eskimos was needed, Hans Suxbey had pleaded; and an excerpt from Hans Suxbey's speech even had been published in California in a 1968 *Sierra Club Bulletin*, intensely read by a thin high school sophomore named Joe West. "We try to preserve species of trees and animals from extinction," Hans Suxbey was quoted. "But we extinguish mankind's distinctive ways of life. What is a man? He is his way of life. Preserve him from extinction. In this increasingly homogenized world any independent way of life has increasing value for its own sake. Think of Eskimo culture as 5000 years of the hardiest men ingeniously creating a distinctive way of life which survived the worst blizzards. But one hundred years of cultural erosion from our kerosene and rifles, our bacon and flour, Family Allowances and outboard motors, transistor radios and so-called schools propagandizing our way of life has almost erased the Eskimo's heritage. Eskimo culture must not die!"

The Fifth Alternative for Canada's Eskimos officially began in 1970 when Parliament voted a small appropriation to indemnify existing private interests in the North and to administer the vast new Eskimo Cultural Sanctuary.

"We must stay out." Even Director Hans Suxbey's specially trained Cultural Instructors, a dozen graduate students of Eskimo ethnology, were withdrawn from the Eskimo Cultural Sanctuary as planned after the first winter. "The natural environment is the true teacher of Eskimo culture," Hans Suxbey had announced nineteen years ago. "Not even I will violate the Eskimo Cultural Sanctuary."

Dr. West wondered how the 112 Eskimos who happened to be on the Boothia Peninsula then had reacted when their rifles or cooking pots were taken away by earnest graduate students. Evidently Parliament didn't think democratic choices extended this far north. These abruptly isolated Eskimos' only opportunity to vote had been with their feet. Now there was antipersonnel radar along the invisible boundary. The windows in the Guards' patrolling helicopters reportedly had one-way glass. Dr. West wondered what these approaching Eskimos thought had happened to the world.

At this distance the Eskimos appeared faceless. Spreading out, they left the sled behind. There were twelve of them, seeming short and stocky in their shapeless parkas.

Dr. West opened his hands. Desperately he smiled. He thought Hans Suxbey had reported to Parliament every fifth year about these Eskimos, barely enough details of their "cultural progress" as observed from his helicopter to support another appropriation for his Guards. Theoretically, for nineteen years no whitemen had talked with these people.

They were returning his smile! With the hoods of their summer parkas turned back, their shaggy black hair gleaming, their wide-cheeked faces smiled so youthfully that Dr. West kept turning his head, expecting to discover a more weathered face, a leader. A young man hurried forward and extended his hand, smooth as a child's. Beginning with a whiteman's handshake, elaborating it into a ceremony, the young Eskimo raised their clasped hands as high as his forehead and then down to knee level and peeked up through his unkempt locks at Dr. West. Shyly they both smiled.

"This person," Dr. West began speaking about himself in halting Eskimo, "has come with open hands as a friend———."

"Eh! One of us? All men speak the same?" The Eskimos crowded around him, all shaking his hand, laughing as if with relief. "That old Peterluk lied."

Dr. West realized this one with the smallest hand was a girl. Her lustrous black hair was tied back in a bun. As if casting aside conventional female shyness, she smiled up at him. He laughed with pleasure. They all laughed as if they had been friends forever.

"This person's name is Edwardluk," the young leader laughed, shaking his hand again.

It was reassuring that this Eskimo was willing to expose his name to a stranger, Dr. West thought, laughing inwardly at the Director of the Cultural Sanctuary. Hans Suxbey would be outraged by such an un-Eskimo name as Edwardluk. Ever since the nineteenth-century invasion by the whalers and missionaries, for over a hundred years Eskimos had been donning the most powerful Biblical names and adding Eskimo endings. But *Edwardluk*?

With the ultimate in hospitality Edwardluk was murmuring: "You must live with us forever."

Dr. West picked up his camera and rifle and reached for his sleeping bag, but Edwardluk insisted on carrying it. As if showing off the power of his manhood, Edwardluk shouted at the girl to carry the big pack. Dr. West watched her bend, squat and heft the ninety pounds of supplies weighing nearly as much as she, but she staggered solidly across the ice toward the sled. Edwardluk shouted encouragement after her with such pride of ownership that Dr. West thought she must be his wife.

"Ha! We go!" Edwardluk insisted that Dr. West sit on the sled and ran alongside shouting: "This person—has killed—a poor little seal—unworthy of a hunter." Edwardluk grinned with so much pride that Dr. West suspected it was a large and fat seal, and he began looking forward to sinking his teeth into seal meat again.

Ten years ago his summer with the wandering Alaskan Eskimos had been the happiest of his life, and now he felt excitement like a child returning to a summer cottage. Shouting, laughing, romping, these Eskimos seemed to radiate happiness as they manhandled the sled across ice ridges. Now trotting beside them, Dr. West warmed to the exercise, feeling better all the time.

As they approached the camp, an amazing number of children swarmed out on the ice to meet them, laughing and skylarking and running alongside Dr. West looking up at him as if he were a giant. Ahead of him in the camp he saw that many of the dark spots were not tents. They were piles of beach stones and driftwood, elevated caches to separate the meat from the dogs, but there were surprisingly few dogs. Beside the largest tent, an Eskimo hurriedly was tying dogs to another sled.

Dr. West noticed no kayaks or umiaks, and he suspected boatbuilding was one part of traditional Eskimo culture Hans Suxbey had not encouraged them to re-create.

As Dr. West walked across the thawing gravel shore, up in the camp dogs yelped. The Eskimo behind the largest tent was whipping his dogs. Yelping, they dragged the loaded sled across the slope in front of the cliffs, surging north along the ice foot, that dangerous ledge of ice clinging to the foot of the cliffs. One shapeless Eskimo lay on the sled. As the man ran alongside, Dr. West saw the long glint of metal in his hand. And Dr. West smiled, imagining Hans Suxbey's outrage because this departing Eskimo was carrying a rifle.

In the camp, Dr. West realized the actual number of sagging caribou skin tents was only about fifteen. At five Eskimos per family that would be seventy-five Eskimos. But so many children were running back and forth, there seemed

more like 175, he thought, smiling down at the brash little
boy who kept grabbing at the stock of his rifle and being
dragged along. The boy stopped. Smiling, he looked back at
the sky.

A distant whining sound in Dr. West's ears grew to a
screech as the F-111B appeared from the west. With its
swing-wings spread, the obsolete fighter flew relatively slowly
over the sea ice from Franklin Strait on over the Boothia
Peninsula, heading east. Presumably it was returning to the
main Cultural Sanctuary Guard Station on the east coast of
the peninsula. Dr. West was not pleased to see the jet fighter
returning from the direction in which his English pilot's
Turbo-Beaver had gone.

"Whiteman's skua bird," Edwardluk remarked, evidently
unimpressed as he stared after the vanishing jet fighter.

This comparison further disturbed Dr. West. "Why do you
call it a skua bird?"

"Chases other whitemen's birds," Edwardluk answered as
Dr. West was afraid he would. "Old Peterluk says its beak
has many rifles. Old Peterluk says there are two white men
inside. Is this another lie?"

Dr. West looked around, expecting to see an old man in
the camp. "Where is Peterluk?"

Edwardluk's smile widened as if in embarrassment. "Peterluk has gone hunting." Edwardluk glanced north along the
ice foot where the sled had disappeared around the point.
"This person thinks Peterluk has gone to pray for more
power. This person thinks Peterluk is afraid of you. Eh-eh,
Peterluk even took his old wife. He said you would be a
whiteman and we would not be able to understand you, but
he lied."

"Have you ever seen a whiteman?" Dr. West supposed
Edwardluk must have been a baby twenty years ago when
the Cultural Sanctuary was established.

"Peterluk said you would be a whiteman," Edwardluk
side-stepped the question, his smile more embarrassed, and he
murmured: "You are so much taller. Are you going to——.
You are a whiteman?"

Dr. West answered softly. "My name is *West*." Trying to
explain the meaning of his name, Dr. West pointed with his

own boldly un-Eskimo nose in the direction the afternoon sun was sinking. "*West* is a good man's name and Edwardluk is a good man's name and we speak the same language," Dr. West's voice rose hopefully. "We are friends forever."

Edwardluk's smile gleamed like the morning sun. "We are brothers, all of us." His hand trembling on Dr. West's arm as if with excitement, Edwardluk guided him into the low-straddling tent of ancient caribou skins.

Children scrambled on an unsteady pavement of flat beach stones. Dr. West stumbled over the bloody carcass of a seal. In the dimness of the tent, another young woman smiled from behind the cooking lamp. "Cut meat!" Edwardluk shouted proudly, and she giggled but obediently snatched up a crude saw-toothed stone and chopped at the bared ribs of the seal.

The other girl finally staggered into the tent carrying Dr. West's ninety-pound pack. With a gasp she tried to lower his heavy pack to the stones without dropping it. Dr. West stepped forward, almost reaching out to help her, but this might be a social error which would offend her pride. So he simply watched her. As she straightened up again, breathing hard in her tattered caribou-skin parka, she looked him straight in the eye, which startled him, and he grinned. To his surprise, she grinned back, not at all shyly, her white teeth gleaming, her dark eyes sparkling. Her gaze was unflinching. *Not exactly the traditional self-abasing Eskimo woman*, he thought, beginning to suspect these isolated Eskimos might be rather different from the traditional Eskimo ideal Hans Suxbey had in mind.

"Cut meat!" the other woman said loudly to her, and both women crouched beside the seal carcass. They giggled in traditional female fashion, and the other woman returned to the lamp, which was the female command center of the tent.

Dr. West stared at the cooking lamp because it was not the traditional shallowly hollowed soapstone slab. Dr. West thought it might have been smashed out of a whiteman's white porcelain bathroom fixture. But it had such a shallow curve it couldn't have been broken from an ordinary toilet or urinal. Nearly two inches thick, two feet long and nearly as wide, its whiteness was disguised by gummed seal oil and soot. Its shape was a jagged oval so shallow he thought it could have been a fragment of—even a gigantic hollow ceramic ball. He gave up speculating for the moment. His main desire was that these people should like him. He didn't want to start asking questions like a nosy ethnologist, which he was not. He grinned, thinking Suxbey wouldn't approve of this un-Eskimo seal oil lamp.

In the framework of sticks above the cooking lamp hung a square soot-blackened artifact. Boiling inside this ancient five-gallon gasoline can, the chunks of seal meat began to bubble their rich aroma, whetting Dr. West's gustatory memory. While Edwardluk courteously made small talk about the early summer, so early the open leads surely would freeze again, Dr. West equally courteously asked no questions of his host. He watched the woman behind the strange ceramic lamp using a bone splinter to press down the long floating wick of cotton grass into the seal oil, shortening the smoky line of flame. He realized these Eskimos had added a wall of clay inside the mysterious concave ceramic object to separately contain the chunks of seal fat. Warmly melting, the fat seeped oil replenishing the lamp.

Since the lamp was the female power center of the household, Dr. West thought the woman tending it must be Edwardluk's wife. With a forked stick she prodded from the can a steaming chunk of meat. Smiling, she dropped it on a floor stone to cool. The other young woman, who had carried his pack, promptly picked up this hot chunk. Smiling down at it instead of up at him, she handed Dr. West the fat-dripping meat. "Best piece for you."

Having lived in Alaskan Eskimo hunting camps, Dr. West unhesitatingly sank his teeth into the juicy meat. Slicing in front of his nose with his stainless steel hunting knife, he chewed heroically, gulped and swallowed, his eyes squeezing shut with delight. "Good!"

With savage joy he filled his stomach with more meat than he'd eaten for five years. To his surprise, he realized he was even outeating Edwardluk. *This is impossible. An Eskimo can outeat any whiteman. Perhaps he's just being polite, allowing me to seem the more impressive eater.*

With unrestrained Eskimo pleasure, Dr. West belched cavernously. Delightedly, the housewife urged more meat upon him until he leaned back on the sleeping platform. The other young woman's folded knees had provided his backrest. "This person will chew your boots," her voice said against the back of his neck.

Dr. West laughed the way Edwardluk laughed. "This person is so pleased that you think of him. But the skin of my boots is always dry and does not need to be chewed. It is called *silicone rub-ber*. It breathes out air from the foot. But it does not breathe in water."

Now the boys were being fed, six of them. The two largest were teen-agers, apparently too old to be the children of the young woman behind the lamp. Then both the young women and five little girls like stairsteps ate, but amazingly little, Dr. West thought.

Smiling like any matron at the end of a successful dinner, the woman withdrew her arm inside the wide sleeve and reaching around inside her parka brought the baby to the front. Its fuzzy head nursed vigorously.

"So many children," Dr. West began so that it sounded like a compliment rather than a question.

"Eh-eh, many sons," Edwardluk agreed with pride.

"Eleven children, more than the fingers of my two hands," Dr. West outwardly marveled, inwardly doubting. "You are both so young."

"More than my fingers and my toes," the woman behind the lamp added shyly.

"You are the mother of more?"

"Three are older than Marthalik," she said, smiling past Dr. West at the young woman whose knees supported him, "and two who are younger but already have babies of their own. Grandfather Bear is pleased with—them."

The knees behind him hardened, and Dr. West turned his head thinking surely Marthalik and the woman nursing the baby had to be sisters. Their smiling faces seemed equally young. Were they lying? This young mother obviously couldn't have produced twenty children, some already older than Marthalik. "You are her sister."

Marthalik's small hand rose to cover her startled giggle.

"This person is only the daughter of my mother, and Edwardluk is my father."

Dr. West blinked at Edwardluk, whose smoothly unweathered face indicated he still was in his twenties. By their thirties, the faces of Eskimo hunters were seamed by wind and frostbite. Edwardluk's wife, smiling behind the lamp, still had the fresh face of a teen-ager. Dr. West wondered why Edwardluk had adopted so many older children. Had their parents died?

"This person wonders what it is like Outside," Marthalik said boldly behind him, her breath close to his ear.

"Marthalik is a bad one who frightens away the boys," Edwardluk laughed. "They are afraid she will ask them to take her *Outside* again."

"This person walked on the winter ice," Marthalik's soft voice added without laughter. "Where the lightning fence does not go, where Peterluk said our grandfathers fled, this person walked because——."

"The mosquito chased her back," Edwardluk laughed, and Dr. West imagined the Guard's mirror-windowed helicopter swooping down.

"What is out there?" Marthalik said anxiously. "This person knows you are a whiteman."

"Outside are many whitemen," Dr. West sighed. "White whitemen, black whitemen, yellow whitemen, more whitemen than all the birds nesting on all the cliffs." He grinned at Edwardluk. "None serve so much good seal meat as you, nor are their tents as warm with happiness."

Edwardluk laughed with pleasure and pride, but Marthalik's hand tightened on Dr. West's arm. "Old Peterluk, he says in the old days hunters traveled far to get good things to eat from the whitemen. No one was hungry. Before Grandfather Bear came down from the sky, all hunters owned loud rifles. Peterluk says——."

"Peterluk is an old man," Edwardluk interrupted, and a hint of unhappiness appeared in his smiling conversation. "Peterluk is a bad old man who lies. Sometimes he boasts he has the only rifle in the world; there was never another rifle."

"Then Peterluk is," Dr. West guessed aloud, "the man with the big sled and many dogs who———."

"Peterluk ran away from you," Marthalik said firmly, her knees against his back, "because you are more powerful."

Dr. West couldn't help smiling at this. He was no warrior but he liked her compliment. From his parka he took out the notebook and looked through the list of names the McGill crowd had given him from their census of twenty years ago. There were two Peterluks listed. One was described as about sixty years old then, so he would not be this living Peterluk. The other's age was listed as twenty-three based on Family Allowance records. The McGill census taker had not seen this Peterluk but counted him anyway because: "Peterluk, years ago, fled with the wife of—another man? Her name was Eevvaalik," Dr. West added.

"Eh-eh, even then Peterluk must have been a bad man," Edwardluk laughed. "Now he flees from you again with Eevvaalik, but she is only an old woman now, a woman who talks too much," Edwardluk added, smiling past Dr. West at Marthalik.

Smiling, Dr. West watched Edwardluk's wife oiling the baby.

"Do you remember when the whitemen took away the rifles?" Dr. West asked her bluntly; if she'd lived long enough to produce twenty children she should remember what happened twenty years ago.

She hung her head. "This person can remember the last caribou."

"That was four winters ago," Edwardluk said loudly, making a spearing motion with his arm, grinning and trying to redirect the conversation to himself, the hunter. "This person speared so many caribou his arm died!" A right-hander, he reared back and threw an imaginary spear past Dr. West, who glanced at Edwardluk's wife.

"How many winters ago," Dr. West asked her deviously, "was Marthalik born?"

Beside his shoulder, Marthalik giggled. Her so-called mother looked confused, studying her fingers as if she had lost count.

"A hungry winter," Edwardluk said loudly, "when Marthalik was born. No caribou. But," he laughed, "we did not leave her on the ice."

"Grandfather Bear would not permit it," Marthalik retorted spunkily. "No one leaves a baby on the ice."

"Peterluk still says babies should be left on the ice," Edwardluk sighed. "But we could not do that even when our other children were starving. Babies must live even if there are no more caribou for parkas."

"There are no more caribou?"

"No more for three winters," Edwardluk sighed, but then he smiled: "This person is a killer of many seals." Proudly he waved his arm toward Dr. West. "Give this big man more meat!"

Dr. West felt Marthalik moving beside him. Her hand pressed a juicy chunk of meat into his. "You eat so much because you are stronger than Peterluk," she said. "That fierce old man, he fled from you with such speed because you are stronger."

Dr. West laughed and chewed his meat; it felt good to impress a pretty woman, even better than when he was Director of Oriental Population Problems Research, which had impressed certain women, but his satisfaction now was more——.

"Even though he is an *angakok,* with powerful magic," Marthalik said emphatically, "Peterluk fled from you because you are stronger."

"Eh!" Dr. West agreed. "Even though he has a rifle——."

Children were wandering in and sagging down against him in sleep. He tried to count them but they kept moving around and he was too full of meat, too sleepy.

It was a pleasure to be an—Eskimo again. Lying back against Marthalik's supporting knees, he watched Edwardluk's wife spreading out the caribou skins. *No more caribou?* Dr. West supposed the Director had not tried to teach his first Eskimos conservation because it was not an authentically primitive concept. Obviously Hans Suxbey's staff of instructors had not taught his Eskimos birth control. Such a large proportion of children indicated the population in the Sanctuary now must be increasing rapidly.

"Where are the old people?" Dr. West muttered. "Everyone in this camp seems—young."

"Eh?" Edwardluk pondered the question while sleepily scratching himself; without his parka he was revealed as a rather wolf-ribbed young man, still lacking that good belly from years of successful hunting and eating which was a primitive Eskimo's pride. "Peterluk says the other old people ran away—out of this land before we remember them. Sometimes Peterluk says the star frightened them away from the Burned Place. Is it the Navel of the World? Peterluk says the reason he camps there is to find more power. But his only power is his rifle. Peterluk tells so many lies, even a whale vomiting a man—alive! All of this happened long before this person was born."

Patiently Edwardluk played with the drowsy children, urging them naked under the caribou skins. They slept side by side in a long row on the sleeping platform. Watching, Dr. West smiled, feeling peace and inner warmth as if he were part of the family. Her plump skin glowing, Edwardluk's wife slid under the worn old caribou skins. "If this person may speak, that old Peterluk never should be believed. He never has good dreams, so how can he understand? He does not even believe in Grandfather Bear's love for us."

Blinking with drowsiness, Dr. West undressed into his sleeping bag. Leaning on one elbow, he tried to count the children now that they were motionless under the caribou skins. Fourteen? He recounted and got seventeen. *Impossible. Maybe some of them are twins—, or triplets or——.*

He glimpsed Marthalik rising sleekly from the caribou skins. His pounding heart startling him, he looked away. He heard a crunching sound, and he watched her. Firmstomached, she was kneeling beside the seal carcass, tearing loose a rib. The sinuous light from the lamp moved on her smooth skin. Her jaws crunched through gristle as she chewed her night snack. And he smiled to himself. All her darkly shimmering hair was drawn back, coiled up on her head as beautifully as if she were a modern city woman. Dr. West felt he had seen her hairstyle before: Phyliss proudly wearing a dark wig to that last performance of the San Francisco Opera Company, Phyliss striding ahead remote.

Loudly chewing, Marthalik was moving. Squatting down, her thighs and buttocks swelling, she bent over the seal's rib cage, her breasts moving forward in the soft light from the lamp.

Dr. West closed his eyes, breathing too hard. Apparently she was at least eighteen, he thought. *None of my business.* Keeping his eyes closed, he tried to count, not seeing sheep. His heart was so quick; even this tired he couldn't relax. *Go to sleep. In two different years you lived with Eskimos as a detached observer.*

Day and night, the Alaskan Eskimo hunting camp had exploded with crude merriment, but he'd had his own pup tent and all those University of California graduate students to look after and set an example for—for some reason, although he'd been only twenty-four himself.

When he was twenty-six, in the Canadian Eskimo town on Baffin Island it already was such a wealthy Co-Op that behavior seemed dominated by middle-class strivers with what they prudishly imagined were middle-class morals. The wife-trading took place in middle-class Berkeley, not on middle-class Baffin Island. Never, he thought, had he seriously experienced any serious desire for any Eskimo woman, and he smiled sleepily. Hardly ever——.

With his eyes closed, restlessly turning inside his soft sleeping bag, he could hear Marthalik walking back across the rattling floor stones. Now she was sliding under the caribou skins. In his warm sleeping bag he buried his face. *Forget it. Sleep, dammit,* he thought. *Among primitive Eskimos the main cause of violence,* he thought with self-cooling realism, *always has been passion. So stay away from their women and keep a harpoon out of your heart.*

Fighting his excitement, he couldn't sleep. Restlessly twisting in his sleepless bag, he turned his back. *My god, how did I end up in here?* Trying to cool his excitement, he deliberately circled his thoughts back into his old grief, his distant guilt. Deliberately he remembered his father's robust face gasping in breathless agony.

His father had been one of the "Flying Doctors of the Sierras." In his memory, his guilt revolved like the blades of the copter descending toward the mountain lake. His father was smiling at the controls, and he was nerving himself to disappoint his father. He remembered his father's raised eyebrows as the copter sideslipped, unable to hover in this alpine altitude. Cheerfully out of the smash his father climbed. "You're all right, Joe. Let's find the patient." The trout fisherman had suffered a coronary. Because the copter was inoperative, they tried to pack him out. Down the trail, Joe still was nerving himself to tell his father. Unhappy as a premed student at the University of California where his father had graduated, Joe had wanted to change his major to anthropology or demography, population statistics, anything instead of medicine, and he told his father this further down the trail. The patient lived. In the airtel in Bishop that night his father died of a massive coronary while Joe bent over him unable to do anything against death.

After that Joe West studied premed so desperately he was offered medical scholarships to three top schools. He chose Harvard Graduate School of Medicine because it was a continent away from Berkeley and his mother, who had remarried so soon—so terribly soon. Against death Dr. Joe West suffered from intern to hospital resident, still corresponding with Phyliss. From a sprightly graduate student in demography, Phyliss was becoming Dr. Phyliss Byars, Assistant Professor on the Berkeley Campus, still single.

In Massachusetts, Dr. Joe West was being reassured by his hospital chief that he might be happier in research. Dr. West's research paper on *Endocrinology of Hibernation in the Arctic Ground Squirrel as a Guide to Hibernation in Space Flight* led to his first research grant from the Defense Department. Now he didn't have to peer down at the faces of dying patients and see his father.

Continuously he wrote Phyliss. She wrote she couldn't marry, "this summer because I've been invited on the Ethnology Department's little study of the Alaskan Eskimos. What we need, and a live one is required by the Regent's because there'll be grad students along, is our own doctor to pass out the aspirin and chaperone the grad students. But who will chaperone us chaperones? Volunteer?"

Before the expedition left Berkeley, Dr. West gave the required physical examinations to the members. Phyliss failed. At this irony she laughed: "You've already signed your contract. You go without me." And he had. Since then their relationship had been strained.

Far from Phyliss, he had been fascinated by the sharp balance of life on the Alaskan tundra. The closeness of death was less disguised than in cities. The expedition's demographer was a pessimist. Population was pressing against starvation all over the world in spite of cheaper birth control devices.

Dr. West thought he was making a second start in his life when the expedition returned to Berkeley and he enrolled in Phyliss's lecture class in demography, population distribution. Earnestly he attended graduate seminars in human ecology. Ecology not-so-simply was the branch of biology concerned with the interrelationship of living things with their environment and each other. By the time he earned his Ph.D. in human ecology he knew how he intended to fight death. He had bargaining power in the military-industrial-academic power complex because he was a rare *interdisciplinary* man. He had an M.D. research background in human glandular processes plus a significant Ph.D. thesis: *Socio-Medical Political Approaches to World Population Control.*

Within three years, his proposal to the Defense Department drew to the University of California the largest federal research grant outside the "weapons" field. The men he recruited for this broad spectrum study had such a bizarre range of talents he was reduced to being another embattled administrator. "Joe, even when you're with me all you talk about is——."

"Dammit, Phyliss, you're the one who's cold." So they'd never quite married. As Director of Oriental Population Problems Research the day came when he was human enough, guilty enough, to try to suppress the most terrible aspect of their research.

Now his only escape from what had happened was sleep——.

He was startled awake by a child scrambling over his sleeping bag. Blearily, he saw that the caribou skin roof resembled a star map, hundreds of little round holes glowing with the morning outside. Each hole, his thoughts squirmed sleepily, marked an exit from the living caribou of a wriggling fly-larva as big as this child's finger which was poking him.

"Hi." Dr. West sat up in his sleeping bag, and the surrounding children giggled. "So you know a better purpose in life," he laughed in English at them as he struggled into his pants, "than making children laugh?"

Outside the tent, the sun's reflection from the gleaming wet gravel and glaring snow patches blurred his vision as he looked for Edwardluk. From the corner of his eye, he watched Marthalik scraping a pegged-out sealskin, her head lowered. She should have made some Eskimo kid a valuable wife, he thought and grinned. She was smiling up at him.

"You sleep so long," she said, "this person thought perhaps your spirit had risen to Grandfather Bear."

"You mean died?" he laughed; was she teasing him?

"No-no! Some day you will understand—when he comes." She rose, smiling again. "This person will boil your meat." While he ate, he teased her a little.

"This person may be small," she laughed back at him, "but stronger than certain men who need wings to fly."

"You mean me?"

"How could that be?" She feigned innocence. "Wave your arms and you will fly like an *angakok* because you are so big and strong."

Dr. West laughed at himself, wondering if Marthalik was considered too quick-witted and outspoken, insufficiently self-abasing to be an Eskimo boy's ideal of a wife.

"Will you help me?" He drafted Marthalik to be his introductory emissary to the women in the other tents. It would be dizzying to attempt a direct age-sex census of so many children running back and forth outside. From the thawing tundra pranced little boys holding up lemmings they had caught to be boiled and eaten. Little girls squatted among boulders scraping off gray-green lichen the missing caribou also used for food. As the hillside emerged from the thawing snow, swarms of children were gathering everything edible. To begin his census, Dr. West visited the mothers in their tents.

As if he were King Charles on a royal visit, the excitedly jabbering women in the tent were rearranging old seal bones, sticks and other important furnishings. Finally, he asked this giggling mother how many of the twenty names she had given him really were her children. The mother hung her head in silent embarrassment.

Marthalik whispered delicately in his ear. "She is being modest. She has had many more babies than her fingers and toes. But the others have married and gone away, and she is ashamed because she has forgotten their names. She was an old woman when this person was born, so she must have had babies as many as three times her fingers and toes."

But the mother appeared to be in her twenties.

Dr. West scowled at Marthalik. She was teasing him again? Her smile faded. She insisted these women never had twins. But he knew the physiological child-producing limit for the human female was less than thirty full term babies. All of these children could not have come from this one mother. He turned to Marthalik to ask why she was putting him on. But Marthalik was walking away. He realized his disbelieving scowl had hurt her feelings. He wanted to rise and hurry after her.

Instead he tried to interrogate this mother as to the ages of her children. He became baffled trying to write their ages opposite their names. For at least eight names, she kept murmuring: "First summer."

"Which ones are seeing their second summer?" he sighed in defeat.

"That winter was too hungry for my babies." Staring down at her fingers, she managed to name only four living children in their second summer, who he presumed were—all two years old?

"These four," she said, "are seeing their second summer. The others are gone to Grandfather Bear," she sighed. "This person used their names again this winter. This time they are alive because the whale fed us."

Dr. West stood up. Wearily he hoped when he'd interviewed enough mothers, the true age-sex census pattern for the camp would become more clear and this woman's confusion about which were her children would be explained. In anthropology courses he'd learned that some primitive peoples have ingenious adoption procedures. "Are many men and women who are your relatives—away hunting on the ice now? They have left their children with you?"

As if he had hurt her feelings, the mother sniffed and turned away.

Retreating to the gravel beach he saw Marthalik sitting alone on the skeleton of the whale.

She lowered her head as he approached. He hoped her feelings weren't still ruffled because he'd scowled at her. He looked down at her bowed head. She looked up at him. Suddenly, they both smiled.

Dr. West's foot poked the whale's rib. "You ate this whale?" he laughed.

She giggled. "The mosquito shot it very fast."

"You mean the Sanctuary Guards' helicopter shot it with a machine gun——?"

"Eh?"

"I think some of the Guards tried to help you." Dr. West knew modern technological aid to these Eskimos was a violation of the whole Sanctuary concept and of the Director's orders. Even from their copter the Guards must have seen there would be mass starvation last winter, and they had risked their jobs, killing the whale.

"Is it permitted for this person to ask a question?" Marthalik was watching his face. "Out there—are they people like us?"

"Didn't Edwardluk tell you? Doesn't your father know?"

"My father says everything has always been like this. He says for me to be happy and babies will come. He says not to believe Peterluk."

"Old men remember the way things used to be."

"But old Peterluk says many men came out of a whale," she protested, ducking her head and shoulders under the arched jawbone. "Would not men drown inside a whale?"

"Perhaps this was an iron whale built by the whitemen."

"Even old Eevvaalik says Peterluk lies, and she is his wife. Eevvaalik say only one man could come out of a whale and his name was Jonah. Every time Peterluk tells his lies, there are more whitemen. He says the whitemen must have killed all the caribou. Is this so?"

"This person does not know," Dr. West replied, "but will

find out. Truly, most whitemen would want to help you—with more food."

These Eskimos seem so well adjusted now, Dr. West thought, if only they had an emergency food supply they might be happier without any other whitemen's help. Perhaps Hans Suxbey, Director of the Cultural Sanctuary, was right when he wrote: *A people are happiest when their whole culture is like a single sunflower with the petals of their religion, songs, sexual customs, artifacts and economy all consistently growing from the flower's single center. Through their distinct history the ancient Eskimos achieved a beautifully unified culture.*

But during the last century the introduction from the Outside of such conflicting cultural petals as whitemen's technology and several religions had caused the flower of Eskimo culture to disintegrate.

Dr. West knew his own presence here already was disturbing this unstable cultural group. What he reported to the Outside, Dr. West thought as he looked down at Marthalik, eventually might result in the disintegration of this small new Eskimo culture. Unless he were careful, he might destroy the essential meaning within her life.

"The whale is a good place to sit," she said, and he sat down beside her.

"Because you are strong," she said, "this person hopes you will see the bones on the hill."

He assumed she meant caribou bones. "Are there still enough seals? Do the hunters say——," he asked, "will there be enough seals this winter?"

He was watching a distant hunter on the shore ice dragging in a small seal. Running happily out were the children. When he turned his head he caught Marthalik smiling at him. Her hand rose. Instinctively, Dr. West took her hand. She blushed, ducking her head.

"There will be enough seals," she murmured, "because Grandfather Bear will come for us from the sky. This person hopes you to rise, too." She had a warm hand as she stood up.

Smiling to himself, Dr. West stood up holding her hand. These Eskimos still were trying to integrate a hundred years of Christian teachings with a million years of animism. *Is this Grandfather Bear anything more than the Christian concept of a Second Coming?* Was she telling him that The Day of Judgment was close at hand?

As he walked up the hill with her, Dr. West thought he should reconsider before turning in any report to those overeager ethnologists and anthropologists at McGill University. *Eskimos aren't faceless dolls to be played with for academic advancement.* He knew the McGill enemies of Hans Suxbey hoped his report could be used in Parliament to break open the Sanctuary. *Those eager anthropologists would invade with more gum-chewing grad students than there are Eskimos.* He shortened his uphill strides, realizing Marthalik had been trotting to keep up with him.

The hill still was shrouded with snow but dark boulders were emerging.

"Many bones here," she said, and her hand sought his again.

Among the dislodged rock piles, scattered as if by the powerful digging efforts of a huge carnivore, he blinked at splintered rib bones, small femurs, crushed skulls. "My god! Hundreds of children."

"This person can remember three winters ago when she was small and hungry. Under the snow we found rabbit droppings and chewed them." Surprisingly, she laughed. "This winter we had the whale."

If so many children died, Dr. West thought quickly, *how is it there are such hordes of children in the camp?* Such an overwhelming proportion of children had to put an exhausting winter burden on the few adult hunters. This child glut appeared even worse than in parts of South America, where half the population was under fifteen years of age. *This Eskimo population must be multiplying even faster than South America's,* he thought. Down there in the *barrios* of South America the attitude toward family planning lagged far behind the Vatican's. Up here in the Sanctuary there was neither whitemen's contraceptives nor traditional Eskimo infanticide. *Each winter there will be more children starving, more women starving———.*

As he squeezed Marthalik's hand, he knew he was going to

attempt whatever help was necessary to shield them from starvation this winter. *You will not starve*, he thought strongly.

"This person will not starve?" She was staring up at him, openmouthed with surprise.

Dr. West blinked. "You heard me?"

"This—this person does not know—what she heard. In her head——."

"I thought too loudly," Dr. West laughed in reassurance, inwardly startled because this hadn't happened to him since Harvard Med School when he used to do beer-party tricks. He'd spooked one tall kid named Tom Randolph so badly Tom transferred to the Psychology Department and still pestered Dr. West every few years, even offering free beer, but Dr. Tom Randolph's receptor tests with him had become increasingly inconclusive. *Thought I'd lost the old feeling*, Dr. West thought. *Marthalik, Marthalik, can you hear me?*

"Soon the fish will come out of the sea," she was saying, looking far down the hill at the river where women were arranging lines of boulders in the estuary shallows for a fishtrap.

Marthalik, you are so pretty. Now he was thinking so hard at her he wasn't breathing, and his eyes blurred. *Marthalik— so pretty.*

Swaying, grinning, he thought this should be one message which must reach into any woman if any message could, but Marthalik was chattering about seal meat. He wasn't contacting her now. He'd never been able to break through to Phyliss. *Marthalik, look at me!*

But she was looking down at the camp. "Tonight this person will hand you the best pieces of seal as if——."

"As if what?" he laughed, challenging her.

Shyly she ducked her head. Walking down the hill she stopped. She struggled to pick up a boulder. "This person needs it!" She looked up at him helplessly.

He picked up the boulder she'd been unable to lift. He thought it weighed perhaps twenty pounds, less than a fourth as much as his pack she'd carried, and he grinned down at her. She was looking away as if afraid to look at him while they walked down the hill. He guessed she was teasing him

again, but he'd never been able to read anyone's mind. He
had enough trouble reading his own. "This boulder has a
pretty dimple like your cheek."

She giggled. But when he bent as if to put the boulder
down, quickly she seized his hand. "Please!" Her face flushed
as if with embarrassment.

"This boulder is as heavy as you are," he joked.

She said nothing as they walked down the hill together.

Toward them children ran giggling and scampering around
him, staring up at him and tittering. Loudly shouting people
flowed out of the tents, smiling up at Dr. West, whose face
was beginning to feel hot. Edwardluk rushed out of the tent
at him with such speed that Dr. West thought for a moment he
was being attacked and almost dropped the boulder. But
Edwardluk yanked it out of his hands. Surrounded by laughter Dr. West retreated after Edwardluk into the comparative
privacy of the tent, but everyone was crowding in. Marthalik's mother placed the dimpled boulder beside the lamp.
"——as pretty as her navel," she was saying in the uproar,
while Eskimos laughed and Dr. West blinked. He thought
he'd learned quite a few Eskimo customs, and this was not
one of them. But he wasn't 100% stupid.

Marthalik was beaming with happiness. Sitting behind him
at the evening meal she handed him the best pieces of seal
meat as she had predicted she would. As if she must make
sure the meat was good enough for him, sometimes she
would take a quick bite, chewing thoughtfully, then handing
the chunk to him. Others she rejected, searching for a better
piece for him.

With a full stomach, warm and comfortable beside her,
Dr. West's pleasure began as a chuckle at himself and grew
into a mighty laugh worthy of a hunter. Beside him Edwardluk's laugh rose from his belly. "You are a strong man.
Eating even more than this person again."

With increasing frequency during the evening Edwardluk
shook Dr. West's hand. "Grandfather Bear will be pleased."
Plainly Edwardluk was more pleased every minute.

In the crowded tent, hot with bodies, children scampered
out of their parkas. Uproariously, hunters told ribald stories.
Dr. West noticed one unobtrusive little boy speculatively

rubbing his finger round and round in the dent in the boulder. Edwardluk's laughter exploded at him, and the boy fled. "That small boy can't even harpoon a baby seal."

Edwardluk tried to dance with barely room for his feet to come down. Guests clapped their hands and swayed. Marthalik snuggled against Dr. West. In the mounting heat, visiting Eskimos were taking off their parkas. But this evening, although her forehead glowed with perspiration, Marthalik did not take off hers. Whenever he turned his face toward her she quickly looked down at his other hand resting on her bootleg. Her ear seemed red. Her cheek was flushed.

"Everyone must rest," Edwardluk shouted through the uproar, and the adults laughed except Dr. West who was looking at Marthalik, whose averted face was red with—embarrassment? She wasn't smiling now.

He squeezed her hand. She smiled a little.

Loudly the guests began to depart. Several girls glanced back at Dr. West, giggling as they ducked out of the tent. As the lamp's floating wick flickered and dimmed, and children dropped into sleep, and Edwardluk's wife slid out of her parka and under the caribou skins, Dr. West removed his hand from Marthalik's waist. With the caution of the experienced and overly responsible bachelor, Dr. West already was trying to foresee the future for himself and Marthalik. In only six days he would be gone. *If the bush pilot returns, would I leave these people now?*

Gently he opened the fingers of her hand, sliding his finger across her spreading fingers. "Marthalik, Marthalik, little one, in five days, six days, this person will be gone. The whitemen's bird——."

Her hand closed around his finger. Turning up her face, her eyes wide, she whispered: "You have told me. But this person thinks—this person hopes—no one leaves this land."

He smiled at that. She smiled up at him, and his finger touched the huge dimple in her cheek. Her huge eyes closed, and she turned her face against his chest. Against his ribs he felt the quick beating of her heart. He touched the smooth rim of her ear. As if startled, her body jerked. She moaned, which startled him.

With all these unpredictable people here, *what if she*——? He too vividly remembered one distant night as a college freshman he'd parked with some indecisive girl who unexpectedly screamed: "Help!" He'd fled out of his own Mustang.

Against the tent wall gleamed Edwardluk's ivory-barbed harpoon. Elaborately asleep under the caribou skins Edwardluk and his wife apparently didn't even need to breathe. Their heads were turned away in the other direction, and they seemed to have fallen asleep as suddenly as if hit on the head. But a little boy was sitting up, grinning at Dr. West. Dr. West scowled threateningly at him, and the little devil's grin widened.

Abruptly Dr. West tried to decide against any involvement with Marthalik—tonight. He started removing his hand from her waist inside her parka. But his rising hand under her breast insisted she must be a mature young woman who——. With excitement he felt the touch of her fingers upon the back of his hand, pressing his hand upon her. Within her parka, he realized she had withdrawn her arm through her wide sleeve as she leaned back. His fingers gently made love to her firming nipple, and she sighed. As his lips touched her ear, he saw far beyond but in compressed perspective that naked little devil still sitting there grinning.

With irrational fury Dr. West wished this budding little fiend would explode in hellish flames. More rationally he dragged Marthalik out of sight into the privacy of his sleeping bag. Her quickened breathing against his throat became as uneven as his thudding heartbeats. His hand smoothing up the cushioned warmth of her back muscles, she slid her parka up over her head. Her trembling hand touched his, guiding his fingers down over the ripples of her ribs to softening warmth, pressing his hand on the huge dimple of her navel, and she shivered.

His hurried hand rediscovered downward that Eskimo girls wear tight caribou skin pants extending down to meet their long sealskin boots above the knee, and he smiled against her cheek. He still was clothed, breathing hard and thinking harder, while his hands helped her squirm from her pants.

In his frustrated excitement he felt like laughing or crying. *As a professional population expert,* he thought,, *should my travel pack have included an assortment of the most modern devices and morning-after pills for young ladies? Not funny, you unprepared idiot.* In the Eskimo Sanctuary he hadn't intended to get involved at all personally.

Gasping, struggling out of his clothes within their wriggling sleeping bag, he reassured himself he could exercise responsible physiological restraints more possible in intent than in practice. Smiling wryly against her ear, he had no intention of abruptly interrogating her with questions such as: Marthalik, do you have a calendar? Marthalik, are you among the 60% who are dependably regular? Marthalik, you don't know?

She wriggled smoothly against his chest and lips as his hands helped off her long soft boots. She moaned as his fingers rose, and inhaled, clamping his right hand between the inner softness of her thighs. She exhaled. In his throbbing excitement while he turned her huge-small body with her moist breath sighing faster against him, lovingly he prepared her.

Dying with his love for her, vaguely he remembered he must remember his responsibility to her. When the time came for him he must be able to interrupt himself.

With her hand clinging to his back, she moaned with pleasure about—babies? In his mounting excitement and their rhythmic smoothness repeating faster and faster into a delicious shudder she rippled wonderfully inward like no woman he had ever experienced or been prepared for and he exploded, everything forgotten.

Gradually his outer consciousness returned. Against his chest he felt the relaxing rhythm of her heart, and on the back of his neck the stroking of her fingers. She inhaled against him, exhaled: "Am I your wife?"

Bombed by the question, Dr. West lay still part of her. To his own surprise he blurted: "Yes. Marthalik, you are my wife." And he felt joy, better than he'd ever felt, wonderfully free to love her now. He held her in his arms, his throat swollen with love as if he wanted to cry. *And why not?* he thought. *And why not!* "Marthalik, you are my wife."

She giggled and snuggled against him. "This person will try to have a bigger navel for you."

Her small hand guided his hand upon that part of her softness, and he smiled, remembering vaguely that Eskimo men loved opulent navels. The deeper the navel the better-fed the wife, demonstrating the greatness of the hunter because his wife had such a wonderfully deep navel, beautifully cushioned in lush plumpness. To Eskimo men, and perhaps to Marthalik, he realized the erotic symbolism of the navel must far surpass the breasts and even the nose.

"Plump wife," he whispered, "you will always have plenty to eat with me, and a navel so wonderfully deep. Such a perfect navel is yours now because I love you."

To his surprise, her finger was making love to his navel, which was neither deep nor opulent, but startlingly stimulated by the circular sliding of her finger. Inward with delicately circling touches her finger was penetrating so deeply his abdomen hardened with sparkling nerve signals radiating downward. *What have I been missing all my life?*

Arousing deliciously he discovered the Eskimos' affection for the navel was based on more than abstract symbolism. Evidently these Eskimos through thousands of years of long winter nights had elaborated that aspect of culture known as physical love with intricate stimulants of touch and movement and communication more powerful than any hurried whiteman's.

Gliding upon him and he within her, longer and more easily they breathed and moved and flowed as one person toward unbearable excitement together as her flesh became his as he surged upon her while she cried out in joy carrying him as if they were falling through space.

In that moment, he saw a dazzling sun beneath him. Falling past asteroids dotted with white domes, he surged upon her toward a green planet as he exploded within her. Dazed, he raised his head and only the dim tent was still there. Lowering his face in exhaustion, he slept upon the smooth safety of her breasts.

Dr. West lived each day and night fully as if it were his last. With her now he felt so free he hoped she would conceive because she kept insisting this would make her so happy. "Your sons will be strong hunters!"

A week ago during that first night with her he'd hurriedly rationalized that the odds of safety against conception that night were a fairly safe five to one. As they lived together in happiness along her twenty-eight day cycle, the odds were narrowing. Instead of wasting his time with that confusing age-sex census which didn't make statistical sense, he learned to make love to his wife's navel with expertise beyond any Eskimo's, or so Marthalik assured him. He felt she loved him so much that anything he did pleased her.

Sometimes upon her as if entering the darkness of space he glimpsed that strange sun again. On their gasping journeys he strained trying to see again that green planet, but standing up in the morning after his oddly recurrent amatory mirage, he laughed simply with the joy of being alive and strong and truly in love for the first time.

Nearly two weeks had passed, and the Turbo-Beaver was not going to appear, he thought. Anyway, he had no intention of returning with the pilot to the Outside. Not yet. These happy people needed him. He wanted Marthalik always to be happy, and for this reason he knew he would have to venture Outside before winter. He would have to get them food——

On unlucky nights when the only seal carcass was bare bones, he listened to these people's night myths. His arm around Marthalik he watched Edwardluk crouching lower than the flickering lamp. He heard the hoarse grunting of Grandfather Bear emerging through Edwardluk's strange guttural voice. Magically, all these Eskimos would become excited, smiling upward and unable to explain what they felt.

Hungrily, Dr. West went seal hunting with Edwardluk on the bay ice. Impressively he shot a seal with his recoilless rifle. It favorably impressed the seal because it floated long enough for Edwardluk to hurl his harpoon. Edwardluk seemed less impressed, even though he admitted old Peterluk could not shoot so far. "That old man's rifle is louder."

"Does Peterluk remember which direction you people came from?"

"Eh?" Edwardluk laughed in confusion at Dr. West's startling question. "Always we have been here. Ever since this person can remember. And before. Ever since Grandfather Bear we have been here, as this person has told you." Edwardluk squinted at the vast blue sky. "If you are to understand—where we come from, you must wait with us for Grandfather Bear."

"No one seems to remember what happened to the old people."

"Sometimes Peterluk says one thing, sometimes another."

"You can find Peterluk?"

"This person always knows where that *angakok* has traveled, and hopes he will stay there."

The next morning on the thawing gravel in front of the tent while learning to cut a seal into the proper pieces, Dr. West asked Edwardluk: "Will you take me to speak with that old man?"

Edwardluk looked north. "Peterluk is in a strong place with his rifle." His worried expression showed he didn't want to go there.

"But he fled from me." Dr. West doubted that Peterluk would shoot at him in any case. All these Eskimos seemed so nonviolent. "Already Peterluk has fled from me."

"To get more power he has returned to the Burned Place. Above the sea on that great rock ledge Peterluk is camped in the Navel of the World."

"But whitemen's magic," Dr. West remarked, "is stronger."

"My husband is stronger than Peterluk," Marthalik laughed, squeezing Dr. West's arm. "And wiser and braver. Even though Peterluk pretends he is not even afraid of Grandfather Bear, Peterluk always lies. He is nothing but an old man. My husband could——."

Dr. West laughed, unable to resist showing off for his wife, and he stood up, towering above them. "Edwardluk, you are a strong man, too! We both are strong men! We go!"

Edwardluk smiled unhappily as he looked around, surrounded by so many curiously smiling faces. What could he do? They went, leaving Marthalik behind, which hurt her feelings. "Who will prepare the camp each night? Without a woman——."

Like a strong husband Dr. West ordered her to stay, to give his letter to the airplane, truly to keep her from the dangerous journey.

On this rough bay ice any pilot would be afraid to land, Dr. West thought as he helped Edwardluk heave the sled up over another pressure ridge.

Across smoother ice the dogs raced over cracks the pressure had closed. Riding the sled, both men laughed with man's third greatest pleasure, a journey.

At first, Edwardluk had said the journey north along the coast might take two sleeps. Dr. West expected to be back with Marthalik within a week. On the bay ice the sled short-cut from point to point, but beyond the next promontory the ice had opened with leads of shimmering water, and they had to work back toward the cliffs. Taking the longer route along the shore ice they had to follow all the indentations of the coastline. Proud he was in such good physical condition, Dr. West trotted over the uneven ice. Hour after hour, his pride kept him moving. That night he was too tired to eat much. The next day he was stiff-muscled. The next day he was slower.

"Soon-soon," Edwardluk's voice kept soothing, and during the afternoon of the fourth day finally Edwardluk halted the dogs at the foot of a massive stone promontory. He stared up toward the gigantic ledge. Then he smiled wanly at Dr. West. "Burned Place up there."

His small hands becoming clumsy, Edwardluk finally tied the sled to a boulder at the base of the promontory. Their noses pointed toward the ledge, the dogs whined. Indecisively Edwardluk picked up his harpoon and set it down again. "Peterluk has so much power in the—the Navel of the World."

As if he were afraid, Edwardluk made no move to start to climb.

Clutching his rifle, staring up toward the ledge, Dr. West wondered: *Navel of the World? A pit or crater up there? The navel symbolizes sexual power to these people, and birth. But this is the Navel of the World. A focus of power?*

The only focus around here which he could think of was of the Earth's magnetic lines of force converging at the North Magnetic Pole. *Which they've never heard of.*

Up in the Earth's ionosphere the magnetically trapped radiation belts did dimple inward here, he thought, above the North Magnetic Pole. Looking up, he half-expected the squat silhouette of Peterluk to appear against the sky.

Dr. West started climbing. Back in the 1950s when he was born, early space scientists had been too concerned about the Van Allen belts, he thought. They'd suggested manned flights should be directed out through this polar hole in the radiation doughnut. *A center of weakness?* Dr. West grinned, hearing Edwardluk finally following him up the sloping cliff.

With his rifle slung over his back, Dr. West scrambled toward the top. Already he could smell seal oil, dog odors, typical smells of an Eskimo camp. Breathing harder than necessary, Dr. West thought he'd heard too many midnight tales of Peterluk's so-called powers.

As he raised his head, from eye level the ledge appeared to spread out as immensely as a football field. Oddly, the top of a tent seemed to be protruding from the solid rock.

When he stood up on the ledge, Dr. West was looking down into a shallow gouge or crater in the blackened rock. The tent was squatting at the bottom, surrounded by fiercely clamoring dogs.

Seeing they were tied, Dr. West walked down over the charred rocks. Under his boots crunched small shards like white china. He realized these might be fragments from the same ceramic material the Eskimos had salvaged to use as seal oil lamps. Cautiously he walked toward the dogs and the dark opening in the tent.

From behind, Edwardluk's hand restrained him.

"Our hands are empty," Edwardluk shouted at the tent.

Dr. West felt foolish standing there clutching his rifle in plain sight.

"We love you," Edwardluk shouted past the dogs toward the triangular opening in the tent. Edwardluk repeated his love so interminably that the bored dogs lay down, whining.

Dr. West supposed this small crater was the dark spot he and the pilot had noticed from the air. By airplane flight this rugged promontory had been only fifteen minutes north of the camp. By dog sled, four days——.

Cautiously, Edwardluk was edging toward the tent's entry, still murmuring about love and peace. At the last moment he stopped because a harpoon had poked out against his stomach. As he backed off, a leathery-faced Eskimo woman emerged, turning the harpoon toward Dr. West.

"Eevvaalik, do not fear this whiteman," Edwardluk's voice apologized.

"Who fears? This person knew many whitemen." In bitterly long agglutinative Eskimo word-phrases she began recalling insulting girlhood experiences with sickly stingy whitemen, while smiling innocently at Dr. West.

"He speaks our language!" Edwardluk bleated in belated warning.

"Good. We understand each other." Her insolent gaze moved downward from Dr. West's eyes to his rifle.

"Eevvaalik," Dr. West began awkwardly, "where is your— husband?"

She laughed or coughed. "You are afraid to say his name?"

In her challenging smile, her teeth were brown stubs. Dr. West wondered how many years she had spent chewing her husband's boots to soften them. Her hair was streaked with gray. He noticed her parka was beautifully decorated with white fox tails and expertly sewn compared with the crude parkas of the young people back at the camp. Her wrinkled face seemed sculptured by frostbite and years of freezing winds, in contrast to the unweathered complexions of the others he had met.

"Your husband is named Peterluk," Dr. West stated. "We have not come to arrest him. We are not with the Guards. We are not with the police. We are—friends."

"You come for fox furs after all these years?" Eevvaalik suggested and smiled, baring her worn teeth. "You have— lipstick?"

"No, but when I return I will bring many things."

"A *Sony* box with new *Evereadys?*" Eevvaalik parroted in English: *"Cleaner than Clean. Don't you Know What's Happening Mr. Jones?"*

"Is your husband in the tent?"

"This is the CBC. This baby-man," she laughed contemptuously toward Edwardluk, "does not even believe voices come out of a box."

"Where is your husband?" Dr. West repeated, hoping the unseen Peterluk wasn't squinting at him now along a rifle barrel.

"All these young people are fools who will starve," she chattered. "All of this land was my husband's, and now there are so many people there are no caribou, and all will starve." Her voice drowned in a paroxysm of coughing. "My husband, sometimes—he says—he will kill you."

Gurgling phlegm, she spat on the dark rocks. As she raised her tortured face with red saliva hanging from her chin, Dr. West realized this was the first case of tuberculosis he'd seen in the Sanctuary. Those young Eskimos didn't even have summer colds.

"Where are the other old people?" Dr. West gently asked her.

She wiped her chin. Edwardluk elbowed Dr. West. Pointing with his stubby nose, Edwardluk was facing the big rocks silhouetted along the other rim of the crater.

"We are your friends!" Edwardluk shouted and began walking toward that hulking rim, spreading his arms like a willing target. "See, this person is Edwardluk. We love you. Even this powerful whiteman loves you."

There was no rifle shot as Edwardluk reached the huge rocks. Among them he disappeared.

Laughter came down from the rocks. Edwardluk came down with his arm upon the shoulder of a massive Eskimo. The bushy hair and lowered head made Dr. West think of a musk-ox. The big hands hung empty. Dr. West was relieved that Peterluk was not carrying his fabled rifle.

As Peterluk approached, Dr. West saw his parka was fringed with ermine tails. As Peterluk raised his broad face, his big teeth gleamed and muscles bulged on the sides of his massive Eskimo jaw.

But Peterluk's jutting nose, Dr. West thought cautiously, suggested a Boston whaling captain in his ancestry. Now Dr. West became uncomfortably aware of Peterluk's avid glances at his rifle.

As if initiating a whiteman's handshake, Peterluk extended his mahogany-colored hand, rough with frost scars. Gripping Dr. West's right hand, Peterluk lowered his bushy head, his eyes disappearing beneath all that shaggy black hair as he peeked down. He seemed to be staring at Dr. West's left leg or rather at Dr. West's rifle which was leaning against his left leg. Dr. West's left hand involuntarily tightened on his rifle.

When Dr. West relaxed his right hand as a hint the handshake was over, Peterluk's suddenly raised eyes glinted through his shaggy hair. Gently, irresistibly, he continued holding Dr. West's right hand.

"*Furs-furs,*" Peterluk's voice murmured in English. "*Furs? Peter has furs. Understand?*"

"Later we will trade," Dr. West replied in Modern Eskimo, tightening his own grip in defense against Peterluk's tightening grasp.

Peterluk laughed in amazement. "You understand us."

"This person is trying to——," Dr. West laughed in relief, quickly explaining he was not a Guard or a policeman. "This person is wondering where are the other strong hunters, the Eskimos who were with you when the whitemen closed off this land."

Peterluk peered past Dr. West's arm, probably at Eevvaalik, Dr. West thought, his own hand beginning to feel numb.

"Many fine fox furs," Peterluk's voice grunted with exertion.

Dr. West had to tighten his own grip in self-defense, hardening his whole arm like a trembling iron bar, trying to harden his hand to protect it from being crushed.

"Eh-eh, you are a strong man," Peterluk laughed excitedly.

Straining there, Dr. West didn't know what to do. Peterluk was smiling like a friend.

"We are friends," Dr. West said hopefully. "You are a

man who understands. You are a strong man who understands where all these young Eskimos come from——."

"Eskimos? *Innuit?*"

"Yes, did they come from the north?"

"Eh-eh, from the north," Peterluk laughed derisively as if he didn't care what he said. "From the north."

"But these people have a legend they were born here on the Boothia Peninsula."

"Humpback monster-man split open," Peterluk began insolently.

"No, not that old legend. Tell me how these young people came to the Boothia Peninsula."

Like an animal's hard jaw, Peterluk's grip tightened. "All lies! There is no Grandfather Bear coming down from the sky. You and me don't believe ignorant things like that!"

"Then why are you," Dr. West resisted, "camped here in the Burned Place?"

"Old woman, close your mouth," Peterluk bellowed, as if he thought Eevvaalik had said something. "She lies. No star fell here."

"A star? If a star fell here years ago, where is the iron?" Dr. West was thinking of a meteorite.

"No star. Bad candles made my navel of power," Peterluk laughed defiantly at Dr. West's face. "Iron box of bad candles."

"This crater was not made by sticks of dynamite," Dr. West retorted, trying to twist his hand free——.

"You think this person lies?" Peterluk shouted like a madman. "Then you don't believe the Egg of God fell here. You don't believe a whitemen's ship poked up its eye on a stick. Like a whale with many whitemen but this person was stronger than—you!"

Peterluk lunged against Dr. West, his other hand siezing the barrel of Dr. West's rifle. As Dr. West strained backward, struggling to free his rifle, Peterluk's head slammed his chest, ramming him backward off balance. Peterluk's massive head with an upward heave like an uppercut struck Dr. West's jaw. Staggering back, Dr. West still managed to cling to his rifle with his left hand. Peterluk was crushing his right hand as they struggled, and Dr. West gasped at Edwardluk: "Help——."

He glimpsed Edwardluk simply standing there with a worried expression like a pacifist. He glimpsed Eevvaalik stepping forward, raising the harpoon.

With that jolt of adrenal fear, Dr. West violently twisted, trying to turn Peterluk for a shield against her harpoon. Both men fell to their knees. Dr. West bounced up so quickly his other knee struck Peterluk's rising face. With new strength in his left arm, he yanked his rifle up, slamming it down at Peterluk's ducking face. Its steel receiver clanged against Peterluk's forehead. Peterluk sank to his knees like a wounded musk-ox.

His rifle freed, Dr. West whirled to face Eevvaalik, who already was running away. Her harpoon had vanished.

Warned by Edwardluk's shout, Dr. West looked down at Peterluk rising with blood streaming over his forehead and into one eye. His huge face lurched straight at the rifle's muzzle, and Dr. West stepped back.

His face contorted, Peterluk took one forward step. With a howl of rage like an injured child, Peterluk whirled, running away toward the rocks from which he had emerged.

Edwardluk was running after him, shrilly shouting: "Father, don't do it. Grandfather Bear does not allow——."

Edwardluk ran back as if shielding Dr. West. "Run because his rifle is louder than yours——."

Dr. West raised his rifle, looking at the silhouetted rocks along the rim. He didn't want to shoot Peterluk, who was the one person who seemed to know what had happened on the Boothia Peninsula. If Peterluk really had a rifle which still operated, he would have the advantage of firing from cover. Dr. West ran, overtaking Edwardluk. He could feel a cold .30 caliber spot on the back of his neck as he ran toward the cliff. Over the edge, they went sliding down toward the tiny sled below. With instant efficiency, Edwardluk freed the sled. Looking up over the sights of his rifle, Dr. West saw no movement or sign of Peterluk against the sky.

When they finally reached the cover of the next promontory, Dr. West mentally was berating himself. *That damned Eskimo almost took away my rifle. I failed to learn anything*

*from him except what a treacherous——. No, I learned
there's plenty to tell when I make Peterluk talk.*

"I'm not through with him!" Dr. West muttered in English,
looking at Edwardluk and wondering what this smiling savage would tell Marthalik. *That I ran? The hell with it! She
loves me. She'll understand.*

Dr. West looked back where the promontory of the
Burned Place, of the Navel of the World, already was hidden
by the next projecting point. *That crazy Peterluk, inside his
greasy head is what happened in this Sanctuary.*

Trying to short-cut across the bay ice while the wind was
shifting, Edwardluk finally had to admit they were cut off
from shore. "Soon-soon we see our camp." Day after day,
Edwardluk led them south, east, north, west among the open
leads, the cliffs always visible on their left hand. Far to the
right gleamed ice islands. Beyond like gray mist lay a real
island. "Over there," Edwardluk laughed cheerfully, "Peterluk says whitemen. Guard Station."

Dr. West was too tired to answer. In this continuous ice
glare, his eyes were killing him. His dark glasses weren't
enough protection from this needle-sharp brightness as his
body weakened. His sighting eye blurred so much he missed
his one shot at a seal. Each day Edwardluk failed to harpoon
a seal, Dr. West's hungry stomach tightened and his temper
grew shorter but he tried to act cheerful, at least half as
cheerful as Edwardluk.

Vaguely, Dr. West thought eight or ten days had passed as
they struggled toward the cliffs, parallel to the cliffs, below
the cliffs, along the slippery ice foot with the sea gurgling
below. In all that time Edwardluk seemed as strong as ever,
and as cheerful. *The man is a saint*, Dr. West thought with
exhaustion.

From the one seal Edwardluk had managed to kill somehow, Edwardluk ate little. "You big man. You need to eat
more." But Edwardluk insisted on feeding the dogs. "So few
dogs, so many of us."

One blinding day there were distant shouts. Children ran to
meet them.

"Where is my wi——. Where is Marthalik?"

"She coming. We run faster," they laughed, "faster than your wife."

Dr. West's face cracked in a chapped smile as he finally recognized Marthalik jogging toward him. Surprisingly, she ran as heavily as a little hippo, he thought, and stumbled to meet her. With joy he squeezed her to him. He thought they had been separated more than two weeks. Feeling her belly pressing against him as he nuzzled her hair, he clasped her swollen waist.

My god! he thought in shock. *She's developed some sort of gigantic fast-growing watery tumor—in just two weeks.* She had swelled up like a balloon. He didn't want to frighten her, but he'd have to take her Outside. To get help, first he'd have to cross all that ice to the Guard Station on the gray island. He'd have to get an aircraft, a gynecologist, get her to a hospital. In the month since he first saw Marthalik kneeling naked in the tent she'd swelled up like——.

Inside the blessed dimness of the tent, Marthalik giggled proudly. "This person is going to have a baby."

Dr. West didn't want to contradict her. There was no use frightening her yet. He laid his hand on her belly. He couldn't feel the baby kicking. Two weeks ago when he left her she had been nicely plump. Before he left, he thought perhaps she had put on some weight during those two weeks while they were making love but even if she'd been a few months pregnant then, such a suddenly advanced pregnancy now was physiologically impossible. *Got to get her to a hospital.* In exhaustion on the sleeping platform, Dr. West lay resting his head against her while she whispered so happily to him.

He was awakened by the knocking of floor stones being moved, by the scraping of gravel. Marthalik and her mother both were on their knees, digging a shallow pit in the floor of the tent. As he sat up, he stared at Marthalik lining the basin-sized hole in the gravel with a caribou skin, her body jerking as if with surges of pain.

My god. This has gone too far. How can I explain to her about a false pregnancy? Surely her mother knows a pregnancy takes nine long months——, Dr. West's thoughts trailed off.

Marthalik was kneeling above the hole when her mother bent behind her with the stone knife. As Dr. West opened his mouth to cry out and lunged forward, her mother sawed up at the seam of Marthalik's fur pants between her legs.

"Eh!" the mother laughed, with her hands tearing the seam open, her own young face gleaming at Dr. West. "She is your wife. ——This person believes more sons are born if the father helps."

Like a sleepwalker, Dr. West knelt beside his wife. Gynecology was not his specialty. The mother pushed him over behind Marthalik. "Put your strong arms around her. Higher! On top of your son, help push him out."

He felt Marthalik's contractions.

Matching his rhythm to hers, Dr. West went through the motions of pressing down his spread hands. He was afraid to press hard. Marthalik never moaned. Feeling more and more tired, Dr. West felt like moaning on and on.

Exhausted, Dr. West heard a small mewing sound beneath them, and the two women were chattering happily. Dr. West lay down. The slippery baby gave one loud cry as Marthalik's mother bit through the umbilical cord. She knotted it while Dr. West worriedly watched, realizing any interference from him simply might hurt their feelings. Happily Marthalik licked her baby clean. Proudly, Marthalik smiled down at Dr. West: "You have a hunter!"

Cradling her baby out of sight inside her parka, Marthalik crouched beside the seal carcass. With one hand she tore loose a great chunk of fat and meat.

"You must eat," she said, seriously peering at Dr. West's face. "You are tired. But this is best piece."

Dr. West grinned, taking the meat and putting it aside. He helped her up onto the sleeping platform.

"This person is a little bit tired from scraping seal skins this morning," she murmured, snuggling beside him under the caribou skin and lovingly stroking his neck. "This person wants to thank you——."

While she slept beside him, Dr. West lay on his back with his son squirming on his bare chest inside his parka. Encouraged by Dr. West's finger, this strong little hunter even managed to raise his head.

"My name is Joe, Joseph," Dr. West whispered, grinning. "Your name should be Speedy."

Exploring, Dr. West stroked with his finger around the rim of the baby's ear. In the cartilage on the top he could feel the little bump, and on the other ear the same. Proudly he fingered his own ear. "That's a West family trait. A dominant genetic characteristic."

Without waking his wife, he fingered the rim of her ear, which was smoothly rounded, no cartilaginous bump. *I doubt any of these Eskimos have that characteristic so—nine months or one month———.* "You speedy little devil, you *are* my son."

The terrible global significance of what he'd just experienced had not hit him yet.

Turning his head toward the lamp, he saw Marthalik's mother was suckling her own new baby. This baby must have been born while Edwardluk and he were on their journey to the Burned Place. "How many days old?" he whispered.

She held up one hand, spreading her fingers and thumb. Five days. Her baby squirmed strongly, getting a better grip.

Dr. West was no pediatric specialist, but he thought her baby appeared very fat and sturdy for only five days of feeding. "How long does it take—inside?"

"To make a baby?" The woman smiled at him as if he were stupid or something. "Perhaps a woman begins when the moon is thin. After the moon is fat and becomes thin again a woman has a baby."

"All women?"

"Of course, all women. Are whitewomen so different?"

Dr. West closed his eyes. *Who is more right? Why should it take nine months?* He thought of hospital premies who emerged fairly successfully after five months. They weren't really ready. But why not a full-term baby in five months? Or four months, three months, two months, one month? Nine months must have been normal for hundreds of thousands of years. Prehistorically it may have become most advantageous for survival millions of years ago when species of manlike animals and their environments were so different.

Why nine months? He knew that many mammals have

much shorter gestation periods. Growth from fertilized ovum to embryo to fetus to fully formed baby could proceed more rapidly than nine months, he pondered, if the prehistorically programmed hormone signals proceeded faster and more efficiently.

How do I know? I've just seen it demonstrated. My son is here wiggling strongly on my chest.

Smiling at that perfect little red face, Dr. West thought that part of a nine-month gestation period must be a waste of time anyway, particularly during the early embryonic stages. *How much growth-energy does a human embryo waste while growing its tail and then absorbing it again?* "And our embryonic gills—ridiculous. Obsolete recapitulation."

A one-month gestation period really is more logical from a uterine standpoint, he thought. *Approximately once a month an ovum descends a Fallopian tube toward the uterus, and the walls of the uterus thicken in preparation. If the ovum isn't fertilized, fails to attach itself, the uterus sloughs off a bloody discharge which is a signal of failure. The womb is unfulfilled and its menstrual flow simply reveals a wasted month, a physiological failure, an inefficiency of the civilized female,* he thought to himself, grinning. *Ovarian efficiency would mean a baby every month.*

For we *Homo sapiens*, a nine-month gestation period may have been one of our prehistoric survival advantages, he thought, when we were in competition with other manlike species. We don't know how long was the extinct Neanderthal woman's gestation period? Or Peking woman's? Nine months happened to be a characteristic of our winning species long ago.

But conditions on Earth now are so different in the same competition for food and living space, he thought. *Perhaps people with a one-month gestation period will have the advantage?*

Not unless they have food, he thought, worriedly looking down at his sleeping wife. Her lips were moving, smiling in her dream.

Like the rest of us they can't understand or admit they're breeding toward catastrophe, he thought unhappily. To save them from starvation this winter they'll need food and other help from outside this so-called Sanctuary.

His snow-burned eyes blurred. What should I do first?

2.
POLAR
BEAR!

SNOWBLINDNESS STALKED HIM LIKE A SPECTRAL WHITE BEAR.
Through his Arctic sunglasses, Dr. Joe West's eyes winced.
His forehead ached from the penetrating white glare.

Across the dazzling ice, shadow-shapes of children and
squatty men romped on all fours. They were pretending to be
bears, roaring and giggling as the bears devoured the children. Watching from their summer parkas with hoods turned
back, the horde of swollen women exposed their squinting
babies to the Arctic sun. Dr. West's eyes pulsed uncomfortably in the glare.

He must leave soon and travel fast before his eyes be-
trayed him. His eyes seemed weaker every day. He had to
leave, he thought. Escape still seemed too strong a word.

"Today we go," Dr. West said (asked).

"Soon-soon we go," Edwardluk agreed pleasantly; his was
the only dog team in the encampment. "The wind will
change. This bad ice will be better tomorrow. We will go."

"Each day you say that." Dr. West felt trapped in a
morass of happy promises and no action.

"Eh-eh," Edwardluk laughed, politely agreeing. "The ice
will be better. Your eyes will be better if you stay inside the
tent with Marthalik. Each day we are more all-the-same with
you, and you will like us more. In the winter the ice will be
safer——."

"I like you now." Dr. West tried not to raise his voice.
"We must travel now. As soon as we reach the whitemen, I'll
tell them how much you helped me. The airplanes will drop
much food for this camp. We must go now before the ice is
worse."

"Eh-eh." Edwardluk unexpectedly stood up as if he were

about to do something besides talk. "Soon as we kill seals to feed dogs, we go!"

Edwardluk trotted toward his tent, and Dr. West followed with long strides, unable to believe this sudden activity.

"First we fill our bellies." Edwardluk flopped down on an ancient sealskin and shouted impressively for his wife to cut meat. "Then we hunt seals together like brothers," Edwardluk sighed happily. "Good dreams will protect us from the bad ice out there. Good dreams will help you like us better tomorrow." With downcast eyes, Edwardluk smiled like a shy little boy and handed Dr. West a thawing glob of seal liver as if it were a valentine. "Best piece for you."

"Do you think I don't like you? Is that it? Because I am going away? But I will return with help for all of you. And I will return for Marthalik and my son. We are of one body. You understand I will return?"

"Eh." Edwardluk's smiling eyes narrowed as his massive jaw crunched through the partially frozen meat. Gulping, he swallowed and crunched and gulped. His eyes closed. His head sagged down. As easily as a tired child, he slept.

Dr. West's thin hands tightened on his recoilless rifle. *These people are so damned lovable, it would be impossible to threaten him. My rifle is useless against him.*

Dr. West's contradictory grin, which also made him attractive to women who were more selective than Eskimo women, his uncertain grin cracked his chapped lips. *If I am a prisoner,* he cheerfully thought his way into a semantic trap, *I can escape. If I am NOT a prisoner, by definition I cannot escape.* He laughed. *Damn! That's a neurotic thought. I've got to escape, I mean, take a leave of absence.*

He stared down at the chunk of meat which was attracting flies to Edwardluk's small hand. It was amazing how these people lacked the gargantuan appetites of other Eskimos. And there was the little matter of babies, their one-month gestation period; even his own son was conceived and born in a month. Too many babies. There were too many small children, tragically more than the environment could support this winter, he thought. *I've got to hurry back for Marthalik and my son.*

If the ice out there weren't so bad he would take her with

him. He would take her with him but when he surrendered at the Guard Station they would arrest him, probably humiliate him, and he didn't want Marthalik to see that. To her, he was a big man, a strong man, a lover. *Marthalik, Marthalik, if I don't leave now, I may never leave.* His smile becoming unhappy, he stared a long time at the tent where she was drowsing. Finally he looked at the snoring Edwardluk and the sleeping dogs. Yesterday, when he tried to order these people to help him prepare the sled, giggling they had diverted him from leaving. Marthalik had rubbed urgently against him, peering up with sweet narrow eyes, urging him to come back into the tent, ducking under his suddenly waving arms of anger. He'd never been angry at her before, and it had shocked him, shamed him.

In her hood the wrinkled face of the baby had flopped back and forth, crying. His son! From Dr. West's inexplicable rage, the people had averted their faces like hurt children. Yesterday his determination to leave had dissolved in embarrassment, remorse, the restfully dark tent and gentle whispering with Marthalik. Yesterday. Today.

In the white glare his eyelids itched. Dr. West knew if he was going to travel he already should have left. *These women, these incredibly wonderful women. I've got to escape now!* Simultaneously, he felt like laughing and crying. *Marthalik, how I love you.* He did not look at her tent. Perhaps lying on the caribou skins she was nursing his son.

His forehead wrinkling, Dr. West looked in the opposite direction, out of the Sanctuary to where the Guard Station was supposed to be. Beyond the shore ice and the dark crack gleamed the veined sea ice with distant islands glittering. They were icebergs. *God help me! I have to cross that!* Edwardluk had told him the Sanctuary Guard Station must be on the gray smudge on the horizon. It was the whitemen's island. He looked back at Edwardluk so happily sleeping. Angrily Dr. West thought: *I can travel there alone—if the dogs are harnessed to the sled, by you——.*

Flies buzzed above Edwardluk's sleeping smile, and his massive jaw moved. He was dreaming. These people, Marthalik, all of them—Dr. West marveled how animated their faces were when they slept, as if their dreams were more real than reality.

Surely I can outthink Edwardluk. I'm the one who should be pulling the strings. I'm not his puppet. He should be mine if I have any brains left at all.

Quietly, Dr. West picked up his sleeping bag. He slid his arm through the sling of his recoilless rifle. He hefted his pack. Heavy-laden he started walking across the ice toward the distant icebergs in the polar strait. He hoped he was setting a trap for Edwardluk. He hoped Edwardluk would not be angry. Perhaps Edwardluk would laugh, "Eh-eh, we go!"

With each step, the silicone rubber membranes in Dr. West's boots exhaled fog. Yet he waded with dry feet through shimmering puddles of meltwater across the thawing sea ice. Like a giant, he strode over eroding stream beds on the ice. Fresh water trickled toward dark leads where the sea surged, where seals could rise.

This summer ice was rotting, dangerous. He opened the vents in his outer parka because to perspire also was dangerous. "Bad, bad-bad," Edwardluk had said, "for whiteman to walk alone on sea ice."

Then you come rescue me, Dr. West thought and walked on and on.

The icebergs seemed no closer, but when Dr. West looked back he saw that the encampment had miniaturized into a cluster of dots.

Like a midget, a midge, a dark speck, Dr. West plodded endlessly across the flat sea ice. He hoped Edwardluk was watching, massive jaw beginning to sag with worry. Dr. West was gambling that Edwardluk would grunt with decision, hitch the dogs to the sled and come out after him to rescue him.

"You will, if you truly like me." Dr. West's pack-straps sawed into his shoulders. His feet plodded on and on across the sea ice. He squinted at the sky although he had given up all hope of being arrested, rescued by a Cultural Sanctuary copter. The only way of carrying his warning message to the Outside seemed to be through hopeful physical exertion, plus guile if Edwardluk fell into his trap.

Above the peak of the iceberg, a flock of dark fulmars whirled. Around the berg gleamed broken ice and dark water where sea birds could feed. Dr. West was surprised that he did not sight a single seal. He circled behind the berg, setting the psychological trap.

Now he was out of view from the camp. Dr. West hoped Edwardluk was harnessing the dogs. *If his friendship is genuine, he'll come to rescue me. If not, he'll come to recapture me.* But there was a third possibility. Edwardluk simply might sleep. But Marthalik would awaken, asking: "Where is my husband?" She would awaken Edwardluk quickly.

From his pack, Dr. West took out a pad of caribou skin and sat down on it. Rifle propped against his thigh, he waited. The trap was set for Edwardluk. And he waited.

Cold rose through the ancient caribou skin pad into Joe West's haunches. Restlessly, he remembered his Alaskan Eskimos had used bear skin pads because they were thicker. But these Boothia people owned no polar bear skins. They said they never killed bears, and Dr. West was inclined to believe them.

The cold enfolded him. From the corner of his eye a small part of the white background trotted across his field of vision. It was an Arctic fox, plume-tailed and oblivious.

Suddenly the white fox stared at him or past him. Dr. West felt a creeping urge to look behind his own back. He remembered that the Eskimos refer to the white fox as the bear's dog. On the sea ice, the fox follows the polar bear, dependent on the bear's kills. The Eskimos say: "Fox on ice, look behind you quick, is bear."

Turning his head, Dr. West squinted at each white mound and fuzzy shadow. At point-blank range, he knew a polar bear would appear more cream-colored than the ice. A black spot would be the nose of the polar bear. The Eskimos say: "Bear hold white paw over nose, bear gone, eh-eh. Bear still there."

"Ha!" Dr. West shouted, standing up. The immense white background remained immobile. From the white mounds, a polar bear's head did not rise weasellike on its long neck.

"Spooked myself. These people talk too much about Grandfather Bear." Dr. West twisted his chilled face in another grin. He didn't want to remember Edwardluk's wide-eyed face above the seal oil lamp.

Like earlier Eskimos, these people entertained themselves with night stories. His eyes closing in ecstasy, Edwardluk had grunted like a bear. "Grandfather of the sky——," Edwardluk's suddenly hoarse voice had croaked. "Sharpen your hunger. We—your children—prepare for you. Open your jaws!"

Dr. West blinked his eyes and shivered. If their grandfather was a bear-spirit, that was all right with Dr. West. Who was he to deride anyone's totems or religious beliefs? But after thirty-six days what grated his nerves was the continuously nonanthropomorphic teleology of their night stories. These people had things backward, he thought.

The mythology of other Eskimos presented bear-spirits as merely helping or hindering man. Man was the end-purpose.

But in these people's stories the bear seemed the end-purpose. The people helped the bear. The people prepared the seals, the rocks, the airplanes, for the bear. This was not the bear on the ice. This was a bear in the sky. The purpose of all life seemed to funnel into the bear.

What their bear symbolized, Dr. West had not found out. But he suspected that a real bear, a hungry polar bear, would make little distinction between a prone man and a seal, and he remained standing, clutching his rifle. The nonappearance of seals in the open water around this iceberg suggested that a real bear was near.

Dr. West's eyes watered with the strain of trying to see everything and distinguishing less and less in the white glow of the ice. The cold soaked up through his feet. His leg bones became conductors of the cold. Sometimes he stood motionless, forgetting to stamp his feet. His vision and time blurred.

The fulmars cried out in alarm and whirled dark wings upward into the white sky, and Dr. West's eyes widened. He turned. He laughed with relief. A line of black specks across the ice became dogs pulling a distant sled.

Dr. West sat down on his caribou skin pad, but his heart was thudding with suppressed excitement, and he stood up. Peering, suddenly he cursed.

There was more than one man approaching. A man trotted ahead of the sled. The dark bulge on the sled was a second man, probably Edwardluk. Far behind, a third man plodded over the ice. Three men was more than Dr. West had bargained for, even though he had the only gun.

By the time they were close Dr. West still had not decided what to do.

"He was watching you!" Edwardluk shouted happily. "Up there he was watching you."

Dr. West looked back and up at the translucent iceberg. If Edwardluk was referring to an actual bear, it was invisible to Dr. West. He squinted at the dogs, who calmly lay down. They had not scented a bear.

"Bear seen us coming." Edwardluk made a circling motion with his wide face and stubby nose, and Dr. West supposed the bear had circled out of sight behind the berg.

"We come to carry back your seals," Edwardluk suggested innocently, smiling. "This person told Marthalik you were hunting, and you would return soon—perhaps with a seal."

The second man stood smiling at the sky. The third man still was approaching. They seemed unarmed. In their fur parkas they reminded Dr. West of three childhood teddy bears. They had been kind and hospitable to Dr. West, and now he couldn't quite bring himself to point the rifle. He didn't want to threaten them with harsh words which would bring hurt expressions to their childlike faces.

He hesitated to ask Edwardluk to go with him outright. Edwardluk would invent so many excuses for returning to the camp, and that is what would happen; Dr. West was afraid he would go back with them, defeated. Smiling like a skull, he tried to conceal his growing anger.

"There is a dead seal under the edge of the ice," Dr. West blurted, pointing with his rifle barrel and walking behind their backs to the sled. Their three harpoons still were lashed to the sled.

"Eh, eh," Edwardluk's voice agreed politely to this lie, "there is a seal but my eyes don't see it yet."

Dr. West's shivering hands were tying his pack and sleeping bag on the sled with fumbling speed.

"Ha!" Dr. West shouted at the dogs as he flopped on the

sled, and to his surprise and relief the dogs lurched forward before he could use the whip. They dashed past the startled face of the third man. Back to camp was where the dogs were hurrying. Slashing the whip with all his strength, Dr. West managed to turn the leader toward the ice horizon.

The sled passed in an arc through the shouting range of the running men, but Dr. West managed to whip the dogs away, the sled weaving a snakelike course beyond the iceberg with Edwardluk running far behind.

I have escaped, Dr. West thought inaccurately. The terrible global significance of what he had observed about these people he had not fully analyzed. Mainly he was fleeing from his contradictory desire to go back to them. *Marthalik, Marthalik.*

He clung to the sled undulating over the ice. The wonder of Marthalik! The dogs were running uncontrollably. The sled bucked over a pressure ridge. Marthalik, in her arms he had been so much more than he had ever been before. If he let go he would fall off the sled and go back. He laughed with bewilderment. It was these women who would be too much for the world.

Up a steep pressure ridge he clung to the sled, and down. The sled runner jammed in the ice. It almost capsized as it abruptly stopped. His sunglasses slid down his nose.

Blinking, Dr. West slid off the sled, hoisted the runner free and shouted at the dogs, who surged forward. Dr. West found himself loping behind the sled, trying to overtake it, running. He tripped, dislodging his glasses as he lunged through the blinding white glare.

Squinting without his sunglasses, almost catching the sled as it skidded across a puddle of meltwater, he fell. Springing up, running harder and shouting angrily at the dogs, he had thought they would stop, but they were veering off to the left, and their loose gait accelerated to an excited rush as if they had scented a seal.

His commanding shouts grew shrill. Desperately he ran a shorter course to head them off, but they were bounding too fast, the lightened sled skipping behind them. Without the sled he was helpless, hopeless. His eyesight whirled with blinding lights as he fell.

From the ice, kneeling upward, gasping with breathless panic, he unslung his rifle. In the glare, his twitching eye could barely distinguish the front sight as it shook back and forth. Aiming ahead of the dogs he fired.

Unchecked, the dogs ran into the blinding distance. He fired again. The lead dog turned end-for-end biting his rump as the other dogs dragged it along. With a crushed yelp, it was mounted by the sled runners as the team swept on. Dragging the writhing dog and the swerving sled, the dog team charged on like troops into battle. They were running suicidally straight toward an open lead.

At the last moment, abruptly they stopped at the edge of the lead, and the sled skidded sideways braked only by the body of the wounded dog from sliding into the dark water. Dr. West ran furiously. With stupid grins, the dog team looked back at Dr. West, their breath fogging. If there had been a seal, it was long gone.

Whiteman, you panicked. Dr. West blundered toward the team's watching eyes and steaming grins.

His unprotected eyes were shimmering and blurring, but he had to recapture the sled before he could go back to search for his dark glasses. His face twisted in pain and guilt as the wounded dog whined and sniffed its shattered spine.

The other sled dogs watched, their tongues lolling out of great grins, while he pointed the rifle muzzle at the wounded dog's ear and pulled the trigger.

His hand trembling, with his knife Dr. West cut through the leather strap and freed the dead dog. Rising, squinting against the whiteness, he tried to see back along the sled runner's trail all the way to the indistinct pressure ridge where he thought he had fallen, where he had lost his glasses.

He was afraid Edwardluk and the other two would have heard the shots, but they should be a long way off near the iceberg. Surely this was a different iceberg. His eyes were killing him!

To reduce the glare, he slit his handkerchief and tied it across his eyes. Almost blinded, he shouted at the dogs, pushed the sled, yelled, cursed, flailed with the whip while dogs dodged in every direction, and suddenly the dog team darted, curved and flowed along their back trail toward the pressure ridge. He intended to allow himself one minute to search for his sunglasses.

"Here are your snow eyes!" Edwardluk stood up holding the dark glasses above his head.

Dr. West tore off the handkerchief, squinted around in a semicircle and did not see the other two men in ambush.

"Hand me the glasses." Dr. West did not point the rifle directly at Edwardluk.

Edwardluk's small hand extended the sunglasses. "Bad dogs run away," his voice murmured as if in apology, and he ducked his head as if ashamed. He shuffled his mukluks on the ice. "This poor person couldn't run fast enough."

"I cannot return to camp," Dr. West interrupted. "I must go find the other whitemen now."

"The other whitemen," Edwardluk agreed like an echo, and his real thinking emerged circuitously. "Bad ice. Wisest dog is dead. This is the dog's fault not to understand you. We do not understand you, but we like you. We want to help you always. When ice is safe, we go. Tomorrow. Each day you will like us better. Tomorrow."

Dr. West became aware of movement behind him, another Eskimo.

"I cannot go back now," Dr. West protested. "You must understand I'm trying to help you. I'll tell the whitemen your babies are hungry. I'll bring back food for the winter. Because I like you," he insisted rapidly. "I like you. Grandfather Bear eat me if I lie."

Edwardluk looked up at the sky, and he laughed. "West, you are stronger than my fear. Eh-eh, you want to go, we go! This person understands so little, but perhaps some day we people will help the whitemen, too. When we are many, we will help much. Help whitemen of whole world." Like a tiny giant, Edwardluk spread his arms and laughed, unaware that the world was 24,000 miles in circumference at the equator, that there were six billion white-whitemen, yellow-whitemen and black-whitemen, that their vast machines rumbled and lurched toward the stars.

"Go back," Edwardluk said to the other two young Eskimos. "Tell Marthalik her husband's safe with Edwardluk.

We will return in a——?" He looked questingly at Dr. West.

"In a month," Dr. West said, intending to allow plenty of time so she wouldn't worry.

"We go!" Edwardluk shouted at the dogs and cracked the whip. The sled rushed off carrying Dr. West, with Edwardluk running alongside, shouting: "There is the island."

Beyond the furthest iceberg on the horizon Dr. West could see the gray smudge. "A Guard Station of whitemen is truly there?" Dr. West knew Edwardluk had never been there, and other Eskimos who approached had been herded away by the Guards' helicopter. Perhaps antipersonnel radar would mistake him for another Eskimo, he thought. The helicopter might try to herd him back into the Cultural Sanctuary. "Has anyone seen the whitemen, spoken to them?"

"Peterluk has been close," Edwardluk shouted, "but the ice was not this bad. If there is much open water, we will have to turn back to the camp. We will try again next winter."

My god, Dr. West thought, *by then I'll be snowblind and the Eskimos will be starving*. If necessary he could threaten Edwardluk with the rifle. They would have to go on. If there was too much open water out there, he would build a signal fire and try to attract the helicopter.

Dragging the sled over pressure ridges, the dogs soon slowed. Tiring, Dr. West trotted beside the sled toward the gleaming horizon. Always there was another crack or ridge.

Helping lift the sled, slipping, tiring, falling, he accidentally jammed the muzzle of his rifle into the ice and rose muttering, staggering after the relentlessly gliding sled. He was encased in perspiration as he slogged into the blinding sun. His thoughts became confused. In his exhaustion, he became suspicious. Perhaps Edwardluk's plan was to wear him out and then seize the rifle——.

When the sled snagged on the thousandth pressure ridge, dizzy with exhaustion Dr. West lay down on the sled. The dogs lay down.

"Eh-eh, you rest in camp." Cheerfully Edwardluk scampered about with seemingly inexhaustible energy simultaneously trying to sight a seal while forcing two harpoon shafts into the ice and erecting a tattered caribou skin windbreak.

"Eh-eh, this person will talk to that seal." Edwardluk hefted the third harpoon and walked away into the blurry distance.

The wind hissed over the ice, bending the caribou skins into a funnel, a wind tunnel directed at Dr. West's congealing body. Edwardluk had vanished. Shivering, Dr. West ceased to know he was shivering until his ears awoke him to the distant grunting of the polar bear.

"Eh-eh," Edwardluk's voice laughed. "He don't find no seals either."

The dogs' voices whined, but their tone was not hunger. Dr. West's eyelids felt glued together. The dogs' voices whined with fear. Alaskan Eskimo dogs would have been roaring with eagerness to rush along the scent of the polar bear, he thought. These dogs were whining.

Dr. West slid his fingers under his sunglasses to his throbbing eyelids. Overpowering light penetrated although his eyes were closed. His head ached with pain messages from his overloaded optic nerves. When he tried to open his eyes, he gasped, drowned in dazzling liquid light.

He was snowblind.

The hoarse coughing sound was so distant he knew it wasn't Edwardluk. Edwardluk was moving here beside him. From the blind distance came a grunting sound as if from an indecisive hog. Dr. West's hand tightened on his rifle.

When a bear is hungry enough, he thought, *it will stalk sled dogs lying on the ice like seals. When a bear is starving it sees nothing but seals, and I am blind.*

"Eh-eh," Edwardluk's voice laughed, "nothing but seals. Give me the rifle. Big noise will tell the bear we are not seals."

"I will hold the rifle," Dr. West replied; he was afraid to let go of it because the rifle was all he had, snowblind and helpless. "I know how to work the rifle."

"This person knows how to work it," Edwardluk volunteered, and Dr. West could hear him moving closer. "Peterluk shot his rifle many times, and this person watched. It is not magic. It is shot with the finger. This person could shoot."

But not at bears, Dr. West thought.

"Close to the bear," Edwardluk answered his thought. "Give me the rifle."

"You would not shoot the bear even if I gave you the rifle," Dr. West replied, clinging to its stock.

"This person would not shoot too close," Edwardluk agreed, tugging at the rifle. "This person is not a bear killer like Peterluk, who will never rise into the sky. This person would only shoot a loud noise so the bear understands we are not seals. Give me——."

"Get back." Dr. West clicked off the safety catch, pointed the barrel down and squeezed the trigger. The supposedly recoilless rifle blasted, kicking viciously. There had been ice in the barrel, he realized, but it had not burst. "I have frightened the bear," Dr. West blurted. "Now there is no need for you to have the rifle."

"If this person had the rifle, a seal could be shot," Edwardluk's voice persisted.

"There are three harpoons," Dr. West replied.

"But your eyes are bad," Edwardluk murmured circuitously.

"I will not give you the rifle."

Further away the polar bear emitted a mooing noise.

"This person watched you while you sleep," Edwardluk said, as if this was more important than the circling bear. "Eh-eh, asleep you frown, you twist. In the encampment it was this way also. You look unhappy when asleep. The same as you, Peterluk is that way. Even with your arms around Marthalik, your sleep-face is unhappy. Are all whitemen unhappy when they sleep?"

"How the hell should I know?" Dr. West slung the rifle over his back and crawled blindly onto the sled. "Let's go!"

"Whitemen do not shoot us—," Edwardluk asked what really must have been worrying him, "—as if we are dogs?"

"No, I was frightened when I shot the dog. I thought they were running away. I thought they were leaving me alone to die. I only shoot things that are leaving me to die."

On the moving sled, Joe West clung to his rifle, his head

muffled in the futile darkness of caribou skins, his eyes
throbbing and flashing with lights of pain. Once he heard
Edwardluk shouting at someone, and his stomach contracted.
He dreamed Edwardluk had circled all the way back to the
encampment. No escape. Then he realized Edwardluk had
merely admonished the dogs.

The sled was moving sporadically as if the dogs were
exhausted again. Finally the sled stopped. Their whining
faded.

Motionless, Dr. West was awakened by the distant crack-
whoosh of a recoilless rifle. *Whitemen?* Dr. West's fingers
crawled along the oddly thin stock of his rifle. He was
holding on to a harpoon shaft. "My rifle. He's stolen my
rifle."

Under him the sled jerked, and the dogs whined, hungrily
straining while the sled creaked immovably because Edwardluk had anchored it to the ice.

Edwardluk's plodding return with a dragging sound was
engulfed by the roaring lunges of the dogs. Edwardluk was
feeding the dogs first, hurling thuds of meat within their
harnessed range. Then he was beating them off. "No more!
Got no more!"

"Here is the seal's liver." Edwardluk must have carried it
under his parka. "Eat. Do not be afraid. This person left a
little blubber by the water for the bear. Eat. Grandfather
Bear will see how we helped this bear. Eat. Soon this person
will shoot a bigger seal. ——You eat. Around us there are
many wide cracks and soon another seal. Then this person
also will eat."

From the distance rose a long-drawn howling roar like a
giant, insane.

"My god! Was that the bear?"

"This person don't know. The bear, it was the bear. A little
taste of blubber wake up bear's stomach. Eh-eh," Edwardluk
laughed nervously. "Bear want to eat world."

"Give me my rifle."

"Eh-eh, he is only a bear." Edwardluk clicked the rifle's
safety on or off; there was no way for Dr. West's ears to tell
which. Edwardluk's voice diminished as he moved away.

"Bear don't like man's smell. Once Peterluk's rifle don't work. He said he lie still and bear sniff him and go away."

The snarling was the dogs.

"What are you doing?" Dr. West meant: *don't leave me alone*.

"This person sees a seal far off. Dogs not fed enough to sleep only fight each other. This person must shoot this other seal." Edwardluk added with practicality: "Your smell will keep the bear away from eating the dogs. Soon this person come back——."

Dr. West groped on the sled for the harpoon shaft, clutching it.

"Best thing is sleep," Edwardluk's voice said, softer, but closer. Instead of leaving, Edwardluk squatted down so close Dr. West could feel his radiated warmth, hear his excited breathing.

"The important thing, will the whitemen like us?" Edwardluk blurted. "We don't harm anybody. We helped you. We want to help everybody because—we know. You don't know what's happening, but we know. We sleep happy all with the same dream because we are here, we are there, we know why."

Edwardluk's voice hoarsened with emotion, with joy, and his hand gently closed on Dr. West's wrist. "We sleep happy because we know that Grandfather Bear will come. He will come down when there are enough of us and——."

Dr. West had stiffened involuntarily, and Edwardluk stopped, as if sensing rejection. Again, Dr. West knew what Edwardluk was thinking: you don't like us. For over a month Dr. West had been bombarded by the confusing love and mythology of these people.

If these strange Eskimos escaped from their cage, from their Sanctuary, Dr. West wondered wryly, would they be scurrying door to door, knocking and disturbing housewives with their joyfully apocalyptic message?

"He will come," Edwardluk's voice insisted, "when we have covered the world for him." Edwardluk's grip tightened on Dr. West's wrist. "Our bodies will reward him for our birth." Edwardluk's voice rose in confidence and joy. "His great hunger is for us, for us. To this world and all worlds, he comes."

Abruptly, Edwardluk released his grip, standing up. His footsteps shuffled away over the ice. The dogs whined with hunger, with hope of more seal meat.

Through the wind drifted loud then softer grunting as if the bear were circling. The wind hissed across the sled. Under the stiffening caribou skins, Dr. West lay shivering and trying not to sleep or perhaps to sleep, to escape. *Eskimos say dream life is real life, beginning while sleeping cold, dreaming cold, awakening into sleep like a wolf inhaling the scents, like a caribou hearing the most distant sounds, like a hand feeling———.*

Smoothly he dreamed Marthalik, warmly moving in love, and he were gasping together. In his arms was Marthalik loving him, and he knew she was more wonderful than any woman he had ever known. Relaxing, awakening, she became cute and dimpled. Rising, she became determined and efficient. Proudly she was nursing his son. Then she was flowing back into his arms, and he dreamed they were moving together stronger and stronger, rising again toward that distant sun. Coupled with her he was dreaming toward the green planet he could never quite see. With indescribable horror he saw the green planet was brown.

Writhing from smoothness, he was falling from the ape forest of his ancestors. He was running, lost from Marthalik. In his dream he was trying to run away from the grunting sounds of the polar bear. The terrified whining of the dogs awakened him. He sat up blindly on the anchored sled. The grunting sound was the bear approaching.

With his finger and thumb, Dr. West peeled one eyelid open and gasped with pain, stabbed by the blinding white light. His eyes flooded with tears. He couldn't see. Along the sled he groped for the two harpoons.

"Edwardluk!" he shouted, and the vast emptiness of sea ice swallowed his voice and returned like a false echo the grunting of the bear.

His hand gripped the harpoon shaft, best weapon for a blindman? To his own surprise he laughed. A bit shrilly, but he laughed. Turning his head to follow the piglike noises of the bear, he extended the harpoon. "Come on you invisible spook! I'm a man, not a seal."

His pounding heart, his surging adrenalin, had given him back his warmth, his liveness. He laughed with surprise that he was not afraid. He felt beyond fear. Much closer than before, the bear growled.

The dogs yelped, violently thrashing the anchored sled, concealing any moving sounds of the bear.

In this uncertain moment as Dr. West continued to awaken, he reevaluated. *These dogs are straining to escape. Escape is so simple!* With this intelligent realization, his atavistic flow of courage froze. With the frightened gasps of a civilized man, Dr. West dropped the harpoon and unsheathed his short-bladed skinning knife.

Of course the dogs will run, he thought. *They'll drag the sled away, carrying me.*

The bear growled.

Tight-muscled with fright, Dr. West lurched along the straining sled, fumbled back along the rail until his hand found the taut anchor strap. His knife slashed.

The strap broke, the lunging dogs yanking the sled from under him. He fell on his elbow on the ice, momentarily stunned by his stupidity as the clamor of the fleeing dog team faded into the distance.

So he couldn't escape, he thought, almost laughing with shock. Was he predestined never to escape from the Eskimo Cultural Sanctuary?

"Edwardluk!" Dr. West started to rise and was warned by a cavernous growl.

He remained in a crouching posture, turning his head in the direction from which the sound had emerged. He was facing upwind, and an odor like rotten meat became noticeable, but now he couldn't hear the bear. The bear must be motionless, staring at him.

Gradually, Dr. West sank down on the ice, his knife hand under his shoulder as he flattened out on the ice, his vulnerable stomach pressed against the ice, his legs pressed together, his shoulders hunched protectively about his neck. His chest pressed against the ice, his heart thudding against the ice. He could hear the hiss-hiss of its breathing, the bear's shuffling advance.

Dr. West made no new attempts to open his eyes. He tried to see backward into the fortress of his bachelor apartment in Berkeley. In stunned amusement he thought: *I can't die here with six months rent prepaid there.* To the right of its fieldstone fireplace, behind the multi-colored medical books on the top shelf, he could almost see his .44 caliber magnum Ruger Blackhawk revolver, a heavy hog leg single-action revolver with gleaming thick cylinder stuffed with six bullets looking fat as thumbs. Almost as if it were reality, his hand closed around—emptiness.

The bear snorted. Motionless on the ice, Dr. West suppressed his breathing. He remembered Alaskan Eskimo hunters laughing how they had behaved in such situations. Prostrate before their bears, they had lived to joke. "Don't breathe," those wizened Alaskan Eskimos advised; "bear never kills dead man."

This polar bear's stench engulfed him. Above him poised the hiss-hiss of its breathing. There was a gurgling sound, the ravenous contractions of its digestive system.

As forcibly as the blunt end of a baseball bat, the polar bear nosed his thigh, trying to turn him over.

Desperately, he wanted to lunge away, but he sagged limply because the bear's quick paw would smash him like a seal if he moved.

He wanted to leap away with a nightmare shriek as the bear's nose clubbed his thigh, his hip, shoving to turn him over, to expose his vital belly. Stiffening, resisting, Dr. West tried to hold his belly pressed against the ice.

With an eager grunt and a series of hisses, the bear's nose burrowed under him, pushing up his hip. He twisted and was clamped——.

A shriek with an agonizing muscular spasm ballooned through his consciousness. His thigh, the bear's crushing jaws. With the squawling vitality of any animal being devoured alive, the former Dr. West writhed, striking the knife blade across the hard muzzle of the polar bear.

With a startled woof, the bear's jaws opened. Dr. West's body rolled away slashing the air and screaming defiance like a cornered animal. Backing away, gasping, he hacked the air with the knife while the shuffling sounds of the bear softened.

He became aware of the throbbing of his thigh. Gummed eyelids torn open, he faced blindly into the whiteness and listened through his own harsh breathing for the silent bear, and remembered who he was.

Dr. West's fingers explored the slippery twitching remnants of his thigh muscle. Hard-jawed, he tourniqueted his belt around his thigh against the groin, and gasped.

"Edwardluk," he gurgled. "Edwardluk, Edwardluk!" he yelled.

There was no Edwardluk. "Edwardluk! Edwardluk!"

His voice thickened. His head seemed to sail away, and he muttered and twisted, resisting. If he fell into shock, he thought, in this cold he would be dead.

Dead, dead, irretrievably dead. All gone. Finished. Nothing.

From hissing wind emerged a scraping sound approaching, as if something were dragging the sled back to him.

"Dogs turn away," Edwardluk's voice wheezed, "from water too late. Sled float. Curlytail drown. Loafer drown." All Edwardluk could talk about was the dogs. "Hump drown." Edwardluk's strong hands were turning him over on his back on the sled. "Wind Runner drown."

Darkness and warmth slid down over Dr. West's head and shoulders, and he realized Edwardluk was giving him his outer parka.

"White Eye drown." Edwardluk was prodding his coldly numbing leg, wrapping his leg in something jellylike within wet fur. "Fished out drowned dogs. Cut up. Eh-eh," Edwardluk laughed feebly, "much good dog meat for everyone. This person cut open Wild Runner for the bear."

With crunching sounds, Edwardluk began breaking apart the sled. Edwardluk murmured he was rebuilding it into a man-sled. Gently, Edwardluk's hands tied Dr. West on a sled so small his heels dragged.

Blind, Dr. West knew they were microscopic specks moving across the enormity of sea ice, icebergs, shore ice and distant ice-scraped islands.

"Ha!" As if encouraging the drowned dogs to pull, shouting Edwardluk strained at the harness, and the jolting hours moved Dr. West through chills and sleep and fever, becoming days of blind agony without end.

Edwardluk's soft voice tried to soothe. "Eat-eat." He was pressing chewed dog meat into Dr. West's mouth.

Edwardluk would shout: "Ha! Forward, dogs!" and Edwardluk's stubby legs would tramp forward, endlessly dragging the man-sled with its raving burden, Dr. West.

"The bear," Dr. West would gasp. "Got to warn them." The Canadian Parliament became twelve pairs of eyes surrealistically floating in a jury box. "Please believe me." *All our growing population pressure is forcing nation against nation in amoebalike growing struggles of the population masses of the world*, his thought writhed. *Believe me, these Eskimos are multiplying so much faster. Like a Bomb!* ——"These people cannot be Eskimos! What are they?"

In his delirium, Marthalik's face rose smiling. He clung to her body. The droning of the airplane transformed snowflakes into parachutes drifting down with swaying food packages. As absurdly as Pop Art, these were decorated in red calligraphy: FAMILY ALLOWANCES, and swaying back and forth, massive jaws crunching.

"Too many Eskimos." *For these happy people what does the bear symbolize?* "Don't feed the bear!" he shrieked.

The giggling Eskimo women slyly were stuffing the birth control pills into their ears. Their bellies inflated. Scurrying children massed. The Earth tipped. From the darkness of space opened the jaws. "The bear!" he shrieked.

In more lucid moments, Dr. West clutched his swollen thigh and thought what a good man Edwardluk was. Laughing, straining, uncomplaining, that was the Eskimo image. Eskimos were cheerful people who fought no wars. It was true. So true. Men of goodwill all over the world would not let the Eskimos starve no matter how many Eskimos——.

The headwind carried the smell of coal smoke, the barking of dogs.

Loud voices were threatening. The sled had stopped. A harsh voice wheezed: "This bastard has a beard! He's a whiteman."

"At his eyes, look," the younger voice murmured on with an accent as if he might have been one of the political refugees from West Germany who'd flocked to Canada since 1984. "Such sore eyes——."

"Lift the dirty smuggler." They were carrying him into darkness and dumped him. "Don't let the Eskimo get away," the harsh voice wheezed. "Kerosene eyedrops for snow-blin——."

"No, wait!" Dr. West gasped. "Leave my eyes alone. I'm a doctor. I must be flown to a hospital with—with Edward-luk."

"If you're a doctor, where's your kit?" the Guard's harsh voice challenged. "You smuggling bastards won't even leave the world's best people alone. Twenty years I've been waiting to catch you." His voice subsided in a succession of wheezes as if he had chronic emphysema.

"In his pack are no trade items," the younger voice soothed, and Dr. West felt the caribou skin being pulled off the lower part of his body. "His leg——," the young voice thickened in a retching sound, and Dr. West became aware of the stench.

"Gangrene," the old Guard wheezed. "Hope the bastard dies."

Edwardluk, Edwardluk, Dr. West thought desperately. "Help——." From his swollen throat his voice squeezed out so distantly it must be nearly inaudible.

"This good man. You will like us," Edwardluk's Eskimo voice was murmuring hopefully. "West says much food here. Dog bite him. Mad dog bite his leg. This person drag him on little sled that many sleeps." Edwardluk must be holding up stubby fingers, still trying to communicate. "Dogs drown. This person drag him all the way across."

"Sea ice over there?" The halting voice of the old Guard was attempting to reply in Eskimo as if he'd spent twenty years cooped in the Station listening to language records, never allowed to speak to an Eskimo. "Big travel. Bad ice."

There was respect in the Guard's voice. "You long-traveling hunter!"

Perhaps they were shaking hands.

Edwardluk giggled with embarrassment. "Pulled whiteman long way. Children hungry. He say much food here."

There was an awkward silence. Already the Guard grievously had sinned by allowing the Eskimo inside the Station. Now he was being asked to further violate the purpose of the Sanctuary by giving the Eskimos food.

In the silence, Edwardluk laughed in confusion. "Will you help us? Many-many people hungry!" Edwardluk must be spreading his short arms. "Many people. ——Here his marker-book."

Muttering, the Guard must be turning the pages. "I'll be damned!"

"He count people. Say not enough seals," Edwardluk expounded. "He count babies. He say more hungry quick."

"The Director should make his own survey," the Guard's voice blurted in English. "This smuggler must be crazy. He's counted too many children. Can't be this many until the end of the *second* Twenty-Year Plan."

"From now is twenty years," the accented younger voice remarked almost maliciously. "But we are not permitted close enough to count. These Eskimos we know are too many already or they would not be starving."

"He say all whitemen love us. We help him," Edwardluk's voice swept on hopefully. "All this way pulling sled like dog."

"What does he say?"

"He says," the Guard's tired old voice muttered in English, "we'll have to crank up the copter more often this winter to chase them back."

"Of their starvation I worry," the young voice blurted. "Of other guards who obeyed orders I think. My *grossvater*——."

"You can think," the old Guard's voice interrupted, "because you're as good as out. Your contract won't be renewed anyway, so you don't have to hang on for your pension."

"But if the Director finds out of the whale last winter which you—we drove ashore," the young voice thrust slyly as if he were leading toward something, "he will cut from his budget you and your pension, *kaput!*——Already didn't Suxbey say the budget is too small to give you medical leave this year?"

"You talk about the whale, and you'll have an accident!"

"No, no, me you misunderstand. No one would know about us except the producer. Think of this Eskimo smiling on the CBC all over Canada, tears in his eyes, children starving."

"And wreck the Sanctuary before I get my pension?"

"The producer said I—we would receive a percentage——."

"To help sink Mr. Suxbey after twenty years?"

"But this trespasser, lying here, if he talks to the press, which he will, perhaps for his own percentage, he or the next man will finish the wreck of the Sanctuary. ——Your pension, *kaput!* My producer is a generous man. But you are in command here. You must decide——."

"Simple. I'm radioing the Director for instructions," the old Guard wheezed.

"Then hurry," the young voice retorted, "if out of life that is all you want. This trespasser anyway is dying."

In terror, Dr. West tried to sit up. In his delirium he tried to speak as Edwardluk's face appeared pleading as if from the TV screens. "Our babies starving." As if in a dream, Dr. West saw food packages pouring from shimmering aircraft and there were always more Eskimos and not enough packages. Dark faces were springing up in the UN General Assembly of his delirium, accusing. Canada's attempted birth limitation of the Eskimos was pushing the angry darker peoples of the world up in the UN shouting: "Racial sterilization! Capitalist genocide!"

The angry roaring was huge aircraft attacking from all over the world with more food, more tents. Like a distant dream, the Eskimos were spreading over his delirium.

"Eh-eh, we fill world," Edwardluk had explained a week ago with lovable simplicity, "until bear comes."

Death gnawed Dr. West's leg, and he tried to sit up while Edwardluk's gentle hands held him down.

"Must speak," Dr. West gasped, thinking: *I must live. I want so much to live.* "I must speak."

"You sleep now," Edwardluk was whispering, holding him down. "He come———."

In his delirium, Dr. West heard the galactic grunting of the bear.

3.
WHO
IS
MORE
HUMAN?

THE MOANING SOUND OF THE AIRPLANE ENCLOSING HIM bumped down. He was carried out feet first.

Under a modern surgical-green ceiling he lay in delirium as a blinding light moved above him and a phantom bear's teeth gnawed his leg. "Scalpel. Suture," a disembodied voice snapped, and years later another voice remarked: "They say a sled dog did this to his leg?"

Writhing feverishly, Dr. West heard the savage howl of a diesel train. With a revolving clarity he decided he must be a thousand miles south of Boothia in the city of Churchill on Hudson Bay at the northern end of the railroad. He opened his eyes.

Now he seemed to be lying in an Intensive Care room. There was an oddly familiar wheezing sound.

"Welcome to Ottawa, sir." On the other bed lounged the blue-and-white uniform of a Cultural Sanctuary Guard.

"Ottawa?" Dr. West blurted in surprise. "Ottawa?"

"Ottawa?" the leathery face of the Cultural Sanctuary Guard mimicked. "Because you're from the States, sir, you've not bothered to learn we Canadians have a capital too?" The Guard's sarcastic smile widened in triumph. "Welcome to the New Ottawa Reformation Center."

"My trial! When was my trial?"

"I expect you're looking forward to the Pasteur injections for rabies, sir? They stick the needle in your stomach and——."

"I'm in prison without a trial!"

"No, sir. This is the finest hospital in Canada. For serious illness, sir, the Cultural Sanctuary always uses this hospital. The prison is outside. Around us."

Dr. West tried to sit up, entangled in drainage tubes, and

in wires presumably transmitting his heartbeat and blood pressure to the monitor beside his bed.

The nurse materialized through the revolving one-way glass wall. "You're disturbing the patient."

"Never did a thing," the Cultural Sanctuary Guard retorted weakly, his leathery old face seeming out of place in this hospital room 2000 miles south of the Boothia Peninsula, and he slumped back on his own bed, wheezing.

"You've been smoking again," she sniffed. "I can smell it. The doctor should take away your uniform. In a hospital gown, you should be guarding this gentleman. From your bed, you should be——."

"Pranging you!"

"You old dreamer. Is this how you earned your pay in your Cultural Sanctuary? Lying around boasting and smoking. Going outside to take away transistor radios from poor little Eskimos. Or stealing their fishhooks. Or shooting down newspaper gentlemen." She winked at Dr. West inaccurately.

"I know which party you belong to—my lass," the Cultural Sanctuary Guard's voice wheezed. "Asinine women like you think they understand more than important scientists and statesmen. Your asinine party would solve Canada's problems with her unprepared minorities by making the Eskimos disappear. We'll save a few Eskimos from your melting pot."

"Please stop disturbing the patient." She pressed her cool hand on Dr. West's forehead between his taped-on encephalogram sensors and winked at him.

One day when the Guard was asleep, she asked Dr. West if Marthalik was his wife.

"Marthalik?" Dr. West realized he must have done a lot of talking those first days while he was delirious. "Yes, my wife."

He lay trapped in the hospital while they attempted massive repairs of his leg while simultaneously torturing him with Pasteur injections. "It was a bear that bit me, not a mad dog," he protested, but he had to admit to himself that perhaps the bear *had* been rabid and this was why it had acted so strangely.

Like a fellow prisoner, the Cultural Sanctuary Guard reclined on the other bed, fully uniformed, setting down his oxygen mask. "Don't plan to escape, lad, while I'm in the can. If you pull off your wires, the monitor will buzz the nurse."

She might be watching him through the one-way glass wall, Dr. West knew. Because his room was narrower at that end, with an oddly trapezoidal pie shape, he deduced these Intensive Care rooms were arranged around a central nursing station but located in a square building. The center was where the warning lights and sensor readout panels and computer would be located, he thought, wondering how to get out. He saw the walls and floor of his room had removable vinyl covering to help maintain semisterility. Whenever his door opened, he could feel air from his room flow outward, evidently an air pressure barrier against outside bacteria. Although the Cultural Sanctuary Guard was a minimum care patient, the hospital staff never allowed the Cultural Guard outside to carry in new bacteria.

One day, while the glass wall was opening, Dr. West glimpsed a nurse at the central console removing a bottle from a pneumatic tube which must extend down to the pharmacy. He supposed the computerized console had the medication schedules of the patients dialed into it by the doctors. On schedule it would order the medical dosages from the pharmaceutical computer downstairs. But there were no stairs. To escape from the ward he would need to use the elevator.

Trapped with his leg in an antigangrene hip boot pulsating, Dr. West had to envy the medical technology in this Canadian hospital. Everything expensive that they talked about in the States, and rarely installed, was here: patient self-service beds, liquid residue diets, electrocephalic sleeping helmets, old-pro nurses.

"You have a visitor." She glowered at the tweedy bacteria carrier, who extended toward Dr. West an unsterile and leathery hand.

It was a hard grip the wizened man had, a commanding gaze. The nurse departed. The Cultural Sanctuary Guard, who had been standing at attention, obediently departed as if he had heard an order from this grimly smiling man.

"Dr. West, I've been most interested by your dossier—your, shall we say, checkered career," Hans Suxbey said. "As Director of the Eskimo Cultural Sanctuary, I've often imagined how it would feel to be—fired. I assume your resignation was not a, shall we say, cover. You weren't sent into my Sanctuary by that Oriental Population Problems Research Project from which you were fired. The U.S. Defense Department surely can't be interested in my innocent Eskimos."

Dr. West smiled like a shield. "I'm up here on my sabbatical, on University of California money, not Defense Department money. Either press legal charges against me or let me go."

"Nothing would give me greater pleasure than for your medical treatment to be completed so you can depart for the States. You raved so deliriously on the various aircraft which transported you here from Boothia, that your accidental crash and heroic rescue by one of my Eskimos earned thirty seconds on the TV news. But you've been forgotten, replaced by more important news such as Ottawa's increasing lead over San Francisco in the new International Hockey League."

"What crash? What happened to my pilot?"

"The English are abominable pilots. Before our aircraft could intercept him he crashed. So much open water in Victoria Strait."

"Your F-111 forced him down or shot him down?"

"Of course not," Hans Suxbey laughed. "But it would have been better for all concerned if our radar had noticed his aircraft on the way into the Sanctuary, while you still were in the aircraft. Even now, your distraught wife is lurking outside the pris—the hospital."

"My wife?"

"So she's not," Hans Suxbey laughed. "I thought any woman who carries her marriage license in her purse must have an ulterior motive. Either she's the most persistent of the reporters or she's been sent by the McGill University crowd who put you up to this."

Dr. West said nothing, wondering if the Director's attaché case contained a tape recorder.

"My former colleagues at McGill have never forgiven me." The Director's face seemed to age. "Because my own career began at McGill, Lecturer in Eskimo Ethnology over thirty years ago, they think I owe them special treatment. For twenty years they have been demanding to inspect, that is, to violate my Eskimo Cultural Sanctuary, even though this would shatter its purpose. Hordes of note-taking ethnologists by their very presence would disturb the cultural pattern of any primitive people. How can my easily influenced Eskimos regain their prehistoric independence and self-confidence if they're to be jostled by professors, with notebooks, and then denigrated by loudmouthed whitemen riding in Sno-Cats and flaunting two-way radios, nylon tents, rifles, canned food, steel knives. My industrious Eskimos may be beginning to recreate bone knives."

"If they don't starve to death this winter——," Dr. West thrust.

Hans Suxbey stared him down. "While you were delirious, your babblings about a one-month gestation period for women, for women, that is, not lemmings, was reported by some gullible spy to the sensationalist press, where your name was printed. Your ravings were quoted. This may have destroyed the remnants of your professional reputation."

Dr. West nodded glumly. "What did you do with my black notebook?"

"You attempted an incredibly sloppy age-sex census."

"At least it shows a disproportionate number of children, suggesting a startling increase in population. Too many hungry mouths, not enough adult hunters, starvation this winter. Where is my notebook?"

"Prehistoric Eskimo culture was shaped by their harsh Arctic environment."

"Implying starvation has cultural benefits which you can't admit to the press or Parliament," Dr. West persisted. "More Eskimos, more starvation, more authenticity in your cultural museum."

"I plan to introduce plastic intrauterine birth control devices into their religious rites in four years when the Eskimo elements of their culture are stronger, and I plan to enter my—their Sanctuary."

"Do it now. Open your eyes to reality in your Sanctuary," Dr. West said, "or there will be too much starvation this winter. Your Guards will turn against you and tell the world what they know. When Canadian voters learn that your Eskimos are starving in Canada, land of wheat surpluses——."

"You're exaggerating. You're threatening me?" Hans Suxbey bleated. "My Cultural Sanctuary's my life."

Hans Suxbey leaned forward, "It's the Boothia Peninsula my enemies want to grab. Members of Parliament would use your lies, any lies, to open the Sanctuary. They hope to strike oil for Quebec. They don't care about my Eskimos. Think what happened to your Navahos when——."

"Since uranium was discovered their living standard has improved."

"True Navaho culture has vanished," Hans Suxbey stated. "And our last Eskimo culture will vanish if liars like you cause Parliament to vote against my annual appropriation. In Parliament that greedy old Etienne LaRue is the tool of the oil interests. In Parliament that reactionary old racist, LaRue, is drooling to destroy me and my Sanctuary and the last Eskimo culture. That senile old paranoid in Parliament for twenty years has been trying to destroy me and the last Eskimos."

"At least the Eskimos in the Co-Ops will——."

"Those aren't Eskimos." Hans Suxbey leaned forward, repeating his old protest. "They're lost as Eskimos. They're simply round-faced Canadians disappearing in the homogenized cultural slurb spreading all over the world from the United States."

Dr. West said nothing, no use arguing with this wild-eyed old man that the real villain for the increasing similarity of cultures throughout the world was not the United States. It was technology.

"You are anxious to leave Canada," Hans Suxbey was saying like an offer to do business.

"Yes." Dr. West was trying to think how he could get back to the Sanctuary and rescue Marthalik before the winter starvation began.

"But when you reach the United States you would talk to journalists and contact my enemies at McGill. Deliberately or not you would help destroy the Sanctuary."

This was difficult for Dr. West to deny. "If you bring me

to trial for violating the Eskimo Cultural Sanctuary, the publicity will do the same thing." Immediately he wished he hadn't said that because—but surely this civilized man wouldn't have him murdered—would he?

Hans Suxbey opened his attaché case on his knees and thrust at him the microphone of the tape recorder. "Whatever lies you tell in the States will be contradicted by your recorded statement." He aimed the microphone like a gun. "Simply tell us how you intended to study those debased Co-Op Eskimos to the west. Your aircraft strayed off-course near our Sanctuary and crashed off-shore. Our more authentic Eskimos rescued you. ——What you say now simply will confirm our press release of last month when you were brought to the hospital. You were quoted, shall we say, through my mouth——."

Dr. West felt the trap close.

"You observed them to be well-adjusted to their environment," Hans Suxbey was saying. "Happy and well-fed, they are succeeding admirably in their use of bone and stone artifacts. While one Eskimo was transporting you to our Guard Station, a rabid sled dog attacked you, severely injuring your leg. You remember raving with delirium, strange dreams like a one-month gestation period——."

"Go see for yourself."

"Shall we rehearse before I switch on the recorder?"

"Yes, rehearse the truth," Dr. West blurted. "Face facts. It's important that you personally enter the Sanctuary this summer, now. See for yourself. Not only will Eskimos starve; suppose for example this one-month gestation trait were not transmitted by inheritance from a mutation. Suppose this increased growth rate of Eskimo embryos has a viral cause, like a cancer, like a communicable cancer which could spread to mothers throughout the world?"

"The ultimate population explosion?" Hans Suxbey laughed. "When you were fired as Director of Oriental Population Problems Research, you went insane."

"No, I admit the one-month gestation period probably did begin as a mutation rather than a virus, but when a people's birthrate rises so suddenly it must be investigated at once.

There's not only starvation for your Eskimos; there may be long-term implications for Canada."

"My next inspection within the Sanctuary is scheduled in my Plan in four years. By helicopter, I'll conduct my next flyover then."

"Four years?" Dr. West bleated. "Flyover? Inspect from an altitude of 5000 feet? You're the one who is insane. You don't want to disturb your cultural museum. You want survival of the fittest Eskimos? In four years when you enter, you'll inspect your museum—of starved corpses."

"Now if you'll relax, we can rehearse something more reasonable for the tape recorder."

"Like hell I will!"

"Then don't." Hans Suxbey snapped the attaché case shut, rose and departed. "Ever."

For another month Dr. West underwent minor operations on his leg, waiting for Hans Suxbey to return or for the hospital to release him. Now that the tendons and remnants of muscle were healing they were giving Dr. West daily physiotherapy—in his room. When he proudly hobbled into the central station, the nurse abruptly pressed an alarm button and an orderly appeared from the elevator and firmly hobbled him back to his room.

"You're not a prisoner," the nurse insisted and the doctors insisted while they cheerfully played with endless minor cosmetic operations on the skin of his leg, and more weeks crawled by while Dr. West practiced walking quickly to the window of his room.

Snowflakes fluttered against the glass. Dr. West stared out at the last brown leaves in the park which surrounded the cylindrical white towers of the prison. With the growing strength in his body, he daydreamed of Marthalik. Through a thin spot in the mirrored one-way glass, Dr. West studied the silhouette of the nurse at the central console. When the wheezing Cultural Sanctuary Guard was in the bathroom, Dr. West opened the closet and studied the Guard's civvies for fit. He knew the Guard was standing on the toilet seat with his head in the air vent smoking a cigarette, which was the Intelligent Man's Cure for Emphysema. Swiftly, Dr. West entered the bathroom carrying the Guard's pillow, and the

Guard's wheezing stopped. When the dim silhouette of the duty nurse left the console to inspect one of the other rooms, Dr. West put the limp Guard to bed, using both oxygen and manual resucitation to start his wheezing again. He crowned the Guard with the sleeping helmet dialed to MAXIMUM. The sleeping Guard's civilian trousers were too short for Dr. West, the old sportcoat lacked modern duo-lapels, but the next time the nurse left her console station, an unstylish Dr. West left the ward by elevator.

He had learned the visiting hours.

On the ground floor he limped away among the visitors departing from the Minimum Care Ward. He limped after them along the concrete path between the concrete towers. As blankly windowless as silos, they housed the "students" at the New Ottawa Reformation Center. At the gate there was no security. It must be the towers which were escape-proof, Dr. West thought as he entered the monorail car, dropping the Guard's quarter in the slot. The mono whined above the sprawling metropolis of Ottawa.

He knew Ottawa was only fifty miles from the U.S. border, but the broad St. Lawrence River would intervene. Probably the hospital would be contacting the police and Hans Suxbey. Dr. West hoped the Director of the Cultural Sanctuary would try to call off a public search because arrest publicity would provide new ammunition for the enemies of Hans Suxbey. Dr. West thought, if he reached the U.S., his delirium already misquoted by the press, who would believe his story of a one-month gestation period in the Eskimo Cultural Sanctuary? He needed Marthalik.

If he sought help at McGill University, he thought those nervous ethnologists might be indecisively helpless. Their instincts would be to guard their research grants. They were afraid to offend the Canadian Government or even such minor political battlers as Hans Suxbey.

"But there is one man here in Ottawa, he won't be afraid— to use me." Dr. West hoped he could use this powerful man as a passport back to the Cultural Sanctuary.

From the monorail he looked ahead to the hill bristling with Parliament buildings. Like a square-sided rocket, the Peace Tower pointed at the afternoon sky as Dr. West limped toward the private office of the most ferocious member of the Canadian House of Commons.

Inside the outer office of Etienne LaRue, Gobelin tapestries swathed the walls. The cut-glass chandelier glittered. The receptionist's desk was Louis XIV, and the buxom receptionist seemed wasted on Etienne LaRue, who was eighty-four years old with a handshake like parchment.

"When I heard your name, Dr. West, I come out!" Etienne LaRue straightened and his eyes seemed startlingly youthful. "That lying Suxbey, weeks ago how he lied the press! But my friends in the hospital have report to me—you seem sane. I wish to believe with you."

Scurrying, the old man led Dr. West to the inner office, where a fortyish man rose ponderously, sliding a bottle back into a drawer.

"It may be useful to speak in front of my nephew," old Etienne LaRue snapped. "Tell him—Henri, listen to him—how the Sanctuary has become a concentration camp of the dead."

As Dr. West opened his mouth, Etienne LaRue's voice rushed on: "That dog in the manger, Suxbey, would seize the whole Northwest Territories. For his Eskimo empire, he is stealing Canada's future living space. He is a maniac! Do not describe for me all the atheistic sexual abominations taking place under his leadership. Each fiscal year I have been pleading with Parliament that we must defeat his wasteful request for appropriation. Always I have said, reopen the Eskimo Cultural Sanctuary to the honest Canadian people to whom Canada belongs!"

Somehow Etienne LaRue didn't leave Dr. West much to tell. Dr. West remembered Etienne LaRue had begun his rise to elder statesman a generation ago on a political platform of linguistic independence for Quebec.

"But there are only a few hundred of these Eskimos," Dr. West kept trying to calm Etienne LaRue. "Only the few Eskimos on the Boothia Peninsula have the monthly gestation period. ——Of course, they do seem different from other Eskimos in other ways. Their complexions are so clear and unweathered, as if they're all quite young. They seem even more good-humored and patient and honest than the Co-Op

Eskimos. With the exception of one older Eskimo who still owns a rifle, they were kind to me. They are wonderful people."

Old Etienne LaRue's face wrinkled as if in disgust. "You— Doctor West, are another visitor from the United States who becomes an expert on Eskimos in a week. Like a child's book, you tell of Eskimos like happy angels smiling." LaRue's voice lowered to a whisper. "Those squint-eyed heathen are barely human!"

Dr. West blinked. This old man was showing himself to be a political dinosaur, who was outside the beliefs of either party in Parliament. Dr. West smiled sardonically. "Perhaps they're not human, by your definition."

"Ah!" Etienne LaRue smiled in instant agreement.

"A one-month gestation period," Dr. West said, "suggests many hormonal differences from other Eskimo women, from human women. Perhaps these should be considered a new subspecies."

"A new species, *mon dieu!* I knew they weren't human."

"Perhaps not a new species because—they do interbreed," Dr. West laughed hollowly, "——with us. Perhaps you could say they are a new race, differentiated not so much by outward appearance as by gestation period and other habits which we will discover. Instead of Eskimos, instead of 'skimos which is a derogatory term, perhaps we should differentiate them from Eskimos by calling them——."

"Esks." This was the first word the nephew had spoken, and Henri LaRue smiled like a hopeful candidate for minor office, his cheeks gleaming with good living, his little mustache neatly trimmed.

"Too pleasant, this word, Esks," old Etienne LaRue retorted. "A longer word telling of sin and filth and treachery must be discovered by my staff. The way these—these Esks are increasing, the whole French language and way of life may be threatened not only in the Northwest Territories but in Quebec!"

The nephew snorted. Evidently he was feeling his oats after his success with his invented word: ESK. "There are only a few hundred of them. Let these Esks learn French. And vote."

"They are not human, those Esks, or any Eskimos," the old man hissed. "None of them. Look at their faces, those grinning devils. Even as a boy I dream of them. Slant-eyed devils, my shouts wake myself up. They are like evil spirits, and these—these Esks must be worse."

Dr. West glanced at the portly nephew, who was eyeing the ceiling. Evidently the old man not only was racially, culturally and religiously prejudiced, he was entangled by senile paranoia in boyhood fears and superstitions. Dr. West stood up to leave.

"*Voilà!* We get rid of those Esks." The old man clutched Dr. West's arm. "Savages no better than dogs. Morals unspeakable. Dogs in the manger is what they are. All that land up there must be freed for—for all mankind!"

Dr. West pulled away. He knew how rapidly the French-speaking population still was increasing due to the increasing baby bonuses supported by increasing sales taxes, and incited by increasing immigration from England's overcrowded New Towns. Etienne LaRue's party wanted more *Lebensraum* for Quebec.

The old man pursued him. "My nephew will lead the investigation. You will guide Henri to the Esks. With my influence, the Sanctuary cannot keep you out even though Hans Suxbey, that moral fiend, denies access to all. Your aircraft will not be shot down."

Dr. West stopped walking away. He thought he could use this old devil.

In the Rolls, the nephew sighed: "Wild goose chase." He proffered a half-pint of Haig & Haig. "Call me Henry."

"You think we are the two geese who will be shot down?" Dr. West asked.

"*Mon dieu*! I hope not! Finally our monetary offering was accepted by the Guard pilot. I hope that fighter pilot is honest."

By commercial jet, Dr. West sat beside the portly Henry LaRue all the way toward Churchill on Hudson Bay. Barring accidents, he hoped to return this way with Marthalik and his baby son. In the Sanctuary, Dr. West hoped to show Henry LaRue the Esks' need for birth control assistance as well as food this winter. Surely old Etienne LaRue would not oppose artificial birth control—if it were for Esks.

Who is human? Dr. West thought, his memory recoiling from his own conversation with that withered Etienne LaRue, who hated Esks he'd never seen. *Who is human? Who is more human? What definition? Physical appearance? Nation? Language? Religion? Birthrate?*

"More than a hobby. Me," Henry LaRue was saying not so humbly. "Perhaps I am the only whiteman in Canada who bothers any more. But my hobbies are difficult things. I have listened to Eskimo recordings. At the hospital I visit the old Eskimos. The Eskimo language has become my——." And he laughed, "——my most austere and intellectual hobby, and yet my uncle disapproves."

Because you are challenging him, Dr. West thought, *deliberately irritating him by pretending to learn the language of the Eskimos—of his nightmares.* Dr. West imagined Henry LaRue's linguistic attainments would turn out to be the parroting of a few long agglutinative word-phrases without wholly grasping their significance to an Eskimo. Henry LaRue was signaling to the stewardess, and she understood, bringing more champagne. As she bent over them, she flinched and giggled, and Dr. West had glimpsed another of Henry LaRue's happy hobbies.

At Churchill's enlarged airport, met by a pilot and staring out at his aircraft, Henry LaRue's smiling facade cracked. "That little plane? It is so small."

Squatting like a fat two-motored duck, the VTOL looked reassuringly large to Dr. West whose previous flight across the tundra and ice to Boothia had been in a single-engined Turbo-Beaver, not a massive twin-engined transport like this.

"Our Order has faith," the pilot laughed, "flying this old Canadair CL-284. You will see her wings and engines pivot to the vertical. You will be set down safely as in a copter upon the Cultural Sanctuary. Of course providing that——." The pilot stopped, as if deciding not to worry his two passengers with his other concern.

But Dr. West knew what it was.

Glancing at the sky, the pilot zipped up his snow-white and

visual orange flight jacket and led them to his white and visual orange striped aircraft. These were the bold colors of the Aerial Order of Pope John, an Order of Involvement flying rescue missions throughout the North while the older Order of Oblate Fathers concentrated on more ascetic obligations.

Seated at the instrument panel, the pilot grinned at Dr. West as if they were going on a great adventure together, which was no lie! Dr. West hoped old Etienne LaRue's bribe to the fighter pilot guarding the Cultural Sanctuary was generous enough. This lumbering VTOL transport would be helpless beneath a supersonic hawk.

Here on the parking apron at Churchill Metropolitan Airport, the priest-pilot did not wait the long wait to enter the crowded airport taxi pattern, or wait some more for clearance from the control tower before scooting out between the deadly turbulence of giant jet transports. Instead, still parked like a car he lifted a switch on the CL-284's instrument panel and an electric motor growled, twisting the wing and its two propjet engines to a vertical position. He started the jet props squealing dust around the squatting aircraft.

Dr. West watched intently while the pilot checked the rpm's of the little tail rotor back there between the rudders. For his own purpose, Dr. West tried to burn into his visual memory the pilot's hand motions in sequence setting the autopilot for vertical takeoff. The twin propjets screamed with exertion, and the VTOL lifted straight up with heavenly stability. The priest-pilot raised both hands from the controls, grinning. Someone else was flying the aircraft upward more safely than any man. It was the autopilot.

At 3000 feet, Dr. West watched how the priest-pilot pivoted the wing and engines to a normal horizontal position without losing much altitude, and the CL-284 whined forward at 300 mph north. With all these automatic systems assists, Dr. West thought he could learn to fly this aircraft more easily than a Turbo-Beaver.

Flying above the whitened tundra, Henry LaRue poked his head between the dual seats shouting louder and louder to relieve his nervousness. "I am not prejudiced like my uncle about the Eskimos in the Cultural Sanctuary. But the money

WHO IS MORE HUMAN?   97

of the taxpayers cannot continue to go down that rat's hole while in Montreal thousands of honest Canadian voters are unemployed. I say the Government must subsidize New Towns throughout the Arctic, as the Russians have done so successfully. Stocked with sturdy Canadian voters from our overcrowded cities, the North will prosper at last. Some pessimists say Canada's population continues increasing too fast because of our increasingly humanitarian Baby Bonus. But I say, look down from this aircraft at all that empty tundra. I say it is impossible for Canadians to increase too fast while there is so much room. I mean all Canadians regardless of religion or race, and for all progressive people there is so much living space here in the North."

The priest-pilot winked at Dr. West as if the North was not that easy. For two hours the CL-284 whined north across a thousand nameless frozen lakes of the glacier-bulldozed Keewatin District. For another hour they winged northwest across the frozen curly-cues of Back River past Lake Macdougall and banked north across empty tundra toward the Boothia Peninsula. "I believe we're over the Eskimo Cultural Sanctuary now," the priest-pilot shouted, glancing toward 12 o'clock high in the sky.

Dr. West saw the metallic speck swooping down from the altostratus clouds. Flashing, it made a head-on pass, for an instant it was an ancient F-111B carrier-launched version of the McDonnell swing-wing jet fighter of the 1970's, overkill as far as their lumbering CL-284 was concerned. "Butcher bird!" the pilot shouted. "There are so many rumors—bush pilots who disappeared. I hope our permission to enter truly has been transmitted to this reckless pilot by the Director."

Dr. West winced as the F-111B made another pass. Someone had lied to the priest-pilot. Of course the Director of the Cultural Sanctuary, Hans Suxbey, had not been informed of this impending violation. Hans Suxbey would have ordered the fighter plane to down them. It was the pilot of the F-111B who was supposed to have been bribed.

Looking back, Dr. West saw Henry LaRue had his eyes shut. His lips were moving. The CL-284 wallowed through the jet fighter's turbulence, but did not change course.

"How do they explain about this butcher bird," the priest-pilot angrily shouted, "to their Eskimos who are supposed to have become innocent—of whiteman's machines."

"When Suxbey descends from the sky—above the Esks in four years," Dr. West laughed with strain, "he could explain this F-111 was a winged god watching over them."

"I thought the Director was to be their only god," the pilot retorted, ducking and grinning and holding his northward course as the F-111B made another pass.

"He's trying to do the best he can for them—from his point of view." Dr. West stared at this priest-pilot who faithfully was refusing to change course in the face of threatening F-111B collisions, refusing to be forced down.

Evidently the pilot was unwilling to commit aerial murder. Flying three times faster than the VTOL all over the sky, the fighter plane burned away its fuel and departed. The priest-pilot appeared to have won.

"Can you recognize the bay?" he shouted at Dr. West, grinning.

They had found it, the familiar bay and the river flowing from the little lake.

"Never have I seen such a big Eskimo camp," the priest-pilot marvelled as he set the CL-284 straight down on the snow-dusted gravel beside all the newly raised winter igloos.

Dr. West swung outside already shouting to the Esks.

"You are asking about a woman?" Henry LaRue shouted, revealing a better understanding of the Eskimo language than Dr. West had expected, and Henry jumped down beside him, interrupting Dr. West's conversation with the Esks. "We came here to count and inspect, not to chase a woman. All these young women look—healthy, well-fed. Do they have the hospitality of the Eskimos in the old days? If necessary I would not want to hurt their feelings if hospitality were offered. I am a bachelor and a serious student of Eskimo—language."

"The important Esk—Eskimo, I am looking for has moved to the next bay," Dr. West said truthfully. "His name is Peterluk, and I think he may have been a witness to the arrival of these Esks."

Dr. West did not mention Marthalik was said to be living in a new camp beyond that next bay.

"Beyond a little hill," the Esk boy murmured as Dr. West maneuvered this unsuspecting guide and the smiling and waving LaRue back toward the aircraft.

In the rising VTOL, the Esk boy sat bravely. He peered down, then up, his mouth opening. "We are near to Grandfather Bear?"

Dr. West shook his head. He couldn't answer that one as the CL-284 sank down toward the white flat at the head of the next bay. When the swirl of snow settled, Dr. West saw a lone igloo. "Peterluk?"

"Bad man," the boy murmured, but he climbed out.

Dr. West glanced at the ancient Winchester Model 70 rifle strapped above the aircraft door, part of the priest-pilot's survival equipment. "I'll stay here and keep her warm," the pilot said, and Dr. West shrugged and climbed out empty-handed, followed by LaRue. If he approached the igloo carrying a rifle, he thought old Peterluk might be happy for an excuse to shoot. That day they had struggled for possession of Dr. West's rifle in the crater of the Burned Place, the Navel of the World, Peterluk had been flung down. Growling with rage, he had fled back to the rocks to get his own rifle, but he had not shot then.

Dr. West realized Peterluk wasn't here to shoot now. Like farewell notes, his dog's droppings were steaming in the intense cold. The trail of Peterluk's sled curved over a low hill.

The young Esk crawled into the entry tunnel, cheerfully shouting. From the igloo his voice came back to Dr. West. "Grandmother! This person happy you wait for us."

In the translucent dimness of the igloo, Dr. West recognized old Eevvaalik seated on the skin-covered ledge behind her strange ceramic seal oil lamp.

"Eh-eh! You——," she laughed in instant recognition. "He is not afraid—of you."

"Eevvaalik, when will your husband return?"

Her weathered face exposed stumps of teeth in what might have been a smile of triumph. "When your airplane was smal-

ler than a petrel bird, already my husband was loading his
sled. He has long eyes."

"He ran off and left you." Dr. West tried to create resent-
ment of Peterluk, so that Eevvaalik might tell the truth for a
change, but she laughed at him.

"My husband says not even a woman should be afraid of
you, you plain whiteman who does not wear a gray uniform,
not even a cap with a red star, so he is not afraid of you,"
she sighed. "He is afraid of what he did not tell you. After so
many winters, in his dreams he cries out like a child."

Stinging snow particles shot across the dim igloo. The two
men, the boy, the woman blinked at the small bright hole
which had appeared in the snow wall. A muffled sound from
outside had followed the rifle bullet through the igloo.

Dr. West smiled apologetically at LaRue and lay down on
the icy floor. "I believe we've found Peterluk."

A second spray of snow and a distant rifle report brought
Henry LaRue erect in the igloo. *Mon dieu*, the man is
berserk—or has formidable humor." LaRue heaved his bulk
toward the low exit tunnel. Head and shoulders committed,
he changed his mind and buttocked back against Dr. West.
"No doubt this Peterluk shoots only at strangers——?"

Both whitemen glanced up at their guide. The young Esk,
with a smile as quizzical as an Eskimo's, was kneeling on the
skin-covered ledge, poking his finger into the upper bullet
hole.

"Get down here," Dr. West ordered, and the Esk peered
down at them, smiled like a Cheshire cat in the dimness of
the igloo and slid down beside them, his hand groping.

The Esk grunted with pleasure, having discovered an unidentifiable glob of meat which the escaped Peterluk must
have left. The young Esk's chewing sounds were punctuated
by Eevvaalik's tubercular coughing.

*Even now while some people walk on the Moon, others
live like this*, Dr. West thought vaguely, waiting for the next
shot.

In the cold stench, Eevvaalik sat above him on the ledge,
trimming the seal oil lamp as intently as if her husband,
Peterluk, were not shooting into the igloo.

"Eevvaalik, a bullet might hit you," Dr. West said. "Come down here."

Another shot smashed through the igloo. Eevvaalik made no move to lie down with the two whitemen. Smiling, she turned her head away from these two whitemen hiding on the floor. "Bullets of this person's husband have eyes—for you—he says."

With a spitting sound the fourth bullet passed through the snow wall.

"Tell her that we surrender," LaRue murmured, brushing snow from his face. "Tell her surrender means we—we whitemen will go away."

Dr. West told her to tell her husband. "Please shout to him."

The flickering flame line from the lamp reflected on her greasy face. She smiled, exposing her tooth stumps. Dr. West knew from the records she was forty-four years old.

"It is not a woman's place to advise her husband." Eevvaalik bowed her head, and a fifth shot spat through the igloo.

Hopefully, Dr. West thought all the shots had been deliberately too high.

"How many bullets did Peterluk take?" Dr. West asked her even more hopefully. "Only the bullets in his rifle?"

Snow sprayed inward, and the sixth little eye gleamed high in the igloo. Dr. West wondered why the priest-pilot wasn't— doing something. There was a rifle in the plane. Would the priest——?

The seventh shot whined across the icy floor between their faces. Ice crystals gleamed on LaRue's cheek.

"*Mon dieu!*" LaRue's hand swept from his cheek to the Esk's arm, "you must go out and tell him to stop shooting."

As if understanding his meaning without needing to understand the words, the young Esk obediently crawled out through the tunnel to the little entry dome where outer parkas are hung.

"He's so much shorter than we are. That madman will notice this boy is a fellow Eskimo," LaRue muttered. "After all, they know each other."

Dully, they heard the eighth shot. No hole appeared in the igloo. Dr. West scrambled along the snow tunnel and blinked at the darkly spreading blood from beneath the boy on the snow glare.

"Murderer!" Until that moment, somehow it had been as if he hadn't really believed Peterluk's bullets would kill. "Murderer. Inhuman!" *I should have stopped the boy from going out.* Whirling inside the entry dome, he saw a coiled line with a massive bone-splint tied to a stone. It was for snagging the floating body of a seal.

Dr. West's arm and momentary exposure of his head did not draw fire. As Dr. West yanked the gasping body of the Esk toward the entry, two more shots resounded from the hillside but no snow kicked up near the moving body. No snow holes spat through the tunnel at Dr. West.

"He died. Peterluk killed him." Dr. West's agonized voice ignited LaRue.

"Savage!" LaRue grabbed Eevvaalik by the shoulder, pulling her down on to the floor. "Why? Why is your husband killing? Ask her, West. Demand to know."

Dr. West asked as Eevvaalik firmly removed herself from LaRue's grip, and climbed back up on the sleeping platform.

Compulsively she trimmed the seal oil lamp. "This person's husband says too many more people hunting every year. There are not enough seals anymore." She seemed to be speaking seriously, truly. "So many hunters on the ice they frightened away the seals of my husband. That is why he shot the hunters on the ice."

Dr. West blinked at this, and told LaRue: "Peterluk has already murdered some Esks who were hunting seals."

"But we do not come to shoot seals," LaRue protested, squirming like a seal on the icy floor, suddenly directing his anger to Dr. West. "You——. If I—if my Uncle had not listened to you, I would be in my warm office. My secretary would be bringing hot coffee *et croissants.* Instead I am being fired upon, frozen, murdered by savages who don't even vote. I do not think all the maniacs are out there. For leading me to this savage I think the maniac is you!"

Dr. West had no reply. It was deathly quiet outside the

igloo. Ten shots had been fired, he thought. Some rifles, old British service rifles, had ten-shot clips. "Eevvaalik, does your husband practice shooting every day because he has so many bullets?"

"Eh-eh, not for many years. In those days the great iron box of bullets on a belt he hid because the angry men from the whale——." Eevvaalik's voice stopped, but Dr. West guessed the rifle must be a model which fired the same ammunition as a machine gun, and over the years Peterluk's supply of bullets now ought to be low.

The eleventh bullet splattered through the igloo.

"*Mon dieu*, that is the tenth shot." LaRue laughed unhappily. "That savage has enough ammunition to drive both the English and French from Canada! I am cold and I do not want to die. Listen, I think we should chop through the opposite wall of the igloo and run for it."

"To where?" Dr. West demanded.

"Toward the plane. Don't be cowardly. Eskimos are all poor shots."

"Running all the way down there would only attract Peterluk's fire. He would shoot at the plane."

"Too much logic. We go! A brave pilot will start the engines when he sees us approaching. Where is that cowardly pilot? Why has he not started the engines?"

"He's damn cold if he's outside the plane. I hope he's still alive.——I hope Peterluk hasn't already visited the plane."

"My friend," LaRue blurted, unexpectedly flopping his arm around Dr. West's shoulders, "so do I. So do I. This igloo is as cold as a crypt. Poof, that was another bullet! He is firing lower. I do not care; I no longer wish this Eskimo's vote," LaRue laughed nervously. "We must run for it." But he didn't get up.

On the sleeping platform, Eevvaalik coughed and spat blood near the two whitemen lying on the icy floor shivering and waiting.

"Doctor, in your fanciful distinction," LaRue said finally, "is this woman an Eskimo or an Esk?"

"She is an Eskimo. Of these people, only Eevvaalik has had TB, the only one. Perhaps Peterluk has it too. The rest, Esks, do not appear to be subject to tuberculosis. They don't even have lice!" Dr. West's voice rose as if it were a means of escape from bullets. "Bacteria and parasitic organisms may not have had time to adjust to body chemistry differences between Eskimos and Esks."

"Fine words and a theory of which you admit you have no proof. Did you not tell my uncle that Esks appear like swallows from the mud, something like that," LaRue's voice rushed. "You have confused the old man—and me. I saw all of these people back in the camp where you picked up the guide, rest his soul, and they were the cleanest, the most happy Eskimos I have seen in my many trips to the North." His voice rose in outrage. "Certainly, they are human! Are you insane? Everyone in my family knows my uncle is insane. I wish I were in my warm office."

"I wish it were true," Dr. West muttered as bullet number twelve or thirteen zipped through the igloo from a new angle.

"Anyway, I don't need to be freezing here to know Eevvaalik is a real Eskimo," LaRue sighed. "My uncle and I have a copy of the old Family Allowance Census taken when the Government still had the integrity to give to these Eskimos food and clothing. They have as much right to Family Allowances as other Canadians," he exclaimed. "Of course this Eevvaalik is an Eskimo. In the old Family Allowance records must be found her fingerprints, her chest X-rays. This Eevvaalik and Peterluk, they are old enough to be listed among the original families of Boothia Peninsula imprisoned in this—this concentration camp."

"Yes, and where are the other original families now?" Dr. West replied. "There were 112 names on the census list made by the McGill ethnologists. But twenty years later I have found only two of them, Peterluk and Eevvaalik." He looked up at Eevvaalik.

Dr. West smiled winningly. "Eevvaalik, where are your father and mother, your sisters and brothers?"

With womanly pride, she smiled back. "Peterluk stole me and my first baby son. My first husband had a—a boat—motor very loud but the whitemen took it away. Peterluk took me—away from the old camp. This person thinks her first husband and other people fled that winter from this land. The whitemen could not keep them in this one land. We are people who travel far."

"But not Peterluk."

"Eh-eh, Peterluk stayed in this land because there were so few people." She laughed or coughed. "He thought this would be his hunting land for him alone," her voice sank, "and for my baby son who died, and other sons this person would have——."

"But it is Esks, hundreds of young people crowding this place, spoiling the hunting," Dr. West argued. "It is not we whitemen who crowd Peterluk. Tell him to stop shooting. Whitemen are friends, men like he is——."

Eevvaalik smiled back. "A good husband never listens to his wife, at least not when there are others nearby to hear them."

"Then go out there to him. Whisper to him not to shoot," Dr. West said with exasperation.

Eevvaalik frowned. "This person might obey you as stupidly as that boy did and be shot. No, this person is not one of her stupid children from the big camp." Eevvaalik wiped her mouth with her hand. "This person knows death. She is Eevvaalik! An *Innuit*! A true Eskimo! Not one of these young fools who think death is the sled to happiness in the sky."

"And Peterluk is different from the young people now in the camps," Dr. West insisted, translating as she talked, because he was trying to convince LaRue how different from Eskimos these young Esks were——.

"Eh-eh, my husband is braver than those meek children in the camps," she agreed. "Our bellies are hungrier than theirs. We do not like to be told what to do. My husband needs much land to hunt."

"Why wouldn't Peterluk tell me," Dr. West explored, "*if* these younger people's night stories are true? Is it because he told them the stories that they now believe? Why won't he tell us where they came from?"

"Eh?" Eevvaalik laughed. "Why do you men always want to ask my husband? This is a woman's question, where babies come from."

"All these people were not born here?" Dr. West asked as another leading question.

"I am the mother!"

Dr. West stared up at her in disbelief while she tittered. "You do not even believe this person is the grandmother," she taunted, countering with an Eskimo legend. "There also was a girl who was carried off by a bear to live in his igloo. She is barren now, but they began from me, and whatever Peterluk tells is lies."

Angrily, Dr. West retorted: "You joke while he shoots at us."

"His power is weak because he is not at the Burned Place."

"So the Navel of the World," Dr. West asked, thinking of his struggle there with Peterluk for the rifle, "is of— importance."

"This person was not there that night."

"What night?"

"This person does not know what night," Eevvaalik replied with an irritating smile.

"Was it the night a sub—a whiteman's boat which swims under the ice—?" Dr. West was remembering Peterluk's lies. "Whitemen came ashore?"

"This person does not know." Eevvaalik answered too quickly, Dr. West thought.

"Then the legend of the man who fell from the sky," Dr. West challenged her with wry humor, "whose back split open so that he bore a son, that is false?"

"Who can say what is false? Peterluk was only a young man then, and how could he recognize his Grandfather?" The woman shook her head with distaste. "No, it would have been better if a bear truly was his Grandfather. His Grandfather! I was but a young girl who had borne only one child when Peterluk stole me, and my son died. Peterluk, how angry he was. He wanted many sons."

She coughed, gurgled, spat blood. From the icy floor Dr. West argued from a new direction. He was trying to talk his way free from Peterluk's bullets.

"Eevvaalik, when you were a girl you remember the whitemen called *doctors*? I am a doctor. Your coughing will become worse and you will die soon unless you are taken to a *hospital*. You remember that is a place of beds and white-women in white clothing. You will be given *injections*. You remember the sharp needles which make people well? Tell your husband to stop shooting, so we may help you."

"You are afraid of my husband," she laughed triumphant-ly. "He is stronger than whitemen, with more sons than you will ever have."

"Are they really his sons?"

"Eh? Is it better to believe all these people began when Grandfather Bear's back split open. No? Then, believe, a sharp needle in a tube of glass," she laughed contemptuously at Dr. West, "as this person lay on the sleeping ledge waiting for her husband. Oh, so big! A whiteman's harpoon that makes love! This person was surprised when she swelled up and had a baby in a month!"

"What is she talking about now?" LaRue hissed.

"She has an active imagination," Dr. West replied. "She's just invented her own artificial insemination for some rea-son——."

"Disgusting. Was that fiend a scientist?" LaRue accused, having missed the point of the conversation, and not clarify-ing his own antiscientific fears rising from his subconscious memories. "I do not approve of any tampering with the human body."

He gawked. Eevvaalik was grinning, gesturing crudely, deliberately catching their attention.

An explosion slammed through the tunnel. The murderous-ly low path of the bullet had ripped between them, and the two whitemen scrambled apart, up on the sleeping platform on either side of the low entrance to the room. The acrid stench of gun powder and the hoarse sound of Peterluk's breathing came from the tunnel.

"Listen my husband," Eevvaalik called cheerfully, "we have two visitors. One is waiting on each side above the door hole."

Peterluk's voice began only a few feet away. "Tell them to come outside."

"They are afraid you will kill them," Eevvaalik answered, compulsively trimming the lamp.

"Tell them to come out or I will break a hole in the side of the igloo and shoot them where they are." Peterluk evidently didn't want to risk lunging blindly through the low entry. "Come out!"

Neither whiteman spoke.

Dr. West watched as LaRue discovered that a lump under the caribou skin was a stone axe. Vaguely, Dr. West thought this flimsy-handled slab of stone would have made Hans Suxbey, Director of the Eskimo Cultural Sanctuary, smile with pride, a genuine Eskimo artifact!

Finally, Eevvaalik called, "My husband, you had better do it, or go away and not do it."

"Woman, close your mouth!"

The three people in the igloo crouched waiting. The sounds of Peterluk's breathing softened. Silence.

"Children who grow big as a man are very good," Eevvaalik remarked like a housewife making conversation during an embarrassing pause. "But too many. Children have children so quick, too many. Never enough seals. When this person was a little girl, my mother told me it was a hungry winter when I was born and she would have left me out on the ice but changed her mind because that day three seals were killed. With meat again she would have milk in her breasts. Eh-eh, customs were wiser in those days. There were not too many Eskimos because enough new babies were left on the ice. Everyone had enough to eat. Better not too many girls to feed, better enough hunters."

Neither whiteman commented.

"You fat policeman come out," Peterluk's voice called inaccurately and more distantly as if he had backed silently out of the tunnel. "Better hurry. Many people coming and they will kill you. You better come out and run away."

"He is not a policeman," Dr. West shouted. "He is a friend."

"Too late for that. So close." Peterluk shouted. "Come out. Run."

"Those many people from the big camps wouldn't kill anybody." Eevvaalik snorted. "They want everyone to love them, but there are too many of them."

"Come out!" Peterluk yelled as if in desperation. "Run fast

to the plane before they catch you. They kill all whitemen."

Neither man moved or reacted to this obvious trap.

Eevvaalik snorted. "These people do not even kill enough seals. They are afraid to kill bears. All they talk about is Grandfather Bear." Eevvaalik's voice rose in outrage. "They are not even Christians!"

There was a muffled gun shot. No bullet passed through the igloo. The silence became so long that Dr. West wondered if Peterluk had shot himself.

"All they talk about," Eevvaalik's voice rambled cheerfully, "is—soon there will be so many of them that their Grandfather will come down from the sky. This person thinks he will merely eat them. That is what should be expected if he is a bear. These people are not Christians."

From the distance there was a shout, followed by three shots fired at the speed a clumsy but hurried man could operate an old bolt-action rifle, Dr. West thought.

"He must be firing in another direction," LaRue hissed, standing up on the sleeping platform with his head and shoulders bent to fit the curve of the icy ceiling.

With the stone axe, LaRue began knocking a hole in the roof of the igloo, presumably high enough, Dr. West hoped, that Peterluk would have to scramble up on the side of the igloo if he were to shoot in at them.

Outside there were strangely cheerful-sounding shouts.

As LaRue chopped upward, light burst through the roof and snow chinks fell inside; standing erect on the sleeping platform, LaRue thrust up his head through the hole in the igloo.

"*Mon dieu!*" Like a turtle, LaRue retracted his head back into the igloo as another shot sounded. "Dozens of Eskimos approaching! He has shot one."

Again, LaRue poked up his head through the hole. "They are coming to rescue us I think. Ah, so many of them. They are showing no fear."

Dr. West heard their voices calling to each other.

"He is running. They have him. They have seized him. They have his rifle." LaRue ducked his head into the igloo. "They have rescued us I hope. There are so many of them we might as well go outside in any case and congratulate them."

When Dr. West scrambled out of the tunnel into the blinding snow-light, he blinked at Peterluk standing with lowered head like a musk-ox among the smiling Esks. None was holding Peterluk.

An Esk handed Peterluk's rusty rifle to LaRue, who glanced at it incuriously, then squinted at the rifle's bolt action. "*Mon dieu*! I think this old rifle is Russian."

Peterluk walked away through the Esks. With Dr. West stumbling after him, Peterluk ran toward the aircraft. Dr. West heard the click-snap of the rifle's action. Would LaRue shoot?

"Don't shoot him," Dr. West gasped unheard as he limped far behind Peterluk.

From LaRue, there was no shot.

The rifle's magazine must be empty, Dr. West thought as his repaired leg muscle tightened. He slowed to a hobble as several Esks passed him. Running alongside Peterluk like playful puppies, they seemed hesitant to violently seize him. Peterluk veered away from them toward the low hill from which his earlier shots had come.

Peterluk's sled and dogs were not visible. Dr. West knew they were concealed behind this hill because Peterluk was circling back. Dr. West took the shorter course up the hill.

His repaired thigh muscle jerked like a poorly constructed android's. Polar bear, not dog bite, he thought angrily of his thigh's great white square of plastic surgery. As he scrambled up the slope his muscles warmed. From the corner of his eye he saw Peterluk change course—away.

Dr. West had won this race. The dogs growled at him. Closer than the dogs was spread a worn caribou skin on which Peterluk had lain while shooting down into the igloo. The ejected cartridge cases were dull and old. Tied on the sled was a battered metal box, an old military ammunition box, he thought. The letters stenciled were Russian. Years ago, it must have contained hundreds of bullets, he thought. Now it was empty.

"I want you, Peterluk," Dr. West gasped to himself. "You know so much more than I——."

Peterluk was running far away, toward the sea, and the Esks had stopped chasing him.

"Pacifist fools," Dr. West wheezed. "You'd be helpless in this world." With his good leg, he kicked the frozen sled runners loose.

With the whip, as ferociously as a real Eskimo, Dr. West lashed the dogs until they understood who was master in a hurry. He was driving the sled under good control when he headed off Peterluk. Back down the hill toward the Esks, Peterluk fled as if he was afraid Dr. West wanted to kill him. Down there LaRue ran to meet him. Hurling the rifle at Peterluk and missing, LaRue lunged at the Eskimo with open arms and bulldogged the exhausted Eskimo to the ground.

"*Voilà!* I have captured this murderer." LaRue shouted triumphantly, twisting Peterluk's arm behind his back so that he growled in pain. "Ask this savage why he foolishly shoots at whitemen."

Peterluk grunted that he had killed no one.

"That Esk is lying dead from your bullet," Dr. West retorted.

"Not people. Not real Eskimos."

"He says they're not real Eskimos," Dr. West translated to LaRue. "Not real people."

"Not real Eskimos? These Esks not real people?" LaRue shouted in outrage at Dr. West. "Maniac. You are wrong. These are the finest human beings in the world. They save our lives while this murderer was shooting. Among the bullets, they seized this man. They didn't have to, but they came to help us. Look at this poor Esk lying shot dead in the snow. He helped save our lives. He died for us. Don't you tell me these people are not human. They are more human than you." He was shouting at Dr. West. "You and my uncle saying these people are not human. You are—are bigots! There should be more of these wonderful people in this world."

"You misunderstand me———."

"I saw your dossier. You are one of those scientific birth control fiends," LaRue roared on. "Who are you to decide who lives and who is not born? Birth control is so easy for you to say if others should do it, other races we don't want

to feed, such as these people who need food. They need
warm clothes. They need protection from fiends like you, and
that atheistic Director of this concentration camp, and also
from my uncle," his voice faded. "Help me tie this murderer."

"We agree there won't be enough food for them," Dr.
West said wearily.

"You want me to agree there are too many of them,"
LaRue retorted. "My uncle, at least he will help me fight
your birth control. My uncle he is old and crazy but he still
controls a few voters."

LaRue's face gleamed as if he were seeing the rising
summer sun. *"Mon dieu!* All these people will have votes."

As if stunned, Dr. West stared at Henry LaRue's gleaming
face. Dr. West stared at the blinding snow. For the Esks and
for Canada if ignorant politicians began using these people,
Dr. West foresaw tragedy growing. He limped away from
LaRue toward the aircraft. He was afraid Henry LaRue at
age forty finally had become a man. This LaRue finally was
seizing a purpose for life. Henry LaRue was shouting after
him: "I'll aid these people. I, too, am a leader! I'll show that
old bigot. I'll show my uncle what I have become."

My god, Dr. West thought, *if he can keep it up he
might——.* On the snow beneath the wing of the aircraft,
Dr. West stared at the priest-pilot's body face down on
frozen blood. Peterluk's longest shot——. Dr. West supposed
the priest's rifle still must be hanging on its straps inside the
aircraft. *This priest is ended on this Earth,* Dr. West thought
dully. *And Henry LaRue has just begun—to help these Esks
survive and spread from their Sanctuary. So many hungry
mouths. Such gentle people. Probably better than the rest of
us.*

The crying sound of a baby pierced Dr. West's conscience.
More Esks were coming from the new camp over the hill.
Closer, muffled in tattered parkas against the wind, they
appeared indistinguishable. But Dr. West's heart leaped. Running toward him——.

"Marthalik!" He seized her, clung to her, and because he
was so much taller he looked down over her shoulder into

the bulging back of her parka, into the wide eyes of the baby.

"My son is well?" Dr. West laughed, squeezing her even closer as if she could become part of him.

Marthalik gasped, breathlessly laughing with tears shimmering down her cheeks. "He is growing strong, like you. This person will run back to the camp and bring him to his father."

Dr. West blinked, staring at the round face of this baby in her parka, who had begun to smile at him. "Who is—this?"

"Your daughter," she laughed proudly, "this is your newest daughter."

"Two children!" he laughed more with excitement than surprise.

"My husband, this person is even stronger than that."

"Marthalik, we must hurry. We will travel to my country. Go back. Bring my son."

"Only your son?"

"Hurry." Dr. West turned back to LaRue, who was scowling from the aircraft to the dead pilot and muttering.

"For an inexperienced but courageous pilot as myself," LaRue was saying, "two motors are too many to control."

"True." Dr. West limped back toward the igloo, seeing Eevvaalik vanish into the entry tunnel from which she must have been watching. "Wait, Eevvaalik!"

He pursued her into the dimly arched igloo. "Eevvaalik, I am a doctor. I will take you to—to a hospital place, you remember? You are sick from coughing. You will be made well. Please come to the airplane with Peterluk."

"No!" She twisted free from his gentle grasp.

"Eevvaalik, you will travel with your husband; Peterluk is going in the plane."

"No," she hissed, avoiding his grasp. "This person wants to stay here until all the whitemen die! This person will rise to Grandfather Bear."

"But you don't believe those young people's legends? You said they are stupid. Not Christians."

"This person," Eevvaalik gasped, "is deciding now what to believe!" Struggling against him, she began to scream and cough, and Dr. West gave up trying to carry away Eevvaalik into civilization—for the moment.

He limped back down the slope to the aircraft, thinking ahead toward LaRue, who would interfere with his plans.

"If we cannot fly this aircraft," Dr. West told LaRue, "I can operate the radio."

"My idea exactly," LaRue laughed with relief. "We will radio the Order of Pope John to fly here an experienced pilot to res—to aid us."

"Yes, that is a good idea." Dr. West instantly agreed, visualizing himself seated at the radio, at the controls of the CL-284, and rising into the air with Marthalik and his son and daughter, and with Peterluk bound and locked in the baggage compartment, and LaRue in the cockpit but violently interfering when he discovered they were not returning to Churchill; he would have to do something about Henry LaRue now.

"——champion of these oppressed people." LaRue interrupted his thoughts, "I, too shall be nominated to stand for Parliament. My uncle finally will be shown I am a man of my own. The little people are my concern, the hungry ones. I will not be simply a politician. From the beginning I will be a statesman."

With deaf ears and darting mind, Dr. West stared at the aircraft and beyond, visualizing Peterluk somehow flown out of Canada to Berkeley, Peterluk strapped on a leather couch, being injected with sodium pentothal. *Now tell me the truth about the Burned Place. You are the one who knows how the Esks began.*

"Already today," LaRue laughed excitedly, "I have captured a murderer."

"True. Like a hero, if you stayed here in this icy wilderness to look after these people," Dr. West suggested, "at least until tomorrow. I could return to civilization first to tell the newspapers how you stayed behind to help them. In spite of my pleas, heroically you stayed to help these oppressed people in the blizzard," Dr. West expanded. "You stayed to study the problems of these starving Eskimos so that all people throughout Canada will learn—that you are a hero, because that is what I will tell them."

"You mean you would try to pilot out this plane and leave me here in the cold?"

"I would tell the news services how you seized that murderous Peterluk, bravely you personally captured him in order to save the lives of us all. Tomorrow a whole planeload of newsmen would fly here to congratulate you on the spot. With cameras for TV they would listen while you expose this whole Sanctuary mess. On TV you would address the voters."

At this, Henry LaRue smiled shyly. "I think you are exaggerating my contribution—a little bit. I will alert the world to the plight of these people. I will speak on the radio now. Now they can send another aircraft with an experienced pilot—to fly us out today."

"True." Dr. West grunted, trying to conceal his raging frustration as he dragged the bound Peterluk to the aircraft. "Help me lift him in so I can lock him in the baggage compartment. As their future leader, give encouragement to all these Esks who are your friends. Two men have died this day———."

Beside Peterluk in the baggage compartment, Dr. West laid the body of the priest-pilot, and looked down at the priest's softly dead face, and then at Peterluk's wrinkled, frightened face, the narrow eyes, the mouth a chapped scar.

"Eh! You think to frighten this person with the dead?" Peterluk's big teeth gleamed. "Stronger whitemen than you have not been able———."

Dr. West slammed the aluminum door against Peterluk's voice because he heard Marthalik's voice calling.

She handed up his son to him. Then she handed up the baby from her parka. He saw Marthalik's face was frightened.

"A woman should not disobey her husband," Marthalik blurted, "but this person could not leave behind our other daughter."

She handed up a third baby, who eyed Dr. West suspiciously. In his hands, this baby felt heavier, larger than the baby from Marthalik's parka. But it was smaller than his son and intermediate in size, Dr. West pondered, and age. Stunned, Dr. West stared down at the three babies crawling on the dented floor of the aircraft. The boy, he knew, was his—that first night. Precociously his ten-week-old son struggled erect. Dr. West thought the second baby could have been conceived that last night before he left Marthalik. Across the ice with Edwardluk and into the hospital, he had been gone over two and a half months since the second baby was conceived. This third little baby, the smiling baby from Marthalik's parka, must have been conceived at least a month after he was gone. He thought he could not be the father of this gleefully smiling baby girl. Wearily, Dr. West helped Marthalik into the aircraft.

"Why are you putting in all these Eskimos," LaRue shouted up from the snow. "You cannot fly."

"To protect them from the wind," Dr. West retorted, moving to block the entry. "I'll radio ahead that you're the hero, the Savior of these Esks. Keep back! Read the newspaper account of how I told what a hero you are before you say too much. Be sure our stories agree. Look out!" He kicked at LaRue's fingers. "I'm going to fire off the jets." With all his strength, Dr. West closed the door of the aircraft against the yelling LaRue.

Out of breath, blinking at the control panel, Dr. West tried to review from memory the intricate movements of the pilot's hands on the controls. LaRue's fists drummed on the outside of the Canadair CL-284.

Experimentally Dr. West operated the electric motor, tilting the wings and engines to a horizontal position, and then returned them to the vertical takeoff position. He stared at the autocontrols, hoping the little electric-powered gyroscope inside the two-axis autopilot was spinning with stability in relation to the planet Earth. "I can't fly this beast by the seat of my pants."

As a warning for LaRue to step back, Dr. West fired off the propjet in the opposite wing. It squealed, idling. "Marthalik," he shouted. "Sit down. No, go back. With that rope, tie the babies on that seat. Wrap them, tighter. Now sit here. With this strap I'll———." He fired off the propjet on LaRue's side, and let them both whine while at the instrument panel he wondered about the rpm's of the tail rotor.

Abruptly he reached for the paired throttles, feeding the propjets.

"Marthalik," he shouted, suddenly smiling with fear. "I love you. You know what that means?"

With a screaming roar the CL-284 rose more reassuringly than his father's copter.

Hands safely off the controls, Dr. West let the autopilot fly them up slowly, almost straight up to 5000 feet. He wanted plenty of altitude when he tried tilting the wings and propjets toward the horizontal and attempted forward flight at 300 mph.

In triumphant forward flight in the direction of Churchill, Dr. West waited until he was sure he was south of the Eskimo Cultural Sanctuary boundary before using the radio. Abruptly he identified his aircraft. Dramatically he described Henry LaRue volunteering to remain behind to help the Eskimos in the blizzard. "Single-handed he overpowered the— the renegade Eskimo who shot the pilot."

"I say, then who is flying your aircraft?"

"Over and out." Dr. West pushed the aircraft into a shallow dive which should worry radar observers when he didn't pull out. As the little ice ponds on the tundra loomed huge, Dr. West leveled off, skimming low toward the west. Air rescue should search for his wreckage on a line between his last radar blip and Churchill, he thought, deceptively flying away southwest in the general direction of Lake Macdougall, but not too near. Low over endless white tundra and nameless frozen lakes he flew for nearly five hours toward the westward dying sun.

Even if he'd had enough fuel, he would have been afraid to turn south all the way into the United States. "U.S. Border Patrol has more radar along the friendly border, more VTOL interceptors to keep airborne people out or in—a super Cultural Sanctuary."

Flying west across northern Canada, he hoped to see the immensity of Great Slave Lake. He hoped he had fuel to reach Yellowknife, where he'd had friendly contacts. He supposed his bush pilot, the English expatriate, was not only missing but dead.

That butcher bird, that Cultural Sanctuary Guard plane

*undoubtedly shot or forced him down on the summer sea ice,
bad ice, same as murdered him.*

In the baggage compartment beside Peterluk was the body
of the priest-pilot. *But I can't risk contacting the police.* Dr.
West felt trapped by his own actions.

Probably he would be arrested at Yellowknife Airport. He
had, in effect, stolen this CL-284 aircraft which belonged to
the Order of Pope John. *What LaRue tells his rescuers and
the police will decide my fate.*

Technically, Dr. West knew he also was guilty of kidnapping an Eskimo woman and her three children from the
Cultural Sanctuary. *What will LaRue say about that? He'll
hesitate to admit I tricked him, forced him to remain with
the Esks, if his rescuers already are telling him what a hero
he is. Over the radio, my last words were how heroically he
overpowered Peterluk.*

*So I'm also aiding the escape of a murderer. If I manage
to smuggle Peterluk, as well as Marthalik and her children,
across the border into the U.S., the legal charges against me
should multiply. Unless LaRue can hush things up for his
own purposes, I'll be extradited back to Canada. Violating
the Eskimo Cultural Sanctuary will be the least of my legal
troubles.* "I've got to think my way out of this now."

Beyond snowbent forests he glimpsed islands in the immense whiteness of what he hoped was Great Slave Lake. To
his right, a glow against the night sky might be the reflected
city lights of Yellowknife beyond the horizon. He banked the
aircraft in the opposite direction, pondering how he could
make the CL-284 vanish. "Should unload Marthalik, Peterluk, the babies, and taxi out on the lake and sink the
evidence. Damn lake looks frozen five feet thick. No holes in
the ice."

Ahead, on an island he saw a speck of light from what
might be an ice fisherman's cabin. Banking over this island to
a snow-white clearing in the darkness he successfully set
down the CL-284. Leaving the engines idling, he helped
Marthalik and the children out into the deep snow and
handed her his rifle. Then he dumped Peterluk out, bound
and growling. Dr. West set the autopilot for vertical takeoff.

Knocking both throttles wide open, he lunged out of the rising aircraft onto the snow.

The CL-284 lifted itself straighter than if a human pilot had been at the controls. As its propjet whining faded upward, he wondered what would happen when the VTOL aircraft reached its ceiling. Would it drift along in the high-altitude wind? Because its wings were twisted in the vertical position, when its fuel was exhausted, when those two straining propjets stopped, it should fall like a brick. That would end the priest's body. He hoped the aircraft's smashed wreckage wouldn't be noticed in the endless fir forests around Great Slave Lake.

They walked and walked, trying to find the lake. Peterluk walked ahead and finally led, pulling at the rope, his hands tied behind his back, the rope connecting him to Dr. West's belt. Dr. West followed, his rifle in one hand, his son carried like a football in the other. Marthalik trotted behind, one baby girl in her arms and the littlest baby girl inside her parka. Dr. West glanced back at her. The force from the rope yanked him to his knees as Peterluk tried to lunge away like a musk-ox. Dr. West's belt broke. Peterluk crashed away through the dwarfish fir trees.

"Come back; you'll die," Dr. West shouted. "With your hands tied behind your back, you'll die." Then he tried to arouse an ancestral Eskimo fear. "This is the land of the Indians. Come back. The Indians will kill you." Peterluk kept running.

Dr. West found the Indians by means of the music from their transistor radio. Beside their cabin an Ice-Cat was parked under the canvas. The two Indians were cool until they saw the money which had the magic effect. Pushing the blocks of frozen fish out of the trailer-sled, they rolled in a fifty-gallon drum of gasoline. "It's a long way to Hay River, man."

Dr. West's money was the carrot, his rifle the stick.

In time and exhaustion the distance was much longer across Great Slave Lake by Ice-Cat than across Canada by plane. "Hay River over there, man. Hot cool town. Topless shows!"

But Dr. West paid the two Indians more money for them

to go straight back to their fish camp without entering the lively city of Hay River. Sourly staring at all that money, they agreed, and their Ice-Cat growled away. He hoped they would keep on going all the way back to their cabin without telling anyone until spring, but that was too much to hope.

In the outlying slums of Hay River, Dr. West's money acquired clothing for Marthalik and little snowsuits for the babies, even a couple of empty old suitcases. In the brand new Hay River Municipal Airport Terminal, no one seemed curious about a tall man, a short "Indian" girl and three babies as he bought tickets to Edmonton.

From that crowded metropolis, they flew south to Calgary. But here Dr. West was afraid to buy a ticket on a Western Airlines plane which would cross the border to Great Falls, Montana, and continue on to Salt Lake City. Dr. West smiled wryly. Entry inspection by the U.S. Immigration and Welcoming Service would catch Marthalik as an alien invader, not even a marriage license.

He knew the U.S. border was tight in retaliation for Canada's irritating new Border Regulations which were in retaliation for the new 1812 orations of U.S. Congressmen of the Pentagon Party who were retaliating for something which enraged them more each year.

Since a direct airline flight into the U.S. might end with Marthalik in a cell, Dr. West and family traveled only as far south as Lethbridge in southern Alberta, and took a bus to Coutts, a growing city subdivided by the U.S.-Canadian border. Across the street stood a new chain-link fence and a sentry box. The fence extended out of town in both directions along the border line.

In a small hotel in Canadian Coutts, Dr. West signed the register: John Smythe, wife and children. The three babies provided moral cover, he thought. No one could accuse him of stealing a young Indian or Eskimo girl for solely immoral purposes. The hotel dick never gave him a second glance, and they went up to sleep, exhausted.

Before dawn, when the hotel detective was long gone from the lobby, and the clerk had gone back to the sofa in the inner office, Dr. West and family checked themselves out.

Having left their empty suitcases in their room, they were able to walk faster out of town.

In silvery darkness, crunching through an open field, Dr. West found tracks and followed them south to a gulley and a suspiciously stretched hole under the international fence. Entering the U.S., he was startled by scrambling sounds approaching up the gulley, and a hollow-sounding clunk. "Damn, damn, damn, dented my guitar. Dad, is this the way to Peace River?"

"Keep crawling north." Dr. West and family hurried south down the gulley in time to find the bearded one's auto.

"He make it?" the pale girl hissed, and drove them back to Great Falls, Montana, where Dr. West finally had the pleasure of boarding Western Airlines.

In a cloud of dust, the Boeing 797 skimmed from the runway on its wheelless aircushion. More tailless than a bat with systems assists, it automatically maintained lateral and longitudinal stability. Its wings folded inward, while Dr. West had a choice of coffee, tea or milk.

Pop-out control surfaces altered the Boeing 797's smoothly wingless fuselage, changing its course as programmed while they dropped in on Helena, Idaho Falls, Pocatello, Salt Lake, Las Vegas and L.A., where Dr. West was startled at how unimpressed Marthalik seemed by the vast Offshore International Airport. "So many hunters and their families waiting and waiting. But Grandfather Bear will not come for them."

More hopeless hunters were waiting in San Francisco's International Airport.

By copter, Dr. West and family rose across the Bay to Berkeley. "Look Marthalik, past all those grass places and big igloos. See, up on the hill, that low white igloo. Your husband used to work there. I was Dir-rect-tor."

"Eh?" she laughed excitedly. "What did you hunt?"

4.

BERKELEY
CAMPUS,
1990

DR. WEST ASKED STEVE JERVASONI TO BE HIS BEST MAN BE-
cause Steve turned out to be his only loyal former graduate
student.

When Dr. West returned unannounced from the Arctic,
striding past the startled Security Guard into what formerly
had been his own Oriental Population Problems Research
Building, he caused more embarrassment than if he were a
leper. Smiling, he forced handshakes from his former grad
students and professional colleagues.

Dr. Fred Gatson, boy wonder bacteriologist and newly
appointed Director, popped out of what had been Dr. West's
office to pump Dr. West's hand. "——just like old times, Dr.
West—Joe. Just because your security clearance has been
canceled by Washington doesn't mean we don't want to see
you here——."

"But you're in secret session," Dr. West interrupted satiri-
cally, laughing as if he were kidding, "conferring whether to
save or destroy mankind?"

"Joe, when they appointed me Director," Fred Gatson
blurted in this gleaming building created by Dr. Joseph West,
"there was nothing personal. I didn't——."

Dr. West tried to grin. "I'm glad to be out of it. Screw the
Pentagon!"

Steve Jervasoni was the only one of Dr. West's former
grad students with guts to follow through on Dr. West's
invitation to visit the big ramshackle second-story apartment
Dr. West had moved into with Marthalik, whom Dr. West
coolly described as his bride-to-be. Steve Jervasoni "volunteered" to be his best man.

At the courthouse, Phyliss stood with Marthalik. Phyliss

had selected Marthalik's full-hipped skirt and flowered blouse. Phyliss's svelte presence was embarrassing to Dr. West, but Phyliss had insisted on helping their wedding. "Believe me, Joe, I've always felt more like your—mother." She had eyed him with what appeared to be disapproval rather than jealousy. "I still can't understand you—bringing this sweet kid down here into this mess we call civilization. You—she can't be that sexy. Can she?"

In the judge's chamber, Phyliss stood behind Marthalik, towering behind her.

"Do you take this man——" the old judge was intoning.

Anxious to help the whiteman's magic work, Marthalik correctly responded: "I do!" so emphatically in English that the judge smiled and coughed.

Marthalik peeked up cautiously at this old *angakok*, this black-robed magician, then glanced up at Dr. West for reassurance. He squeezed her warm hand, and Steve Jervasoni poked him with the ring.

"With this ring I thee wed." Dr. West lifted Marthalik's moist hand with her small fingers spreading like all of nature to him, and his throat hurt with a startling emotion, more confusing to him than joy.

As he slipped on the ring, she inhaled audibly, peering up at him as if worried whether she had done right in this whiteman's ceremony. He nodded. Her smile blossomed like a little girl's, and Dr. West thought he'd written her age on the license as twenty-one. He could just as well have written eighteen or another guess.

"I now pronounce you man and wife," the judge intoned.

Marthalik closed her eyes, prettily tilting up her lips. In a smiling instant, Dr. West guessed Phyliss had coached her as to this whiteman's ending to the ritual beginning. Feeling her mouth in trust beneath his, Dr. West humbly hoped he had done the right thing not to use good sense. Marrying Marthalik was beyond good sense. Hand in hand, they hurried out to the car, laughing.

"You're my wife," he said happily in English.

"I'll boil your tea!" She seemed to be learning English more quickly than a child.

"You're my wife," he repeated as they slid onto the back seat.

"I'll boil your tea!" Where she'd picked up or assembled this useful sentence, he didn't know—Phyliss or television.

In modern Eskimo, he announced proudly: "You are the wife of my house. You will boil much meat when I bring home a fat seal," he laughed, "or a *grad-u-ate stu-dent*. If I'm lucky on the hunt, I'll bring home *full pro-fess-ors* more powerful than walruses."

"This person herself thinks," Marthalik murmured in Modern Eskimo, rubbing her face against his shoulder, "you are joking with her. *He* is a *grad-u-ate stu-dent*." She pointed her small nose toward Steve Jervasoni, who sat alone in the front seat, driving, and Dr. West finally realized that Phyliss was gone.

"This person herself thinks," Marthalik's soft voice ventured, "that you should speak always to her in your own language so that she will learn. The man speaks. The woman must learn to understand."

"Then you'll boil my tea?" he laughed in English.

"I'll boil your tea," she answered proudly in English.

As she peeked out of the automobile past the huge new Regional Shopping Center along Telegraph Avenue, she clutched his hand. He tried to imagine how confusing the whiteman's world must be to her. In this strange world she had only him to cling to. *My god, what am I doing to her?*

As they ran upstairs to their apartment, playfully she elbowed him. Laughing and gasping on the porch, they struggled. As he picked her up, her accidentally swinging tennis shoes banged open the door of their wedding igloo.

The baby-sitter, a co-ed from Free U., stood up with her mouth open. Dr. West dumped Marthalik on the couch. "Boil tea!"

The co-ed stared at him as if he were a brutal monster.

"I'll boil your tea," Marthalik gasped happily in English and scurried into the kitchen.

Little Joe wandered sleepily out of a bedroom and tried to climb Dr. West's leg. "Wha-wha? Daddy."

Dr. West picked him up and walked toward the crib in the dining room in which Little Martha already was standing up, holding on with only one hand and grinning two teeth with accomplishment.

Steve Jervasoni was knocking bashfully on the half-open apartment door as if he didn't know whether he should bring in Marthalik's forgotten corduroy coat or not. "Sir—, Joe, you want me to drive to a supermarket and buy you folks some groceries?"

"Come inside and entertain my daughter," Dr. West commanded, paying off the slack-jawed co-ed, who fled. "Just pick her up," he challenged Steve. "Already she weighs nineteen pounds."

Steve squinted down cautiously at Little Martha's diapered toplessness. "I guess she's more accustomed to being carried in her mother's parka?"

"She won't wet you. Pick her up. These last two weeks I've discovered what fatherhood is," Dr. West laughed faintly, worrying whether the University would renew his contract, worrying how he was going to support a wife and children and baby-sitters and a tutor for his wife.

"Soon-soon! I'll boil your tea," Marthalik called happily from the kitchen. "Hello Steve."

"Maybe I should get married," Steve laughed. "Marthalik have a sister? You know, seriously, just being around her makes me feel good. Maybe Eskimos are better than other people. When she smiles, I almost feel an aura, a radiation, almost like love—for all humanity."

At that moment Steve looked more like nineteen than twenty-nine. After junior college, he'd served his four years in Army Biological Warfare, followed by two years at State College, and now was in his third year of graduate work at the University of California.

Like the perfect housewife, Marthalik bustled from the kitchen carrying a tray with the steaming teapot and four paper cups. Dr. West noticed a slight wiggle or waddle to her walk which had increased since yesterday. Soon her next pregnancy would be noticeable. Sooner, her hot tea would melt the waxed seams of those paper cups if she poured——.

"It is the custom in this big village," Dr. West said quickly in Modern Eskimo, anxious not to embarrass her in front of Steve, "we drink hot tea only from heavy cups, the big cups with flowers, the cups on the ledge above where the stream flows out. These thin cups of *paper* are for cold water. The heavy cups are for hot tea."

"Eh-eh," Cheerfully she picked up the tray again. "A woman does as her husband wishes."

As she hurried back to the kitchen, Steve looked at Dr. West. "Translated?"

"Learn Eskimo yourself," Dr. West laughed, for it was a difficult agglutinative language as complex but more consistent than English. "Learn Eskimo. Then go up to Boothia and steal your own bride."

"The Canadian Government might not approve," Steve laughed, "nor might the Eskimos."

"Marthalik isn't an Eskimo." Dr. West watched Steve blink.

"Quit your kidding, sir," Steve grinned with embarrassment and looked down at his shoes, expensive appearing cordovans for a nonscholarship grad student. "Sir, when you get a new research grant, I hope you'll acquire my contract from Dr. Gatson. We don't seem to be attempting really basic research since you were—since you resigned."

The next morning Dr. West entered the office of the Dean of the Demography Department at the University. He had two purposes in mind.

First he picked up his next to last sabbatical paycheck and turned in a required synopsis of his proposed sabbatical research report. It would analyze any population growth trends he observed within the Boothia Peninsula Eskimo Cultural Sanctuary. Deceptively, his synopsis indicated his report merely would be another age-sex census. From the synopsis, the report promised to be of only academic significance, merely confirming he'd been earning his sabbatical paychecks through required self-development in his approved field of study. He smiled. When he'd collected enough evidence from Marthalik, the real report would startle the Dean of the Demography Department into orbit! Dr. West would become a boy wonder again in a candy store of rich research grants, he hoped.

Second, Dr. West was anxious to see if the University's offer of contract renewal was in his professorial mailbox. He knew this time the University would offer him less than his bonanza negotiated three years ago. Then he'd just won that huge grant from the Defense Department for his proposed Oriental Population Problems Research program. He had been a hero. Consequently, with the University he had negotiated what was termed a Koufax contract, his paychecks reflecting in a small way the 1.8 million dollars he had attracted from the Pentagon to the Berkeley Campus.

Now he was out as Director. He had offended the Defense Department's cornucopia. His three-year University contract had expired. His bargaining power was gone. If he failed to turn in a sensational sabbatical report, he thought his last year's high pay probably would suffer the maximum cut, 25%. Even so, he still would be one of the most highly paid members of the faculty, so highly paid it was possible the University would try to trade him off to another university which had a lot of money but a weak Demography Department.

The annual ninety-day negotiating period had begun in the U.S. If he refused to report to another university campus, he thought his university might stall along in negotiations with him until the ninety-day negotiating period was almost over. Then it would be too late for him to start applying for positions elsewhere. He would have to take the 25% cut anyway. So he decided to sign his contract at once. But his mailbox was empty. No contract yet.

He was sure they would offer him one. In fairness to him, after all that Defense Department money he had brought in, the University would offer him some sort of contract renewal, he thought. They wouldn't declare him a free agent. At worst, they would try to trade him.

The University might try to trade him to another university for a lower-salaried man but they wouldn't simply drop him during the ninety-day negotiating period, he thought. This once-a-year negotiating period applied to all universities and to all professors who wanted to continue doing business with the Defense Department. Three years was the unbreakable length of such contracts. A former Secretary of Defense had devised these regulations for academic salary negotiations, trading and recruiting, after remarking that some research professors most vital to the national interest were job jumping or being recruited to rival universities so frequently their productivity was impaired. "They spend more time traveling from coast to coast, pursued by moving vans, than in trying to straighten out their disorganized commitments to the Defense Department."

Dr. West stared into his empty mailbox and hoped the University would not cut him. As a free agent now, with less than ninety days for him to locate a comparable position elsewhere, he might have to accept a minor position.

"You ever teach?" The scratchy voice startled him because it belonged to Dr. Darwin; that academic outlaw was standing behind him here in the Dean's outer office with a recruiter's smile.

"What are you doing on campus?" Dr. West laughed; at one time Dr. Darwin had been his buddy here in the Demography Department.

Although highly regarded by his graduate students, and after working hard through three three-year contracts as an Assistant Professor, Dr. Darwin had failed to be promoted to Associate Professor, and struck out. Too few of Dr. Darwin's population research papers had been accepted for publication by the professional demographic journals, and he was out. Released as a free agent, no graduate university had offered him a contract. He was an outlaw from organized academics, and was teaching lecture classes in Berkeley at Free U., where there were young and unruly students known as undergraduates.

"I'm recruiting you, that's what I'm doing," Dr. Darwin said.

Dr. West laughed again, not meaning to sound contemptuous. "I'm surprised our Kampus Kops even permit a talented talent raider like you to enter our Demography Building," he kidded, "or even drive through Savio Gate."

"Oh, the University police never bother me," Dr. Darwin laughed, "unless I park my car in an administrator's space. Now if you were at Free U., we've no monthly parking fee."

"I'd have to look for a space along the streets and in distant alleys?"

"No, the kids set out sawhorses to guard a teacher's parking space. We need another teacher of General Population Problems who can also teach Physiological Aspects of Reproduction—doctor."

"If you mean me lecture to a big class," Dr. West laughed, for he had been more the research-executive type, working with small groups of respectful grad students while he was Director of Oriental Population Problems Research, "I've had no experience as a dramatic performer."

"If I can, you can. On my recommendation, I think the Student Hiring Committee would agree to give you a one-semester tryout," Dr. Darwin persisted. "If you draw big crowds, there's big money. If you're good, every day those kids will be dropping their dollar bills in the entry boxes, and you'll know you're being appreciated."

"You're still lecturing in that former furniture warehouse?" Dr. West smiled, inwardly wincing at the thought of being graded by his students every day; he wanted nothing to do with Free U.

Free U. was making another comeback. When Dr. West was in the last class of undergrads on the Berkeley Campus, Free U. already had been growing. The year after he departed east for Harvard's Graduate School of Medicine, undergrad education at Cal. had been discontinued for financial and other reasons. As a consequence, Free U. had blossomed until it encompassed 10,000 students during the 1980s, spreading to old rented buildings all over Berkeley. So many idealistic professors were attracted and such ambitious young student administrators were elected each year that the undergraduate curriculum became more substantial than at the state colleges.

The examination schedule was solidified, eliminating the relaxed amateur students. National-standard courses were instituted and eventually required, driving away any eclectic searchers after Truth and other eccentrics. Free U. achieved B.A. degree granting stature. It became an accredited springboard to all the important graduate schools except the University of California, where there was professional jealousy because——.

The Health, Education, and Welfare Department had

granted Free U. a fifty million dollar credit for acquisition of land for a permanent campus. The student body voted to accept the slum clearance land on both sides of Telegraph Avenue which the Housing and Redevelopment Authority offered to them at a bargain price of fifty million dollars. The student body president signed over the credit and accepted the deed. The student body had voted to use this potentially valuable commercially zoned land as security so that a major insurance company loan could finance construction of the permanent campus buildings. But a developer of regional shopping centers offered Free U. 100 million dollars for the cleared land. The student body sensibly voted to accept. A hundred million dollars divided equally among 10,000 students is $10,000 for each student. Some got married, combining their capital for a sound financial start in life. Irritated by outcries from Washington, more idealistic students flew away to the International Human Be-In in Paris. "The sensible time to enjoy money is when you're young enough to enjoy it."

Gutted of its wealthy students, retaining few of its disillusioned faculty, overwhelmed by the annual influx of new students from high schools into the same old overcrowded Free U. rented buildings throughout Berkeley, Free U. was making another comeback.

"Sure, I'm still lecturing in a warehouse," Dr. Darwin retorted to Dr. West. "Who needs a billion dollar concrete edifice? A college is for the students and teachers. At least we don't have professionally entrenched administrators. If your contract isn't renewed, visit the former beer parlor that's our administrative headquarters. Visit our classes. These are real live kids again. They want to interact with a real live teacher instead of a ghost on TV."

But Dr. West was edging out the door, worrying why Dr. Darwin seemed so sure his university contract might not be renewed. "Your lecture classes are so big," Dr. West murmured, "even bigger than the 1970s."

"They wouldn't be so big if we had more teachers," Dr. Darwin pursued him.

"Ha!" Dr. West struck back. "If there were more teachers

there'd be less student dollars per teacher. The kids won't go above a dollar per lecture."

"They might, they might. We plan to negotiate with the kids. But what the hell! Regardless of the $1.00 or any future $1.25 per lecture, the real satisfaction in life is having an audience if you're a real teacher."

"I'm not a performer." Dr. West hurried along the hall because he had to go home and pick up Marthalik and take her to that innocently unsuspecting obstetrician within a half hour.

"Could you perform for $1000 a week?" Dr. Darwin pursued him. "Two lectures a day, ten lectures a week, plus individual student conferences the rest of your time. Two lectures a day, a hundred students in each, that's $200 a day. In a five-day week, that's $1000."

"But if they skip a class they save a dollar," Dr. West retorted, hurrying down the stairs, not asking whether even half a class showed up for any lectures, because this would only encourage Dr. Darwin to keep talking.

"In order to take the final exam for credit," Dr. Darwin panted after him across the ground floor lobby, "kids have to produce receipts from at least half the lecture hours. I can't attract the co-eds like you could, but I'm grossing $850 per week. My only expenses are my pro rata share of the warehouse rent, heating, lights and student janitor service. I'm netting more than an Associate Professor at the University of California."

"Good." Dr. West dodged between silent electric autos, wondering if the innocent obstetrician he had selected for Marthalik would end up as famous as Dr. DaFoe, a semimythical Canadian who delivered the unremarkable Dionne quints.

"And I have no research deadlines to meet," Dr. Darwin's voice trailed after him toward his car. "Without research and publications scalps to collect, I have so much time to meet with my students individually. I'm working a solid ten-hour day with kids, a lot more than I'm required to, but these are real live kids. Believe me, real teaching is wonderful."

"What do you think my graduate students were—dead people?" Dr. West retorted, cornered against his car. "I was teaching them———."

"Then there's our merit bonus," Dr. Darwin shrugged. "At the end of the semester, when the students vote for the outstanding instructors, what a pleasure to receive a merit bonus from the kids!"

"I hear that some teachers have received more eccentric treatment."

"Young people are lively, but each semester my own bonuses have grown bigger. I'm learning——."

"Thanks for asking me," Dr. West blurted, scrambling inside his Olds Electro-Drive and simultaneously worrying about his university contract and about Marthalik's surprising attitude toward her approaching visit to the obstetrician. She had acted insulted at her husband's apparent lack of confidence in her ability as wife.

"It is so easy to have babies by oneself," she whispered finally in the obstetrician's waiting room. "This person never has needed help. I simply kneel over a hole dug in the earth of the tent. The hole should be lined with a caribou skin."

Dr. West sat beside her, staring at a dog-eared medical journal in the waiting room and saying nothing.

"This is so stupid," she persisted in Modern Eskimo. "My belly has only begun to grow big. I won't have my baby for at least a week."

"You speak truly. But it is a whiteman's custom for a medical *angakok* to look at the mother first. This brings good luck for the baby." Dr. West accompanied her into the examining room. He had decided not to confide in the obstetrician about the one-month gestation period because the obstetrician wouldn't believe him, and would think he was a nut.

The obstetrician moved with practiced sureness and a curious smile which faded as Marthalik resisted.

In outrage, Marthalik finally submitted to the examination. In answer to the question as to the date of conception, Dr. West told the obstetrician that he could not even guess the approximate date. At the end of the examination, the OB innocently predicted Marthalik could expect normal labor pains in about three months. Dr. West asked for another appointment this Friday. The obstetrician blinked, evidently realizing the husband was even more difficult than the wife.

Dr. West insisted that he record a handprint now—of Marthalik. Turning a dull red, the obstetrician tried to smile and humor him. "Normally it is the handprint of the newborn baby we take to eliminate any worry as to positive identification." But Dr. West insisted, and the obstetrician suddenly laughed. "First time I've ever handprinted a mother."

"We'll be back in four days," Dr. West said.

"If you wish, but I wouldn't worry about a thing," the OB laughed, steering him out the door. "She's young, has borne previous children, has outstanding muscle tone. Since this is your fourth child, there's no reason for you to suffer such acute symptoms. Don't worry!"

In four days, it was the OB who was suffering acute symptoms. In only four days, Marthalik had swelled up like a balloon. The OB feared a huge watery tumor and insisted that a heat print of the uterus and fetus not only was justified, it was imperative. When he inspected the blurry picture of the nearly full-term fetus, the OB glared at Dr. West as if suspecting a bad joke. "This is a different woman. This is a different baby. It will be born within six weeks. Different woman——."

"Compare handprints of my wife."

Making another handprint of Marthalik and comparing it with the one in his files only made the obstetrician angrier. "Even my nurse—someone in my office is in on this so-called joke. Switching handprints has to be an inside job. Mr. West, if you're not satisfied with my services and are trying to make a fool of me I would recommend another doctor. You still have six weeks."

"I'm satisfied." Dr. West was not satisfied, worrying that this OB might prove too unadaptable for his purpose. The OB would undergo a shock in three days. But to change doctors now would frustrate Dr. West's whole purpose.

In three days, the obstetrician was called to the hospital to deliver the baby. When he recognized Marthalik, he called in a specialist. "You won't be billed for his time, Mr. West. If necessary, I'll pay him out of my own pocket. When I deliver this baby, which should be a simple procedure, which is supposed to be a simple procedure, and I've been delivering babies for thirty years including many premies, I expect no problems, and the incubator and my usual assisting physician for interesting cases are ready—but I want an expert witness."

Dr. West smiled. This was exactly what Dr. West wanted, witnesses. Marthalik had an easy birth, a baby boy who gave one squawl, then lay on the OB's rubber gloves, seeming almost smiling with confidence in this cold and drying new world.

"Full-term," remarked the specialist, and shrugged, coldly eyeing the obstetrician.

The OB became embarrassed. Evidently he had given the specialist and the other doctor the impression that the baby would be premature. Plainly the OB had lacked the confidence to tell them his patient had progressed from the apparent six-month to a full-term pregnancy in one week, and now he had no intention of doing so. Before the witnesses could depart, Dr. West desperately whispered to the OB that he handprint Marthalik in the presence of these two doctors and get their signatures on the handprint. Surprisingly the OB nodded in agreement. With odd expressions the two doctors signed and left.

The OB peered at Dr. West. With a deductive hypothesis worthy of Sherlock Holmes, the OB laughed hopefully. "Is it possible, you'll be bringing your wife—to my office again—in a couple of months?"

Dr. West returned with Marthalik in a week. With nervous hands, the OB personally did the pregnancy lab ten-minute test and other exam procedures. "I suppose I don't know much about Eskimos. But this heat print suggests she's already in her second month of this second pregnancy. I never imagined that Eskimos——."

"Marthalik's not an Eskimo," replied Dr. West.

The OB stared at him. "Will you do me a favor and bring your wife in every day except—of course, Wednesday. Your daily appointments could be at 6:00 if that is convenient. No charge, no charge at all." The obstetrician smiled with boyish excitement as if he were about to make a great medical discovery.

In less than a month, this baby was born before too many witnesses. Some of them clutched Dr. West's arm and virtually demanded a repeat performance.

"Visit Canada," Dr. West retorted with a narrow smile. "Put pressure on the Canadian Government and demand to be allowed to inspect the Boothia Peninsula Eskimo Cultural Sanctuary. There's nothing unusual about Marthalik. Believe me, a one-month gestation period is normal for Boothia Peninsula Eskimos—if they are Eskimos."

He was feeling fierce because the University finally had notified him that day his contract would not be renewed.

"Go to Boothia," he told the reporter, "and see if I'm lying. Those poor people are multiplying so fast it's like the next hundred years of the world's population explosion compressed into the next ten. Unless those bureaucrats in Ottawa hurry up and introduce birth control instead of endless food, Canada could be submerged by Eskimos. No, call them Esks. They're not the same as Eskimos. They're something new. But their hunger is as old as mankind."

Dr. West had only one more sabbatical paycheck, and already five children to feed. He intended to practice birth control from now on. Five children were more than enough. In this crowding world, in his crowding apartment, he lectured Marthalik on when to take The Pill. Conscientiously, she seemed to follow his instructions.

Each morning when he rolled out of bed to type exploratory letters to colleagues at other universities, not openly applying for a job, Marthalik already would be up, boiling tea, pouring milk, spooning baby food, nursing the smallest baby, frying ham and eggs for Dr. West.

Like Icarus at the breakfast table, he devoured his ham and eggs regardless of cholesterol consequences. Like Icarus at the typewriter, he hammered wings of words beginning his Boothia report, planning to impress the universities who soon would be competing for his services. He thought U.C. would regret making him a free agent just before he became famous. But to be recognized in the academic world his report first needed to be published in a professional journal, which meant a time lag of months, if he were published at all. Unfortunately, when he was on the Boothia Peninsula he had spent more time making love to Marthalik and then traveling to the Burned Place to try to question Peterluk, than in gathering the detailed statistics which would impress the editors of a professional population journal.

He regretted working up his age-sex census from memory. Hans Suxbey had his notebook. He wished he could provide more statistical clues as to the rate at which these pseudo-Eskimos really were increasing. It was an unprofessional report.

One important factor in any population's rate of increase was the average age at which marriage began. How soon did each generation begin breeding the next generation? From his questioning of Marthalik he was confused as to how fast an Esk child would mature.

Watching Little Joe riding his tricycle round and round the living room, already chirping whole sentences in understandable English although he was less than a year old, Dr. West knew Little Joe hadn't inherited such precocity from the West side of the family.

To his dismay Marthalik became pregnant again as promptly as if she'd spit out birth control pills when he wasn't looking.

When he stared at his daughter, Little Martha, whose physical father he had believed he could not be, he thought he could see some of his characteristics. Fingering the cartilage of her ear, he even thought he could feel the West family lump. Eva, the third child, who also could not be his, also had his ears, he thought. So did Little Sam, and also the new baby they had named after the obstetrician. All five of them equally appeared to be his children, he pondered, although Little Martha and Eva could not be. But he felt they were his. Was this too much fatherly pride? No. "Marthalik, we've had enough children."

But Marthalik refused to accept an intrauterine device. "Children are so nice, Joe. They are our purpose in life. If you love me, you will permit me to have children."

Stubbornly, Dr. West not only was gulping guaranteed

sperm-suppressant capsules, he was making double sure by using condoms.

To his dismay, Marthalik became pregnant right on schedule. He didn't think she had been unfaithful to him. He had his pride. Who had been alone with her? Steve Jervasoni. Impossible. He wasn't going to question her or accuse him. He could not believe she had been unfaithful to him.

"Marthalik, six children will be enough! This next baby must be your last."

"But this is why we are alive—to have children, Joe. My babies are my purpose."

"Marthalik, in your village——." Dr. West paused in embarrassment. "Sometimes husbands would be gone for many days hunting seals on the ice. While these husbands were gone, their wives would sleep with other men?"

"Sometimes yes, sometimes no."

"If some women did not sleep with other men while their husbands were away, did they miss having a baby?"

"Why should they not have babies? Babies come because the woman has thought faithfully about Grandfather Bear—and even if she hasn't."

"No men are needed?" Dr. West smiled at this startling innocence as to the facts of life.

"Yes, this person thinks a man is needed—the first time. Young girls do not have babies until they have known a man. After that, perhaps a man is not needed if a girl continues to think good thoughts."

"Or even if she doesn't," Dr. West murmured realizing with relief that he was the physical father of all six of her children. She had been physically faithful to him. Even Little Martha and Baby Eva, who apparently were conceived and growing in her womb during the two months he was 2000 miles away in Ottawa imprisoned in a hospital, were his children.

Nervously he thought of tropical fish he owned when he was a boy, multiplying until his little aquarium was overcrowded with red platys. Forced to buy a second aquarium, shrewdly he had transferred only the swollen female to the new aquarium. To avoid being overwhelmed by more platys, as the female gave birth he netted out her babies and guiltily flushed them down the toilet. Momentarily the lonely female platy appeared slim. With relief he had thought he was freed from killing any more babies. But in a month, she was swollen again. Without any contact with males, miraculously she was giving birth. Swimming weakly above the gravel were more baby platys. In defeat, he had traded both aquariums to another kid for a telescope.

"Marthalik," he muttered, stroking her arm, "you are a fountain of life."

There seemed two possibilities. Either his male sperm survived much longer than the normal two to three days in her uterus and Fallopian tubes; this seemed unlikely. Or on up in the narrow Fallopian tubes, perhaps into the ovaries themselves, his sperm that first night had impregnated all her partially developed ova. Did some hormone delay their growth? Hundreds of ova still might be waiting their turns to ripen and descend through her Fallopian tubes. As if from a savings bank for babies, these prefertilized but undividing ova were descending into her vacated uterus at monthly intervals. Triggered there, each grew from cell to embryo to fetus.

After a month each baby emerged smiling into the world.

With five little children already crowding the apartment, a sixth on the way, and Little Joe tackling his leg, loudly shouting like a two-year-old although he was barely five months old, Dr. West had no intention of finding out how many more babies his wife could have. "Dammit, I'm not trying to breed a touch football team."

They needed a bigger apartment but his last sabbatical paycheck was devoured by grocery bills, even though the kids were small eaters like Marthalik, and by clothing bills, even though each child's clothing was passed down to the next younger one. The oldest, Little Joe, seemed to be outgrowing his overalls overnight. And there were overdue bills from the hospital for the delivery room. Until now Dr. West hadn't comprehended how expensive marriage could be. Bills were piling up so fast it was terrifying.

In his letter to his former Harvard school buddy, Tom Randolph, he inquired about a position at Duke University where Dr. Tom Randolph now was Director of a new research project reportedly rich with Pentagon money. Tom's reply was friendly but so vague.

Tom had been so cautious in mentioning his own project that Dr. West suspected Tom suspected the Defense Department had rescinded Dr. West's security clearance. Although Tom didn't say so, obviously he couldn't or wouldn't help Dr. West meet the Dean of the Demography Department at Duke. In spite of the help Dr. West had given Tom at the beginning of his career, Tom wasn't going to stick his neck out one inch for Dr. West.

"Screw you, Tom." Dr. West mailed off his hurried report: "A Preliminary Analysis of a Population Growth Trend on the Boothia Peninsula" to the *Journal of American Population Scientists*.

"When this is published, recruiters from a dozen universities will be phoning me," he muttered, hoping against hope.

Trying not to think of the weeks he would have to wait in torment while not hearing whether the *Journal* had accepted or rejected his paper, Dr. West wondered if he ought to start a popular article in simple but terrifying language aimed at one of the newsstand magazines. Perhaps he should be aiming at the *New Saturday Evening Post* or even at one of the thick women's magazines like *Good Apartment-Keeping*. Even publication here might help him get a grant from some government agency. He knew the cancellation of his security clearance had been simply because he no longer was in a Defense Department funded project. He hoped it wasn't a permanent cancellation because a certain general considered him insubordinate. Hoping for a grant from the Department of Health, Education, and Welfare, he daydreamed of returning to the Boothia Peninsula as director of a major project. He would name his project: *Institute for the Study of the Shortened Gestation Period*. "Vitally significant research if this shortened gestation period is a trait which might also appear in other parts of the world."

He thought the Canadian Government might let him enter the Sanctuary. Right now, a Parliamentary Committee was questioning Hans Suxbey, embattled Director of the Eskimo Cultural Sanctuary. The elder LaRue was chairman of the vilifying committee. Old LaRue must have Hans Suxbey sweating.

"I'll bet, within a year, the whole Eskimo Cultural Sanctuary will be abolished by Parliament." Dr. West leaned over his coffee cup toward Dr. Darwin. "I've got to get back into Boothia with cameras, grad students for census takers, and tape recorders, before the Esks' myths are altered even in their own minds by loudmouthed newspaper interviewers. I've got to beat *Life*."

"You have the advantage of being married to Marthalik."

"Yes, *Life*'s bringing out our picture-story in the next issue, and this may help me get a grant. I've got to get back to Boothia."

"I hear through the grapevine that ethnologists over at the State University in Palo Alto," Dr. Darwin remarked, "have snitched a copy of that synopsis you submitted to Cal. They are applying to the Canadian Government for a——."

"Damn! Spies from that diploma farm won't get into Boothia yet. Of course Henry LaRue, the younger LaRue, candidate for public office, has been in and out and in again."

"Oh, the hero?" Dr. Darwin laughed. "I saw the rebroadcast of that CBC program. LaRue dramatically translates for this young Eskimo man whose babies are starving."

"That was Edwardluk, the Esk who dragged me to the Sanctuary Guard Station."

"Then all this talk about babies starving is true?" Dr. Darwin asked. "There's a solid reason a chapter of the SAVE THE ESKIMOS LEAGUE is being formed here at Free U.?"

"The Canadian Government already is air-dropping Family Allowances. The Esks should survive this summer ok, and they'll be a bigger problem each winter."

"You have a growing family problem yourself," Dr. Darwin thrust. "You can still pay for your own cup of coffee, but next month, who knows? I invited you here for coffee to tell you I'm confident the Student Hiring Council will accept you as a lecturer in population problems."

Dr. West stood up, abruptly pushing a dime beside his coffee cup. "I'm thinking about it, I'm thinking about it." He was worrying that some weird things had happened to teachers at Free U. He still was hoping to find a job elsewhere in some graduate university.

"Did you know the Defense Department has blacklisted you?" Dr. Darwin said. "They even mail Free U. copies of their latest blacklists. We throw them in the wastebasket."

Dr. West went home and tried to balance his checkbook, but his hand was shaking so that he got a different answer every time. All answers said: not enough money. Another month and he'd be overdrawn.

"Even if my professional journal article is published, there'll be no cash payment, no quick money." He stayed up late hammering into the typewriter a first-person article: "Population Explosion in the Arctic," aimed at the *New Saturday Evening Post*. "When you think about it, future Esk numbers could become—overwhelming—if the Canadian Government—for political and religious reasons—does not attempt forcible birth control of the Esks. That's what's needed——."

In the bedroom, Dr. West studied Marthalik's sleeping face. Even in her sleep she was smiling.

My love, he thought, *are you dreaming of me or of Grandfather Bear?*

As she turned restlessly, under the sheet the bulge was there. His face twisted in mental pain. He couldn't ask her to have an abortion now. But this sixth baby had to be the last.

When this baby was born, he thought, he could hardly ask her to undergo a hysterectomy. Even severing her Fallopian tubes was a major abdominal operation. The safe abortifacient pill he had given her three weeks ago without explanation hadn't aborted the ovum, or the microscopically shapeless beginning embryo. Evidently her hormonal balance was more stable or adaptable than a human woman's. *Something's got to be done—which won't hurt her, won't frighten her, won't turn her against me.* "I do love you, Marthalik."

On Saturday morning when Marthalik had gone on an exciting expedition to the supermarket all by herself, and Dr. West was playing with his five children on the living room rug, Steve Jervasoni dropped by. "Thought you'd be interested to hear, we've finally evaluated those tests we began at

Sierra Women's Reformatory while you were———. Very interesting."

"So?" Dr. West didn't want to listen, but what could he say? While he was Director he had arranged for the test. Now it seemed weird to him how his originally broad proposal, which won a Defense Department research grant and erected a white concrete building on the hillside behind Cal with gleaming brass letters over the open door spelling out: *Oriental Population Problems Research,* had been narrowed.

The door to widespread basic research on the social-religious-physiological approaches to population control had been slammed. From the original staff he had recruited, all the sociologists were fired due to pressure from the Pentagon. The social psychologists and mass communications experts were gone. The ethnologists were gone. The religious experts were gone, Taoist, Maoist, Marxist, Buddhist, Moslem, Protestant, Catholic, Cao Dai, Animist. Some had gone even before Dr. West was fired. But their empty desks had been refilled so quickly. Enlarging the edifice, a specialized lab was being erected by the ever-generous Defense Department.

Dr. West's original proposal for Oriental Population Problems Research had been a study of all avenues toward control of the population explosion in the Orient. Advertising, psychological, religious, chemical and bacterial approaches to population limitation were to be pretested. Then the most humanely promising approaches were to be evaluated in the Orient. Efficiency of population control was to be only one of the criteria for evaluating any proposed approaches. The effect of any method upon the people *as human beings* with social and psychological traits as well as physiological plumbing was to be evaluated. Each nation and within each nation each identifiable social or religious group and within each group each individual should be considered.

What will be the long-term effects of this particular approach to population limitation upon this woman—and her husband? With fewer children, will they fear there may be no one to care for their graves, to worship their bones after they become ancestors? What substitutes can be offered for these truly human needs? At the end of the first year, Oriental Population Problems Research still had been a diversified and hopeful program.

But someone in the project evidently was reporting continuously to the Pentagon, because the pressure already was on Dr. West.

On the telephone, the General said: "Dr.—uh, West, explain to me why we're spending money for this crap."

Dr. West tried, and the General's voice brightened: "I get it! Attack on all fronts."

But the phone calls from the Pentagon became more frequent. "Dr.—uh, West, I hear only your bacteriological boys have been making real progress. Seems to be your only effective attack."

"That's just one approach," Dr. West had insisted, "and it hasn't been tested even in a controlled environment. There are so many implications——."

Theoretically, a nation might become able to control another nation's birthrate without that nation's consent, perhaps even without that country's knowledge. Only after several years might its leaders become frantic at how rapidly the birthrate curve was falling. Belatedly they would begin trying to find out why. Was it disease, or malnutrition, or declining national morale, or a change in social and religious attitudes, or the result of foreign propaganda urging birth control? They might not discover who had attacked their country with a genocidal weapon as deadly as nuclear bombs, or had intervened with humane wisdom.

The next phone call from the Pentagon barked at Dr. West: "Your bacteriological boys have perfected a surefire attack."

"Hardly that," Dr. West had replied, "we're just beginning the first pretest of the bacterial strain."

At Sierra Woman's Reformatory there were a hundred volunteers between the ages of twenty-one and twenty-five. Isolated, these women had developed slight colds, a temporary burning sensation in the abdomen and groin, and even before their uneventful recoveries the phone was ringing in Dr. West's office.

"Great work, Dr.—uh, West. Now you can expedite R and D on this successful attack."

"General, several years will be necessary to evaluate the physiological effects and much longer for the psychological effects."

"Anything you say, Doctor. Great work. We evaluate your program at the end of the fiscal year."

At that meeting Dr. West was forced to admit that the biological-bacteriological research had made the most apparent progress, and he accepted the additional money to enlarge that wing of the building.

In a few months the phone rang louder than usual. "Dr.—uh, West, we understand the bacteria you used at that women's prison wasn't strong enough. It pooped out."

"Hardly that," Dr. West replied. "For the safety of us all, naturally we have been breeding only self-attenuating strains."

"Huh?"

"As the test women transmitted and retransmitted the disease from one isolated cellblock to another the virulence of the disease declined."

"It pooped out."

"Of course," Dr. West replied, "it was supposed to——."

"You're kidding?——Dr.—uh, West, we're paying for results. Your bacteriological boys can give us better results than that. Now!"

This had launched Dr. West's jet trips to Washington. His desperate confrontations were ended when the Defense Department suggested to the University administrators, if they hoped for continued funding for this and other research programs, the present Director of Oriental Population Problems Research named Dr.—uh, West, should be replaced.

Dumped into his sabbatical leave, Dr. West had fled; from further conflict he had escaped to the Arctic, but now he lay on the living room rug in his Berkeley apartment with his five children crawling all over him while he listened to Steve Jervasoni.

"The hundred lucky fellows from Chino Men's Prison have really been producing," Steve Jervasoni laughed. "After two years, a better percentage of those gals than we hoped finally have managed to get pregnant. In the outlying cellblocks where the infection was least virulent, most of them are pregnant."

"Good. I'm relieved the way their Fallopian tubes are reopening. Just as our first gynecological studies indicated, most of the stoppage was due to swelling rather than permanent scarring. Good."

"Bad," replied Steve Jervasoni. "The Pentagon is pressing us to start human testing of Dr. Gatson's virulent strain."

"Dammit!" Dr. West stood up. "Those military minds have been juggling H-bombs on the tightrope of extinction for so long they've lost all sensation of danger. Dammit! Accidental transmission of Gatson's favorite bacteria outside the prison——. God! Why would even the military want to develop anything that can't be used, that couldn't be sprayed on Asia. Do they think we could medically isolate America while infection sweeps the rest of the world sterilizing all women and men until——."

Steve Jervasoni's restraining hand was on his forearm. "Dr. Gatson still thinks he's on the trail of the antibodies for a protective inoculation."

"Bullshit! That's what little Freddie Gatson was saying two years ago."

"Maybe yes, maybe no," Steve Jervasoni replied, sitting down again and absently ruffling the dark hair of Little Joe's head. "What I'm wondering is whether the mild and safe temporarily birth limiting strain we tested at Sierra Women's Reformatory would have any effect on Esks. Let's face it," Steve sighed, "now that the Canadian Government's feeding them, there's going to be an awful lot more, and if they're all as uncooperative in birth control as Marthalik——."

"Probably little or no effect on Esks," Dr. West retorted. "My kids haven't even caught cold. No sore throats or secondary bacterial infections. Marthalik's never ill. No, she did have a sore throat once."

"Then this mild strain might not be able to limit the births of Esks in a few years when Canada needs help."

"Who knows? Unless something like this is developed, I think Canada will have a lot of Esks. And a lot of starvation and a lot of lynching of innocent Esks."

"And you'll have a hundred children by then, a hundred of Marthalik's children to feed, clothe and educate," Steve Jervasoni replied.

"Very funny. You've observed Marthalik's preg again."

"This is a safely self-attenuating bacterial strain."

"Marthalik?"

"You said it, I didn't." Steve stood up.

"Forget it," Dr. West retorted, and failed to forget it.

The day Marthalik produced his sixth child, Dr. West discovered Steve Jervasoni sitting on his doorstep.

"Wouldn't the baby-sitter let you in?" Dr. West asked wearily.

"When do you bring Marthalik home?" Steve's fist bulged awkwardly inside his coat pocket as if he had a sixth finger. "*Life* still taking pictures? Next month they'll have lost interest in your seventh baby. Eighth. Ninth." Steve took out a stoppered glass tube and blurted: "Giving you this from the lab, I guess I could get twenty years in the Federal Pen——."

"Bacterial spores? Dammit! Damn you! Good stockpiling characteristics?" Dr. West asked bitterly. "Storable to Pentagon specifications?"

"Until you have to do it," Steve murmured, "in this culture medium the spores could survive for months—years at low temperatures like in the Arctic or in your refrigerator."

"You think some day I'll open this tube in desperation?" Dr. West demanded. "You think I'll say: *Marthalik, breathe——.*"

"But not around here. Fairly safe, self-attenuating but ——."

"I can't do this," Dr. West said and glared at Steve but did not hand back the glass tube.

"It was your—you gave me the idea," Steve muttered and departed with his head down.

His face blank, Dr. West walked into his kitchen. Carefully enclosing the tube in a polyethelene bag, he transferred part of the culture medium to an empty nasal inhalator can. He put the polyethelene bag, which contained both the glass tube of bacterial spores and the inhalator can of spores, in a Mason jar. Opening the refrigerator, he hid the jar at the back behind a six-pack of lager beer.

He thought Steve was a contradictory character, supplying the bacteria and then acting as if its use was morally wrong. Even Steve's outward personality seemed contradictory. He acted more awkward and shy than Dr. West. Yet Steve was the newly elected president of the Graduate Students' Forum. For such an introvert to be elected president of anything seemed strange. But Dr. West suspected that few other grads had the free time or motivation to sit as moderator at interminable meetings where U.S. foreign and domestic policies endlessly were argued.

Surprisingly for a bacteriologist concerned with infective means of limiting the world's birth rate, Steve favored larger families in the U.S., speaking quietly from his central seat on the platform. "It's a matter of our national survival. In the international competition, the Chinese are——." Steve had repeated the Pentagon's line, urging an increased income tax deduction per child. "Our whole economy will be stimulated. More children mean more consumption, and for the unemployed more jobs demonstrating to the world that our system still works best. A return to our American tradition of large families is in the national interest."

After Marthalik returned in the *Life* Magazine limousine from the hospital proudly carrying her new baby, Dr. West hired a full-time sitter. "Goodbye Little Joe, Daddy and Mommy are going on their first vacation."

Dr. West was relieved how easily Marthalik left her children. "This person does not worry about children once they are born," she laughed wistfully. "Always someone will take care of those who are born."

Dr. West almost asked her if she was more concerned about those who weren't born yet, but with husbandly wisdom he kept his mouth shut. He drove their Olds electric to the shingled cottage overlooking one of the last private beaches in California. He had borrowed this old wooden cottage from a rich but short-haired artistic type who was a friend of Phyliss's. Locking the chain across the long dirt driveway, Dr. West helped Marthalik carry two-weeks' supply of groceries into the cottage.

"Warm waves. No ice." Across the deserted beach, Marthalik ran to him, her flawless skin beaded by the sea.

Breathing hard in her first bathing suit, she had a stocky figure by whitewomen's fashion standards, but very nice, Dr. West thought. *So very nice. Because I love you, you have a beautiful body.*

"My husband," she giggled as he squeezed her, "this wet person is making your shirt wet; you are so strong!"

"Are you happy here?" He released her.

"Like this we sat," she sighed, sitting down beside him on the salt-whitened log, "like this on the bone of the whale. This person's heart felt quick like a bird held in the hand. A very strong man beside me with his own rifle even stronger than Old Peterluk, you touched my hand. Until you saw me, this young girl was so careful." She rested her cheek against his shoulder. "With you, so strong, this person was ready for her children to begin."

"Now we feel close again like that," he suggested hopefully, "because there are no children between us now. Do you think that?"

"This person thinks she does not miss them. No matter where we are, we will have new babies for us to love."

Inside the beach cottage, Marthalik peeled off her wet bathing suit. She was most beautiful lying down.

"Marthalik, first we must breathe this." Sitting on the bed with his arm around her, he opened the inhalator can, and in her trust she didn't even ask him what it was, and inhaled, and he wanted to cry.

Breathing deeply from the can, he stood up.

"My husband, are you feeling well?" Her hand sought his leg.

"It is a custom here," he muttered, walking away from the bed, "as when the hunters are preparing to go out on the ice after walrus, the night before—they do not sleep with their wives."

With his back turned, for an instant he imagined her flushed with fever from the bacteria, moaning and writhing on the bed. He wanted to cry.

From the bed, she giggled. "My husband, you are not going walrus hunting. It is not a walrus you are going to harpoon."

He had to smile, his pulse racing. Probably she wouldn't

even have a fever. Turning, he looked down at her lying there. Looking up at him, she stretched luxuriously. And he had to laugh, he was in such a burning agony of desire. There seemed no medical reason why they shouldn't, particularly if he took old-fashioned precautions, so why was he torturing them both, denying nature? His face twisted in a grin. He was burning like hell's fire. He thought with wry amusement: *continence might not be quite so difficult if I were 5000 miles away in Rome."*

Entwined in the morning, they both sniffled with what he said were lovers' colds. Marthalik's temperature was only 99 degrees. His was 101. Dulled by a headache, he worried in how many ways Marthalik might differ in her physiological reactions from the women used in the testing of this bacteria. Those female prisoners reportedly had temperatures of 100 to 101.

The next day she said she felt fine. Her temperature was 98.2, normal for her. She bustled around the cottage. He lay in bed with 101.6, feeling burning pains like acute prostatitus. Finally he slept, burning and revolving until he dreamed he was her, part of her, within her. In her swollen shut Fallopian tube, he was trapped like an ovum. Like a tiny embryo growing bigger and bigger, he couldn't get out. He woke up sodden with sweat. If the blocking of her Fallopian tubes resulted in such an ectopic pregnancy she would have to undergo a major operation to save her life, he thought, a more dangerous operation than any uterine abortion.

"My husband, you must eat something." Cheerfully, she fed him canned peaches for breakfast.

As his temperature descended, he began to suspect the bacteria had left no effect on her. For controlling the spread of Esks, this mild bacteria might be useless. Perhaps the Esks could be affected only by a bacteria so virulent it would sterilize all humans, he thought. Esks seemed so much more durable than humans. He squeezed her strong little hand, thinking, *My love, what are you?*

The next day he felt so much better he knew she was as human as he was. "This game is called checkers," he explained, and she learned amazingly quickly, but he managed to beat her every time, while she nodded: "It is proper that the husband is wiser in the fighting of these little men."

Five days later she was surprised and alarmed to discover a menstrual flow. "This person has not bled since she was a girl, since she met you."

"That is because each month until now you had a baby." Dr. West smiled because the family limitation bacterial infection was a success.

"Is this person—sick?"

"Your body has been given a chance to rest."

By the end of the two weeks their last groceries were eaten. He felt confident they no longer were active carriers of the bacteria. The women in the prison had not been carriers after one week. None of the men had contracted the infection when they were admitted to the cells two weeks later.

"My husband, my body is so empty. Where is my baby?"

"It's time to go home," he said, and packed their clothes in their suitcases, which he left in the cottage.

Going outside onto the wooden porch, he stared at the red drowning sun. For a moment his confidence drained. How ironic if he caused the spread of the bacteria and it mutated, becoming more virulent. Ninety years after the last human birth, he thought, a world crowded with Esks shoulder to shoulder. "The meek shall inherit the Earth."

"Eh?"

"Your people are meek, Marthalik. That means they don't fight each other. They don't get angry. Always smiling, they are better than the rest of us—but I don't think they will inherit the Earth."

To Marthalik's openmouthed surprise, he told her to take off her clothes.

"My husband, in this country, it is not done out-of-doors."

"Marthalik, we're merely going to swim in the ocean. It's dark. Take off your clothes. Don't be a prude." He threw all their clothing on the wooden porch, and led her by the hand into a grippingly cold ocean.

While he shivered, she giggled trustfully, plumper, female, more resistant to cold water. Hardening his muscles, he ducked completely under and rose. Seizing her shoulders, he ducked her. Bubbling, she did not resist. Gasping, she clung to him as they waded out.

"My husband, it is not a woman's place to ask questions but——."

"No, don't go back on the porch." He led her to the car, took his extra key-card from his illegally installed spare key-holder under the fender, and inserted the magnetically coded card into the trunk lock. "Here—a towel, and some of your clothes I brought from home for you."

He said: "Put them on!" Naked he ran back to the house, and when he returned she had laid out his extra clothes for him.

"My husband, you have forgotten our suitcases."

"No, we will leave them. It is a new American custom," he said, unlocking the driveway chain.

As they drove away, bumping across the railroad tracks, curving toward the coast highway, her voice rose. "My husband, look back! A brightness like a campfire on the roof. Look back, is our cottage burning?"

"I can't look back when I'm driving," he blurted, driving out of sight. "You saw the red light from a fishing boat." He doubted if the cottage was insured. He would have to pay for it. But he had taken every precaution to minimize the unlikely risk that anyone else would be infected. As he drove, he worried.

When Marthalik did not produce a baby the following month, emotionally he began to pay for what he had done to her.

"What is wrong with me?" she complained, compulsively rubbing her small stomach as if this would help make a baby grow there. "Where is my baby?"

"You already have six children to take care of, and me."

"This person feels so——. Not accomplishing anything. So lonely with herself." For the first time Marthalik was speaking negatively like a whitewoman. "This person feels as if her life lacks——." She stared helplessly at the ceiling as if unable to express her inner feelings.

In the night she groaned and thrashed in a nightmare, and he held her in his arms. "My love, what is it?"

"Eh? ——Dreaming. All right now. Hold me."

In the morning with coy smiles she tried to be attractive to her husband. Now when she needed him most, he felt separated from her.

"When will this person have a baby?" her voice persisted, while his sexual desire waned, and he paced the streets, anxious for his teaching adventure at Free U. to begin.

The finance company had been willing to loan him only $500 on his future prospects when they learned he would be teaching at Free U. Nervously he organized and reorganized his lecture notes. To get out of the apartment, he took Little Joe for long walks.

Not yet a year old, Little Joe ran across the lawns and shouted and laughed with the round-eyed children. Already Little Joe appeared as large as a four- or five-year-old, but his coordination seemed similar to a three-year-old's. When children pushed him, Little Joe smiled instead of crying or pushing back. Smiling at his smile, strange children strangely didn't push him again. They romped around Little Joe as if enjoying the radiance of his magic smile. "Daddy, they love me. Everybody loves me!"

That sleepless night, only two days before he would have to face Free U., Dr. West lay on his elbow listening to Marthalik's groaning. Beside him, asleep, her face twisted in pain while she mumbled: "For you—we will fill—for you—this person is trying——."

Awake, she tried to maintain her smiling face. Accidentally upsetting an empty glass, which didn't even break, she broke into tears. Steve Jervasoni stared at Dr. West. With increasing frequency, Steve had appeared at the apartment to play with the kids or to chat with Marthalik if Dr. West was out taking the children for a walk.

"She doesn't understand," Steve blurted at Dr. West as the two men stood outside by the curb. "A terrible thing has been done to her without her permission. Have you told her why?"

"You know I haven't told her. Goddammit, what could I tell her? I sterilized her—perhaps forever."

"She has this terrible need."

"Tell me something I don't know!"

"I feel so guilty," Steve's voice persisted, "for bringing you the bacteria. Because you asked me to——."

"That wasn't how——."

"She was the happiest person I ever knew," Steve's voice rushed. "I—we felt so wonderful just sitting in her presence, enjoying her smile. Have you considered an operation to reopen her——."

"She's my wife, not yours!" Dr. West went in the house.

He had to sleep. Tomorrow was his first lecture at Free U. Half-remembered stories of the laughter and booing, of the humiliation hurled at inadequate lecturers, left him sleepless beside his restlessly sleeping wife. He tried to reassure himself that he'd be lecturing at Free U. for only one semester. But the *Journal of American Population Scientists* had rejected his paper, asking for more substantiation that his wife was not merely a "gynecological phenomenon." The rejecting editor added: "Your age-sex census of the Boothia Peninsula Eskimos is not of a professional level. If any Eskimos, other than your wife, do tend to have shortened gestation periods, we can assume a reputable expedition soon will confirm it." But Dr. West lacked the money to return to the Boothia Peninsula, even if the Canadian Government permitted him to enter.

Free U. was scattered all over Berkeley. With a hollow feeling in his stomach, he walked stiffly toward the former furniture warehouse. Past an ancient signpost in the alley, proclaiming this as Reagan Boulevard, he entered the enormous room. Clomping on the wooden plank platform, he wrote across the blackboard what he considered most important while the coughing and chattering of entering students grew. To his dismay, he saw they were ambling past the padlocked entry boxes without putting dollar bills in the slots. There must be an explanation——.

With surprise and excitement overlaying his discomfort, he saw that he was packing the hall. All the chairs and benches filled with gum-chewing faces. A stocky youth in conservative knickers scrambled onto the platform, his bow tie askew. "Employee Relations," he introduced himself, shaking the hand of the employee, Dr. West. This student executive extracted his watch from his wescot, then glanced at the

chattering audience. "Lecture Course in Population Problems," the youth shouted into the noise. "J. West, Probation-
ary Lecturer."

Chattering continued among the low-waisted, short-skirted
co-eds until resoundingly the youth fired at the high wooden
ceiling. A splinter fell to the platform. Nodding encouraging-
ly at Dr. West, the student leader blew across the twin
barrels of his derringer.

Dr. West's mouth opened but no sound emerged.

He had been advised by Dr. Darwin to open his first
lecture with a fresh but safely pretested joke, or if he didn't
want to gamble on a joke, to hurl a shocking introductory
statement at the co-eds in the front row to make them pull
their knees together and sit up straight. A dramatic opening
to hook the audience at once was necessary if he were to
compete against the nationally syndicated TV professors. But
Dr. West's throat was so dry he pointed at the blackboard,
voiceless. He hoped to hook them with this visual teaser:

Date	Human Progress	Estimated Population of World in Millions
25,000 B.C.	Hunting and seed gathering	5
8000 B.C.	Deliberate farming, villages	7
1 A.D.	Roman and many Asian cities	250
1650	Scientific start	500
1960	Birth control pills tested	3000 (3 billion)
1980	World census	5000 (5 billion)
1990	This year	7000 (7 billion)

"Back in the 1960s," Dr. West's voice creaked, "population
experts predicted a world population of about seven billion
by the year 2000. They assumed correctly that there would
be increasingly widespread use of The Pill. They predicted
three-month antiovulation injections such as medroxy pro-
gesterone. But they underestimated nationalistic pressures to
maintain high birthrates. Right now in 1990 we've had to
update our prediction for the year 2000 to nine billion." He

took a breath. "There'll still be room for the tourists who reserve earliest for Yosemite and Yellowstone."

Hastily he chalked on the other blackboard: WHAT IS THE MAXIMUM POPULATION THE EARTH CAN SUPPORT?

"This is an unfair question," Dr. West said, "because I didn't ask WHEN, what year. Given about sixty peaceful years of cooperation, it is estimated that mankind could organize this planet to support a maximum population of twenty billion by the year 2050. This future twenty billion would have about as much food available per person as with our seven billion today."

Dr. West inadvertently let his gaze fall to a co-ed's knees, and he stared at his notes. "In only ten years, that is, by the year 2000, there will be nine billion of us. Medical progress reducing infant mortality in Asia, Africa and South America has continued to outrace birth control programs. Population contests between military-industrial nations are escalating. World population has continued doubling every twenty-five years. But assuming nine billion in the year 2000, we may not have eighteen billion in 2025, and we won't reach thirty-six billion in 2050 if there's only food for twenty billion then. It appears that famine, disease and war may control more population than The Pill."

"The maximum population the world can support at any given time is balanced on a precarious pile of interlocking—factors." He was afraid he was getting too abstract and losing his audience.

"Think of a three-legged race. I mean, at a picnic where you and your boyfriend's legs are tied together and you try to run. Your name is Potential Breeding Power, and you are a fast runner. His name is Food Production. He's a plodder, but you're tied together. If Breeding Power runs too fast, Food Production can't keep up, and both of you begin to stagger."

A girl giggled, and Dr. West's voice improvised: "Suppose there were a sudden increase in population———." He didn't know where his sentence was going and realized subconsciously he'd been thinking of the Esks. "Such an increase that our food distribution system begins to—to stagger—with lowering standards of living even in America and Europe, causing political unrest, decreasing production, revolution, chaos, a breakdown of our delicately balanced technology?" He let the question hang, and started telling what was happening in South America.

When he noticed the stocky student standing, swinging his watch back and forth by its wescot chain, he realized his hour was over. "Next meeting, old Thomas Malthus, his Theory still haunts us."

Students stood up, but Dr. West compulsively raised his voice, talking faster. "I hope you'll all be here next meeting. Young Thomas Malthus from his eighteenth-century essay became the most influential population—uh, philosopher. *The power of population,* Tom Malthus said, *is greater than the power in the earth to produce subsistence for man.* Do you believe that———?"

But the students were hurrying out; not one left a dollar.

Dr. West stood openmouthed.

"Good beginning," the stocky student said. "Bet you win at least half of them. Bet you draw at least a hundred dollars into the boxes next meeting when formal enrollment begins."

"Oh!" Dr. West laughed. He was in a cold sweat.

"We grade you at the end of each month," the student leader said. "You'd better improve your enunciation by then. And I think you'd be rated D or F in *Looks at His Audience.* Maybe a C in *Organizes His Material in a Comprehensible Manner.* But you certainly rated at least a B today in *Sincerity,* and that's most important with some of us."

Dripping wet, Dr. West still had two more lectures to deliver that day.

When he trudged home, he grinned weakly at Marthalik, and maneuvered among his clinging children and collapsed on the couch. This went on for several weeks, while Marthalik's loud dreams kept him awake at night. In the daytime, she had become strangely withdrawn, not even cheering up when Steve Jervasoni visited.

"I hear you're drawing bigger audiences than Dr. Darwin," Steve said, and lowered his voice when Marthalik went into the kitchen. "Seriously, why don't you let me take

Marthalik to a doctor with a psychiatry background—since you just keep putting off———."

"You'd put her under sedation?" Dr. West whispered from his blurry weariness, for he had been trying to rewrite his article for the *New Saturday Evening Post* at night after grading papers while trying to make sense from Marthalik's nonverbal nightmares. "And interrogate her—the origin of the Esks, is that the real reason you———."

"No, you're overtired. I just want to help Marthalik," Steve protested, his face pained.

"I already tried pentothal with her—and LSD," Dr. West whispered. "Neither exposed what she's seeing—in her dreams."

"I don't care about that," Steve retorted. "It's Marthalik I care about."

"You think I don't care about her?" Dr. West stood up waiting for Steve to leave.

One day when Dr. West wearily wandered back from class to the apartment, there was a strange middle-aged baby-sitter with the kids.

"Where's my wife?"

"Was she *your* wife?" The baby-sitter looked embarrassed.

Dr. West saw the strange envelope on his desk, read the note and told the baby-sitter to get out. Then he telephoned the police. "Is there a Missing Persons Bureau?"

Marthalik had vanished from Berkeley. So had Steve. The police couldn't find them anywhere in California.

Marthalik, are you all right? I deserve—suffering. But Marthalik, please———, he thought each night.

"Find my wife." But he did not show the police the note.

His life seemed shattered like an Arctic ice floe. Every day at Free U. he had to lecture to keep the money coming in to pay two shifts of baby-sitters and a housekeeper. At night he played with his children. "When Mama come home?"

"She's gone on a long vacation, Little Joe." Dr. West couldn't believe that the police were unable to find Marthalik or Steve in the United States. "Steve wouldn't take her back to the Arctic———."

"He didn't even leave you a note?" Dr. Darwin stirred his coffee.

"No," Dr. West lied with shame. "The police located Steve's folks in Detroit. They said they hadn't seen much of him since high school. Then he went to a junior college, and then into the service, four years in the Bacterial Warfare Section, came out as staff sergeant, and studied bacteriology at L.A. State." Dr. West stared out across Berkeley at the fog shrouding San Francisco Bay. "He wasn't outstandingly bright for a grad student, no scholarship grant-in-aid, but Steve was my most dependable team member. He was the only one who remained—loyal to me—after I was—canned as Director."

"So where did his money come from?" Dr. Darwin asked, smiling cynically. "Did he have an outside job?"

"No. Any spare time, he used as Treasurer and then President of the Graduate Students' Forum."

"A grad student can't live without money on top of his G.I. Bill checks."

"Don't tell me you're one of those paranoid professors," Dr. West began, "who still suspects every student is a——."

"Conveniently planted inside your Oriental Population Problems Research program," Dr. Darwin interrupted triumphantly. "There he was. Every day he could report."

"Our Government didn't need reports from Steve. Behind my back, Fred Gatson and three or four more of my so-called colleagues continuously were bitching about me to the Pentagon. Steve at least stuck with me. Until he stole my wife——."

"Was that in character?" Dr. Darwin laughed dryly. "Was Steve the passionate type?"

"How can we know—even ourselves?" Dr. West's face twisted in pain. "I hope he is in love with her. I hope he's looking after her."

"In this neatly numbered population," Dr. Darwin persisted, spreading his arms, "where computers should be able to trace any man, cooperation from within Government is necessary if a man wants to disappear."

"Bullshit! We're not animated IBM cards yet. A man and a woman still can disappear together." Dr. West's voice rose.

"At least I believe he loves her and is looking after her. You, you're practically implying Steve Jervasoni is a Government employee such as CIA, who stole my wife following orders as cold-bloodedly as if she were a dog for vivisection. God! I hope he does love her."

Each day, each night, Dr. West listened for the phone. In another shattered part of his life he worried about the care of his children. Now that old Peterluk had been located in Yellowknife, Dr. West was worried that he himself might be extradited to Canada as a witness against Peterluk. No charges had been filed against Dr. West for violating the Sanctuary or perhaps kidnapping Marthalik. Evidently someone in Canadian politics preferred to give Dr. West no publicity.

Peterluk was tried for shooting the priest-pilot of the Order of Pope John solely on the dramatic testimony of the younger LaRue. This Hero of the North was running for Parliament, where his uncle was demanding abolition of the Eskimo Cultural Sanctuary. In newspaper accounts Dr. West wasn't even mentioned. When Peterluk was convicted of murder and given an indeterminate sentence at the New Ottawa Reformation Center, Dr. West breathed more easily. He needed to stay here in Berkeley to help his motherless children grow up.

What do you do with six children growing so fast their clothes have to be let out or exchanged every month? At one year they looked like six-year-olds, but talked like three-year-olds. Physically they looked old enough to be starting school.

Although Dr. West hired a retired schoolteacher as a reading readiness tutor, he knew eventually he'd be contacted by an Attendance Administrator from the Public School System. Already a woman from the Child Welfare Bureau had visited. "We're concerned about these children—without their mothers. Where are their mothers?"

When Dr. West maintained that he was the legal father of all six children, the woman's thick eyebrows rose as if she thought he was a bigamist, and rose higher when he insisted Marthalik had been the mother of all six.

"Didn't you see the *Life* article?" he asked.

Physically all six children now appeared to be between three and six years of age.

"None are twins," she muttered, lowering her eyebrows in a thoughtful squint. "The older children should be enrolled in school. Where are their birth certificates?"

The Public School System pounced. "In spite of the apparent validity of their birth certificates, physiological readiness for school increasingly has been recognized as the most important criterion for admission. The larger three children obviously should be given placement tests."

The tests showed Little Joe, Little Martha and Eva had the approximate mental ages of three-year-olds. "Because they are physically ready but not mentally ready, they must be placed in the Special Class."

"You mean for retarded children?" Dr. West protested. "They're not retarded. They're advanced for their ages. Show me another eighteen-month-old child who knows his addition combinations. Little Joe does."

"But surely he's really at least five years old. The operative from the Child Welfare Bureau informs us the birth certificates and *Life* article may have been a publicity stunt. A Guidance Administrator will investigate your noncooperation. Surely, your children need to associate with other children."

"They do. After their lessons. In the park." Dr. West spent hours playing catch with them.

Soon Little Joe was as large as a nine-year-old boy. When he tried to play baseball with other boys his size, he couldn't hit the ball.

"You will. You will," Dr. West kept reassuring him. "You just haven't had as much practice as they have."

By the time Little Joe's coordination was as good as a nine-year-old's, he looked like a twelve-year-old. Finally placed in an ungraded classroom in the regular neighborhood school, Little Joe seemed embarrassed surrounded by "little kids." But his reading level was only third grade. He was two years old. By the time he was two and a half, he was reading and doing arithmetic at a sixth-grade level, but he was as large as a fifteen-year-old who should be in junior high.

"Joe, please believe me. You'll catch up, Joe." Dr. West had dropped the "Little" from his son's name.

The boy stood a massive five feet three inches tall, appearing muscular like a giant among grade school children. But he was no bully. Even when he was unhappy, Joe smiled.

Dr. West couldn't smile. Within six months, Joe would be three. At the calendar age of one he had looked like a six-year-old, at two like a twelve-year-old. Physically he had matured six times as fast as a hu—as other children, Dr. West thought. In six months, when he was three, Joe might be looking at girls as if he were an eighteen-year-old. "Nothing but trouble! But he's such a good kid." Dr. West thought all Joe needed was time for his mental age to catch up with his physical growth. Joe had been promoted three grades in the last year, but he had grown six years physically.

At what might be physically eighteen, Joe needed scissors rather than the electric razor he bashfully asked for, but his voice had deepened and he was a powerfully built young man five feet nine inches tall. Smiling, he appeared like a football prospect in junior high but he didn't block. When he was knocked down, he stood up smiling while smaller boys tittered. But suddenly Joe became "a star" in basketball and then baseball, and he was very popular in junior high school. He laughed and joked with budding girls.

It was Little Martha who was overtaken by trouble. Dr. West's housekeeper had purchased her a bra the month before, and now she was in junior high school and giggling a great deal. Whenever Dr. West looked at her he was reminded of his wife. He felt like crying. How old had Marthalik been when he married her?

Already high school age boys shouted at Martha. She wasn't a "Little" Martha anymore. A brash high school boy telephoned her at home, asking her for a date. Smiling with pride and hope, she asked Dr. West. He said no. Her smile faded while he tried to explain why she was too young to go out on her first date, why she wasn't like other girls.

"Daddy, I can't believe I'm only three years old."

What problems we create, Dr. West thought in anguish, bringing children into the world. Alone he thought: *No, my bringing my children to Berkeley was what caused the problems. On the Boothia Peninsula, they would have grown up at the same rate as other children there and entered smoothly into a simpler life as Eskimos.*

But his children couldn't go back and squat in frigid tents gnawing at seal bones. "They don't even speak Eskimo. They're—Americans."

Marthalik and Steve seemed to have vanished from the face of the Earth. Dr. West had finally shown the police Marthalik's note, the Missing Persons Bureau had what seemed a good way of tracing her, but found no record of her. If Steve had taken her back to the Boothia Peninsula, Dr. West was sure he would have heard about it. Dozens of eager-beaver ethnologists, gynecologists, social workers and professional journalists had entered the former Sanctuary. Dr. West's own first-person article had been purchased and rewritten by *The New Saturday Evening Post*. He used all that money to pay bills. Before he could expand it to a book, a professional journalist who "parachuted on the spot" had published a book complete with ferocious attacks by hordes of spear-hurling Esks and other nonsense. Dr. West's own manuscript dragged on, not completed.

In the three winters since Dr. West had carried Marthalik away from the Boothia Peninsula, the Canadian Government had forestalled starvation with larger and larger food deliveries.

"So their Public Health nurses still are having difficulty teaching family planning. That's Canada's problem," Dr. West told Dr. Darwin. "I've enough problems here. My kids——. Joe wants a car. Already he's talking about a college education."

Dr. West was grossing $20,000 a year from his lectures. After paying his share of rent, lights, janitorial services in the former furniture warehouse, and miscellaneous expenses, such as printing of course outlines and tests, he netted $16,-000. This was about a plumber's take-home pay in the continuous price-wage inflation. It was about what he would be making if he started at the bottom again as an Assistant Prof at the University of California.

"You keep talking about the satisfaction of teaching undergrads," he accused Dr. Darwin. "But at Free U. we lecture to such large classes we have so little time for face-to-face two-way communication with individuals.

Teaching was more satisfying for me, I was doing more real teaching, when I was a research professor at Cal working closely with only a dozen grad students. That was real teaching, the ideal method of education for both professor and student." He was restless. He felt the world had passed him by. He dreamed of Marthalik.

Dr. West's biggest problem was Little Martha, who was not little. His housekeeper snidely reported Martha was pregnant. Evidently someone reported this to the Child Welfare Bureau, because a woman with bushy eyebrows appeared with a sternly satisfied expression and a photostat of Little Martha's birth certificate. "This proves you're not a fit father, Dr. West. Your daughter is only three years old, and she's pregnant! You failed to give these little three-year-old children the parental protection they deserve. You're not a fit parent."

At the hearing, Dr. West lost his temper and his six children. "I tried! You think you can do better?" he shouted up at the judge. "Little Martha will have another baby in a month. What will you do? Put the baby out for adoption?"

"Please sit down," the judge asked gently.

"In a few years," Dr. West shouted, "how will you feed their thousand grandchildren?"

"Dr. West, I should hold you in contempt of court. If you cause further disturbance in this courtroom, I will order you held for a psychiatric examination."

Alone in his terribly empty apartment, Dr. West smashed the mirror. He kicked the bed until it collapsed. Sitting on the floor, he thought of Hans Suxbey, founder and Director of the Eskimo Cultural Sanctuary. During Suxbey's last appeal before the Parliamentary Investigating Committee, when it became evident they would recommend against any future appropriation for the Sanctuary and that they would recommend abolishing the Eskimo Cultural Sanctuary, Hans Suxbey had lifted a revolver from his coat pocket. While old LaRue sat like a grinning dinosaur, unafraid, and other Members of Parliament tipped over backward in their chairs in their haste to leave the room, Hans Suxbey had blown out his own brains.

Dr. West went to his bureau drawer. Opening it he took out Marthalik's note, smudged and crumpled from reading and rereading. *My husband,* she had dictated in Steve's handwriting, *this person loves you. This person has gone away with Steve. It is hoped the operation will help this person have more babies.*

"That's all you wanted, Marthalik, to bring more babies into the world." Dr. West walked toward the kitchen. "More children to be penalized because they are different from humans. More and more children. Until there are too many Esks for us whitemen to feed, then the anger of the whitemen will rise against the Esks."

He opened the refrigerator. "We humans are descended from savage animals. You Esks are meek, multiplying toward misery. So who will inherit the Earth?"

Yesterday the expedition to Boothia from the State University at Palo Alto had published their preliminary report. They had counted 4000 Esks. Statistical analysis of the birth rate, which was in excess of 10,000 per thousand women per year, the maturation rate to breeding age, three years; and death rate, a few statistically insignificant accidental deaths; and present age distribution, approximately 70% of the population were children two calendar years of age or less, had caused the eager geniuses from Palo Alto to estimate that the Esk population was doubling every year.

"Multiplying into misery, Marthalik," Dr. West picked up a crayola left by one of his children on the kitchen linoleum, and he savagely scrawled on the ivory-toned wall:

1	—	this year —	4000 Esks
2	—	next year —	8000
3	—		16,000
4	—		32,000
5	—		64,000
6	—		128,000
7	—		256,000
8	—		512,000
9	—		1,024,000
10	—		2,048,000

"That's not many Esks ten years from now, only two million or so Esks in a world population with nine billion humans," he laughed savagely. "But the Canadian economy would rupture itself trying to feed that many Esks. Canada will try to get rid of them and not by means of mass sterilization or genocide. Canadians are too civilized. They'll try to export their problem. The world can absorb two million Esks so easily."

Defacing the ivory-tinted wall of the kitchen he scrawled:

11	years from now	4,096,000
12		8,192,000
13		16,384,000
14		32,768,000
15		65,536,000
16		131,072,000
17		262,144,000
18		524,288,000
19		1,048,576,000
20		2,097,152,000

"Only two billion, give or take ninety million, twenty years from now. That's controllable, that's feedable, only two billion Esks against a human population of twelve billion. Surely forced birth control, machine guns and starvation can administer Esk family planning, maintaining the Esk population at a useful two billion cheap laborers throughout the world. But let us hope human politicians are sufficiently intelligent because the doubling process involves a subjective deception. As long as the total numbers are much smaller than you are, you can laugh it off. They seem small."

On the wall above the sink he scrawled with his black crayola:

21	years from now	4 billion
22		8 billion
23		16 billion

"My god, what happened?" he laughed to his imaginary audience. "All of a sudden they outnumber us and there wouldn't be nearly enough food for humans plus Esks, or even for Esks plus humans. But we will have slaughtered the Esks by then."

He thought of Little Joe, not so little, waving goodbye as the Child Welfare lady urged him into the electric bus, and Little Martha peering wistfully out the bus window. Dr. West's throat hurt as if he were going to cry.

"My god, with what birth control methods will they torment all the millions of Esks of the future? What of all the Esks who have intermarried with the human population because Esks are lovable people. Whom do we sterilize, whom do we push into the ovens of Auschwitz?"

"My children are mine as well as Marthalik's." He had read in that morning's paper how the food barges were on their way north. "No one will starve. No one will suffer— yet."

Summer was melting the Arctic ice, and in the Canadian Parliament the newly elected M.P., LaRue the Younger, had won his debate. Before winter, the Canadian Government would resettle the overcrowded Esks throughout the North. "They'll open our Frozen Frontier," LaRue had orated, "and Canada needs more willing and cheerful laborers in the cities. Land of the Future, Canada must grow!"

"And scatter the Esks throughout the Canadian population," Dr. West muttered, "so that even the safest birth limitation bacteria could not be used—again. Marthalik? Dammit, where are you? Your children are being doomed to misery, starvation and death!"

He kicked the refrigerator. Sweating, he opened its gleaming door.

From the refrigerator he took the polyethelene-wrapped glass tube and stared at the gray culture medium within. With trembling hands he found empty fruit jars in the base cabinet. In a big sauce pan he warmed gelatin for a culture medium. His heart hammering, he opened the glass tube.

For hours he helped bacterial life awaken and multiply in spreading plaques of life upon the gelatin within the fruit jars. "My god, look at those little bastards multiplying whether they want to or not. Their population must be doubling every hour."

Now he needed an ingeniously simple means of transporting and disseminating the bacteria in the North.

5.
THE
SPRAY
CANS
OF
DEATH

WINGING ABOVE THE OPENED HARBOR ICE, THE IMMENSE FLOCK
of male sandpipers crowded down on the thawing tundra.
With menacing squeaks and dueling beaks, the fragile sandpipers hopped at each other. Flurrying wings they battled for
nesting territories close to the tiny pond.

Too many sandpipers? Dr. Joe West rested beside his
heavy pack and tried to force his thoughts ahead to the
Arctic bay, where the ragged tents were crowding. A squeaking sandpiper fled past his boot. Dr. West's imagination
recoiled from the distant bay, which had become a harbor.
He stared into the tiny pond, where wriggling swarms of
mosquito larva already were pupating.

Already there was a bloody whine behind Dr. West's ear.
He slapped the back of his neck. "Dammit, I don't want to
end up like a criminal—even though I will be——."

Through the mosquitos, he focused his binoculars against
the bleak natural harbor. "I don't want to be a martyr."

The distant growling of the tractor-truck trundling food
cases out of the beached LST was punctuated by a gunshot.
Probably some bearded amateur humanitarian shooting at a
seagull! Dr. West glared through his binoculars at the flam-
boyant amateur lettering across the hull of the chartered
landing ship. BOOTHIA PENINSULA OR BUST—NEW YORK SAVE
THE ESKIMOS DAY COMMITTEE.

"No matter how many you feed there'll be more." Dr.
West shook his head in a haze of mosquitos and refocused his
binoculars at the tent city rimming the harbor like dirty
snow. With its explosive rate of growth those canvas tents
would spread all the way inland to this pond before——!

Dr. West blinked. His nervous system tingled from surfacing childhood guilt as he recognized through the binoculars, magnified and standing in compressed perspective beside a distant plywood cabin, the uniformed man, Mountie—Police Inspector—Canadian policeman—cop, cop, cop!

On the surface, Dr. West knew the problem was how to distribute the aerosol spray cans to the Esks without being traced. The depths of his problem were more disturbing.

He had landed his float plane on newly named LaRue Lake, the long pond located an hour's hike inland up the river through the boggy tundra. No secrecy here. Two seaplanes and an amphibian already were tied up like spiders as if their pilots expected wind. For their fragile aircraft, the lake was safer than the exposed bay. A grinning Esk had peered out of a single tent, probably a guard for the planes. Many muddy boot prints converged on deeper tracks, a trail left by all the airborne whitemen who had hurried down the little river valley to the bay to inspect the multiplying Esks.

Through his binoculars, Dr. West studied the cop—the Mountie walking away from the plywood cabin and its tall radio mast. Striding past stacked supply crates, the Mountie moved down the beach toward the bearded characters lolling in front of the LST.

Like a beached whale, the landing ship vomited the tractor-truck with another load of food cases. Up beside the tents of the Esks, no one seemed to be guarding the supplies. Perhaps during the past winter the R.C.M.P. had discovered that the Esks were even more obedient, less tempted to thievery than Eskimos. Dr. West frowned.

Hordes of Esk children were romping around the boxes. Dr. West could not see any guards. He put away his binoculars.

Glancing at the vast Arctic sky, he hoisted his pack, heavy with the disguised containers of aerosol spray. He plodded straight into the village. Concealment was impossible anyway.

While the children scampered around him, Dr. West walked stiffly to meet the Mountie, who was striding up from the beach in a swarm of mosquitos.

"Sir—I recognize—you are Dr. Joseph West." The Mountie managed to seem glad to see him. "As you predicted, sir, we've a—rapidly growing community." The Mountie had a warm handshake. "It is—it is an honor, sir, to meet you. Sir, I've always considered you as the—the discoverer of these—people. A pleasure to meet you. Why don't we continue on to my cabin. Your flight, walking from the lake, you must be tired and hungry, sir." He reached to relieve Dr. West of the weight of his pack.

"Thank you," Dr. West muttered with embarrassment, allowing the Mountie to take the surprisingly heavy pack.

For the moment, the Mountie was too courteous to ask if he had a landing permit. No doubt the politician, LaRue, had warned the R.C.M.P. to be on the lookout for Dr. West.

Inside the cabin, mosquitos hummed across plywood walls lined with books, stereo components and photosatellite maps of the Boothia Peninsula. Evidently the Mountie expected a permanent assignment here.

"Here's my landing permit." Dr. West handed it over with a belligerent smile. "Surprised?"

"No, sir. Headquarters radioed me to be expecting your aircraft." The Mountie acted like a stolid type who would not expose his surprise even if a little green man from Uranus four-lettered on his R.C.M.P. hat.

During tea and mosquitos, Dr. West opened his heavy pack. He lifted out a tape recorder, and a strobe light with the largest size battery pack, and a bulky battery-operated 16mm movie camera. Due to efficient forethought, all this equipment used the same size cylindrical interchangeable batteries. None of the equipment would work, because each battery enclosed and concealed an aerosol spray can.

Dr. West glanced from the tape recorder to the Mountie's mildly interested expression. "I'm looking for Eevvaalik, that old woman whose husband was jailed," Dr. West announced, and the Mountie's eyelids flickered.

A year ago, Cultural Sanctuary Guards would have kept Dr. West out, but their replacements, the R.C.M.P., evidently approved letting him in for some reason.

During the winter, the Canadian Parliament had listened with increasingly affirmative nods to impassioned attacks by members of LaRue's party against the whole Cultural Sanctuary concept. No one hesitated to speak ill of the dead Director, Hans Suxbey. As Hans Suxbey had anticipated in the Committee Room when he shot himself, Parliament overwhelmingly refused to pass their annual appropriation for the Eskimo Cultural Sanctuary. "Starvation camp——. Concentration camp——. Free our starving Eskimos——. Eliminate the Sanctuary."

When carry-over funds were exhausted, the Sanctuary Guards had been withdrawn, and replaced by Mounties and smiling politicians, *Life* photographers and amazed gynecologists. Disturbed Family Allowance administrators had landed on LaRue Lake and plodded across the tundra to gawk at the multiplying Esks.

The Canadian Government's Family Planning nurses already reported that the Esks showed discouragingly negative attitudes toward customary birth control techniques.

When the rumor reached Ottawa that Family Planning nurses were injecting Esk women with a six-months ovulation delay hormone and assuring the women it was a flu shot, there was more outraged oratory from old Etienne LaRue in Parliament. "This, it is not only murder of unborn spirits. It is government deception." The nurses were withdrawn.

But Dr. West suspected the bureaucrats still were holding their fingers up to test the winds of change.

In Canada, from one side blew the dinosaur's breath of old Etienne LaRue, opposing any population limitation for the Esks or anyone else. Whether the Esks might vote for his party was unimportant, he said, smiling because the birth control shots proved ineffective.

On the other side were increasingly disquieted administrators and politicians responsible for providing the food, clothing and well-being of the rapidly increasing Esks. Unless something sensible were done, Canadian income taxes would have to increase.

"You're quite lucky, sir," the Mountie was saying, "to locate old Eevvaalik. She was brought to this camp two weeks ago. Our doctor tells me she is quite ill, TB."

The thought flashed through Dr. West's mind, when he fled again from the Boothia Peninsula, he should take Eevvaalik back to civilization with him. Kidnapping? Three years ago, when Dr. West had taken Marthalik and the bound and growling Peterluk, Eevvaalik had refused to go. Now would she harshly scream and fight and cough? This might be his last chance. In California, he could get professional help in interrogating her. Depth hypnosis aided by pentothal injections might expose what Eevvaalik claimed she could not bear to remember. Unreasonably sometimes she claimed all the Esks were her children. But what had created the first Esk? Locked in her greasy head——.

"This way, sir." As the Mountie led him through the aimless crowds of smiling Esks toward old Eevvaalik's tent, Dr. West's heart leaped.

For a moment he'd thought he glimpsed Marthalik. Then he saw this was another Esk girl who looked like his wife. He felt like crying.

"In this tent," the Mountie was saying. "Eevvaalik?"

The tent was Canadian Army surplus and looked it. Eevvaalik crouched in the dim corner beside her strange ceramic seal oil lamp, empty. Dr. West unslung his heavy pack.

"Eh-eh," she laughed, immediately recognizing him. "It is The-Whiteman-Who-Was-Bitten-by-a-Dog." Coughing, she gasped: "Tell this person of her husband——."

"Peterluk has much to eat. He has a warm place to sleep," Dr. West answered. "The Government would not let me go in to see him in the beautiful white tower."

"A warm place?" Eevvaalik said hopefully. "This person wishes to be there also."

At this, the Mountie left the tent.

Dr. West smiled at Eevvaalik as he knelt beside her and felt her pulse. In a way he was sorry that her weakness had drained away her crusty independence. Probably she was the only real Eskimo in the camp. Mosquitos whined.

"You would like it in Ottawa," he said, meaning California, beginning to think she would go with him to the plane with no trouble at all.

"Eh-eh," she laughed. "What is this warm place called?"

"The New Ottawa Reformation Center. They say each

person has his own igloo in the tower." Dr. West laid his hand on her brow, wishing he had brought a thermometer.

"Peterluk needs a woman," Eevvaalik laughed. "This person will be stronger soon." She slapped her bony chest. "This person can still do it with Peterluk the way he likes." She managed a feeble leer at Dr. West. "So you take this person to her husband."

"Soon-soon," Dr. West sighed, regretting he had not even brought a sleeping injection from his medical bag now seeming so far away in the plane on LaRue Lake. "Sleep."

Ignoring the mosquitos wheezing in the tent, leather-skinned old Eevvaalik slept.

This tent seemed the only place where Dr. West could escape the thousands of eyes. Swiftly, he opened the back of the tape recorder, took out the batteries. Prying off the top of a cylindrical battery he removed a small orange aerosol can labeled MOSQUITO SPRAY.

With his heavy-bladed hunting knife he dug hard-packed filth-clotted gravel from the floor of the tent. He refilled the battery with gravel. Jamming on the top, he fitted the battery back into the tape recorder. By the time he had operated on all the batteries in the tape recorder, in the battery pack for the strobe light, and in the battery-powered camera, he had sixteen aerosol cans labeled MOSQUITO SPRAY.

He was sweating with haste and fright as he removed the rigidity boards from the square pack, dovetailed the boards together, and opened the little package of box nails. He hammered the box together using the butt of his hunting knife. The outside of the box was stamped: MOSQUITO SPRAY—NEW YORK SAVE THE ESKIMOS DAY COMMITTEE—334, a nonexistent but likely looking invoice number.

If he had planned all of this sooner, if he had made the terrible decision earlier, Dr. West thought, he might have planted this box in the freight car to Churchill on Hudson Bay or in the LST when it was being loaded. He might have avoided this risk. But here he was.

Ahead of the Government's plan to resettle the Esks, he might have been able to place these terrible cans in the next food shipment, and never return here to the Boothia Peninsula. But here he was. "What makes me do these things?"

It was as dim outside as it would ever be. The crazy orange sun was looping down to the horizon and would rise without setting.

Dr. West withdrew his head back into the tent. With his expensively worthless photographic equipment strewn on the gravel floor, he fitted the wooden box containing the aerosol cans into his pack. Their spray would not kill mosquitos.

As he tried to walk outside past hordes of playing children, they followed him. Like Eskimo children they didn't keep regular sleeping hours. Here it was midnight. They ran ahead of him toward a stack of unopened wooden crates stamped: DEHYDRATED FREEZE-DRIED 218.

Children swarmed ahead of him onto the crates, giggling. Little girls hummed and flapped their skinny arms.

My God, I can't really do it, Dr. West thought. *Let the Government do it. They've got to, eventually.* But most Canadian economists insisted their country was underpopulated. He thought of China, India still increasing. And South America!

More disillusioning, in the U.S. during the 1970s when use of The Pill was most widespread the birthrate had tumbled down. Belatedly the Pentagon became frantic because the future supply of scientists and soldiers was diminishing in comparison with unfriendly countries whose birthrates remained high.

U.S. economists became disturbed because industrial production had been geared to a population growth rate of about 3% per year and this slump to a 1% population increase per year was leading into an endless recession. Even the increased antiballistic missile spending and overseas military exercises no longer were obscuring the gap between immense production and lagging consumption. As unemployment increased, the work week was shortened. As U.S. population growth slowed, there was less active demand for cars and houses because there were fewer young consumers because of The Pill. Formerly, half the population had been under twenty-five years of age. Now the proportion of young people was declining. Future consumers were lagging, failing to emerge because of The Pill. The stock market continued to decline. Corporations geared for continuous growth were frantically demanding more Government help, more pump priming. As one of the least inhibited telecommentators put it: "The opinion media must lead the massive educational program for mother priming."

Four children became the minimum family size shown in television advertisements.

Finally awakening, the Federal Government improved Income Tax deductions to $1000 for the first child, another $1500 for the second, and $2000 for each additional child, plus the $1200 for husband and wife, so that a man with five children on an income of under $10,000 was free from income tax. New excise taxes increased the costs of birth control pills. Newspaper publicity was given to patriotically large families. The population growth rate began returning toward 3% aided by the Federal Family Allowance Bonuses which rewarded the parents with the financial equivalent of a new car each time they produced a new baby.

Thus, in spite of the vast array of birth control methods available in this richest country in the world, the patriotic U.S. population should double during the next twenty-five years to a happily predicted 500 million while the stock market skyrockets.

This rate of increase was tortoise-slow compared with the Esks.

"What got for us?" The roundly innocent face of an Esk boy peeked over the supply crates close to Dr. West, and the suddenly grinning boy opened his little hands; he was a clown.

"Nothing. Everything." Dr. West answered.

Laughing, all the children began jabbering at once. Their Modern Eskimo dialect sounded clumsier somehow than Dr. West remembered of children he talked with three years ago, before he carried off Marthalik.

Now these children were the next generation. With other Esks as models for growing up, would each generation be more crudely hewn than the last?

Dr. West asked if any of them could read. He pointed to the marks on the boxes. None of the children grasped what he meant. They didn't know about—reading.

Dr. West doubted they would have the opportunity to

learn. They would be adults in three years. How long would they live? No one knew yet.

Except for old Eevvaalik, these Esk children saw only inexperienced Esks as their models for growing up. "Do you hunt walrus?" Dr. West asked. "Do you play at hunting walrus? Harpoon? Seal?"

"Wal-rus?" Already these two-year-old children, who looked like twelve-year-olds, didn't know what walrus were. Due to the outspreading population pressure around this harbor where the supplies were landed, these Esk children might not even see a seal. A little girl climbed onto Dr. West's lap. Smiling not so shyly, she reminded him of Little Martha, his first daughter. "Tell me of our Grandfather in the sky."

"Once there was a great white bear who looked down from the stars," Dr. West began, but since he last was on the Boothia Penninsula the myth must have been crystallized in a new order, because the children giggled and began telling him the story.

"That star. That star." They were pointing, but in the sun-faded Arctic summer night the star was invisible to Dr. West.

"That star flying to this place closer all the time," the boy explained patiently. "That is how we began. Grandfather Bear send part of himself ahead. He say be fruitful and multiply and prepare this place for me."

"What does fruitful mean?" Dr. West asked. "Multiply?"

"Don't know yet," the boy answered solemnly. "But— when we have covered the world, Grandfather Bear will come. And once again all of us will become one. It will feel so good."

The children giggled and laughed and clapped their hands, echoing: "Will feel so good."—"Will feel so good."

Like children everywhere, their attention was shifting, and they lost interest in Dr. West and ran away to play. Dr. West listened to their shrill voices in the distance while he removed the wooden box of aerosol spray cans from his pack and left it among the bigger wooden crates. He walked away, his heart beating faster instead of slower.

What are you doing? Dr. West's young-old face twisted as

if a spear was probing his heart. *I'm doing what has to be done now. The thing which can't be done once the Esks have spread through the Canadian population.*

But do you know what you are doing? Dr. West blindly hurried away, thinking of Marthalik's gently smiling face across the breakfast table in California. Anxious to please him, at first she had repeated that she was glad not to be bothered with a baby: "I dream about many babies. Something, Grandfather Bear from the sky? Silly dream." Like the waxing moon her restlessness increased each month, and she cried out in her sleep, but to him she laughed with embarrassment: "Eh-eh, it feels strange not to have a baby every month. Feels strange not to accomplish anything."

And now Marthalik was gone. *Steve and Marthalik. Marthalik and Steve.*

Do you know what you will be doing to these people psychologically? Why? Dr. West punished himself as he pushed into Eevvaalik's tent and shoved his photographic equipment back into his emptied pack. *Can I even predict their physical reactions to this pathogen?*

He winced at the thought of children playing with the orange cans.

Endospores of the bacteria were "sleeping" in these aerosol cans marked MOSQUITO SPRAY.

It was true that this was the self-attenuating strain; fading like the ripples from a stone dropped into a pond, as the bacterial infection spread outward through the population its virulency would weaken outward to nothing. It could not infect the world. From a single source, it could not even engulf a small country.

But Marthalik was the only Esk on whom the birth-limiting bacteria had been tested. Although he needed to act quickly because the Canadian Government was preparing to resettle the Esks throughout the North, from a scientific point of view he knew he had acted too quickly, insanely. One Esk was not a valid test sample.

"All members of a species will not react exactly the same to a new disease." In his mind, on a graph, a bell-shaped curve confronted him. The vertical margin of the graph counted people. The horizontal margin rated virulency. Individual reactions tend to group along a bell-shaped curve. On the left-hand "lip" of the bell curve are few people with surprisingly slight reactions to a disease. The great majority of people, indicated by the hump of the curve, have the typical illness. A few down the other side of the bell curve suffer violent reactions.

Dr. West's face tightened like a death mask. If the virulent side of the bell graph had a cutoff appearance, the researcher would be looking at an abstract line of corpses.

"God, forgive me!" Dr. West couldn't know *where* Marthalik's mild reaction would fit on a bell-shaped curve of the entire infected Esk population.

I tell you I had to act now before these people scattered. Dr. West wondered if he had spoken out loud. Eevvaalik was staring up at him wide-eyed.

"We will go now," Dr. West said quietly, and he knelt beside Eevvaalik and began to help her up.

"Eh-eh, this person stand by herself." Eevvaalik swayed while he supported her arm, and as she shuffled across the tent floor she was temporarily halted by a paroxysm of coughing, and then she continued on out into the garish Arctic day-night under her own power. "Eh-eh, big sky."

Her legs sagged, and Dr. West supported her while the mosquitos whined.

Dr. West knew he was going to need strong helpers to carry Eevvaalik all the way across the tundra to his plane. He hoped the Mountie was asleep. Quietly, Dr. West drafted four Esks. Unquestioningly they tried to obey him. Finally, two of the Esks understood—observed from him how to form a carrying chair of their interlocked hands for Eevvaalik. The other two Esks wandered along behind. Dr. West was beginning to think he would get away with Eevvaalik.

The Mountie blundered toward them, his hair still rumpled with sleep, his eyes blinking in the weak midnight sunglow. Dr. West realized that an Esk must have been instructed to watch constantly, and the Esk had run to awaken the Mountie.

"Sir, if she is so ill," the Mountie mumbled, "you'd best take her to my cabin." He added apologetically: "Our doctor isn't here. Gone to Walrus Point Encampment two sleeps ago. Put her in my cabin. I'll send a boy for the doctor's reserve kit, if you want to give her something."

Dr. West started to speak and couldn't. It was now or never.

The Mountie blinked at the pair of Esks. "You, you, walk slow. Carry old woman to big cabin."

"Eh? Not old," Eevvaalik protested faintly as they carried her away from Dr. West.

"Sir, you'll want some tea." The Mountie's hand closed on Dr. West's arm and steered him toward the cabin.

It was as if the Mountie knew how Marthalik had been removed to California and didn't intend to let Dr. West fly off with Eevvaalik as well.

Dr. West felt suddenly old. As he walked, he resisted the urge to glance toward the stack of crates. He wondered if the Esk spy had witnessed him hiding the box of spray cans. Would the Esk tell the Mountie of the little box the whiteman had left among the crates?

"You, you put her on the floor. Over there by stove," the Mountie was ordering the Esks as they entered his cabin. To Dr. West the Mountie smiled wanly. "I'm not afraid of a little TB."

"Eevvaalik's was an arrested case of TB," Dr. West said. "What was the doctor—how was the doctor treating her?"

"Don't know, sir. I thought antibiotics cured that sort of thing nowadays, but—are the germs, sir, getting ahead of us? I'd thought she was better."

"Have you seen TB among the Esks——?" It was a rhetorical question. Dr. West was nerving himself to walk defiantly out of the cabin and hike to his plane, to flee.

"None, sir. Esks all seem sound as Canadian dollars," the Mountie laughed wearily. "Healthier than the rest of us."

"And multiplying a hell of a lot faster," Dr. West blurted, realizing he was going to stay and see it out to the end no matter what happened.

"One chap had a crate fall on his foot today, sir. Bloody mess. He's not complaining of much pain, but Esks don't," the Mountie's sleepy voice rambled on. "Bloody mess. Sir, since the doctor may not be back for days, I was hoping you'd have a look at this injured Esk. Not now, sir. After you've slept."

Dr. West knew the Mountie didn't intend for him to leave. He was the mouse. Was the Mountie the cat? He sat down on the corner bunk.

Swirling with thirty-six hours of exhaustion, Dr. West slept among the whining mosquitos.

When Dr. West awoke, there was an intermittent hissing noise within the cabin. He opened his eyes, and watched the Mountie moving around in the cabin with one arm upraised, waving a little orange can. A masking odor of artificial pine trees drifted down upon Dr. West's face. Breathing quickly, Dr. West raised himself on one elbow.

The Mountie lowered the orange-colored aerosol spray can. "You've had a good sleep, sir. ——Canned bacon for breakfast, sir?"

Dr. West couldn't open his mouth to answer. His contracting stomach was about to crawl out of his mouth as he watched the Mountie using the mosquito spray.

"Any time I wake up," the Mountie's voice chatted on, "I call that meal my breakfast. I miss not having fried seal liver. This spray must be the slow-acting kind. Ah, see that mosquito! Still circling around like a skua. Skua's a fierce gull. Nearest thing we have to a vulture. Sir, do you want your eggs sunny-side up? Those bearded chaps from New York may think themselves better than uniformed men, but the girl, skinny little thing—she's the cook in their landing ship, made me a present of this dozen eggs. A uniform always appeals to the women, sir. Never fails. Made me a present of this strawberry jam. How many pieces of bacon will you be having, sir?" He sprayed near the frying pan.

The scent of artificial pine trees blending with the overpowering odor of frying bacon whirled and thickened. Dr. West blundered outside and threw up before an interested audience of young Esks. They were impressed by his dry heaves for a few moments. Then, giggling, a boy chased a girl through the crowd, spraying her face with another orange can. Dr. West imagined her engulfed in a fog of invisible bacterial spores.

When Dr. West blundered back into the bacon-reeking

cabin, the mosquitos were whining unabated. The spray seemed harmless to mosquitos.

Eevvaalik was awake. Squatting in the corner, she was devouring Dr. West's unfinished breakfast.

"Here, sir, a good cup of tea will swish out the stomach, I always say." The Mountie cheerfully waved his hand at a mosquito. "When you feel fit, I hope you'll take a look at the Esk with the crushed foot." The Mountie evidently intended to keep Dr. West as long as he could.

Dr. West knew the Mountie had been in communication with his superiors by radio. Were they belatedly reviewing the "kidnapping" of Marthalik? That might necessitate telephone calls to authorities in California. Reputedly the R.C.M.P. were sticklers as to legal procedure, careful as to the rights of a suspect.

This Mountie might suspect Dr. West was attempting to make off with Eevvaalik, but proving that to a judge would be difficult if Dr. West denied the intent. Dr. West stood up.

After inspecting the crushed foot of the grinning Esk, Dr. West told the Mountie he wanted to walk to his plane to get his medical bag. Instead, the Mountie sent an Esk to get the bag.

In that irritating moment, Dr. West hoped this damned, smug Mountie would be susceptible to the endospores from the aerosol can. In males the infection sometimes produced uncomfortable and embarrassing symptoms like prostatitus. In twenty-four hours he would know———.

In twenty-four hours the Mountie appeared crestfallen. Perhaps in his latest radio conversation, the R.C.M.P. had told him to forget his suspicions. No warrant would be issued. Dr. West felt like telling the Mountie to go to hell. He felt like walking off to his plane without looking back. He might get away with it.

"Sir, there's a woman having a bit of trouble giving birth," the Mountie muttered, blocking his path.

With so many Esks around all day, the Mountie produced one inescapable case after another for Dr. West, whose irritation exploded.

"Serves her right for having one every month!"

"I know you don't mean that, sir. She's a mother."

"Of course she's a supermother."

"Sir?"

"She'll produce so many children that your children won't have room to sit down."

"I'm a bachelor, sir."

"You're a human being. You'll be one of an inundated species."

"Sir, are you talking about birth control? We were warn——. Anyway it doesn't seem to do any good. The Family Planning nurses said the Esk women WANT to have more babies."

"And just what did the nurses do to prevent it?"

To this question the Mountie colored with embarrassment. "This and that, sir. Pills and all. When they found out what the pills were for, the Esk women threw the pills away."

"There are other female methods than pills."

"I'm a bachelor, sir. I—not instructed in the R.C.M.P."

"Like diaphragms?" Dr. West continued maliciously at this Victorian-uniformed Mountie. "Diaphragms," Dr. West repeated. "I suppose those wouldn't be practical if the women resisted. And intrauterine devices, little curly-cues of plastic or stainless steel. Even with cooperative women there is a 20% expulsion rate. Did the nurses try hormone injections on the Esk women? Technically, science is equipped to control births in any number of ways. Some hormone injections prevent ovulation for six months. Admit that they tried injections."

"Sir, now these Esk women won't even let the doctor hypo them for blood tests, or measles preventative shots, or——."

"You mean some fool told them what the birth control injections were for?"

"Sir, you can't inject people against their will." The Mountie's face was sweating. "You can't just seize people and inoculate them against having babies. Our whole Canadian democratic system——." The Mountie sat down red-faced.

"Let me take your temperature," said Dr. West.

"I'm all right, sir. I'm never ill."

The Mountie's temperature was 100.

"I'm all right, sir. Do you think an outsider has brought in the flu? Those bearded types in the LST, they do a lot of coughing. I've eaten several meals with them. I'm never ill, sir, but I'm concerned about our Eskimos." The Mountie peered out the door. "They used to be quite susceptible, sir. Back in 1972 we had severe influenza which started in Baffin Island. We tried to quarantine. We watched it spread on the map——."

"I'll go outside," Dr. West said.

The Mountie opened his mouth as if to protest. Whether from concern that Dr. West also might be a flu carrier or that Dr. West might make an unauthorized departure, the Mountie did not say.

Dr. West observed some of the children were sitting rather than racing around. When he dipped the thermometer in the alcohol tube, women squeaked with fright and edged away. Apparently the women were afraid he was preparing to inject them—with a new kind of no-baby needle. This was confirmed by the laughter of the men. Children were giggling.

After much instruction and demonstration to ensure they did not bite off the thermometer, Dr. West began taking children's temperatures. Most of this small group were running temperatures of 99.

The Mountie appeared behind him, breathing hard and keeping away from the Esks. Mosquitos clustered on his blotchy face. "Sir, do you think—I think I shall order an immediate quarantine of this village."

From a distance, the Mountie told certain men to carry his words through the village, guards should be appointed, and so forth.

While Esks might be more obedient than Eskimos, as the day dragged on Dr. West observed several groups departing. Their fellow Esk guards hurried after them, gestured, tried to explain. But Esks never use force, Dr. West thought. The Esks accepted life as cheerfully and noncombatively as if it were a dream soon to be ended. Soon guards and departees all were laughing. The guards waved good-bye. The departees trudged north along the coast toward one of the smaller camps. They had no sleds, no dogs. The Esks bred so much faster, that their dogs had become a rare minority with larger appetites than Esks. Most of the accessible seals had been killed, and the younger Esks wore only war-surplus khaki. When winter returned, Dr. West thought, there would be misery and death.

"At the least, this epidemic will slow the birthrate," Dr. West muttered in self-justification, "and give the Canadian Government time to formulate a policy, before the western hemisphere is overrun." He realized he was talking to himself again and closed his mouth. Western hemisphere overrun sounded—ridiculous.

At least this epidemic will demonstrate, for the first time on a large group, what planned bacterial population control can accomplish. "Quickly, cheaply, almost humanely——."

By the next day Dr. West's confidence was shaken. Some Esks showed symptoms of the disease, but mild symptoms on the bell-shaped curve. Marthalik's must have been a severe case.

Few Esks showed temperatures of as much as 99.6. Plainly Esks were more resistant than humans. Not only were they completely immune to TB, they were only mildly affected by this population control disease.

It was the Mountie who was sick. His temperature had risen to 102 degrees.

Dr. West discovered the bearded humanitarians in the LST were running temperatures of over 101 to 103. The two *Life* photographers were confined to their tent. The bleary-eyed Mountie radioed for airborne medical help.

Dr. West stared down at old Eevvaalik shivering in the blankets of what had been Dr. West's bed. Her temperature was approaching 103 degrees. He lost his nerve and began to cool her with damp rags. He forced aspirin between her dry lips. She whined at the bitter taste.

"Let this—person," she protested, "—find happiness. Do not—do things——. No. Eh-eh." She laughed or coughed. "You not sick—don't know."

He tried to force another aspirin.

"Pah!" she spat it back. "You don't know."

Unexpectedly, she said: "You don't even know—this person is the mother of everybody. Eh-eh."

"Yes, I know that." Dr. West knelt beside her, gently

agreeing with whatever she said. He glanced at the tape recorder but the batteries were filled with gravel. "I know you are the mother. Who is the father? What did he look like?"

"Terrible, this person feels terrible," Eevvaalik moaned. "This person, eh-eh, won't remember until you make her feel so good."

Even now, was she still teasing him, holding back her knowledge for some last advantage? Dr. West did not know.

Eevvaalik was prattling feverishly about her youth, when she was a young girl. "Eh-eh, in those days, few *Innuit* (Eskimos), many seals. This young person was so fat and beautiful. Now this old person is burning. Tired. Sleep. Want to sleep," she cried out in sudden pain. "Help me! Want to sleep."

By contrast, the Mountie kept getting out of bed. He staggered between the window and the radio closet, where his two-way radio equipment was housed. "Sir, until the medical aircraft reaches us, and it never will, what with fog and mechanical difficulties and false promises, sir, we've got to do something for these people."

"They're not as sick as you are."

"Sir, the old woman looks like she's dying."

"Not likely," Dr. West answered with more confidence than he felt. "She—and you are the two with the highest temperatures."

"I'm responsible for all these people, sir. I should have kept this disease from spreading. The operator at Seal Camp says fever has already reached there. Says some of my people arrived there yesterday. Why don't you do something; you're a doctor, or were a doctor." The Mountie staggered back to the radio closet without waiting for a reply.

Dr. West bent over the fitfully sleeping Eevvaalik. He had started both Eevvaalik and the Mountie on a course of terramycin capsules, to keep down any additional bacterial infections. Against the bacteria now spreading its secondary poison through the narrow tube structures of their bodies there was a specific antibiotic, and he did not have it. It would not have been available to him without a risky theft from the guarded laboratory in California. It was a classified military secret, as were the bacteria in the spray cans.

Dr. West smiled bitterly. For accepting Steve Jervasoni's stolen starter sample of this population control bacteria, for conspiring in the theft of a military secret, already he was liable to prosecution by the U.S. Government. If the spray cans and the bacteria were traced to him and he was taken back to the U.S.—he remembered what happened to men who stole other military secrets——.

"Now the radioman at Stone Bay says it's popped up there." The Mountie was clumsily charting the new locations of the illness on his wall map. "It's what we did during the flu epidemic," he muttered ineffectually. "The date of appearance and where the visitors came from. I keep telling them to cut off every camp from every other camp. So many Esks traveling, spreads and spreads."

The next day the promised medical plane still had not even taken off. Engine trouble was reported, and the Mountie blundered around the cabin, flopping down on the bed and sleeping fitfully.

By now, R.C.M.P. radio operators up and down the coast were comparing virulency of the disease in their respective encampments. The bacteria had spread south from one coastal camp to the next until mild cases were reported in the fifth camp. Only a few mild cases in the fifth camp——.

"Here, we had it worse, but now we're getting better." The Mountie stared out the doorway.

The Esk children were becoming more active. The disease was running its course.

At Dr. West's suggestion, the medical aircraft was diverted to another camp. The Mountie seemed to want the aircraft here first, but he agreed, temporarily.

The next day as his fever declined, the Mountie scribbled more detail into his chart—as if a map showing the spread of the disease magically could control the disease.

"I can't understand this," the Mountie said. "It seems to have stopped going south. In the fifth encampment, they say there are visitors from the fourth encampment but no one in the fifth encampment has it bad enough to matter. A few slight fevers. Do you think it's halted here?" He pressed his thick finger against the map.

"Yes." Dr. West didn't wince, but a clue was stalking him.

On each of the five encampments to the south, the map contained the Mountie's scrawled date for the reported arrival of visitors. "Everyone's done a terrible job of not keeping visitors out, sir. More inefficient than during the flu. So many more people now, but it's no excuse, sir."

In the village immediately south of them about 50% of the Esks reportedly had been sick. In the second village 20% to 25%, in the third village less than 20%, in the fourth village 10%, and in the fifth village there were only a few with a mild fever or other symptoms.

"As it went south, the disease died out," the Mountie murmured. "It's not like flu, is it, sir?"

"No, it isn't," Dr. West agreed.

At the map, staring at the opposite extension of the disease in a northerly direction, Dr. West began to have a trapped feeling. A clue as to the origin of the disease was beginning to take shape on the map.

"The two villages nearest north of us had it as bad as we did," the Mountie said, talking to himself. "Then it faded, weaker in each of the next five villages. So it took a total of seven villages to wear out the disease going north, but five going south."

He turned and stared at Dr. West.

"The two north camps where they had it as bad as we did," the Mountie said, "their radio operators both report they noticed orange cans, mosquito spray cans like we've been using here. Traveling Esks——."

Outside, there was the roar of the boat-shaped medical aircraft circling the harbor for a landing.

The Mountie's face widened with relief and he walked back into his radio closet and closed the door.

Dr. West knelt by Eevvaalik's sleeping form. As he lifted her wrist to feel her pulse he knew she was dead.

When the Mountie came out of the radio closet, he stared at her, then at Dr. West's drawn face.

"She's not the only one dead, sir. I didn't want to disturb you before the aircraft arrived, but about a dozen people are

reported dead to the east of us, and a spray can. Older
people. They were camped beside the empty Cultural Sanctuary Guard Station, the only old people."

"The last of the real Eskimos," Dr. West blurted, and felt
sick as if this Mountie and the whole world were closing in
on him.

"I think so, sir. I think the disease was strongest where the
spray cans were, sir. Here, there, and in the two camps to the
north where visitors carried mosquito spray cans. I've had
men on the lookout for cans in the other camps but no sign
of them. I know the disease is mildest in the camps furthest
away from the cans. You're a doctor. How do you explain
that, sir?"

"Probably a bacteria with self-attenuating virulency," Dr.
West answered with calm desperation.

"I've never heard of that, sir."

"There's a lot you haven't heard of!" Then Dr. West
managed to control his voice. "Think of bacteria as microscopic blobs like strings of grapes, typical bacteria each excret-
ing tissue-destroying poison as an incidental by-product. The
toxin is what makes the person feel sick. Virulent bacteria,
we say."

Dr. West stared out the open door to the harbor where the
big tilt-jet flying boat had landed; now the Mountie had
reinforcements. "Where was I? Bacteria multiply so rapidly,
a new generation every half hour, millions of bacteria within
a person," Dr. West laughed unexpectedly. "Every hour there
is the possibility of hundreds of bacterial mutations. Bacteria
with slight genetic alterations may be more virulent or less
so. Here is the surprising thing. A single mutated bacterium
may be—born, which is less virulent, excretes less poison and
arouses less resistance in the body of the person. Perhaps for
that reason, it and its descendants are able to multiply more
quickly through the next few bodies than the competing
bacteria of its species. The mutated mild bacteria may win
the competition. Bacteria compete for living space, too.
These less virulent but more fertile bacteria squeeze out their
old-fashioned relatives and take over."

"From the poisonous ones, sir? Like the meek shall inherit
the earth? Hardly that, sir?"

"In self-attenuating bacteria that is what has happened."
Dr. West laughed as if in triumph. "The less poisonous had a
built-in survival advantage. They've spread through the Esks
with less and less symptoms, until they could infect the world
with no noticeable effect, no harm."

"The bacteria, sir?" The Mountie was staring at the map.
"Surprising to me, sir. The opposite would be so much
worse——."

"You mean more and more virulent mutations. For some
bacteria this does happen. But it makes no difference to the
bacteria as long as multiplication can proceed most rapidly."
Dr. West watched the airmen walking up the beach toward—
him. His voice faded: "Like it or not, life's basic chemical
command simply is to survive and multiply."

"It is true there will be too many Esks, sir." The Mountie
was staring at him. "Is that what you're really talking
about?"

"What do you think? This planet was yours first! They're
only Esks."

"Perhaps, sir, but this is a civilized country." The Mountie's eyes scrutinized Dr. West. "Are you saying Esks are not
fully human, sir? Saying things like that, Hitler soothed his
Germans to pop off the Jews, by saying—other races——.
Are you saying Esks aren't human?"

Dr. West retorted: "Thirty-day gestation period and you
still think Esks are human? ——Those stupid bearded kooks
in the LST," Dr. West gasped, "they are the humans. Stupidly feeding a new and competing—species. Esks. Human? The
Esks? No, *not* human unless monthly births from each Esk
woman is an historically human characteristic. ——Mutated
humans? Hell, no! In an Esk there are too damn many neat
mutations at one time. They aren't human. You are the
humanitarian idiots bringing food so the Esks can multiply
until——."

"Sir, we can't let people starve! Listen, sir, those bearded
chaps in the LST, at least they obeyed the law and handed
me approved invoices, lists of all the food they brought in.
All imports approved. That is required by law. Look at these
approved lists on my desk. Shipping number 334 is for 500

cartons of prefolded paper diapers. It is *not* for a little wooden box full of bloody cans of MOSQUITO SPRAY!"

Dr. West looked away as the Mountie's voice rose.

"The Esks brought the wooden box to me." The Mountie's voice broke as if in pain. "I said, open it. How could I know? I said, just what I need, mosquito spray. I took an orange can. I said, you chaps take the rest. Sir, I even showed them how to press the knob on top to make the spray come out. Sir, I did it—the bloody hell! What was in those cans? People died. People died." Mosquitos whined around the two men.

Dr. West's mouth was so dry he couldn't answer.

"People died, sir. People died." The Mountie looked down at the lump of bedcovers where Eevvaalik's body lay.

"But you didn't even get sick, sir," the Mountie blurted. "I think you brought those spray cans from California, sir. The R.C.M.P. will trace them back to where they were manufactured. You needn't speak without advice from your counselor-at-law. Sir———." The Mountie's voice trailed off, and he started out the cabin door.

The words ARREST and MURDER remained unspoken. All day they had been flying through Dr. West's consciousness like savage-beaked skuas. Now they fell at his feet. The worst had happened. There was nothing more he could do.

Dr. West's face twisted in a smile of numb relief as the cheery pilots and doctors from the flying boat blundered into the cabin and shook hands all around. The Mountie was too courteous to mention they were shaking hands with a murderer. They all sat down and had tea.

Voiceless, Dr. West tried not to think ahead to the trial. In Ottawa would they strip him morally naked before the world?

6.
THE
MODERN
PENITENTIARY

ALONE IN THE COMFORTABLE APARTMENT WHICH WAS HIS cell, Dr. Joe West chewed the inside of his cheek in self-torment. Quivering, his scalpel exposed the tiny pituitary gland of the Arctic ground squirrel on his work counter.

"Blind fools!" His real guilt was so much worse than the angry orators in the United Nations General Assembly had shouted.

Racial murder? Unpredictably, twenty-two Canadian Eskimos had died. The Ottawa court convicted him of murder.

"I'm guilty of worse——." His face twisted. Apparently less than 20% of the Esk women had developed any significant infection or even temporary swelling in the tubes from their ovaries. A few of the Esk children and men had a day or two of mild fever. Not a single Esk died. Their resistance to human pathogens was so much stronger than he'd expected. While Eskimos died, Esks had continued happily eating and breeding and breeding and breeding——.

"Damn me! Instead of my controlling their birthrate, I'm their Santa Claus!"

It was his murder trial which attracted worldwide attention and aid to the hungry Esks. Ironically, it was his trial which awakened humanitarians and politicians to the plight of the overcrowding Esks. Rapidly multiplying Esks starving——.

During the year of his arrest, while his trial dragged on, the counted number of Esks increased from 4500 to 8000.

Both the malicious Chinese Government and the embarrassed United States Government were air-delivering food, baby clothing, portable barracks.

"Blind fools! Like providing food and shelter for lem-

191

mings." Dr. West's youthful face winced, gaunt as a pension-er's.

The first rumor Dr. West had overheard as he was led to his bulletproof glass booth in the Ottawa courtroom for sentencing: a Chinese VTOL aircraft had "evacuated" more than one hundred starving "Eskimos," surely Esks, from Canada's Boothia Peninsula. Like an infectious boil, the population pressure of the Esks finally had burst.

The last rumor he had heard before he was delivered to this prison: hundreds of Esks had asked to be permitted to emigrate to China. "We are loved in that free country." Evidently Chinese agents had been planted among the Esks. In the Canadian Parliament there was a Great Debate. Esks if they so desired would be permitted to go. "Few will, I say. Let the few malcontents go, and relieve our taxpayers of a few Family Allowances." When the huge Chinese VTOL jet transports began landing, to the amazement of Canadians not a few Esks but 4000 Esks opted for China. This was fully half the total Esk population at that moment.

"God! What's happening out there?" Trapped in the New Ottawa Reformation Center, Dr. West knew he should make a second attempt to escape—at once.

His cell was frighteningly comfortable. "Safe as a womb."

Already the friendly staff were changing him. Outside, the Esks would change the world.

The hiss of increasing air pressure alerted Dr. West that the outer door to his suite was being opened. Ignoring the Ceiling Lens, Dr. West hastily wrapped the dissected squirrel in metallic-green Christmas paper; he was not allowed news-papers. Dropping to his knees, he hid the squirrel under the compressor.

As he lurched to the sofa, his abdominal incision tugged. His heart thudded more quickly than the compressor pumping coolant through frosty copper tubes past his work counter to the huge insulated cage.

It was an ingenious but scary means of escape.

Peering out through the double glass window of the cage, a single chilled Arctic ground squirrel (*Citelus undulatus*) still resisted hibernation. The other squirrels slept under the sawdust. This lonely squirrel shrank back as the inner door to

Dr. West's suite moved open. With her upswept hair and neat blue uniform, Nona walked in with a therapeutic smile.

Dr. West stiffened, his face twisting. Every time he saw a woman in here he wanted to cry—*Marthalik*. Or shout with rage. *Marthalik, where are you*? Not even during his trial, his last months in the outside world, had Marthalik or Steve contacted him. *Not even tried to contact me*. Sometimes as he lay in his cell he imagined Marthalik making love with Steve, and pounded his fist against the mattress. *That's why she went with him. Not to have an operation*. Marthalik and Steve had vanished as if from the face of the Earth. But when he saw a woman there was Marthalik for an instant.

His pulse racing, Dr. West couldn't remember whether he'd shaved as Nona walked toward him. Every day for a week, at 10:00 A.M. she had entered his suite, made his bed, done his dishes and tried cheerful conversation.

Her blue uniform no longer reminded Dr. West of a guard or airline stewardess. Through his insane glass wall, he was staring at her eyes.

"Merry Christmas, Student." Nona laughed, but her self-assurance visibly fell away. "This is supposed to be a present to you from the staff. But I don't know what's in this package." She wasn't smiling now. "I didn't have anything to do with it."

Dr. West reached for the package, which was wrapped in grinning Santa Claus paper. He felt as if he could almost reach Nona through his imaginary glass wall. His fingers closing around the bottle-shaped package touched her hand. His muscles tightened. After a year alone in Territorial Prison, and then in the bulletproof glass booth while on trial, and then in Classification Prison, always alone and cutoff, Dr. West could not quite break through the illusion that there was a glass wall——.

"Gurgles like a fifth of rye," he remarked with a weak smile, cautiously shaking the package.

"I doubt that." Nona sat herself down on the coffee table, still breathing hard as if she had been hurrying to her hour-a-day appointment with him. Always she seemed to be perched on the coffee table, her knees pressed together, her hand tugging down her blue uniform skirt.

"That's Christmas on your head," Dr. West stammered, not sure what he meant to say.

Her silvery flower-shaped hair decoration of foil, tinsel and yellow-green mistletoe rustled as she raised her face with dimpled pleasure. "Thank you," she said.

After a moment she said, "There's still a package in your hand——."

Dr. West's fingers stripped down the red and white Santa Claus paper, exposing the clear glass neck, and laughed with confusion. "A fifth of gin?" He stared at something worm-shaped and pink drifting back and forth in the alcohol. "I'll be damned! It's my appendix."

"I'm sorry!" Nona blurted. "What a horrid thing for the Medical Officer to send."

At her upturned face, Dr. West blinked, more surprised by her shocked reaction than by the fact the Medical Officer would send him back his appendix for Christmas. Dr. West's smile hardened as he silently read the note: *Mr. West, our pathologist reports——.*

That first night in his suite, Dr. West had lain waiting for his fever to rise. The dull pain spread. His abdominal muscles became rigid. He vomited, crawling toward the bathroom. As he had hoped, the Ceiling Lens was transmitting, and thirty floors below in the basement where 240 TV screens were banked, the Night Observer noticed and telephoned the Medical Officer.

Dr. West had expected to be rushed out of his solitary cell into the elevator, and down, then out through the icy Canadian night to the hospital building. Apparently that was someone's plan. Perhaps an orderly had been bribed. The rectangular hospital seemed to have more escape possibilities than these tall cylindrical towers of the New Ottawa Reformation Center.

From a distance the towers had resembled concrete grain elevators. His return glimpse, as the armored car had delivered him toward the penitentiary, had shifted from the towers to the Canadians massing in the sleet. PRESERVE OUR ESKIMOS a placard read.

Flailing their signs, the screaming mob broke through the police line and halted the armored car with their bodies. SAVE

OUR ESKIMOS. A sign hammered against the bulletproof window. HUMAN LIFE IS SACRED. A contorted face pressed against the glass, recognized Dr. West. "Kill the bastard!"

Dr. West had closed his eyes. They were right.

Shivering inside warm Tower #3 that first night, finally alone in his solitary suite, still shivering Dr. West had hung up his gray denim trousers, and the capsule fell out of his cuff. He had blinked at it. On the pink gelatin was scratched HOSP-APP. At first he did not realize what the APP stood for. With irony he thought the capsule might contain cyanide from his billions of TV admirers who had witnessed his trial and conviction for genocide and were outraged there no longer was a death penalty in Canada. Their dead Eskimos were lovable people, easily idealized. "Tool of capitalist genocide!"—"Communist fiend!" the confused Canadians had shouted after him.

Swiftly, willing to accept whatever it contained, Dr. West had gulped the capsule and lain down. His actual crime, his ineffectiveness was more terrible than the billions knew.

The numbing of death did not come. As his temperature rose and his symptoms proliferated, Dr. West realized that APP stood for appendix. Someone was trying to get him out. Someone must believe him.

Fever engulfed him in delirium. A potent capsule! He imagined he saw Eskimos entering his suite, and he shouted with terror.

The Medical Officer's fingers were pressing his rigid abdomen. "Nurse, best take a rectal thermometer reading from this chap."

The massive whiteness of a polar bear loomed over the Medical Officer's shoulder, and Joe West had yelled.

To his dismay, instead of carrying him out to the hospital, gauze-masked monsters wheeled a portable operating table into his suite. "Best give the patient a spinal."

Mirrored in the reflector of the portable overhead light they were turning his body. Their yellowish rubber hands gleamed. A grease pencil marked a line from his navel to his hip. He felt the numb tugging of the scalpel.

When the appendectomy was complete, a masked face had bent over him. "I say, West, your appendix appears remarkably healthy. In retrospect, your symptoms all seem rather odd. You've made me feel the fool. Was this another one of those unnecessary operations?" The Medical Officer had turned away. "Best deliver his appendix to the pathologist."

Now, for a Christmas present, or a warning, the Medical Officer had returned his appendix in a bottle with a note. *Mr. West, our pathologist reports that a foreign substance, probably ingested, raised your white blood count and induced other symptoms typical of peritonitus. As a former medical man, you may have a more specific explanation?*

Why not feign a brain tumor next time. We would welcome the exercise. Merry Christmas from the staff, New Ottawa Reformation Center.

P.S. Looking forward to your continued presence during the New Year.

Dr. West's bitter grin sagged while he turned his head from side to side as if searching for a window to the Outside. Windowless concrete. He stared past Nona at the concave wall and violently stiffened, his fist crushing the note.

Her voice intruded: "Did he write one of his funny-type notes?"

"Funny? My sense of humor's dead. I'm dead. Don't waste your hour in here with me. Don't waste the taxpayers' money. Get out, dammit!"

Instantly he was sorry. Terribly lonely.

She looked up at him. To his surprise, she moved toward him, smiling. Her hand——.

He stiffened. "Get out. While you can, go!" he shouted. "Get out. I can't stand your—is it sympathy?"

She edged toward the door but turned around, her face solemn. "If you want, you can apply for someone else, a different Social Therapist——."

"No! What choice has a rat in a trap?" He looked her up and down. "Bait, is that what you are? Get out."

"After you've been here a while," she answered softly, "you'll realize this is like your home. You'll feel differently. Please, if you want to—you can apply for a different——."

"No, dammit, I want to get out of here! At least you—get out!"

After he had caught his breath, he realized she was still standing there. Trying to hold his voice from trembling, he said: "You don't scare very easily do you?"

"Sometimes. But I'm not scared of you."

"I'm sorry. But I've got to get out of here. I forget you have problems, too. Here you are a woman alone all day with us murderers and maniacs."

"I'm not alone."

"Do you mean that physically or spiritually? ——Outside, they'd lynch me," Dr. West said finally. "In here you people try to make me feel comfortable but won't even tell me the news."

Wryly he smiled. "There was a prophetess named Cassandra. Now I know why she wailed. A man, a prophet, would have battered his head against a marble pillar. Cassandra could foretell what was going to destroy Troy, but no one would listen. She warned them not to drag the wooden horse into Troy. No wonder she wailed. Helplessly knowing what is going to happen but not being able to do anything is so much more painful than——."

"Aren't you being rather dramatic," she remarked. "That wooden horse, isn't it in a school book about Greece?" Turning away from his tormented face, she walked into the kitchenette and opened the sliding doors which concealed his sink and electric stove. She boiled water. "Instant coffee?"

"So you're the unshakable type," he laughed bitterly. "Must help in a madhouse like this."

"I believe in living along from day to day." She sat down on the other end of the sofa and smiled at him over her steaming cup. "Now that you've had your tantrum for this day, I'm going to tell you something which may give you a second one."

"No, I'm through," he said, smiling faintly. "Your child psychology has overpowered me."

"The Pharmacist asked me to ask you——," she put down her coffee cup. "——if a hypodermic was, shall we say, overlooked and left in your cell. During the first three nights after your appendix operation the nurse gave you sleeping injections. In a government institution like this everything has to be accounted for even if it's all used up like a one-shot disposable hypo. Anyway, the nurse must have become confused in her equipment count. A used hypo is missing. Of course she had other patients to visit, but you're the newest in this tower and this has never happened before, so the Pharmacist wonders, if you still have the hypo, would you return it——."

"I haven't any hypo."

"Good. I'll ask the Recreation Officer if he'll start the search in someone else's suite. The Administratrix has told him to search, so he has to search."

"That's all right." Dr. West leaned back on the sofa. "The Recreation Officer can start here. I won't feel persecuted. He's my buddy," Dr. West bluffed, and nodded at the insulated cage, the compressor, the centrifuge, the gleaming glass equipment, all of which the Recreation Officer cheerfully and ingeniously had acquired for him—with Dr. West's own impounded funds.

Dr. West's heart palpitated as he remembered the dissected squirrel concealed under the compressor. But he went on talking. "The Recreation Officer showed the Administratrix my hibernation study proposal. I may be repeating old metabolic and glandular research, but it's more therapeutic for me than weaving baskets. He says he got her approval by suggesting Tower #3 surely must be more enlightened than Alcatraz, San Quentin—some prison where they once let an old lifer raise canaries. So the Recreation Officer's my buddy, and I raise squirrels. He's welcome to search. ——When is he likely to——?"

"He'll probably start someplace else." She put down her coffee. "At least two students who've been sick and visited by the nurse are former drug addicts and might steal hypos, I suppose——." She looked solemnly at him, and he was surprised how small she really was. Her hand on the couch was fragile compared with his. "The truth is," she laughed, "some men in this tower are—rather scary. That's why in your suite I feel so much better—with you."

Dr. West recognized the pitch, the helpless bit, and he almost smiled with pleasure. He not only felt protective, he felt almost possessive. From the sofa, she looked up at him, smiling with her eyes as if she knew that he knew, and he felt his imaginary glass wall dissolving.

"What are you smiling about?" she said.

"I was just thinking that we——."

The outer door hissed. Dr. West's muscles contracted like a criminal's caught in the act. The inner door shoved open.

"May I come in?" said the Recreation Officer, already in and sniffing his toothbrush mustache in his most characteristic gesture; he had an old face but his mustache and hair were black with dye. "I can come back later." His unreadable gaze bounced off Nona's face, and he stared at Dr. West. "I've been asked, shall we say, ordered, to search for a small useless—uh, item in your suite."

Dr. West grinned. "Nona told me it was a hypo. Feel free to search away. I'll help any way I can, but I haven't got a hypo for you. I wish there was a prison grapevine so I could tell you who's got the hypo."

The Recreation Officer failed to smile. To Dr. West's surprise the Recreation Officer's usually sly sense of humor was gone, blank.

But Dr. West kept trying. "Since this is my one and only happy hour with this sweet young thing, I would be happier if my suite were searched during the following hour." Dr. West grinned hopefully. "I promise not to go away, sir, since this is my therapeutic hour. Sir, as you said, you could come back later."

"No, I'm already here, so I'll start here," the Recreation Officer replied. "She can vacuum this dirty floor whether I'm here or not."

Dr. West tried again. "Sir, if you could come back later, after Nona's gone—I need to talk with you alone."

Dr. West was careful not to glance toward the compressor. Beneath it the dissected squirrel was hidden, and Dr. West was afraid Nona's reaction would be revulsion when it was discovered. He thought the Recreation Officer's reaction would have been mild interest if the dissected squirrel had been in plain sight on the work counter.

Unfortunately, Dr. West had concealed the dead squirrel, as if guilty of something. Now the Recreation Officer's reaction when he found the bloody package might be suspicion.

Dr. West knew the Recreation Officer lacked the medical background to put two and two together, but if the squirrel were shown to the Medical Officer—that intelligent man would recognize this was not merely a squirrel autopsy. The squirrel had been cut open for another purpose. The Medical Officer would ponder this problem and knowing Dr. West's controlling motivation was escape——.

"——in the kitchenette," the Recreation Officer was saying, opening and closing drawers. "You haven't even done his dishes yet, Nona." He opened a cupboard. "A more logical hiding place for a hypo would be—the bathroom."

Dr. West began to perspire. He knew he needed to maneuver both of them out of the suite in order to dispose of that dissected squirrel. If the Recreation Officer continued searching, eventually he would discover the body of the squirrel.

The Recreation Officer spent a surprisingly long time banging around in the bathroom. All it contained was a medicine cabinet, toilet, basin and tub. The bathroom was located in the narrow inner end of the suite.

Whenever he had sat in the tub Dr. West could hear the eight elevators humming up and down the central shaft of the cylindrical tower. His thirtieth floor suite was shaped like an eighth of a pie. The center of the pie was occupied by the huge open shaft, which contained the elevators and the air-conditioning ducts. The elevators were code-controlled. To escape without an elevator would be a long fall.

The Recreation Officer emerged from the bathroom, smiling beneath his toothbrush mustache. "I took the liberty of searching your medicine cabinet." His smile widened. "I deduce from the bottles and tubes that you suffer from piles." His smile spread so wide it almost appeared malicious. "Not a very romantic ailment for a world famous Arctic adventurer—for a convicted mass murderer——."

Dr. West blinked with surprise. Until now, the Recreation Officer always had treated him with human respect, never mentioned his crime.

"You've murdered more people," the Recreation Officer remarked, "than the rest of the students in this tower combined, and you top it off by stealing a worthless one-shot hypo."

"I haven't got your hypo."

"You're a disgusting example of futility. Do you know, if you'd simply applied for a hypo, if you needed a hypo, I would have purchased you a dozen. But during your second or third night in the tower you didn't know that yet, did you? So you stole one."

Dr. West did not reply. He was wondering if the Recreation Officer had just planted a hypo in the bathroom. From a friend, the Recreation Officer inexplicably had turned into tormentor.

"I brought you scalpels, didn't I," the Recreation Officer persisted. "Enough scalpels to butcher a dozen women."

"Please, sir," Nona protested.

"Don't you approve of humor?" the Recreation Officer asked her. "You and I are both on the staff—to assist in therapy, to make the students happy. Isn't that right?"

The Recreation Officer strode across the room toward the entry and kicked Dr. West's bed. "What do they expect me to do, split the mattress to find your hypo?"

"I haven't got the hypo." Dr. West stepped forward, his sweating face twisted in an answering smile. "From what I've been told, the policy of this prison, excuse me, educational institution, toward the so-called student is——."

"——to treat the disturbed student with respect," the Recreation Officer interrupted in a singsong voice. "Make him feel this is home. Rebuild his feeling of inner worth. —— Nona, have you been reciting our *Staff Book* to this filthy murderer?"

"No, she hasn't, Dad," Dr. West retorted, smiling harder, losing control. "You did, remember? Where's your warm father image today? ——The student is to be drawn into a warm familylike relationship and, I quote, encouraged to lower his defensive barriers. In the New Ottawa Reformation Center he is considered reborn. It is the purpose of the staff to offer the student so warm and reassuring an emotional environment that he will find the inner support he failed to feel in his childhood. Strengthened, basically changed, he can return to society. Isn't that right, Dad?"

"Back off!" The Recreation Officer spoke like an angrily barking dog. "Because you're younger, stronger, more sarcastic doesn't mean you can't be spanked, figuratively spanked, no, literally spanked————." He walked away from Dr. West, lifted the top of the insulated hibernation cage and plunged his arm into it.

The one conscious squirrel squalled with fright.

For the last minute, Dr. West had been considering goading the Recreation Officer to such anger he would stop the search and rush out of the suite. But now Dr. West's heart was hammering, his fists clenched, and he realized his own self-control was so uncertain that the Recreation Officer might be successfully goading him. Perhaps the Recreation Officer's strange behavior was intended to goad him to violence. Then would he be transferred? Was that the Recreation Officer's intent?

Nona, her face pale, her lips narrow, was shaking her head in warning at Dr. West. Silently they watched while the Recreation Officer distastefully lifted out a handful of sawdust.

"What a stench! I noticed it as soon as I entered your suite. Are you sure they're not decaying instead of hibernating?" The Recreation Officer reached deeper into the cage. "The stench, is it to discourage us from looking for the hypo? ————Is this little beggar dead?"

By the tail, the Recreation Officer raised a hibernating ground squirrel. "Since you formerly were an expert on Arctic ecology, among other things, I would have expected you to play with something more typically Arctic—such as those beastly little lemmings which you reputedly compared to Eskimos."

"To Esks. I explained to you the difference between Eskimos and Esks. I talked for hours when you listened so sympathetically, Dad," Dr. West added savagely. "You ought to be intelligent enough to differentiate between Eskimos and Esks. As for lemmings, they don't hibernate."

The Recreation Officer shrugged, dropped the limp squirrel back into the cage. "Dear me, you're right. You told me no Arctic animal truly hibernates—except these putrid ground squirrels. I'm not going to search through this stinking mess for the hypo. I'm going to recommend that the contents of this cage be emptied down the incinerator."

"I haven't got the hypo," Dr. West repeated, watching the Recreation Officer step to the wider outer end of the suite where the compressor chugged erratically.

Concealed under the compressor was the dissected squirrel. The compressor unit vibrated against the white concrete wall.

The wall was smooth concrete, slightly concave because it also was the outer wall of the tower. Like a cylindrical concrete grain elevator the tower had no windows, and its exterior construction was both economical and escape-proof, and functional in other ways.

The Recreation Officer glanced from the compressor to the concave white wall spread out behind it like a wide-angle screen. "This noisy compressor must intrude into the corner of the picture, or do you never turn on the projector any more? For emotionally disturbed students, for you, I recommend a minimum of two hours per day." The Recreation Officer smiled infuriatingly at him.

Dr. West stepped violently toward the compressor, the Recreation Officer and the blank wall. At first, while recovering from his appendectomy, he had lain for hours watching the moving scenery on that wall, his only substitute for a window. Trying to ignore the subliminal cartoons pressing him back against childhood, his favorite escape had been following movies of the surf flashing white along the northern California coastline on the wall. At first he'd stared helplessly. The artificial window had been his only release from claustrophobia.

"Nona, don't leave," Dr. West said, without looking back, knowing she was still sitting on the coffee table. This caused the Recreation Officer to glance back at her.

Dr. West's hand darted into the compressor case.

The compressor unit consisted of an electric motor humming at high rpms and revolving a series of larger and larger gears, the largest turning least rapidly and most powerfully, forcing the piston of the air compressor in and out no faster than a frightened heart. Last week, when Dr. West had assembled this jerry-built contraption, he had set an oiling can to drip at five-second intervals on the moving elbow of the compressor, and now, in this instant, his hand reset the nozzle of the can to dribble rapidly.

As the Recreation Officer turned back to the compressor, a fine mist of oil rose against his blue uniform. Dr. West already was walking away. There was a moment of silence as if the Recreation Officer had not yet realized what had happened. "Your damned machine is leaking. There's little droplets all over my coat."

At this, Dr. West turned back. "Either oil or coolant. If it's coolant—the coolant is strongly alkaline, irritating to the lungs." He wrapped his handkerchief protectively around his hand and rushed at the compressor, turning his head aside, as if from poison gas, holding his breath while he readjusted the oiler to its former rate of one drop of oil every five seconds. "The coolant will decompose cloth. It should be soaped off the skin as soon as possible."

The Recreation Officer sniffed the back of his hand and glared from Dr. West to Nona. "The least you could do is help me search," he accused her. "Damn, my hand is burning!"

Seated on the low coffee table, Nona stared down at her own hands, cupped on her lap. "Sir, my job is to maintain a close relationship with my students. The Administratrix never asks us to involve ourselves in searches———."

"You have the soul of a—they let anybody into civil service these days!" The Recreation Officer dashed out of the suite, scrubbing his hand with his handkerchief, and the elevator hummed.

"I'm sorry," Nona murmured. "He's never acted before as if making a search was—beneath his dignity. Normally, he's a nice man. Maybe he's having problems Outside———."

"Oh, sure———. Nice man." Dr. West sat down on the sofa in order to stop shaking. "The staff has to stick together."

"I'm telling you the truth. I've never seen him like this." Suddenly she smiled. "On duty, we're supposed to be saints and let you students have all the tantrums."

Perched on the low coffee table, she pressed her legs together and tugged down at her skirt. She was peering toward the compressor. "Is that a Christmas present underneath? Sort of green shiny paper."

"You'll have to wait till Christmas to find out," Dr. West said and reached forward, seizing her hand before she could stand all the way up and escape to look under the compressor.

Pulled forward off-balance, she raised her eyebrows as she smiled down at him, and plumped down beside him on the sofa. "You didn't need to let go of my hand."

Dr. West grinned with embarrassment, knowing he should try to get her to leave the suite as quickly as possible, so he could dispose of the squirrel. "Do you think my ex-buddy, the Recreation Officer, is likely to pop back in here unannounced?"

She shrugged, jiggling her shirt-waist. "He might." She smiled, glancing at him from the corners of her eyes. "I don't think he will though. He probably went down to the basement to wash and gulp coffee and brood. This was supposed to be his free hour. That's why he was assigned to help search. Next hour he has to be smiling again and sympathetic because he must face his next appointment with another one of you exasperating students."

"Exasperated is the word. I feel like I'm in a fishbowl." Dr. West jerked his head at the Ceiling Lens.

Nona looked up, then down as if she were staring through thirty floors to the basement. "Privacy is mostly in your head. There are 240 screens down there but only one Observer on duty since the budget cut. Mainly the Observer keeps his attention on the red-tagged screens, the new admissions. After all, they're the men most apt to set their suites on fire or slash their wrists or—uh, develop appendicitis."

Dr. West almost smiled at that. Then he asked a leading question. "When the clock says it's night, and the luminous panels dim, and finally I turn out my reading light, there's still a dim red glow in the dark. I deduce I'm also spied on by infrared transmission?"

"You are a bashful one! The night Observer has only one set of eyes. He's worked here for years, and he's seen everything. He's so bored he's slyly wired one TV to watch Outside hockey games." She giggled. "It takes my own inside alarm system to get any protective reaction from him."

Dr. West laughed in surprise. "Inside alarm? Don't tell me,

if a buxom member of the staff is grabbed by a student and squeezed, does that set off her built-in electronic alarm button, gongs clanging, red lights flashing——."

"You tease! That depends on the member of the staff." Nona stood up unexpectedly.

As if in pain, Dr. West leaped to his feet, reaching for her elbow. But her other hand pressed lightly against his chest, and her gaze shifted from his eyes to someplace over his shoulder.

"The clock says your time's up."

"Listen, Nona, seriously, I need you now." He was startled that he was begging.

"I wish I could stay, but I'm hired to look after my students equally. I wish I could stay, but my 11:00 till 12:00 man is expecting me. It's his hour. He's a terribly nervous, disturbed old man. He has no inner resources at all. He's sitting there expecting me——."

"But what about *my* hour? That damned Recreation Officer used up my whole hour bumbling around in here. Listen, you wouldn't understand but I've been hung up in—hell—a glass wa—dead until today and now I need you."

She stepped closer to him. "I'll be back tomorrow. Since you're described in the files as a cerebral type, you can get along," she teased, then added seriously: "I'm so happy you came out of your withdrawal." She smiled again. "Some sillybillies on the staff were making bets you would turn into a vegetable."

"A vegetable? Listen, tell your 11:00 to 12:00 man I'll trade my whole hour tomorrow for thirty of his minutes today, now."

"I'm flattered—I think. But he's unadaptable. I'll dicker with him for you, but don't hold your breath. I won't be back for at least a half hour, if at all—lover——."

"Dammit, Nona," Dr. West almost grabbed for her, then laughed wryly, trying to hide himself behind a sense of humor. "You're playing with dynamite. Nona, is that what you love—playing with human dynamite?"

"That's my job. I'm supposed to civilize——." She winked and went out through the hissing door.

Alone, but perhaps not unseen, Dr. West was careful not

to glance at the Ceiling Lens. To conceal what he wanted to do, he knew that turning off the lights in the suite during waking hours would be the wrong move. That simply would attract the attention of the Observer. Innocently he ambled toward the compressor, knelt and removed the gleaming green package, and walked to the sink. He went through the motions of washing the dishes Nona had neglected to wash, and in the sink he cut the ground squirrel into quarters and ground it down the disposal, all the while bending over the sink, obscuring his actions from the Observer, who might be watching but more likely was not.

Dr. West did not glance at the hiding place of the steel needle he had removed from the hypo. The needle was sticking in the fiberboard partition between the kitchenette and the bathroom. He had extracted the nail which originally supported the lightly framed print of a voyageur portaging a canoe. The screw-in base of the hypodermic needle now served the same purpose as had the head of the nail. Thus the needle was concealed in plain sight.

Two weeks ago, Dr. West had smashed the relatively large plastic plunger of the hypo for which they now were searching, and flushed it down the toilet.

While in bed after his appendectomy he had confused the nurse in her hypo count: like the old shell game. Having stolen a full hypo rather than the empty they thought was missing, he had injected its contents into his empty nose drops bottle, which stood on a shelf in the medicine cabinet next to his eye drops bottle, which he had filled with a second sedative injection the following night while the nurse's attention was distracted by a white wad of paper he had ricocheted off the concave wall—after telling the nurse he had seen a white mouse in his cell.

Now Dr. West visualized the Ceiling Lens above his head without looking at it. If he stacked the kitchen chair on top of the coffee table and climbed up and taped a paper towel over the Ceiling Lens, the blankout probably would attract the attention of the Observer who might send someone to investigate, which would be most embarrassing.

A shy and diffident man, Dr. West wanted privacy, needed privacy.

Even the bathroom lacked privacy. There was a separate Ceiling Lens in there. Dr. West blinked in realization. The staff all had said there were 240 TV screens in the basement. The tower was thirty stories high with eight pie-shaped suites to a floor, so that there must be 240 suites. But there were *two* Ceiling Lenses per suite, one in the main room, one in the bathroom, so why weren't there 480 screens in the basement?

Wrong! He had forgotten the *third* Ceiling Lens in the entrance passageway between the inner and outer doors. It was to reveal attempted escapes or ambushes by students who had gained the code for opening the inner door. Why weren't there 720 screens in the basement?

As his hypothesis germinated, Dr. West smiled. One Ceiling Lens was in the main room of the studio apartment, the second in the bathroom, and the third in the entry hall next to the bathroom in the narrow end of the semi-pie-shaped suite, a total of three Ceiling Lenses per suite. Therefore, there should be three times 240 TV screens in the basement, a total of 720 screens, but there were only 240 screens. Dr. West squinted, trying to visualize how the designers of the remote TV system managed to project 720 pictures to only 240 receiving sets. He nodded. From each suite three pictures were transmitted onto one screen.

In television baseball games, it was customary to show the pitcher winding up and at the same time in the corner of the screen show a separate picture from a separate camera of the runner taking his lead off of first base.

Dr. West assumed that the pictures from his bathroom and from the entry hall were projected as overlaps in two corners of the main picture from his suite. Thus, very likely there were two privacy spots within the main room of his suite. But which two corners of the four corners of the screen, which two corners of the main room would contain this privacy overlap?

Unfortunately, the shape of the main room was not square, and could not fill a square TV screen. From the concave white outside wall of the suite, the two side walls tapered inward. The slice of pie narrowed where the bathroom and the entry hall stood side by side, both abutting the central elevator shaft.

If, on the TV screen, the bathroom and entry hall were moved down and out to the corners of the screen there would be only a partial overlap because the main room was narrowest at the top of the screen. But there would be some overlap, some place to hide from the Observer.

Dr. West walked into the bathroom. It was about eight feet long. At this wider end, it was five feet wide. He glanced out at the kitchenette in the main room. On the TV screen, if the bathroom were moved down into the unfilled corner of the screen, it would overlap the china cabinet, the dumbwaiter pipe which delivered frozen foods, and his refrigerator.

Since the private actions Dr. West had in mind couldn't be conducted in such a small refrigerator, he walked to the other side of the main room near the inner entry door.

The entry hall, which he couldn't enter, also appeared to be five feet wide, and he supposed it was the same length as the bathroom, eight feet. He looked back. The coffee table, sofa, easy chair and standing lamp were grouped near the center of the main room. Beside him, his bed already stood against the side wall, but probably was exposed because it was too far down on the TV screen. It was too near the wide white projection wall to be in the TV overlap——.

Standing with his back to the bed and his calves pressed against the foot of the bed, imperceptibly Dr. West pushed the bed along the side wall until the head of the bed was near the entry door. If he moved the bed any closer, Nona wouldn't be able to squeeze through the partially blocked door. Nevertheless, virtually the entire bed should be concealed by the overlapping picture transmitted from the entry hall. In the upper-left-hand corner of the TV screen in the basement, the bed would be hidden, he hoped.

Because he was by training a conscientious man, he began to cross-check. He stared at the entry door. Perhaps, the Ceiling Lens in the entry hall only operated when someone was entering——? Not likely. More threatening was the probability that the TV system had been designed so that every inch of the suite could be scanned. By throwing a switch, the Observer could shift the overlapping pictures from the upper corners of the screen to the lower corners. But why would he do that with 239 other cells to monitor? But he might. With so many unknowns and embarrassing possibilities, Dr. West felt nakedly exposed. "Dammit, I'm no monkey in a zoo. There's more than one way to——."

Dr. West smiled with excitement, hurried across the suite to his work counter and collected a ball of twine, a scalpel and some safety pins. On his trip back to the bed he dragged his wooden work chair. Listening for the hiss of the outer door, he pushed down the pillow and set up the chair on top of the bed. He tied two chair legs to the tubular iron head of the bedstead.

Hastily, he stretched a string from the high back of the anchored chair down over the bed to its tubular iron foot. Fumbling with knots, spreading blankets over the string, pinning blankets together, pinning edges of blankets to the mattress, he worked as rapidly as a camper when the rain-drops begin to fall.

His face contracted with uncertainty. That two-faced, un-predictable Recreation Officer might return——.

The outer door hissed, and Dr. West jumped like a man awakened by an alarm clock. Across the suite he carried the scalpel, which he had used to cut string, to the work counter and turned, breathing hard, as the inner door opened.

"Surprise," she laughed, "my 11:00 to 12:00 man was so grumpy when I asked him why he hadn't shaved he said I was a worse nagger than his daughter. My heavens, he would have *given* you the rest of his hour. But he'll feel differently tomorrow, so I traded—gave—him your hour tomorrow for his remaining forty-five minutes today. You're looking at me like—my eye shadow's on upside-down." She giggled. "I talk too much. Whenever I'm uneasy I talk too much. I don't know why I should be in a tizzy but whenever—well, we don't really know each other. We're friends but we're still sort of—strangers."

As Dr. West walked toward her, she stepped sideways and the back of her leg came in contact with the bed, and she whirled, startled.

"My heavens! A tent!" She pealed with laughter. "A tent.

A tent," she giggled, "I'm going to have to explain a few things to you. You're so new here you don't know the rules." Then her laughter stopped. "I'm sorry. I'm not laughing at you. I'm laughing at the tent. I think it's cute."

Dr. West took hold of her upper arm.

"You don't need to look so serious and earth-shaking," she breathed. "Life should be fun. It is fun, a tent! You are the most ingenious man I ever did see. Safety pins! A tent flap. Wasn't Omar Khayyám a tentmaker, too?"

She put her head inside the tent. "Oops, am I psychic? I never did make your bed. I talk too much don't I?" Head first she vanished into the tent, as Dr. West's hands guided her in.

Forgetting even a sidewise glance at the door, Dr. West followed, the tent shaking as she disappeared under the blanket roof. From the Ceiling Lens only the tent was visible.

"My heavens," her voice emerged from the tent, "a chair for a tent pole! Not so fast! It's crowded in here. You have lots of ingenuity, but I'll unhook it. Ah———. That's comfy. Next time I'll buy C cups. Mm, you're hurting. Gently, even if I talk too much. That's better, so much better. Easy now, no hurry. You're hurting———. That's better. Yes———. Oh."

"I'm sorry, such a hurry," Dr. West's voice gasped. "More than a year I've been alone, Nona, trapped in jails alone."

"That's all right, lover. Let me rub your neck, your back and in a little while———."

"A year is so long for a live man. No, a dead man———."

"Well, now, I wouldn't say you were quite dead," she giggled.

"But a whole year! A year passes. What's a year?" He laughed wryly, "I shouldn't feel sorry for myself. Those Mars expeditions were gone for more than a year, and married men at that. Listen, I feel better. I can take anything."

"Now you're cheering up. Already you're changing for the better. I may not accomplish much in life," she said, "but at least I'm accomplishing something when you smile, Student. Squeeze me. This is your chance to change, and you'll change, really change and return to the world. We Canadians do like to think we're somewhat enlightened. After you graduate, lover—remember me."

"Graduate, hell!" Dr. West's voice blurted, "Sentenced to life——."

"No, you're not. You can't be. All Ottawa sentences are indeterminate."

"I'm not a fool! I know I'll never be freed."

"You have the same right——," her voice exclaimed unsurely, "to graduate as any other student. I'm sure you must. Why else would the staff go to all the trouble and expense of getting you all that equipment, the cage, the compressor. It's occupational therapy. The Recreation Officer——."

"That two-faced psycho? Not only did he try to humiliate me in front of you, he showed a vicious attitude toward you."

"Please," she protested, "you already have enough adjustment problems without developing a persecution complex. The Recreation Officer just had a bad day. Even Recreation Officers are human."

"He's not your husband is he?"

"What? What a stupid and unexpected question. Certainly he's not my husband. Just because I have a ring on my finger doesn't mean—well, why don't you simply try to enjoy life here in your suite."

"And don't ask personal questions," Dr. West's voice filled in.

"No, I'm happy to answer personal questions. We're in an awfully personal position right now, and you can get as personal with me as you want—if you promise me you'll let the Recreation Officer start out again tomorrow with a clean slate. All is forgiven?"

"Could it be that he's jealous of me?"

"Uh-uh. I'm also Den Mother to five other students. He's never acted this way before. I'm sure he's not jealous. I only know the man in a professional way, and he's rather old and quite professional."

"Not today he wasn't professional," Dr. West's voice insisted. "He didn't even finish searching my suite. What has he got, a triple personality? At first, after my appendix operation, he showed no real interest in me. He wanted me to

THE MODERN PENITENTIARY 213

take up microscopy as a hobby merely because Tower #3 happened to have an unused microscope."

"Yes, my microscope boy graduated. He has a technical job now in the Saskatchewan oil fields," she said proudly. "Oil core drilling samples are full of the tiny shells of——. He wrote me a beautiful letter."

"I told the Recreation Officer, for my occupational therapy I didn't want to weave baskets," Dr. West's voice swept on. "I wanted to review a line of research I began before when I was Director of Oriental Population Problems Research at the University of California——."

"My heavens, what has population problems got to do with hibernation?"

"Nothing, except that birth and growth and hibernation all are dependent on glandular activity. My original medical specialty was endocrinology, glands, but as I was saying——. All of a sudden the Recreation Officer took a personal interest in me, went to great trouble to acquire equipment for me, told me how he cut through red tape. We had long talks. He was interested in the squirrels. I thought he was my buddy."

"He just got up on the wrong side of his bed this morning, his bunk, perhaps," she laughed. "He's a retired naval officer, your navy, by the way. But he's Canadian born——."

"Born in hell," Dr. West's voice muffled, and there was quiet.

"Mmm, that's better. Don't nibble me too hard. Forget, mm, everything. Think about me——. Has all that isolation made you too sensitive? See——. You're ticklish. Lover, that big white square, that scar on your leg——?

"Would you believe a bear bit me? You're warm and smooth, the end of the world."

"What do you mean by that?"

"I don't know," Dr. West's voice breathed.

"My heavens, you're certainly trying to find out," her voice squealed in delighted alarm.

Dr. West's voice hoarsened. "Listen, I fell, Nona, Nona ——."

There were sighing sounds and finally her voice. "Yes, that's it, wonderful, wonderful——. Now!"

From the tent there was no coherent conversation and finally quietness.

"Darling, so nice——," her voice sighed, "so relaxed."

"Nona, I feel wonderful," Dr. West's voice laughed, and after a while in an even tone of voice: "I've been wanting to ask you, in one of the towers here—as a fellow student of mine, have you seen—don't laugh—a middle-aged Eskimo? Fierce looking man. Not the stereotype of an Eskimo. Not lovable. His name is Peterluk, from the Boothia Peninsula."

"You've asked other staff members that question," her voice answered cautiously. "I'm mainly familiar with this tower. Not a single Eskimo in this tower——."

"Could you find out?"

"No, it wouldn't be ethical. That is, each student has his—privacy."

"Privacy?" Dr. West laughed, giving up on Peterluk momentarily. "That's what we enjoy. After a little kiss, let's you and me break out of this prison."

"Now you've regained your self-confidence," her voice teased him. "Don't get overconfident. I still work here. I like it here. You are my student, my job."

"To charm us cons away from reality?" his voice laughed.

"Would you rather be in one of those gigantic penitentiaries in the States—with 5000 criminal types, all supposedly male. March, march! No privacy. Fellow prisoners to teach you better ways to stick up filling stations. Guards who shave and aren't as—ahem, sympathetic as I am. Now would you trade places——?"

"You do have nice smooth skin," his voice exhaled, "but here I've never seen another prisoner. When I tapped on the walls, nobody answered."

"Which would you rather have——?" her voice insisted.

"We're really all in solitary, the 240 men in this tower, and I don't know how many other towers."

"Ten towers," she said. "It's not solitary unless you think of it as solitary."

"Twenty-four hundred men. How many women? Divide by six?"

"You always try to be too precise," her voice laughed. "Our men are changing and graduating all the time. The average stay is less than a year. Thousands and thousands." Her voice grew serious. "I think of a stream of men being reborn."

"I think of thieves and murderers, criminals, myself, crouched in their cells waiting for you." His voice rose. "Listen, I'll never get out of here. For political reasons, I'll——."

"Oh shut up. Don't act so egotistical. If you want to act like a pessimistic, guilt-tortured little boy, go ahead and roll in your own mess." In the blanket tent rose the bulge of a head. "Until you take a more positive attitude, you jolly well won't roll on the sheets with me."

"You mean it, don't you," his voice softened, then exclaimed with wry laughter. "I understand too well! So simple but I don't know how effective. Solitary confinement is the stick and you're the carrot. I've been given donkey ears."

"You stubborn donk," her voice laughed, "don't you see any further than your big nose? You men in here can't be deeply changed by rewards and punishments. Outside, carrots and sticks certainly failed to civilize you or you wouldn't be in here. All your life you've been rewarded and punished but you wouldn't conform and you ended up in here."

"I need to get out. There is a great need for me to get out. Outside, the Esks are——."

"Sweet, harmless, law-abiding people. There's no use talking about Eskimos in here. Listen, we want you to like it in here. Lover, when you adjust—we love you."

"My god, Nona, are you going to give me the family bit? The Recreation Officer already shoveled it on me—during his friendly period." Dr. West's voice rose with anger. "The staff is my family. I am provided with a new childhood, loving and secure, so that I can grow up to the world again. Strengthened by my secure second childhood, or is that the wrong terminology? With new inner security we criminals graduate from our prison families into the world to be law-abiding and patient and sympathetic with our fellow man. Bugles please."

"It works. The family-group produces the———."

"Yes, Mom. But Dad was nasty today. Was he cranky because he thought I wanted to get in bed with you?"

"You don't need to be that sarcastic," her voice said.

"I'm sorry. But my eloquence gets—poisonous. How can you bring yourself to lie beside a murderous maniac like me? The civil service ought to give you a medal. If you're supposed to feel motherly toward me, you don't have to. Just leave me, please, I———."

"I love you."

"I should accept that as it is, now. You also love five other men in five other suites."

"Yes, I love men. I love women. I love my children. I try to love everybody."

"Next you'll tell me you also have a husband to love. I was hoping—and I wasn't so jealous of my five invisible cell-mates," Dr. West's voice stammered, "but I was hoping that ring on your third finger left hand was just for—show."

"Every evening after work I take the monorail back to the apartment district. Did you get much of a look at Ottawa?"

"I saw those angry people waving signs at me."

"I have three children, three little girls. The oldest puts the TV dinners in the oven before I get home. After supper I help them with their homework. On the rug even the second grader mutters at her homework. The older two have begun to giggle about boys, and the oldest is only sixth grade, my heavens! Then we watch TV and no one wants to go take the first bath. When my angels are asleep, I think—they're another day older and stronger and wiser, I hope. I sit watching TV. Me, I'm another day older. I crawl into bed."

"I wish I were there with you."

"You are. Squeeze me hard. You're in bed with me right now."

"That wasn't all that I meant," Dr. West's voice replied. "At the moment I feel more protective than———."

"You needn't be. I can get along very well, thank you," she said. "Except when my children were helpless babies, I always worked, worked as an IBM operator, even when my husband was working." Her voice for the first time rose in anger.

Her voice tried again more softly. "My husband was a nice guy, he really was. I didn't just love him because he was the father of my children. He was a sweet guy, not scheming, not adjustable the way we have to be. Everything's changing faster and faster, and he got quieter every time they automated away his job. What did I do? Did I give him inner strength? No, I began to earn more money than he did, and he said less and less. When I brought my—our kids home from my father's into the kitchen, I ran to turn off the gas."

Her voice sank. "I tried to give him artificial respiration."

"It wasn't until then—after then," her voice laughed unhappily, "I learned what brief animals we are. You're all horny schemers. If you and I were Outside, don't expect that a dinner date downtown and a cinerama will make me—owe you anything just because I haven't got a husband. You understand me?"

"So you got the perfect job here. No, I'm oversimplifying you."

"Yes, I'm simple. I'm just a simple bundle of mother love. Always cheery. Pardon me for sounding cynical with you, but my other students happen to be such uneducated children. They wouldn't understand."

"Or notice you're not perfect, I hope," Dr. West laughed. "I hope not. You're our only hope. Don't hurt us. You are too powerful. Without your personal love this would be solitary confinement and we convicts would go insane. Right now you are miraculously changing me and five other men."

Dr. West's voice suddenly probed. "If any of your prisoners fail, I mean, are released and then hold up a liquor store, do you have such a masochistic and guilty view of yourself that you believe you are responsible for the failure of this man?"

"I don't understand you?"

"As with the failure of your husband."

"What are you saying?"

"Nona, do you think you are so God-awful powerful that

if we cons fail it is because of something you did or didn't do?"

"I don't understand. Not one of my students has become a recidivist. I've worked here four years. Twenty-two of my students have graduated. None have gotten in any trouble with the law."

"You misunderstood my question."

"Of course I'm holding my breath about a few of my boys," she said. "They all get pretty fair jobs because we've retrained them, and the Government subsidizes, pays their employers during the first year."

"So they get along without you?" Dr. West's voice laughed suddenly. "Marry girls just like you?"

"You *are* a flatterer. My students write to me, some of them, and I save the letters and photos. One boy is going with a woman a little bit older than he is, but very pretty. I shouldn't have said that. What I meant to say was she looks enough like me to be my sister."

"No doubt the Government wishes you could be divided more than six ways."

"Silly. The whole purpose of the Government's reformation policy is to help them—you—stand on their own feet when they go Outside. Someday, you'll——. Now you stop that," her voice sighed.

"Nona, you're so warm, so smooth——."

"I think you just want me to stop preaching at you."

"Nona, what I want——."

"Lover, turn your wrist the other way. My heavens, if your wristwatch is correct and I'm sure it is, your borrowed time is up."

"You aren't going to leave me like this?"

"Sort of let me up, lover. Where's my bra? You're lying on it."

"But I was just beginning."

"But you've no more time today," she laughed. "Be here tomorrow? On second thought, I won't be back till Wednesday. You traded away tomorrow. Oh, there's a run in my stocking. Now stop that! You can wait till Wednesday, lover."

The blanket tent shook and Nona's legs swung out. She

fumbled for her shoes. "Where's my comb?" Zipping up the hip of her blue skirt, she clicked on high heels to the door. There was a departing hiss as the inner door opened and closed. Dr. West was alone.

Dr. West emerged from the blanket tent. He stared blankly at the huge cage where the Arctic ground squirrels slept in artificially induced hibernation. Then he smiled and squinted up at the artificial afternoon in his suite.

The luminous ceiling panels were synchronized to a clock and rheostat. There also was an OFF switch, but if he left the panels alone the evening would come gradually, and then night. Then Tuesday. On Wednesday morning at 10:00——.

He smiled down at the coffee table where she had sat looking up at him. He hurried to dismantle the tent, folding the blankets, his pulse racing, his face hot with suppressed memory. For an instant he pictured her inside the tent, moving. The view was too powerful—and he laughed and shook his head, and blinked his eyes. "Wednesday, Wednesday, hurry up, Wednesday."

He vaulted over the couch, grinning. Tomorrow was only Tuesday but——: "When Tuesday's here, can Wednesday be far behind?"

He reached for a glass tube on his work counter, and grinned at the Bunsen burner in his lab setup. He felt young. If he softened the glass tubing, bending, twisting the glass, he could make something for her. "A glass giraffe to make her laugh?"

Behind him, the inner door hissed open. With a surge of warmth, wanting to believe she had returned already, Dr. West whirled.

"Surprise," the Recreation Officer said. "I'm off duty now— Doctor. Before you get too well adjusted in here, I'm to deliver this."

Beneath his toothbrush mustache, the Recreation Officer forced a smile as he flapped down a manila folder on the coffee table. "You wanted news of the world, didn't you?"

"Get out." Dr. West stared at the folder with its projecting newspaper clippings as if he were looking at a snake. Obviously it did not come from the staff. It was from Outside.

"I'm sorry," the Recreation Officer's voice said. "I apologize for my eccentric performance this morning. Nothing personal, really."

"Get out, and take it with you." Dr. West felt no desire to open the folder.

"I'm not trying to frame you, Doctor. I'm the one who should be disciplined—for bringing these clippings into your suite."

"You tried to trigger me to violence during your so-called search. You tried to—wash me out. I assume you're trying again. Get out!"

"It's a pity no one will leave you alone," the Recreation Officer remarked. "Look, we can be frank. I've done two things at great personal risk. One, during my search this morning I disconnected the audio bug to your suite. Two, this noon in the basement I damn near electrocuted myself. Your Ceiling Lens no longer is transmitting. Instead, I've spliced a projector to your transmission line in the basement. If the Observer should happen to inspect your TV screen, he'll see what you were doing two days ago. Your screen is showing a replay of your old micro-video tape forty-eight hours long. I hope you weren't doing anything suspicious during the last 48 hours since I started my video tape recorder. I hadn't time to review forty-eight long hours of tape."

The Recreation Officer pointed at the manila folder. "In any case *now* you don't need to try to earn brownie points in here by claiming you don't want to break the rules. No one is watching you. You—sit down and read a year's clippings. What has really happened during this year you've been isolated in a series of jails? Weren't you the doctor who was so concerned about the Esks increasing?"

"Right now, I don't give a damn what's happening Outside. Get out."

"She's all heart, Nona really is," the Recreation Officer said slyly. "She's the best woman in Tower #3. I don't blame you for forgetting your purpose in life."

"What are you trying to do? Goad me to break out of here?"

"I don't know. I'm not paid to think. I'm sure this tower is escape-proof. You should be intelligent enough to get yourself moved." The Recreation Officer began spreading clippings from *The New York Times, MacLean's Magazine, Life, Time, American Medical Journal, Arctic Review,* completely covering the coffee table. "I'm supposed to say to you: hospital or the Cold Room. You're the one with brains!"

The Recreation Officer spread more clippings on the work counter and more clippings on top of the insulated cage. "I didn't realize so much had been written in the last year about the Esks," the Recreation Officer's voice went on. "I suppose all of these are from a clipping service. That they———."

"Get out!"

"They didn't tell me exactly why you were discharged from your position at the University of California, or why you returned to the Arctic. But I'm beginning to understand why you tried to infect the Esks. The newspaper accounts at the time of your trial simplified you for the simple minds of their simple readers as simply a murderous maniac. But now the *New York Times* seems to be having second thoughts on the matter."

"Get out!" Dr. West's voice rose with alarm as the Recreation Officer actually did walk out of the suite leaving Dr. West alone with hundreds of clippings and articles staring whitely at him from the terrifying world Outside.

Dr. West chewed his cheek in self-torment. Until today with Nona he had been preparing for an escape with almost suicidal calm. Now he didn't want to take any risks. All he wanted was Wednesday, when Nona would return.

Swaying, Dr. West imagined himself gathering up the clippings, eyes averted. Without reading, he would soak the clippings in the bathtub, tearing and squeezing the paper into dying lumps. He would not read what other men were thinking about the Esks, the research that must be going on, perhaps the frightened admissions in scientific circles that he might be right, that the terrible thing he had attempted was justified. "I won't read. I'm a prisoner and safe. Tear them up and flush them down the toilet without reading———."

"That heartless son of a bitch." Dr. West was under such stress he was speaking out loud. "Mysterious sons of bitches who're paying him—I won't read. What do you want me to do? I can't hoist the world on my shoulders. I already dropped it. Very funny." Dr. West stared down at the clippings on the coffee table.

His flashing arm swept clippings fluttering onto the floor. "I refuse to destroy myself. I will not read."

Dr. West dropped to his knees and hands on the floor, his head throbbing as he read of the multiplying Esks. An estimated 16,000 divided between China and Canada by next year, he thought. "Not very many yet." An agnostic, he began to pray for guidance.

No one entered Dr. West's suite the next day, which was Tuesday. Not by happenstance, the Recreation Officer had telephoned to the Tower from Outside saying he had the flu and would not be reporting for duty for a day or two.

Nona did not enter Dr. West's suite because of the exchange of his Tuesday hour to her 11:00 to 12:00 man. She paused outside Dr. West's suite and did not enter, and went on to the adjoining cell.

In the basement the Observer, monitoring the red-tagged screens, yawned and glanced at a hockey magazine.

At 5:00 P.M. when Nona went off duty she hurried to the monorail because the hairdresser's would close at 6:00. In the high-speed car suspended above the city, as Nona found a seat she recognized the Man, the back of his head, the Man.

A week before this short-haircut Man had sat down beside her and at first she hadn't realized his conversational ploy about the New Ottawa Reformation Center was more than casual. Then she had become quite abrupt, because her first loyalty, her life was tied up in the Reformation Center, and she was afraid the Man might be someone preparing to bribe her. She had left the car so she would not have to hear where his conversation was leading.

Now, the same Man, short-haircut, was sitting in front of her. When she got off, and rode the escalator down to the ground level, she hoped he wasn't following.

In the evening, after supper, Nona played jacks with her smallest daughter on the floor, while the Tuesday TV news blared half-heard everyday topics, neo-Maoists, unemployment, the third Mars Expedition, hockey fights, the underprivileged Esks who had been resettled in China.

"Mommy, your new hairdo is so pretty."

At this, Nona laughed with pleasure. "Now go to bed." And soon she slept herself.

Wednesday morning at 10:00, Nona entered Dr. West's suite with her hair up and gleaming and her heart beating unexpectedly. She stopped.

Stripped to the waist, Dr. West was lying on his back on top of his bed, his jaw sagging like a dead man's, his eyes closed as if he were sleeping.

"Student?——He isn't breathing. His heart——?"

She rushed to telephone the Medical Officer. She ran back. Her frantic hands shook Dr. West's body. The push of her hand against his terribly cool chest stimulated a shallow gasping breath, then nothing.

"Please, please." She flung herself upon him, mouth to mouth, trying to breathe for him, endlessly——.

With exhaustion, her own heart was fluttering. Her fingernails were fastened in his cold flesh.

"Keep going," hissed the Medical Officer's voice. "First I'm going to give him a shot of adrenalin." After awhile the Medical Officer said: "Get off. I'm going to attempt external heart massage."

A half hour later, sweating, the Medical Officer stood back. "This is the man who feigned appendicits." He stared at the thermometer. "72.6 degrees, and only one or two shallow breaths per minute, if the room temperature sank to 60 degrees, I suppose his body temperature would follow it down. The crazy fool induced this somehow. For a reason——."

"Do something for him!" Nona protested. "I'm going to telephone the hospital."

"No, first telephone the Tower Administratrix. She's in command here." For the first time, the Medical Officer looked around the suite and noticed the shambles. "Bloody butcher shop!"

On the work counter lay the opened squirrels. Beside them stood the centrifuge and red-brown stained glass tubing. "He was a murderous maniac," the Medical Officer's voice croaked.

"No, he wasn't. They were hibernating. They didn't feel

anything," Nona gasped. "I don't believe he cut them open, I mean, he cut them open with a purpose."

"He bloody well did," the Medical Officer muttered, stooping to pick up a hypodermic needle from the floor. "No plunger. Used the rubber bulb from his nose drops bottle. This is the needle from that missing hypo. May have injected a sedative in himself to start the downward metabolic slide."

The Medical Officer's fingers turned the rubber bulb inside-out. "A goo, an extract. Of course he would have been aware that massive injection of any foreign protein in a human being should cause fever. Quite odd, no fever, just the opposite."

"Do something!" Nona's voice persisted. "For all you know, he may die any minute."

"This involves legal as well as medical decisions." The Medical Officer appeared relieved when the Tower Administratrix arrived.

The Medical Officer laughed nervously. "Quite diabolically, this man has trapped us between killing him or doing something he wishes." He tried to explain. "Human life is sacred, we say, so we have to save him. We have to take him from his cell to the hospital building."

"We have no right to increase his chances of escape. It would be unwise to take him to the hospital building," the Administratrix replied. "I was so long in arriving here because I received a telephone call from the police at the border of the States. They searched the luggage of what turned out to be our Recreation Officer from this Tower with his mustache shaved off. They found $10,000 in small bills."

"Nevertheless, I believe the medical problem the former Dr. West has prepared for us is this," the Medical Officer muttered. "If we leave him as he is, he will die. Alternately, if we attempt to bring him out of his hypothermal coma he will die."

"My god," Nona breathed. "You already shot him with adrenalin to bring him out of it."

"A natural mistake. I'm hoping—it already appears that he has not reacted to it—I hope. Perhaps he has buffered his system against such an eventuality—I hope. As I was saying, if we try to bring him out of it his metabolic activity will increase. His system will begin to react in a typical defensive manner to the foreign protein and his temperature will rise. This will increase the violence of his reaction to the protein. Violently, his body will attempt to defend itself against the foreign protein, raising his temperature higher and higher until he dies."

"No doubt he planned this in order to be taken to the hospital building," the Tower Administratrix asked. "Could we simply leave him here? Assign a nurse."

The Medical Officer smiled at this. "Much more than a nurse is needed if we really believe in saving human life regardless of cost. His life processes should be electronically monitored. His veins should be connected to the kidney machine, and a pacemaker to his heart, or he will die. I suspect his body now is in a delicate equilibrium. His metabolism is too sluggish to react to the foreign protein. No reaction, no disease. What is needed is speedy consultation with experts in human hibernation research, who may know how, who have the equipment to bring him out of this condition, alive. In the States, hibernation research is being conducted in connection with the space program, I believe at the University of California."

"Strange coincidence," the Tower Administratrix said. "Not a coincidence. According to his files this man formerly was director of a medical research program at the University of California. Population Control. Do you think, interlocking medical staffs with their hibernation space transit program ——? If he hopes we will fly his body to California, he is unreasonable. An attorney in California may be waiting to file habeas corpus, legal trickery, bail——."

"I wasn't suggesting that," the Medical Officer said. "I simply was suggesting we make a reasonably humane effort to keep this man alive. Surely he can be adequately guarded in our own hospital building. I want to telephone the University of California. Perhaps a complete change of blood——?"

The Tower Administratrix shook her head. "Look for a note," she said sharply to Nona. "Suicide. A note."

On the coffee table lay a manila folder. Nona opened it. Empty. Swiftly she looked around the suite.

Something white showed under the huge insulated cage and Nona knelt down, reaching under. A single newspaper clipping had fallen behind the cage, and her cold hand drew it out. "FURTHER ESKIMO INCREASE NOTED."

"You didn't smuggle this in, did you?" the Administratrix asked Nona. "The Recreation Officer!" The Administratrix answered her own question and turned back to the Medical Officer. "If people outside could bribe the Recreation Officer so easily, how much easier to bribe the underpaid orderlies in the hospital. You yourself determined that this student's so-called appendicitis attack was feigned in order to get him out of my Tower and into the hospital."

The Medical Officer shrugged. "He'll die here."

Nona's hand clamped on the Administratrix's arm. "You're not going to let him die!"

"Is that a question? I'm sure it's not intended as an order," the Administratrix replied. "Nona, this is my responsibility. I know you. I know you're thinking somehow you failed him. You didn't. This man's urge to escape was too strong. He has taken too big a gamble. He can't escape."

"You can't let him die," Nona repeated.

"The best guarded building outside of the Tower," the Administratrix murmured, "is the Cold Room. There, no decision would be irrevocable. It starts a new problem, but——."

"That would be the place for him, the safest place." The Medical Officer stared down at Dr. West. "He ignored my warning when I sent him back his appendix in a bottle. Such powerful motivation is driving him. Alive, conscious, he would try again to escape. I think we are agreed this student has shown himself not amenable to therapeutic reformation. The Cold Room——."

"But he's not an incorrigible psychopath," Nona protested. "He hasn't attacked the staff." She turned from the Administratrix to confront the Medical Officer. "You both want to evade——."

"I'm wholly in agreement with the Administratrix," the Medical Officer continued. "The man has shown himself to be dangerous, suicidal. No regard for his own life. How much regard would you expect him to show for yours?"

"I believe he is essentially a good man, better than you," Nona retorted, but they weren't listening.

"To preserve his life in the Cold Room," the Administratrix addressed the Medical Officer, "I assume he should be cryofiled as quickly as possible. The legal steps can be justified post-factum."

"Yes, before irreversible physical deterioration takes place," the Medical Officer apologized in Nona's direction. "In five or ten years when we learn how to thaw them out——."

"You can't do this without a court hearing," Nona cried. "The two of you standing there can't convict, sentence and execute him."

"Execute is an unfair word." Instead of growing angry, the Administratrix put her arm around Nona. "It's not your fault. I'm sorry you're emotionally involved with this man, but then you're emotionally involved with so many of them. That's why you are so good."

"Please!" Nona stepped back.

"Nona, there's nothing you can do," the Medical Officer said. "Nona, you still have five. Do your best for them."

"You damn weak bootlicker," Nona cried at him. "Would you tell that to a mother whose baby has died? Would you say, so what? You still have five?"

"If you need to shout, Nona, do so at me," the Administratrix said, lowering her head. "Forget that I am your superior. If you want to accuse me, do so. It is I who must bear the responsibility."

"Please," Nona gasped.

"You did your best for him. You only had him—was it two weeks?" The Administratrix's hand closed around Nona's wrist. "Now go home, take the rest of the day off, tomorrow off, all week off. You are our best. All I can hire is an untrained substitute to take care of your students until you return. Don't feel guilty about your absence."

Without looking at Dr. West's body, Nona walked out of the suite. She went to her 11:00 to 12:00 man as if nothing had happened. The day, the night——.

That night on TV a politician stated that the anticipated increase of Eskimos would be a blessing. They could be trained as government nurses and guards. Eskimos needed less pay from the taxpayers. Increase would be good for Canada, which still had plenty of room. Nona could not sleep remembering Dr. West.

In the morning when she entered the Tower, Nona went to the office of the Administratrix.

"Nona, you're looking unwell." The Administratrix stood up behind her desk.

"I couldn't sleep, thinking he may have tricked us," Nona said slowly. "How do you know the body in the bottle-drawer in the Cold Room is his? Perhaps his real plan was a switch of bodies."

"Well, surely——," the Administratrix blurted.

"The Cold Room is guarded," Nona pressed on: "the drawers are locked, but last night who worked in the cryogenic preparation room; who prepared the body?"

"I don't know. One of the orderlies!" The Administratrix grabbed the phone.

"I want to go with you to identify the body," Nona said.

The Cold Room consisted of tiers of numbered drawers containing huge metal thermos bottles of liquid nitrogen maintained at minus 196 degrees centigrade.

As the Guard unlocked the drawer, Nona memorized the number. When she looked down through the periscope at Dr. West's rock-hard white face, Nona shivered. "Yes, that is the man."

Now she could tell exactly where he was.

That night in the monorail car, to her alarm the Man with the short haircut was not there. The night before, still frantic from the terrible scene beside Dr. West's body, she deliberately had sat down beside the short-haircut Man. Surprised, he had seemed perceptibly disturbed, trapped, hiding behind his newspaper while she told him she didn't want money, she wanted Dr. West to be removed from the Cold Room.

"There are thousands of drawers in there," he had murmured. "Find out the drawer number." And he had left the monorail car at the next stop.

Tonight he was not in the monorail car, nor waiting at her

stop. As she walked past the magazine rack and the soda fountain, a dark young man tried to pick her up. She kept walking. "What is the number?" he was murmuring.

She paused in the crowd by the bus stand. "I won't tell you the number of his cryodrawer until you show proof," she said slowly, "that there is someone qualified to bring him out of the Cold Room and then out of his—hibernation."

The dark young man seemed startled. "I'll find out," he said, and walked away.

Nona watched him thread his way through the crowd into the icy night. Her face felt old with determination. Dr. West or whoever he was—the man who built the tent with chair and blanket—he was hers, still in her care.

Her jaw hardened. Her teeth felt as if they were about to crack. It was even possible that these two men, short-haircut and dark young man, were maneuvering to kill Dr. West. They might be some of those emotional Canadians who waved SAVE OUR ESKIMOS signs and wanted to lynch Dr. West. Or might be inadequate rescuers. She knew she must deal with them with great caution.

As Nona stepped out into the razor-sharp Canadian night, the stars were glittering like ice. She tipped her head high. Invisible up there she knew U.S. astronauts were supposed to be coasting on the long voyage to Mars, sleeping all the way in their hibernation capsules.

At that moment Nona did not differentiate between their chemical hibernation in which their bodies rested at 45 degrees, safely above freezing, and Dr. West's totally different protoplasmic condition, frozen rock-hard in liquid nitrogen, from which no man had been thawed without horribly self-destroying rebirth defects.

"It truly is possible to rescue a man from hibernation," Nona murmured in vaguely misplaced hope.

In the cold she hugged her arms across her body feeling hope as when she had carried each of her unborn children.

Breathing hard, Nona stared in the direction of the New Ottawa Reformation Center.

"You'll get out," she whispered. "I'll get you out."

Dr. West became aware that he was alive. Blindly engulfed

in the prickling of his spreading nervous system, he was aware of intensifying light. His eyes must be open. Out there, a granulated blur moved, but Dr. West was unable to move.

Totally paralyzed, he lay trapped within his body prison, increasingly frantic as his consciousness increased, like a white mouse writhing faster and faster within the prickly hot oven-cage which was his unconnected body. From his eyeholes, his granulated vision signaled to his brain a gridlike pattern. His memory darted. His consciousness steadied as the wire grid reminded him of a shortwave heating grid he had noticed in restaurants to cook huge roasts of beef evenly and almost instantaneously from within. He was burning.

Failing to raise his head, he realized his chest was encased in a thoracic respirator. Into his neck a tube was gurgling. Two tubes extended to a gleaming machine at the edge of his vision and he realized it must be a new design of recirculating arterial machine he hadn't seen before. Although he hadn't known it before, evidently, they already knew how to drain the DMSO-Ringer's solution from the thawing body and replace it with blood so swiftly his revived brain cells apparently had not been damaged by temporary oxygen starvation. Until now, he had not known it already was medically possible to revive cryocadavers to complete consciousness.

He could move his jaw.

A pleased face peered down at him. "Can you hear me? Move your jaw again if you can hear me."

"Yes, I can hear you," Dr. West's joyous laugh gurgled. "So good to be alive."

The face raised its eyebrows in surprise.

"So quick," Dr. West laughed. "You freed me from my thermos bottle and thawed me so quickly."

The face frowned, glanced at someone else and nodded.

Another face appeared, vaguely reminiscent, an old and vulpine face. Had he known—the son of this man? Harvard Med School? This couldn't be his roomie, inarticulate Sammy Wynoski, could it? Sammy would be only about forty years old. This withered face looked sixty and worried as it bent closer. "Can you see me?"

"Sammy?" Dr. West asked.

"Yes."

"How long?" Dr. West croaked. "How long I been—gone?"

"Sixteen years. Two presidents." Dr. Samuel Wynoski shrugged as if in apology. "We've made it into the twenty-first century. It's 2009. For a long time we've known how to——."

"Am I still in Canada—the United States?"

"We're across the Potomac River from the Capitol," Dr. Samuel Wynoski murmured." You're in the basement of——."

Sixteen years——. Why would anyone want me now?"

Dr. West remembered that Sammy Wynoski had specialized in chemopsychiatry. Back in the 1980s when Dr. West was Director of Oriental Population Problems Research supported by a Defense Department grant at the University of California, reportedly Dr. Wynoski was with a clinic in Washington, D.C., which had a consultant contract with the Central Intelligence Agency. He still was——.

Each day Dr. West's strength increased but his confusion did not. He was anxious to find out about the U.S. outside. Leaning over his bed, his muscular "teacher" persisted in talking about China. "They already have over a billion Esks." The cleancut man's jaw hardened as if in suppressed anger as he evaded questions about the U.S. and lectured on and on about China.

Dr. West remembered, while he was on trial the Chinese had recruited nearly half the population from the Boothia Peninsula, approximately 4000 Esks. Now he wondered what had happened to the remaining 4000 Canadian Esks. Sixteen years had passed. *Marthalik?* he thought and asked: "Do Esks grow old?"

"They look about the same as they always did." His muscular teacher shrugged and smiled grimly. "Western hemisphere's relatively unchanged," he repeated. "A.O.K. here. But in China there is a solution to the agricultural problem. Tomorrow you'll be interested in looking at our latest satelphotos of Szechwan Province."

"Why? Why the hell should I be interested in China now? I want to know what's happening in the United States!"

When Dr. West was disconnected from his pumps and pacemaker, and wheelchaired to the office of Dr. George

Bruning, who was no medical doctor, the bland-faced Deputy Director of the CIA leaned forward over his desk. "You have us to thank for being alive. Years ago, under another presidential administration, one of our Canadian agents somehow acquired from a female informant the filing number of your cryodrawer in—was it the New Ottawa Reformation Center? But that administration didn't consider you of national importance, not enough to justify, shall we say, violation of Canadian sovereignty in order to remove you. In those days, Washington simply considered you an unusually unpopular mass murderer."

Dr. George Bruning smiled, and Dr. West thought he recalled the Deputy Director of the CIA as a much-photographed astronaut-scientist of some twenty years ago.

"We of what the newspapers term the Harvard Circle of the Agency," Dr. Bruning laughed, "try to be more creative than those old Agency pros of the 1990s. We do think you are of national importance."

Evidently so, Dr. West mentally agreed because the CIA had gone to the trouble of stealing his 2000 pound thermos bottle from the Cold Room in the New Ottawa Reformation Center. "When can I go upstairs and see the sun?"

"You're safer in the basement."

But each day as they briefed him on China, even renewing his Chinese language training, Dr. West became more restive. Why would they waste so much time on an obsolete Esk expert who had been out of circulation for more than sixteen years and knew nothing of what had happened in the rest of the world? He was no China expert. He had no intention of volunteering to go to China, which sounded even more dangerous and chaotic than twenty years ago.

To his surprise, one day a strangely aged Fred Gatson looked in at him. That balding boy wonder, who had replaced Dr. West as Director of Oriental Population Problems Research at the University of California, still seemed embarrassed. "You look pretty good, Dr. —uh, Joe, my boy. You look better than the rest of us."

"Why are you here?"

"I work here." By training, Fred originally had been a bacteriologist.

And another shockingly aged boy wonder also worked here. Dr. West hadn't seen him face to face since beer after Harvard. "It's good to see you, Tom."

As he watched Tom Randolph's calculating eyes, and remembered how Tom as an undergrad dynamited the Quad and never was caught, Dr. West didn't know whether it was good or not to see Dr. Tom Randolph standing here eyeing him. Their last contact had been by letter some nineteen years ago when Dr. West was back in Berkeley, married to Marthalik, and desperately trying for a position at any major university. He had written to his friend Tom at Duke, where Tom was Director of a parapsych research program funded by the Pentagon. Tom's reply had been cordially unhelpful, probably because he knew Dr. West was on the Defense Department's blacklist. At that time, Dr. West had felt angry because he was the one who put Tom on to psych as a grad student. Dr. West had scared the hell out of the kid with his own parlor-trick thought transmissions, and fascinated him even more. Because of Dr. West, Tom had gone on to fame and fortune, while Dr. West had given up parapsych as an unfruitful hobby. Now Tom was working for the CIA. "Can you walk yet?"

Dr. West's heart pounded alarmingly the day he finally walked, and Dr. Sammy Wynoski reassured him: "Not my specialization but I've been told the shortwave thawing process results in slight depositing of cholesterol fat within the arteries. You know, arteriosclerosis."

"Like my heart muscle isn't getting enough blood," Dr. West laughed, trying to conceal his fear of death as a tiny fist of pain squeezed his heart, and he sat down.

"You're being given an anticoagulant to lessen the temporary danger of clots. For minor chest pains due to overexertion, I suppose you should be carrying trinitroglycerine tablets." Dr. Wynoski shrugged. "We're not likely to lose you now," he laughed reassuringly. "Our cardiovascular consultant tells me our chances are better that your heart will repair itself than if surgical replacement with an androidal unit is attempted. We wouldn't want to lose you."

Apparently they were so reluctant to lose him, they wouldn't even let him go upstairs. "I want to see the sun."

"You can catch up on your knowledge of the world from down here," Dr. George Bruning soothed. "The Canadian Government has been frantic since they discovered their thermos bottles at the New Ottawa Reformation Center had been—shifted. They surmise you're in the United States. Because you are a convicted mass murderer second only in notoriety to the fabled Adolph—was it Eichmann, and your escape has aroused such outraged world-wide publicity, the U.S. Government is making every effort to apprehend you, if you should be in the United States."

In confused anger, Dr. West glanced at the concrete ceiling of the basement of the Central Intelligence Building.

Dr. George Bruning, Deputy Director of the CIA, laughed. "You can't go upstairs. The FBI is looking for you."

And Dr. Tom Randolph laughed as excitedly as an undergrad. "We have a better use for you than they do. You're the subje—the person in the United States with the ideal characteristics and past history."

Apologetically, Dr. Sammy Wynoski inserted a needle into Dr. West's arm. "You're lucky to have such a fine head of hair, Joe. You haven't aged like—uh, I—have."

Dr. West's consciousness faded, seeming to flicker for measureless weeks while he repeated and remembered whatever they told him to remember, and forgot whatever the disembodied voice, which sounded like Tom Randolph's, told him to forget.

7.
AIR FORCE VERSUS CIA

HUNTED BY THE FBI AS A CONVICTED MASS MURDERER—AND concealed by the Central Intelligence Agency for some baffling purpose, Dr. Joe West plodded across the dark runway. His footsteps clumped toward the silhouette of the aircraft.

His legs felt impossibly heavy. Swollen. But he thought his legs were as thin as when he was an undernourished scholarship student at Harvard Med School.

Imaginary heavy legs? Dr. Joe West's mouth split in a confused grin. Psychosomatic elephantiasis? What drugs had the CIA given him these last confusing weeks?

His face was prison-thin as he plodded toward the aircraft. Staring at the cavernous air intakes under the variable sweep wings, Dr. West recognized the bomber as the last of the air breathers.

Takeoff is rocket assisted, lot of Gs for my circulatory system, he thought nervously, remembering a startling amount about this SCRAMjet bomber he'd never seen before.

Probably when 2500 miles per hour or some God-awful starting speed was attained, the bomber's ramjets would become operative, and it would flash much faster like a torch through the night. Too fast!

The exertion of walking made him gasp. His heartbeats faltered. At his side his CIA bodyguard urged him on, and the distance to the bomber became excruciating.

Imaginary heavy legs? *Imaginary* was what one of the excitedly smiling faces in the Harvard Circle had assured him. But in another room in the basement of CIA headquarters another doctor had reassured him that any slight swelling

235

of his legs was merely a mild side effect from a mild sedative. Contradictory liars! Had they saved him or traded him
off? Not to the FBI——.

His legs dragged like anchors as the Air Force ground
crew boosted Dr. West up the steel ladder toward the belly
of the intruder bomber. In his bemused condition the tiny
orifices pitting the stainless steel skin of the bomber looked
like pores. This damned airplane was designed to fly too low
too fast! To protect its fuselage from the meteoric blaze of
air friction, did the pores exude sweat? He'd been told that
several of these SCRAMjets had crashed.

I don't want to burn, he thought, almost panicking as they
shoved him up into a confining metal tunnel in the aircraft.
As he crawled within the glittering tube, it hummed around
his eardrums and clinked and echoed. Someone was crawling
close behind him.

His legs dragging, Dr. West crawled with the strength of
his arms and shoulders. His damned legs felt twenty pounds
overweight. During surgery had they left in more than spong-
es? His face twisted in an uncertain grin. His muscles shivered.
His eyes blinked.

Mild sedative? Bullshit! He felt as disoriented as if he'd
undergone narcohypnosis.

His straining arms pulled him into the cramped electronic
countermeasures capsule of the bomber. Unexpectedly his
head bumped the low ceiling, and his eyes widened with
claustrophobia. The angry world closed on him like a fist. He
tried to turn. Not enough room for two men in here!

But a nameless Major was struggling in beside him. Massive and radiating heat, the Major grunted. The pressure door
clunked shut, sealing them in. Like twins in a womb they
squirmed and politely elbowed each other. Side by side, Dr.
West realized they were seated facing backward toward the
tail. Against him, the Major's blue eyes loomed so close they
blurred.

"Let me fix your crash—I mean—safety harness." The
Major's laugh was high-pitched for such a huge man. "Here's
your crash helmet, you CIA bastard! They——." A metallic
shriek exploded. Lurching forward, the bomber howled along
the runway, hurled itself.

Facing backward, Dr. Joe West felt his eyeballs bulging as if almost left behind while acceleration dragged the nylon straps into his chest. Gawking down at the one tiny heat-insulated viewplate between his boots, he glimpsed discolored clouds. The dark mountains of the California coastline were backlighted by the sunrise. Incongruously, obscenely reversing itself, the sunrise sank back into the mountains. Dr. West realized the bomber had activated its ramjets and was outspeeding the turning Earth. The dimming dawn drowned. The darkening Pacific Ocean glittered as this lone bomber hurried to overtake the night.

The Air Force Major squirmed. "Hope you—I mean—Central Intelligence—you spooks can't just send us off and kill us—without telling us the mission?" The Major's laughter rose like the safety valving of a steam boiler. "The generals shook our hands too much. The brass didn't level with us at the briefing."

"I wasn't at the briefing," Dr. West muttered.

"Why don't you CIA spooks—use your own black planes?" the Major again laughed explosively. "The way your Deputy Director is—buddying around with the President—your Central Intelligence already owns more manned aircraft than the Air Force. So send one of your own black clunkers. This SCRAMjet bomber cost fifty million bucks, and we got damn few of them."

Dr. West didn't know what to answer. His head hurt.

"That was a controlled-environment tank they hoisted into our bomb bay," the Major's voice persisted. "Too heavy. Hell of a long takeoff run. Heavy spray tank. Too heavy. So tell me we're going to spray crops."

Dr. West couldn't answer.

The Major shoveled sarcasm. "I mean—the Air Force is not officially at war, you know. I can't speak for the CIA. Have your spooks got Presidential approval for this mission? Does *he* know what's in the spray tank?"

"He may. I don't," Dr. West retorted.

"Like hell you don't," the Major laughed, squirming, trying to readjust the leather holster on his hip.

Dr. West contorted his body, trying to give the Major elbow room. He thought the Major was showing too explosive a personality. It was difficult to estimate how this Air Force officer would react if he recognized Dr. West. At least the Major was not piloting the bomber. Dr. West wet his dry lips.

The aircraft's flight steadied. "Autopilot's switched to astroinertial guidance," the Major said. "Up front Colonel Meller can take his nap. But I got a personal reason for finding out what's in the spray tank."

Dr. West wished the Major would shut up!

"You look sort of pale," the Major laughed. "Sick?"

Speechless, Dr. West shook his head. His eardrums were killing him.

Strapped to his side as closely as a Siamese twin, the Major eyeballed him. "You feel OK?"

Dr. West blinked at the Major's enormously close face. Plainly the Major had not recognized him from the TV news, and Dr. West tried to relax. Seventeen years ago in Canada, when people recognized Dr. West they tried to kill him.

"The Colonel up there in the control module and you and me, all three in the hot seat," the Major persisted. "We'll fry together, so what's in the spray tank?"

Dr. Joe West furrowed his brow. Clumsily, he tried to scratch his armpit without elbowing the Major. Within his nylon flying suit, Dr. West's body was perspiring in the padded cotton rags of a Chinese commune worker, deceased. He couldn't remember if he had been told what was in the spray tank.

Something alive was crawling up his ribs. Hungrily, it bit. Dr. West's gaunt face lighted in his pained grin. Evidently for authenticity the Central Intelligence Agency had salted his rags with genuine Chinese Communist fleas.

Another bite! Grinning like a befuddled skeleton, Dr. West imagined when his last drop of blood had been drunk, the fleas would arise in unison and shout: "Paper Tiger!" Then in glorious self-defense and in order to preserve international peace, the fleas would infiltrate the Major.

But the Major would not be another Burma or Pakistan. The Major's profile, twelve inches from the Doctor's eyes, appeared massive and forbidding. His teeth were grinding with tension. The Major would not negotiate with fleas. Or Chinese——.

The Major's thick forefinger poked the black box on the Doctor's lap. "That's wired to the spray tank. Hey, this dial is at 98.6 degrees! Is that Fahrenheit? That's the temperature of the human body. What has the CIA got us carrying?"

Dr. West smiled wryly. He still couldn't remember. He wasn't sure. He had known yesterday. He tried to think back into his scrambled-egg brain. Narcohypnosis, those sons of bitches.

"How should I know," Dr. West's mouth answered as if it had been trained. "I'm only a biotechnician who twists the dials and gets his ass shot off." But he remembered he was a medical doctor! "I'm not even CIA." That was true. Even his mouth wanted to disassociate him from the CIA. "I wasn't even at the flight briefing. You were."

"All they showed us was a turning point at the end of our fuel range." The Major opened his hand, then flattened it like a wing, and thrust! "Target a couple of hundred miles inland on the deck—minimum altitude. The Chicoms are more apt to accidentally knock us down with a tree or a hut roof or a radio tower than with AA missiles," the Major laughed, his forehead beaded with sweat. "I need to know what's in the spray tank?" He unzipped the front of his flying suit, revealing an Air Force blue Lemay jacket.

Dr. West's throat clicked, not much of a laugh. Here he was with an agricultural commune costume concealed under his flying suit, but the Major was in Air Force blues. He hoped this was only an oversight, a typical lack of coordination between Air Force and CIA as to escape dress. Their costumes didn't match. Obviously one man could not eject without the other. Aircraft this fast didn't carry parachutes——.

"What's in the spray——?"

"If the plane is hit——?"

The two men spoke simultaneously, but the Major proved to be the more courteous. He answered the Doctor's question.

"If we're hit, blooie!" The Major's teeth flashed white.

"I mean if we're only damaged."

"They'll never touch us. You're not sitting in one of your black-painted CIA clunkers now. This is the real Air Force. The Chinks haven't upgraded their AA missiles in thirty years."

Dr. West scratched his flea bites and supposed the Major probably was accurate. For the last forty years the Chinese had been concentrating their lagging industrial capacity on gigantic million pound thrust solid fuel ICBMs with big dirty hundred megaton warheads. Their patient international strategy had been continuous political infiltration and minimum warfare. Their opportunistic expansions into Burma and India had been shielded from U.S. countermoves by the avowed Chinese policy of massive nuclear retaliation.

The Chinese did not bother with modern antiaircraft or anti-ICBM systems. In the UN General Assembly the Chinese representative alternately stated that no umbrella was needed for their two billion-plus population and that all umbrellas are futile. When he was in a benevolent mood, the Chinese representative would smile and state that huge countries like the United States and China were equally vulnerable.

In the back of Dr. West's skull he realized, remembered, that this aircraft was aimed much deeper than a few hundred miles into China. It would be penetrating far beyond its fuel point of no return.

"Major, rephrasing my question, what happens to us if the plane has, say, mechanical difficulties?"

"Doc, you don't sound very confident about the maintenance procedures of your Air Force. Suppose we have a quadruple flameout right now over the Pacific," the Major laughed. "Forward in the control module, lonely old Colonel Meller pulls a lever. Blooie! His capsule ejects. Our sealed capsule ejects straight up, and at the top of the arc we get all lose and weightless like we're modern young guys in the Space Corps and not obsolete old manned aircraft personnel. Our drogue chute opens, then our big chute jerks open, and we come down to Earth. No sweat. We float in a whole Pacific Ocean of sweat. What I need to know is what's in our spray tank, Doc?"

Dr. West sat rigid. The Major twice had addressed him as "Doc."

"What dirty soup is in our spray tank, Doc," the Major's voice persisted.

Dr. West couldn't speak. He was afraid in a moment the Major would say, cat to mouse: "Doc, is your last name West?"

"You feel OK?" The Major's voice asked.

Dr. West pointed at his mouth, made swallowing gestures, shook his head. He couldn't speak, nauseated, his memory roaring at him: *Dr. West. Dr. West. Murderer. Genocidal murderer.*

The ramjet bomber howled and shuddered, and Dr. West realized it was slanting down into the denser atmosphere. Already the bomber was more than half way across the Pacific. The viewplate between his boots was black as the night beneath, mirroring his eyes.

"What's in the spray tank, Doc?" The Major sounded personally concerned. "You're too old to be a CIA biotechnician. I mean—they're kids in their twenties, just knob twisters. You're someone big. When those CIA spooks shoved you into the aircraft, one of them slipped his tongue. I heard him call you 'Doc.' So I figured you got a Ph.D. Maybe you're even a member of the Harvard Circle in the CIA. You must know what we're flying into——."

To Dr. West's relief the Major was proceeding along the wrong track. He still had not recognized Dr. West.

"That spray tank was airlifted into Edwards Air Force Base in a big old C-5," the Major persisted. "Word is the C-5 flew in from Arkansas. Pine Bluff, Arkansas. An arsenal there. Even I know that's where they breed the microbes. You're a top scientist or CIA or both." The Major slapped his pistol holster. "You're not expendable like me. I mean—this mission must be crucial. Is this the beginning? The spray tank? Are we going to kill millions of Chicoms?"

"No one will die."

"No one will die—my ass!" the Major exploded. "We'll be crossing the Chink coastline in a few minutes. In a few more minutes we'll reach our turn around point. We can't go any farther, and by that time something will happen, courtesy of you CIA spooks. I don't even think I want it to happen! The President said we would never be first to use germ warfare!"

"What do you want?" The Doctor's fear and rage and frustration exploded against the Major. "You're damned hysterical for an obsolete military mind who has been eating out of the public trough for twenty years! What do you want? A nice clean antiseptic hydrogen bomb?"

"Just tell me the mission, Doc." The Major's voice became surprisingly patient. "Colonel Meller and I got a right to know what we're risking our lives for. That spray tank may be warmed to 98.6 degrees but it's no nutrient solution for babies. There's no three-eyed Chink dragon monster swimming in that tank. I mean——," the Major closed his eyes.

Evidently the Major was listening to the Colonel through the intercom. He peered at Dr. West. "Instruments indicate we just crossed the Chinese coastline north of Canton."

"Hey!" the Major exclaimed. "Less than fifteen minutes and we got to turn around. Doc, what are your orders? You better start spraying!"

Dr. West sat there. "When the red light comes on—on this box, the sequence will begin." He remembered that much.

The aircraft shuddered as it rammed through the thickening atmosphere. A fiery glow engulfed the view plate beneath the Doctor's feet. ——We must be down on the deck, the Doctor thought, imagining mountains and cliffs and radio towers looming ahead.

The bomber was dependent upon the precise functioning of its terrain-following radar.

"You'd better press that spray button! We're nearing our fuel point of no return," the Major shouted louder than was necessary. An excited smile began squirming across his face. "There's no time left. Do it. Give it to him. We're as low as we can fly. Dust Mao III's armpits. God help the Chinese and all of us!"

Dr. West glanced at the trembling face. The Major's reactions seemed to be oscillating between excitement and revulsion.

"We're gonna give it to 'em! What are we giving the Chinks? Q-fever?" the Major's voice raced on. "Pneumonic plague when you press that black box on your lap? Mutated scrub typhus? Terrific? Terrible! I can see the black box is set for fifteen minutes spray duration. God! That's a long time. Fifteen minutes! Flying slowed down to 2000 miles per hour, fifteen minutes makes a spray line 500 miles long!"

"I'm not stupid," the Major shouted. "There's ten hours of night over South China. Ten hours before the sun dries out your aerosol microbes. Ten hours of damp night while the sleeping Chinese breathe. For ten hours the wind will blow. You CIA spooks always know which way the wind is blowing. Even if it's blowing only ten miles per hour across our spray line, that's a hundred miles the aerosol fog will sweep before the daylight comes. The Chinks! God! What's the incubation period?"

Dr. West did not know what to answer.

"I'm not stupid," the Major laughed excitedly. "We even studied arithmetic at the Air Academy. Five hundred miles of spray line multiplied by the wind carrying the fog a hundred miles across the line, covers five thousand square miles. No, that's fifty thousand square miles! How many sleeping Chinks in our fifty thousand square miles?"

"Unfortunately, very few," Dr. West retorted, and immediately regretted it.

"Very few? Like we're not really flying over China?" the Major laughed, and his face twisted in an agonized grin. "Wish the radar that's tracking us was our own. ——I wish this was an exercise over the Pacific. I mean—like when I was in the last FB-111Zs and I was so young I was unkillable. ——Hey, Colonel," he laughed, pressing the throat button of his helmet mike. "Colonel, tell me this mission is an exercise."

The Major stopped talking. Listening, he closed his eyes. He coughed. The Major coughed uncontrollably.

The Major's huge face whirled. "You CIA bastard!" he yelled into Dr. West's face. "The aircraft's captured by its own autopilot. Colonel says he's smashed the cockpit portion of the autopilot and he still can't gain control. Hidden somewhere on this aircraft is an operating autopilot you bastards have wired in. His electric controls don't control anything anymore. For some reason you bastards want to make sure we can't come home."

Consciously, Dr. West had not known this. But he must have known this was a one-way flight because his organism experienced neither violent surprise nor additional fear.

With disappointment, Dr. West wondered: After all the political trouble the Harvard Circle of the CIA had risked in stealing him from the Canadian prison's Cold Room, after all the valuable time the Harvard Circle had spent to rejuvenate him, to reeducate him and to carry out parapsychological preparations, after he had begun to think he was important again, they had decided he was no better than an expendable technician. Wasted. Expendable.

On the black box on his lap the red light flickered. Without thought, his thumb pressed the button as if it had been trained.

"Drop the spray tank!" the Major was begging the Colonel through his throat mike. "Save fuel. Save minutes. Listen, Colonel, we're not working for the CIA———."

Abruptly the Major closed his mouth as if the Colonel had said something abrupt to him.

From his holster, the Major hauled out the heavy .45 automatic pistol. At a range of six inches, its muzzle hole looked big enough to fall into. But Dr. West's thumb remained on the button. He ignored the gun.

"I'm not going to blow your brains out," the Major gasped. "I wanted to see what you'd do, you bastard. Colonel thinks it's possible the Air Force brass agreed to let the CIA do this to us. If that's patriotism, then I'm a motherless child."

The bomber howled and bucked through updrafts. Dr. West knew the aircraft was laying a trail of aerosol fog across the formerly desolate mountains of South Central China.

"They should have told us," the Major blurted. "I'm a professional. I should have been given the chance to volunteer. The Colonel and me, we're going to complete this spray run on the chance that the Air Force did agree to—sell us out. You CIA bastard, we've decided to complete the spraying mission."

The Major waved the almost prehistoric .45 automatic ineffectually. "Now do you feel better or worse, you bastard?"

Dr. West surreptitiously had managed to raise his thumb from the button. At first his thumb had not wanted to release the button, as if it had an overtrained one-track mind of its own. The flickering red light stayed on, and Dr. West knew the spraying was continuing anyway. Probably, if he never had pressed the button, a backup mechanism would have initiated the spraying. Probably he was not only expendable; he was superfluous.

Dr. West's mouth twisted with the quick pain of his thoughts. The Major had just stated that the Colonel and he had "decided" to complete the spraying mission. But the aircraft was flying itself, as predestined as a missile. It would be too cruel to point out to the Major that no room had been allowed for human decisions. Plainly, the Major needed to believe he had "decided." The Major still was clinging to his illusion of free decision.

"I would like to blow your brains out," the Major repeated, and savagely hand-operated the slide mechanism, ejecting an unfired cartridge from the automatic pistol.

Dr. West looked away. He wondered if other military personnel still wore .45 automatics. His own grandfather had kept one beneath his folded T-shirts in the top drawer. Way back in World War II, his grandfather had carried it at Kasserine Pass. He said he never fired it. Vaguely, Dr. West remembered that the .45 Colt Government automatic was— had been Model 1911. 1911? Four generations of officers must have carried these hand-cannons. Before the First World War, this very heavy caliber automatic had been designed to knock down charging bolo-waving Moro tribesmen, or so his grandfather had said——.

The spraying aircraft bucked savagely, whether from an antiaircraft missile explosion or a mountain updraft Dr. West did not know. The Major cursed, and Dr. West smiled because it felt good to know that someone else was more frightened than he was. The Major was quite a character——.

The Major appeared to be about forty years old, and obsolete. He had picked the wrong armed service. There now were five armed services competing for younger men. The most clean-cut young men who wanted to completely leave this crowded world volunteered for the Space Corps, and made world-televised crash landings on the Martian craters. More subtle young men with a flair for foreign languages joined the CIA, which had acquired its own submarine navy and VTOL air force to deliver its armored vehicles and heavily armed guerilla war experts. The Navy still owned shoals of old nuclear subs and one hulking aircraft carrier and the arrogant Marines. The Army had enlarged its aerial cavalry, aggrandizing with its SST aerial delivery system the delivery of "iron" bombs, and triumphantly skimming its GEM tanks over BOTH land and sea, while politically seizing the Air Force's latest obsolete ground-launched antimissile system. The poor old Air Force was left with its BAMBI space-launched antimissile system, its vast seedbeds of ICBM silos, a few transport planes for senators, 900 triple-purpose VTOL swing-wing FBA-211 three-pilot interceptor-bombers, plus only a dozen of these big intercontinental SCRAMjet bombers, and the Major and his .45.

"If by any chance you CIA turncoats have rigged the autopilot to deliver our aircraft to the Chinks," the Major blurted, "I *will* blow your brains out."

"If we land anywhere we'll be too lucky," Dr. West retorted. "Right now we're spraying across the interior of China. The people down there have been indoctrinated for three generations that we bring germ warfare. They'll greet us with yells and shrieks and fingernails and sharp hoes."

At this, the Major showed his big teeth. "You're full of fun and games." He thudded his .45 automatic against his knee. "Chinks won't make me apologize and curse my country on international television. Your two CIA jerks, what were their names, Johnston and Mitsui? Pitiful performances. Doesn't the CIA issue cyanide capsules? Couldn't those two jerks swallow? In the Air Force we don't need cyanide capsules." He waved his .45 like a magic wand. "If we crash, I'll use the first five bullets on Chinks."

Dr. West remembered that his grandfather's .45 automatic contained a seven-shot clip. The Major would be hoarding two final shots.

Dr. West remembered the tortured face of Johnston replayed on TV tape.

The televised faces of Johnston and Mitsui had been bounced off the Telstar satellite confessing to everything from dropping virulent hepatitus bombs to potato bugs. Their agonizing scenes had set record Nielsen Ratings for their nonpaying sponsor, the Chinese Federation of Nations, and sold American mothers on some advantages of isolationism.

The aircraft quivered. The red light on the black box on Dr. West's lap flickered out. The spray run was complete.

As if on cue, the bomber exploded.

Dr. West, who had rejected life, who had willingly faced the mob, who had made the hard moral decision for Eskimo genocide, who had faced his conviction and the angry fist of world opinion, Dr. West screamed for life.

In total darkness his body was whirled, slower and slower. He floated in his nylon safety harness, weightless as a drowned man.

An abrupt jolt whiplashed his neck. The swooping side-to-side revolving swinging rocking slammed his head against the wall of the capsule. Dr. West finally realized the capsule had been ejected from the bomber, and the capsule's parachute already had opened.

In the hoarse breathing descending pendulum silence of the capsule, Dr. West's hand crept to his slippery mouth. He bit his hand. The capsule was descending regardless of what he did. The explosion, the ejection from the bomber had been programmed. The smiling faces in the Harvard Circle of the Central Intelligence Agency had delivered him to China.

"Why me?" Those smiling sons of bitches, what had they planned for him to do? "I never volunteered for this!" he gasped. "You sons of bitches, my narcohypnosis has worn off. You may think you conditioned my responses like an experimental animal's. I've got news for you. It's worn off. I'm free!" Whatever program was in his skull, as it emerged Dr. West determined he would snafu it, foul it up.

"I'll sell out, I'll bug out, I owe no allegiance to a country who would do this to a man. I've got one ambition, to save my neck and to hell with you!"

The capsule struck the earth. His head slammed down. Dr. West raised his head in the blinding darkness of the capsule. He shook the Major's slack shoulder. A gurgling sound———.

With shock, Dr. West felt his foot was wet. He groped down. Too much liquid to be blood. The gurgling sound was more distinct when he stopped breathing.

Water was leaking into the smashed bottom of the capsule.

A one in a million spot landing, Dr. West wondered. Instead of striking the mountainsides in this formerly desolate western interior of Szechwan Province, had the capsule descended into a precipitious river valley where water was———. Szechwan Province?

"Those sons of bitches!" Until now he had not remembered the landing was to be in Szechwan Province. "Memory—triggered!" He realized the landing of the capsule had unblocked data the CIA had drilled into his memory. Now he could even visualize the map. The terrain, changing sets of spy-in-the-sky photographs were riffled before his inner eyes.

The slender fingers of Dr. George Bruning had paused beside an oval dot on the aerial photo. "Another new irrigation reservoir." Dr. Bruning's calmly intelligent face smiled across the table at him.

"You son of a bitch," Dr. West said to the darkness of the capsule.

Dr. George Bruning was no medical doctor. He was a former boy wonder, a former geophysicist, a former scientific astronaut whose two lovable children and smiling wife and publicity in *Life* mag had resulted in his election to the House of Representatives. His political defeat by a movie star two years later resulted in his appointment to the President's Scientific Advisory Staff. He was photographed playing croquet with the President. He was promoted to Chief Scientific Advisor.

The unexpected defection of Australia to neutralism resulted in wholesale firings in the Central Intelligence Agency.

Dr. George Bruning was appointed by the President as Deputy Director of the CIA. George might be inexperienced in the use of cloak and dagger but he soon showed himself to be an organizer. His own agency emerged within the Agency and gained the newspaper label "Harvard Circle." By a noncoincidence, not only had Dr. George Bruning and his four top assistants attended Harvard as undergraduates, so had the President of the United States.

"So what's the big deal?" Dr. West hissed, struggling to unbuckle his nylon safety harness, while no explanation, only odd details, emerged from the outer layer of his memory—instructions.

He remembered that there was a special landing kit attached under the seat. A detail, but it was a remarkable feat of memory because he had never looked under the seat. His hand felt it though. He could visualize its contents laid out on a white table. Total partial recall.

"You sons of bitches, you're rationing me details." Dr. West's hands lifted the metal kit and attached it to a prearranged hook inside the voluminous padded jacket of his Chinese commune worker's costume.

"You're all very stupid if you think I can pass for a Chinese just because I'm a student of Oriental population problems." Dr. West knew his laughter was freighted with hysteria. Plainly he was outfitted in this agricultural commune costume for some reason other than to pass as a Chinese during interrogation by Chinese.

Water continued to gurgle into the capsule. Dr. West's nostrils detected the faint yet fetid odor that emanates from streams polluted by humanity. There were no sounds of people outside the capsule.

Not even a frog croaked in what must be night outside.

From his escape kit, Dr. West's hands detached a small, heavy, no larger than a woman's compact, radio. He remembered it was an automatic signal sender. In order to extend the aerial his hands were trained to locate the upper air vent in the darkness, to twist it open and project the aerial like a collapsible fishing rod into the Chinese night. Dr. West crouched in the blackness of the capsule with his legs in the rising water and his thumb on the signal-send switch of the miniaturized ionospheric-ricochet radio beacon. He knew it was broadcasting a continuous signal to someone.

He supposed his body had been trained in a mock-up of this ejection capsule, but he couldn't remember that yet. "You chose me, didn't you trust me? Only part of my memory, part of my conditioning has been unblocked. But I won't wait for the cues like a trained dog. I'm going to tear apart your conditioning, Sammy, you son of a bitch."

He remembered Dr. Sammy Wynoski inserting a needle into his arm.

He remembered before that, the first face he recognized after his rebirth out of the cryothermos bottle from the New Ottawa Reformation Center had been Dr. Sammy Wynoski's vulpine face, startlingly aged. Not so startling, thirty-three years had passed for Sam since they said good-bye, each clutching his graduation award from Harvard's School of Medicine.

While Dr. Joe West returned to California, and finally achieved the exalted position of Director of Oriental Population Problems Research at the University of California, was canned, discovered the Eskimo population explosion, lost Marthalik, and was imprisoned for "attempted genocide," Dr. Sammy Wynoski said he'd been quietly specializing in chemopsychiatry. He had an increasing number of weekend jobs as a medical interrogation consultant for the Central Intelligence Agency. When fellow Harvardman George Bruning was appointed Deputy Director of the Agency, Sammy Wynoski had answered his country's call, his Harvard buddy's phone call, and became a full-time member of the Harvard Circle of the CIA.

Thus when Dr. Joe West and Dr. Sammy Wynoski parted consciousness this year in the basement of CIA headquarters, they were at opposite ends of a hypodermic needle which Dr. Sammy Wynoski was apologetically inserting into Dr. Joe West's arm.

"Joe, you haven't aged like—uh, I—have——," Sammy muttered.

Passing out, Dr. West had been in no condition to reply then, but now——. "You bunch of amateurs," Dr. West muttered, crouching in the flooding capsule. "Have you got any rational plan for me? What do I do next?"

Beside him, the Major groaned. Dr. West's pulse rate jumped. His wrist gave a nervous jerk of its own volition.

"Where's my gun?" the Major's voice blurted, and then he whispered, "Any Chinks out there? ——What you doing?"

"Nothing," Dr. West's voice replied soothingly. "Our best hope is to stay in the capsule." For some reason, his fingers twisted his wristwatch to the underside of his wrist.

"Damn capsule—flooding," the Major grunted. "We got to get out of here fast." From the thrashing, it sounded as if the Major was having difficulty disengaging himself from his safety harness and assorted intercom wires and oxygen tubes.

"We stay here!" Dr. West's voice stated, his pulse rate accelerating as if readying his body for violent combat. He realized—he remembered, when he tipped back his wrist as he was doing now an injection needle emerged from his wristwatch.

"If the faceless airman becomes uncooperative," a disembodied voice had explained, "simply prick him with the wristwatch needle." Otherwise Dr. West was to wait. He was not to kill the purposely "faceless" airman until the proper strategic moment. Dr. West began to shiver. He had not remembered this until now.

He had no intention of murdering the Major. He had no intention of murdering anyone, not even a Chinese.

"Those sons of bitches!" Dr. West blurted, in his memory studying Dr. Sammy Wynoski's apologetic face.

"Yeah," the Major wheezed, probably also referring to the CIA and the two men collided in the darkness.

Dr. West realized he almost had jabbed the Major with the needle watch. With his other hand, Dr. West tried to unbuckle the wristband.

His fingers struggled against his orders. His fingers wouldn't obey him. He felt as frustrated as a spastic as he gasped and sloshed about in the water. The wristwatch fell off his wrist. Success! One victory against the Harvard Circle.

"You all right?" the Major demanded.

"Yes, fine. I feel much better. Let's get out of here. You're in command, Major."

"I'm going to unbolt the hatch."

"Hadn't we better wait in the capsule?" Dr. West's smooth voice suggested.

"But you just said for us to—let's get out," the Major hissed; Dr. West was contradicting himself.

"The ignorant Chinese peasants can't reach us, can't torture us if we stay in the capsule." Dr. West's mouth talked fast. "Yes, they'll think the capsule is one of theirs. Our best hope is for the People's Militia to reach us. Still better is for the Maoist police to find us before the people lynch us. The capsule isn't sinking anymore. The water isn't rising. Probably we're mired in a rice paddy. Our only hope is to stay in the capsule."

"You gone crazy or something? A minute ago you wanted out——. Get out of this capsule!" The Major bodily shoved Dr. West through the hatch into the mud.

Under Dr. West's submerged hands was the bristly feel of newly transplanted rice seedlings.

He lifted his gaze up a steeply terraced mountainside to the night sky.

Behind him, the Major thrashed out of the capsule into the mud and sloshed about in the darkness. With a gasp and a curse, the Major slipped off the crumbling edge of the narrow terrace into the rice paddy below. These terraced rice paddies were little wider than a man's arm span.

The capsule had not descended into a river valley. Dr. West saw that they had landed on a mountainside so steep that all this terracing would have been uneconomic for man. Immense labor would be required for the limited number of catties of rice the mountain could produce.

The odors of the terrace-makers permeated the night air.

"Stinks like human—fertilizer," the Major scrambled back up the hand-packed mud slope. "Millions of Chinks!"

"Not Chinese." In his memory Dr. West visualized photographs of only five years ago showing these mountains desolate and dry, completely uneconomic for rice cultivation. During the last two or three years, incredible energy had been expended on these mountain terraces. The mountains were too steep, the terraces too small for efficient use of machinery. Human cultivators would consume too much rice, more energy laboring here than the submarginal rice harvests would replace. Yet these mountains had been laboriously terraced, magically irrigated, freshly hand-planted with bristly new rice seedlings.

"The moon is rising." Like glittering liquid steps, the terraced rice paddies shimmered down the mountainside into the dark canyon.

"I smell smoke," the Major whispered. "Millions of Chinks down there."

Dr. West did not bother to disagree with him. Turning, he looked for the dim whiteness of another giant parachute, but there was no sign of Colonel Meller's escape capsule.

The Major held up his shining wet hand, feeling for the direction of the night breeze. "Bad! I'm afraid the wind is coming from where we sprayed. Hell of a note if we get infected by our own spray. Got to move out of here fast!"

Again, Dr. West did not bother to disagree with him. Dr. West's hand reached into his nylock flying suit and groped into his commune worker's rags, where his fingers closed around the handle of a dagger he had not known was sheathed there.

The Major pulled at his shoulder. "Move out! You may be inoculated against—whatever it is, but I'm not."

"You don't need to be terrified of this microbiological," Dr. West's voice replied smoothly. "Probably it is a bacterial infection of the staph-strep group——."

"Let's go, let's go!" the Major interrupted.

"A mild infection may settle in the Fallopian tubes and in the spermatic ducts."

"Sterilized," the Major grunted in partial understanding. "Kill 'em before they're born. Yeah, kill Chinks before they're conceived. Yeah, typically CIA. ——Let's get the hell out of here."

"I'm just guessing about bacterial spray." Dr. West was remembering the young-old face of Dr. Fred Gatson, bacteriologist.

Harvard grad Fred Gatson had been even younger than Dr. West when they were the big wheels in Oriental Population Problems Research. When Dr. Joe West was fired as

Director, amazingly, Dr. Fred Gatson had been appointed to replace him.

Dr. West thought. Fred had no compunctions about breeding more virulent "birth control" bacteria in those days even though they had potentialities for sterilizing the human race, exterminating mankind. They were more menacing than atomic war.

When the CIA "freed" Joe West from his life sentence and imprisoned him in the basement of CIA headquarters, Dr. Fred Gatson reappeared with a receding hairline. It turned out Fred had left Cal and scrambled still higher up the ladder of success. Dr. Fred Gatson now was a member of the Harvard Circle of the CIA. Facing Dr. West, Fred appeared uncomfortable but determined. In Dr. West's memory, Fred opened his mouth. He was speaking, presumably about his latest accomplishments, but he appeared unhappy.

In his memory, Dr. West could see Fred's lips moving, but he couldn't hear his voice. What Fred was telling him seemed blocked out of his memory. In frustration and hope, Dr. West wondered if a bacterial mutation finally had been developed which would sterilize or even kill Esks but not humans. If so, this spraying flight over China should be the culmination of his life. Had they finally begun bacterial control of the Esk population explosion before it overwhelmed the world?

Suspiciously, Dr. West felt no happiness. He didn't believe such an Esk-selective bacteria finally had been developed. He didn't believe this was what Fred Gatson's silently moving mouth had said. Fred's words had been censored from his surface memory. Why had the CIA delivered him to China?

"This spray doesn't affect people," Dr. West's voice said reassuringly to the Major. "You don't need to fear personal sterilization. The bacterial mutation is quite specific." Dr. West couldn't believe what his mouth was saying. "It only affects Esks."

"Eskimos? They're people. Same species. So it *will* affect me. You're lying so I won't panic," the Major blurted. "But I have no intention of panicking. Let's get away from this capsule! Double-time! If Chink peasants catch us here where we sprayed, I mean—we won't father anything. They'll butcher us. Right now I'm not worried about my virility. Let's get out of here."

The Major's heaving chest made a close target but Dr. West managed to uncurl his own fingers from the handle of the concealed dagger. Those CIA sons of bitches were determined he should kill someone. Dr. West was equally determined he would not kill anyone.

"We'll have to take the escape radio," Dr. West's voice said.

"What radio are you talking about?"

"Continuous signal sender." Dr. West removed it from the capsule. It barely filled the palm of his hand.

Hope returned to the Major's voice. "The CIA *is* looking out for us! Is a CIA snatch plane going to pick us up? Or is this a guerrilla wavelength?"

"Guerrilla——," Dr. West lied; it was the communications wavelength of the Maoist Police.

"Let's go!" The Major was pulling at him again, making Dr. West's involuntary nervous system clench as if he had been conditioned to kill—— .

"Doc, our best chance is to get far far away from this capsule before daylight shows it to the Chinks down there." The Major needed to clutch at any hope. "Then we hide and wait for the guerrillas."

Dr. West tried to keep up with the Major as he lumbered and splashed along the terraces. Joe West suspected there were few, if any, Chinese asleep down there in the canyon. His legs dragged. His legs felt so heavy——.

His hand refused to let go of it, but he wanted to throw away the signal sender. Why should he obediently give himself up to the Maoist police? "Those CIA sons of bitches!" Dr. West couldn't make his fingers let go of the signal sender. "They really conditioned the carrying of this radio into my skull."

"What?" The Major looked back.

"Nothing." Joe West staggered on.

With devilish energy, the Major began clambering up the sides of terraces, ascending the mountain like a monkey up a giant staircase. Dr. West's legs grew heavier and heavier, and he gasped for breath, dragging himself up over terraces mainly by the strength of his arms. His legs felt like swollen corpses. "Mental elephantiasis? Imaginary heavy legs? Hell!" Dr. West wondered when he would remember exactly what they had done to his legs.

"Hurry up," the Major hissed from far above.

But Joe West was already exhausted. He gasped for breath, and his heart thudded unevenly. As he struggled to climb over the lip of a terrace into the next paddy, the muddy signal sender slipped out of his hand. The tiny radio slid back down the terrace wall. Dr. West clung there, then triumphantly bellied over into the rice paddy, leaving the radio.

His hands wanted to scramble back down and search for the signal sender. "Oh, but you can't make me do it," he whispered. "No CIA assassins sitting safe in Washington give me orders." He crawled forward across the paddy and struggled up the terrace above, leaving the radio lost in the darkness. "To hell with Harvard! I'm free."

The Major came sliding back down. "Let me help you. That's OK, you're not in shape. Let's go. I won't leave you, Doc."

The Major unmercifully hoisted Joe West to his feet. Supporting him, urging him, dragging him, the Major hauled Joe West up the terraced side of the mountain. Dr. West's legs kept sagging.

"That's OK, do your best," the Major gasped. "We're Americans. We'll stick together."

Dr. West wondered what the Major would say if and when he discovered Dr. West was wearing a Chinese commune worker's clothes under his nylock flying suit.

"Doc, Doc! Hey, where's the little radio?" The Major began to shake him, to search his outer pockets.

"In my hand. No, I dropped it."

"You dropped it?" the Major shrilled. "You just dropped our only chance."

The Major scrambled back down the terrace, leaving Dr. West lying in the mud listening to the Major sloshing about below him. There was not one chance in a million that anyone could find that signal sender in the dark.

Dr. West lay there listening to his own uneven heartbeat. His heart sounded like a candidate for an electronic pacemaker.

"Best way to beat the Harvard Circle—for my heart to stop." Dr. West stared up at the moon: the Harvard Circle peered down at him from his imagination.

Dr. George Bruning—Deputy Director, CIA.

Dr. Sammy Wynoski—Chemopsychiatrist.

Dr. Fred Gatson—Population control expert; bacteriologist.

But there were two more members of the Harvard Circle: Dr. West's irregularly beating heart cued one of them out of his blocked memory.

Dr. Einar R. Johansen had not been a direct acquaintance of Dr. West's, but Dr. West had recognized him in the basement of the CIA headquarters. The eccentric Dr. Johansen was so easily recognizable. He was only slightly withered by the thirty years which had passed since Dr. West regularly saw his protruding face in medical journals. In those days Dr. Johansen had been the nation's most inventive heart surgeon.

More recently Dr. Johansen had earned a Ph.D. in bioelectrical engineering from Harvard. He was better known now as an inventive neurosurgeon than as a heart surgeon, and still better known for his press conferences. Reportedly he was the doctor who said: "The older I get, the softer my head, so the more I soak up. I learn more now than when I was a kid of forty. At this rate, when I'm eighty I'll revolutionize medicine." This enraged the A.M.A.

On pop-science TV shows, Dr. Johansen played with electric eels—without wearing rubber gloves. He was ingeniously grounded against electrocution. He was the first surgeon to design and install an electronic heart pacemaker which was powered by the patient's neuron electricity. No internal batteries to wear out, no wires to fray. "My pacemaker lasts as long as the patient. Yes, longer!"

The A.M.A. disapproved of such jovially self-advertising talk. Dr. Johansen's picture no longer appeared in medical journals. His smiling horseface appeared in space journals. NASA had retained him as a consultant to the Bio-Power project. The goal was a subminiature solid state transmitter utilizing a lifetime power supply from the electrical energy of the astronaut's body.

Where had the transmitter been implanted, the leg, the buttock? With a pained grin, Dr. West's teeth gleamed in the moonlight.

Dr. West remembered Dr. Johansen's wrinkled face bending over him. An operating table? "Before I'm through, sir," the old voice croaked, "you'll be a veritable electric eel. Hah!"

Then the anesthetic engulfed him.

Dr. West lay in the muddy rice paddy. His legs ached. He knew the Harvard Circle had not gone to all that trouble just to install a duplicate signal sender in his leg.

High below the stars an aircraft droned overhead, its red and green wing lights flitting. Dr. West knew the CIA had not commandeered an Air Force ramjet to fly him over China merely to spray the Esks. An expendable technician could do that. Yet the plan must have something to do with the Esks. The CIA had selected him, and he was the man with the most unpopular theory about the Esks. He was the man who had been convicted of attempted genocide of the Eskimos. He was the most unpopular man in the world.

If the Maoist police caught him alive, if they recognized him, remembering him as Dr. West, the Mass Murderer of the Helpless Eskimos, the Chicoms wouldn't kill him if they realized he was Dr. West.

The Chinese Federation of Nations joyfully would use him for political purposes. Other Americans had confessed to anything. Dr. West knew he was no stronger than they——.

He smiled with the ultimate fear and fumbled into his layers of wet clothing for the dagger. The Maoists would have enjoyed parading him. Even Mao III, who had been neither seen nor photographed for three years, had expressed the desire to face "the murderous Dr. West, eye to eye!"

Dr. West struggled to remove the dagger from its sheath. "Those fools, those stupid CIA sons of bitches!" If the Chicoms took him alive, their glib diplomats would use him like acid to dissolve any last world goodwill the United States had managed to retain. Piously the Chinese representatives would tell the General Assembly: Any nation who would parachute the murderous convict Dr. West upon another nation must be guilty of more than germ warfare, more than genocide——.

Dr. West spat in the mud. He was unable to make his hand draw out the dagger. "You poor bastard. You're as helpless as an imperialist potato bug complete with implicating little parachute and U.S. insignia on your wing covers. Even the CIA can't be that stupid. They *must* see one move beyond what I'm seeing."

The Major emerged grunting over the edge of the terrace. "Found it. I'll carry the signal sender now."

Dr. West opened his mouth. He wanted to tell the Major that the signal sender was tuned for the Maoist police wavelength, but he couldn't get the words out. Instead he followed the Major across the rice paddy and up the next terrace, and the next, and the next——.

The Major came back and helped him again. "Do your best. Easy does it, old man."

Dr. West was not an old man, at least he had been a vigorous young man when he was sentenced to prison. Theoretically, sixteen years in the Cold Room shouldn't have aged him. But his legs were an old man's legs, unbelievably heavy.

"When we get to the top," the Major gasped, "I'm hoping there'll—uninhabited canyon on the other side. We can hide until—guerrillas trace—our radio signal."

"In China, no place is uninhabited anymore," Dr. West said.

"You got the wrong attitude—mustn't give up—your CIA guerrillas—come for us." The Major raised the tiny radio signal sender—which was squeaking their location to any Maoist police radio location finding equipment within a radius of fifty miles.

By the time the Major had half-carried Dr. West to the top of the mountain ridge, the moon was rapidly descending toward the mountains of Sinkiang. The flat top of the ridge glittered the moon's reflection.

"Irrigation reservoir up here," the Major gasped. "Look at the big pipes and hoses and pumps. Never knew the Chinks had it in 'em!"

"That's a high voltage power line leading down into your uninhabited canyon," Dr. West said.

"Doesn't mean there's Chinks down there. Never give up!" The Major led the way down the other side of the mountains.

They fell down terraces, sloshed through rice paddies, tripped over irrigation pipes, slid down endless terraces into the faintly humming canyon. This was how the Maoists had forced impossible mountains to yield rice crops. At the bottom of the canyon the power line would lead to an atomic generator plant.

At the bottom of the canyon, the two men scrambled over an enormous concrete pipe. Dr. West heard the water rushing inside. With unlimited atomic-electric power the Chinese were piping water across vast distances. With an unlimited number of obedient hands, the Maoists had ordered terracing of mountains previously considered "impossible for wet rice cultivation."

Impossible these tiny rice paddies were for Chinese commune workers who needed at least 1800 calories of rice-energy per day. If Chinese tended these inefficient vertical fields, they would need to eat the entire harvest in order to survive and multiply. There would be no surplus. But Dr. West knew that these tiny paddies were hand-tended by beings who could not only survive; they could labor from dawn to dark and multiply like rabbits on only 600 calories of rice-energy per day!

As the Major led the way across the dark canyon, he stumbled over the sleeping body of the Maoist solution to the agricultural problem.

"Don't strangle him. Don't kill him," Dr. West hissed. "The man's an Esk."

But the Major tightened his grip on the gurgling throat. "Got to kill him. Would yell for help."

"He's sure to be an Esk. I assume he's descended from at least three generations of Maoist conditioning. I believe if I ordered this Esk to go back to sleep, he would go back——."

"You assume—you believe," the Major panted angrily. "I now—he stinks like a Chink." There was a vertebral crunch, and the body shuddered and quivered like a dying fish. "He was a Chink!"

Dr. West did not try to explain how he knew the man was an Esk merely by standing near him.

Dr. West followed the Major down the canyon along the side of the roaring concrete pipe. Someone, perhaps a thousand miles away, turned a rheostatic switch which electromagnetically opened giant valves, and the roar of irrigation water within the pipe increased. Ahead of Dr. West, the sky grew white with dawn.

The Major's gaze darted frantically from side to side. He appeared to be searching for a place of concealment, but all the natural vegetation in the canyon had been gathered, plucked, uprooted to feed the miserable cooking fires of the Esks. The two men threaded their way among sleeping lumps of cloth.

Around dead fires, the faces of the sleeping Esks were animated, twitching, smiling, baring their teeth, seemingly more alive than when the Esks were conscious.

Clutching his .45 as though it was his mother's hand the Major tiptoed on, then looked back. It was evident he wanted to turn back. The further down the canyon they went, the more numerous the sleeping Esks. The brightening dawn illuminated the Major's frightened face. He kept glancing up at the terraced mountainsides for some place to hide. Yet he stubbornly continued down the canyon.

In the canyon, sleeping clumps of men, women, children, lay clustered together for warmth—all around the two quietly walking men. The Major's hand closed on Dr. West's shoulder, transmitting his shivering fear to the Doctor. "Tell me they're Eskimos," the Major breathed. "If they're Chinese——."

"Chinese would be awake and screaming at us right now," Dr. West whispered. "The Esks don't pay much attention to us. Observe, the Esks sleep intensely—as if they're on another planet when they're asleep. Look at that smiling face. We've tried truth drugs, but no human has been able to learn what dreams the Esks have. Awake, the Esks don't know. It's as if the Esks lead *two* lives, concurrently yet separately. That is why the Chinese word for them is Dream Persons."

A buzzer sounded, resounded up and down the canyon. Blankly, the Esks stood up. There was none of the yawning and stretching, eye-rubbing and giggling, hawking and spitting which would have characterized real Arctic Eskimos or Chinese or Americans. The awakened faces of the Esks began to smile. The men and some of the women started climbing the steep trails among the rice terraces, their hoes already in their hands. Efficiently they did not urinate until they stood in the rice paddies. Up there on the terraces, the Esks began hoeing without breakfast.

"What do we do now?" the Major whispered, still shivering as if he expected to be assailed by screaming Chinese with upraised hoes. "Do you think they've sent someone off to telephone for the Chinese soldiers?" He pointed at an overhead wire.

Dr. West looked down at the Esk children crowding around smiling. And he was smiling. Their faces reflected his smile, lighting up with joy almost like children's faces anywhere. Little Joe——. Little Martha——.

Dr. West squatted down and tried to talk with them, using the central Eskimo dialect he had learned in the Arctic. He tried introducing Cantonese words, then Mandarin Chinese——. He looked up at the Major and shrugged and wearily smiled and shook his head. "These people—the Esks have increased millions of times in numbers since I identified them in the Arctic twenty-two years ago. Individually, they—each generation has deteriorated as to outward awareness and adaptability. The original little group I studied in the Arctic— they were excellent imitators of the Eskimos. But these people, these children, they're almost nonverbal. They're not imitating the Chinese. They're not trying very hard to imitate anything human."

A heavily pregnant woman prodded one of the circle of boys and made upward motions with her hands. Evidently the boy was big enough; he should be up there working on the rice terraces. He appeared to be about six years old.

"That boy is about a year old," the Doctor said. "The wonderful and terrible thing is that these people's bodies mature so much more efficiently than ours. Their prenatal development is as perfectly straightforward as if God had had a plan—this time."

Dr. West became excited and disturbed as he always did when he launched into the subject that had overwhelmed his life. "Why should our human fetuses take nine months to be born. Because of our evolutionary history on this planet, the growth of our embryos follows the old paths, gills appear and are absorbed. An obsolete tail begins and disappears. Primitive appendages from our evolutionary past are recapitulated. This is our heritage from the billions of years of changing life forms on this Earth." Dr. West hurled the bitter question no one could answer. "Now we are among people whose babies are born in a month and mature in three years. That does not reflect the evolutionary history on this planet. Now tell me if the Esks are human?"

"You murderer!" the Major hissed unexpectedly. "Finally I've figured out who you are. You genocidal maniac! You've *got* to be Dr. West. On the TV news, your escape from Canada about six months ago. You narrow maniac, are you telling me the Eskimos aren't human?"

"These Esks aren't. The Eskimos are, if there are any real Eskimos still alive. Don't tell me even a calloused military mind like yours has been softened by the '*Esks are Eskimos, love the Eskimos*' campaign."

"You murdered harmless Eskimos. Look at these little children. We just sprayed 'em," the Major bleated, as if it had been a death spray.

The children scrambled about unconcernedly. A little girl clung to Dr. West's leg.

"Don't tell me that little girl isn't human," the Major said. "She is human. Look at her little hands, her ears, her eyes, you murderer."

"You were happier when you thought we were spraying Chinese children——," Dr. West retorted.

The Major made an abrupt move with his .45, and let his arm drop down hopelessly. "You're insane, criminally insane, you were convicted of genocide and sent to a prison for the criminally insane. The Eskimos are the world's happiest, most cooperative people."

"And you believe that murderers should be executed," Dr.

West challenged, hoping the Major would fire the gun, kill him, foul up all the intricate, unknown plans of the CIA.

"These *are* people," the Major pressed. "Call them Esks or Eskimos, they're just as human as we are. Right home at Edwards Air Force Base, whole crews of happy Eskimos are working at the base, more of them all the time. Wonderful obedient happy people, and you tell me they're not human."

"You sound like a bleeding heart or a Maoist," Dr. West retorted. "A rehash of the half-truths when I was crucif— excoriated before the United Nations General Assembly. You're remembering the Chinese Communist Party line."

"You're the traitor. Genocidal maniac is the truth," the Major added more calmly. "That whole U.S. Administration was voted out of office at the next election."

"The U.S. Government was innocent," Dr. West replied, "but a lot of voters believed the Communist Party line. It's funny now. My guilt rubbed off all over, even though only I made the decision to use the bacterial spray cans. If you believe the Chinese fulminations of seventeen years ago when I was convicted, I made old Adolph Eichmann look like an innocent saint. I was the threat to all the yellow skins and brown and black. I was the racial butcher."

"——because the Eskimos weren't bothering anybody." The Major couldn't keep his voice steady. "It wasn't their fault that radioactive cesium is concentrated by the lichen-caribou food chain. The Eskimos always had eaten caribou. None of you wise-guy know-it-all doctors told them not to——."

"The extreme mutational theory has no basis in fact. When will you stop confusing Eskimos with Esks?"

"They're the same. It's a word trap, a phony word trap to justify your plan for world genocide of the Eskimos. The Eskimos can't help it if they've started multiplying fast."

"Major, you don't know anything, except what you've recalled in bits and pieces from old TV newscasts of seventeen years ago when you were about twenty-three and so busy with girls and booze you weren't paying any attention to the rest of the world. How old do you think I was then? How old do I look now?"

Dr. West thought his own face looked about forty, which was his theoretical physiological age. His calendar age since birth was fifty-six. He felt his damaged heart laboring as if he were seventy-six.

The Major blinked. "You're damn well preserved. In prison you weren't in the sun. Or were you in the freezer? In prison is where you'll go again if we ever get out of here. Right now I need you. You talk Chink to these people. Tell them to hide us. Tell them we will free them from the Chinese. We'll give them self-determination, food, real clothing, medical supplies, if they'll hide us from the Chinese."

"Oh, brother!" Dr. West laughed savagely. "You are terrified! Why not promise them guns and ammunition——."

"Sure, we'll drop guns. Some of their people must be the guerrillas."

"Don't you wish it were so!" Dr. West taunted. "These people aren't Eskimos. These people aren't human. These are *Esks*. Throw away your expectations of human behavior. Esks don't behave that way. Do you see any Chinese guards? Humans this miserable would need guards. Esks aren't human. They don't revolt. They feel no need to be guerrillas. Or to vote. They don't need to. They're getting their way. They're getting what they want—or what something out there wants for them. They're filling our world!"

"Tell them to hide us. That's an order."

"Very rapidly they're filling our world."

"Tell them to hide us, damn you!" The Major's .45 was raised again.

"Where can they hide us? Under their bodies?"

"They must have houses someplace." The Major peered about.

Shrugging, gesticulating, Dr. West tried to communicate with some of the women. He asked if they felt well. They said they did. "They say to climb over that ridge, over the hill to the next valley," he lied. "They say hide on the hill."

He regretted his lie as they struggled up the terraces. His mouth had lied before he had a chance to think. It was as if the Harvard Circle of the CIA had drummed into his skull that he must go to a hilltop. The signal sender would have more range from a high place. Was that it?

His heavy legs ached and dragged. His heart thudded. He was exhausted. He couldn't make it all the way to the top of the mountain. It was a mountain of endless terraces, giant steps too big for any man. The world whirled dazzling bright as Dr. West fell in the mud.

"You got to get up." The Major was pulling at him. "Saw a copter out there. A little speck, zigging around like it's looking for something. You don't think the Chicoms are tuned in on our guerrilla wavelength?"

Dr. West stared up at the muddy little signal sender in the Major's huge hand. "Possible." That was the truth. In fact it was the understatement of the year. The CIA radio was tuned to the Maoist frequency.

"How do I turn this thing off without busting it?"

"Don't turn it off. Probably the helicopter is simply supervising the Esks," Dr. West's mouth lied. "To turn it off, you would have to break it. Then the signal sender would be done for, and so will——."

"All right, let's go, we can still reach the top." The Major tried boosting him up the slippery wall of a terrace. "Got to reach the top. Irrigation pumps up there, I think. Can hide underneath. Won't be seen from air." The Major wheezed and gasped for breath, plainly feeling his forty plus years and a candidate for a coronary.

Dr. West fell again. "Leave me." He had difficulty enunciating the words. "I don't want you to die for me."

"No, got to help you. In spite of everything we're on the same side, Doc." With strength and tenderness, the Major helped Dr. West climb. "Some time—when you got time— you got to prove to me—those Esks down there—are different from Eskimos. I don't believe it. I'll never believe it."

When the two men finally wormed under the throbbing irrigation pump on the crest of the mountain, Dr. West regained his breath and spoke intently through the roar of the pump. "If you could compare their chromosomes you would see that their genetic coding, the DNA recipe which guides the growth of an Esk, is too neat, too perfect, too repetitive among different individuals to be—human."

Deaf to a maniac's ravings, the Major peered out clutching his .45 as savagely as if it were an antiaircraft weapon. "The copter's moving to a new position—like they're sure as hell—looking for—something."

"The simplest misexplanation is yours, that the Esks are mutated Eskimos." Dr. West continued talking at cross-purposes to the Major. "Ockham's razor, an old scientific rule of thumb, suggests if there are several possible explanations for a mystery, pick the simplest. Mutated Eskimos is the simplest explanation. It is the most conservative explanation. It is the explanation picked by so-called reputable physiologists. It is the explanation people want to continue to believe."

"The copter's moving out over the valley where we were——." The Major stopped.

The Doctor's hand closed around the dagger within his layers of clothing and he kept talking as though each sentence might be his last. "Mutations usually involve a single trait or related set of traits. But any honest study of the Esks shows they differ from human beings in hundreds of ways, physiologically and psychologically."

"The copter is moving from position to position like they're trying to get a radio-location fix on us. Do you think this signal sender——?"

"And the Esk child acts happier and more cooperative than a human child, and efficiently grows into an adult in three years. Eating only 600 calories of food a day, an adult Esk outworks a Chinaman. And breed, breed like lemmings! For what purpose are the Esks overrunning the Earth? Why are the Chinese, we, everyone letting the Esks multiply?"

"The copter's heading in our direction."

"The simplest misexplanation is that the Chinese are using the Esks for politico-economic purposes. The Esks ease the Chinese agricultural problem. The Esks produce farm surpluses. The Esks produce favorable balance of trade. The Esk manpower frees Chinese manpower to police India. But all this is the superficial explanation. It does not reveal the underlying——."

"Copter straight for us!" The Major began smashing the signal sender with the butt of his .45.

Dr. West could not stop talking. He expected to be stilled forever. "Even our President seems to believe the simple-headed explanation, that the Chinese are using, breeding the Esks as part of the Endless War, simple power politics. ——But I believe the Esks are using the Chinese!"

The clattering wail of the jet copter chewed through the roar of the pump.

Under the iron pump, as if cued by the sounds of the helicopter, Dr. West's hand pulled down the zipper, opening his flight suit, and freeing the quilted Chinese blue cotton within.

The copter squatted down. It was small, with a plastic bubble cockpit. The Major stared at the indistinct faces inside—and then down to his .45 and then to Dr. West.

As the copter engine squealed to a stop, the Major stared unbelieving at Dr. West. "You've got on a coolie costume. All planned! Nothing for me. Good God, what was intended for me?"

Dr. West tried to release his own fingers from the dagger inside the padded Chinese coat. "I don't know. I swear to you I don't know."

The black boots of a Maoist policeman sprang from the copter to the Chinese mountain top and ran toward the pump. The Major rolled, firing his booming, deafening .45 automatic three times. The Major's wide-eyed face twisted back toward Dr. West, and the round eye of the .45 followed too slowly.

With surgical precision, Dr. West's hand thrust the dagger into the auricle of the Major's heart.

Dr. West, the man, sobbed.

In helpless anguish he lay within the body he had not been able to control. A Chinese hand disengaged his fingers from the dagger.

"Liu," exclaimed the excited young Cantonese voice above Dr. West's body, "where could he have gotten such a dagger? It is a Mark III dagger."

"My eyes can see it is a Mark III dagger," the copter pilot retorted. "He killed the other Big-Nose with it—which is strange."

"Liu, with care we should tread. Perhaps the Mark III dagger was issued to him." The young Cantonese voice quickened. "Great care. He is wearing commune clothing, but he has the white corpse-face of a typical Big-Nose, and yet there is the radio signal to explain. See, here is the little transmitter, which told us to come rescue him. The other Big-Nose must have smashed it. I think this man who is alive may be an important personage. Peking should be notified. Extensive photographs should be taken for the record or our buttocks may be burnt." The black boots ran back to the copter.

"You, yes, you—yes, *you!*" the copter pilot nudged Dr. West with his boot toe. "Did you understand our words?"

Dr. West feigned unconsciousness.

"He does. He understands us," the copter pilot shouted.

The returning young policeman with the camera backed off, and the copter pilot followed. Like doctors in consultation, in sinister whispers they argued. Then the young Maoist policeman advanced warily toward the patient. "It is with great regret that official regulations require us to bind your wrists to your ankles," he blurted. "I, for one, would never do such a thing." With professional expertise, he knotted the ropes.

The ropes were not tight. The young Maoist policeman had been careful not to interfere with Dr. West's circulation. Having already tied him so he could not walk, the two men had to hoist Dr. West and carry him to the helicopter.

"For a thin man—very heavy!" the young one gasped.

"Big bones. Primitive skeleton. Typical Big-Nose," the pilot retorted.

"Did you notice the wrists of the dead one are hairy as an ape's!" The young voice echoed the racial disgust. "Weak blue eyes. Shot at me twice."

"Three times. So close to your belly even a drunken sot imperialist should not miss. Either you are dead or there was something wrong with his bullets."

As the helicopter scuttled upward, it sideslipped violently. Its door flew open. The sack in which the Maoist policeman had collected the battered signal sender, the dagger, the .45, and Dr. West's CIA "escape kit" slid across the dented aluminum floor toward the open door. The young policeman fell to his knees, snatching at these sliding objects. Dr. West considered lunging from the copter—to fall forever.

Contorted forward on the seat because his wrists were tied to his ankles, Dr. West leaned toward the open door.

8.
OUR
MAN
IN
PEKING

THE COPTER LURCHED UPWARD, SLAMMING ITS DOOR SHUT, and the Major's hard head flopped against Dr. West's bound feet and wrists. The Major's blue eyes were white-rimmed in the futile stare of death.

Dr. West closed his own eyes. Whiplashes of self-flagellation slashed through the numbness inside his skull.

I can't rationalize that those bastards in Harvard Circle killed him. When he turned the muzzle of the .45 at me, all my vainglorious hopes that he would kill me turned into lies. Instinctively I dodged from the nothingness of death. My mind and body joined in thrusting the dagger with all my strength as if he were an enemy. God help my friends! My hand would have killed him even if I had been free from narcohypnosis, and I may have been free. Now I may be free——.

The copter tilted. Dr. West stared down at the truncated mountain peaks. *Those sons of bitches in the Harvard Circle should be happy now. The Chinese have me.*

Tiny reservoirs, thin pipelines, in every direction the Chinese world was terraced and glittering with microscopic rice paddies. Ten years ago these had been barren mountains, but now the myriad multiplying hands of the Esks were changing the world.

Seventeen years ago in the Arctic, I thought I was free to act like God. I thought I realized the implications of the group of Eskimos on the Boothia Peninsula who suddenly and mysteriously were multiplying.

By the next summer the damned fools in Ottawa and Washington were sending in icebreakers followed by whole barge-loads of food. "Human life is sacred," they said. "No one must starve."

In those days, the Canadians cheerfully planned to resettle any "surplus" Eskimos throughout the Northwest Territories. Canadian Government officials admitted that the birthrate of the Booth Eskimos was "Startling" but "We can hardly drown the little beggars just because their mothers refuse to swallow the birth control pills."

With a bush planeload of luggage, I flew back to the Boothia Peninsula. Having made my decision, I felt tremendous freedom to act. Gambling with people's lives was my everyday work when I was a young doctor in hospital residency. At that time, seventeen years ago when I landed my float plane on LaRue Lake, the staphylococcus strain which specifically infected the Fallopian tubes and spermatic ducts had not been fully tested on a broad sample of human races but I acted.

The Esks turned out to be immune to ordinary human infections.

But camped near the refuse heap of the former Cultural Sanctuary Guard Station, twenty-two old men and women, real Eskimos, died. They should not have died, but they died from this minor staphylococcus infection.

The tragedy became much greater than my life or death, or the death of the twenty-two Eskimos. It was my trial for attempted genocide that focused the attention of the world upon the hunger of the rapidly increasing Esks. The Swedes and Russians sent food.

In the United Nations General Assembly the Oriental bloc seized upon my guilt and twisted it into the guilt of Canada and the United States. The Chinese and other nations sent massive aid. Evacuation of surplus Eskimos to any country willing to accept them and pay the transportation costs began. Huge Chinese jet transports swooped down. The Esks spread——.

This is my crucial guilt, that my own actions aided the spread of Esks. My trial attracted attention to them, so the Chinese "rescued" them. I should have killed myself in prison. I should not have lived to see a billion Esks in China alone.

The helicopter veered, and far below was exposed the gray overcast that shrouds any modern city. The copter pilot chattered through his radio to the ground.

Baring his teeth, Dr. West lunged at the door of the helicopter. As his skull rammed the door outward, his eyes glimpsed nothingness.

Surprisingly strong hands dragged his head and shoulders back into the helicopter.

"Liu, this one would have fallen to his ancestors—but he paused."

The blades of the helicopter whirled through the thickening smog. The continuous squealing agony of its jet engine lowered. With a bounce that slammed Dr. West's face against the floor the copter landed, and the Maoist policeman kicked the door open.

"You're my responsibility no more," the young policeman laughed with relief, and Dr. West was dragged out of the copter by noisy black-uniformed young Chinese. "The Interrogator must think this Big-Nose is a big fish," a girl's voice excitedly laughed. Another voice asked: "Has proper caution been taken to telephone Peking, Capital of the World, Praise be to Mao III?" A second girl's voice laughed: "Liu, you handsome pilot, where are you studying tonight?"

An inhaling gasp quieted the black-uniformed crowd on the heliroof of the massive concrete police headquarters.

"Has no protection been taken against infection?" an authoritative voice demanded. "You are all quarantined! Orderly, place the assassin on the cart. ——No, don't wheel him this way. Take him down through the freight elevator."

Dr. West was to recognize this cold voice again after he had been stripped, sprayed, fumigated, and pricked for a blood sample.

He lay on a cold operating table.

"Cover him with a sheet." It was the voice of the Interrogator.

The ceiling was enameled white.

"Make him comfortable with a 2 cc injection."

Dr. West began to relax. He felt warmer. The effect was similar to a narcotic the Harvard Circle had administered.

"You will be interested to know," the disembodied voice

said smoothly in English, "a large proportion of the working people in the United States, and the intellectuals such as yourself, as you no doubt know, are in sympathy with the peace-loving aims of the Chinese Federation of Nations. When I say interested I mean you will be interested to know that we already had been notified of your war-mongering flight by many highly placed sources in the United States. The exact flight plan of your intruding aircraft was known to us, and proper authorities had been notified, and of course your obsolete aircraft was tracked by our radar and our excellent interceptors, which could have shot it down at any time had such an order been given."

Dr. West listened to the intense voice but had difficulty following its meanings.

"You will be interested to know that in a few hours our excellent medical technicians will have positively identified the aerosol spray which descended from your aircraft, and no doubt they already have several cures for it. You need not fear symptoms from your own exposure to the spray. We will inoculate you against its effects. To confirm our already excellent diagnosis please tell us what virus is involved."

Dr. West awakened slightly. He had assumed, guessed, that a bacterial agent of the staph-strep group had been used. This bacterium should be easily recognizable by culturing and microscopic inspection. Why was the Interrogator talking about a virus? Pathologists and technicians tend to blame a virus when NOTHING can be found.

"What virus were you forced to spray against your will upon helpless women and children? Each word you speak will save the life of a child——."

Dr. West knew that the only effective resistance when undergoing interrogation is to say nothing. As in a psychological test, anything you say, lie or truth, will be filed and cross-filed, so that the more you lie, the more clearly the watery rings of truth will rise through the pool of lies.

Dr. West tried to say nothing.

But his mouth opened. As his mouth began to speak, Dr. West realized that this would not be a two-way dialogue between himself and the Interrogator. Three points of view were present. The third was speaking from his mouth now.

The Harvard Circle had entered the interrogation room—in spirit, a damn treacherous spirit!

"I am Dr. Joseph West," his mouth announced. "I am the man who attempted to exterminate the Eskimos." What was the Harvard Circle trying to do to him?

"We are aware of who you are." Then the Interrogator whispered something aside to someone else. "Answer our questions please," the Interrogator continued. "Do not volunteer extraneous information. We know everything already. Answer our questions quickly," the Interrogator's voice rose. "What is the viral agent?"

"I am Dr. West," his mouth repeated, "Dr. Joseph West. This can be easily checked. No doubt there are photographs of me in your news archives. Dr. Joseph West, I was convicted of Eskimo genocide. I am acknowledged to be the greatest expert on the Esks, Eskimos, Dream Persons as you term them."

"Answer the question! What is the virus?" The Interrogator sounded nervous. "What's the virus?"

Dr. West stared at the ceiling grill. Something had winked, reflected light, a glass lens behind the grill. No doubt they were filming and recording——.

He tried to move his arm, but it was strapped, and something was pressing into his wrist. No doubt his pulse and perspiration reactions were being taped——.

Those sons of bitches! The Harvard Circle really might have notified Chinese Communist agents in the United States that his aircraft was coming over!

"Your Mark III dagger is a forgery! Your pulse becomes abnormally fast," the Interrogator's voice said. "You feel guilt and fear—but be assured we will do nothing to harm you. We bow down before the immortal thoughts of the Spirit of our Grandfather Mao: All men should be treated both with justice and mercy. Therefore feel free—to tell us the virus! ——Then begin by telling why you murdered your companion."

What speeded Dr. West's pulse rate was grief growing to rage. Those CIA sons of bitches callously had prepared him to murder the Major. One minor maneuver. The spraying, their ejection in the capsule, the dagger, the signal sender, the stabbing, he thought all were intended to increase his chances of being taken alive by the Maoist police. All were intended to give him an aura of importance.

"I am Dr. Joseph West," his mouth repeated with sickening fatuousness.

"Damm it!" Dr. West shouted. "How the hell do I know what was in that spray. They let me think it was a bacterial agent to sterilize the Esks, to demonstrate to you that selective sterilization of the Esks is possible. And it may be possible!"

"Good, we are glad to hear that you will cooperate. In typical fashion, your Central Intelligence Agency has tricked you. What virus do you think the spray contained?"

"Why do you keep saying virus?" Dr. West retorted. "In English translation can't you differentiate between virus and bacteria? Tell me in Mandarin Chinese."

"Ah?" And in Mandarin the Interrogator painstakingly tried to describe a virus.

"Still a virus?" Dr. West said impatiently. "If you want a virus, I'll give you three guesses. One, a virus with a long incubation period. In about twenty-one days the Esks will undergo interesting changes. Personality reversal. Cute. Changed into what they really are. They'll tear you apart." Dr. West gasped for breath, unsure whether he or the Harvard Circle was lying now. Sometimes he had a vicious sense of humor.

"Number two," he laughed. "The spray could consist of distilled water. No wonder your medical personnel are baffled. But don't let it baffle you. It means the spray run was a decoy. The CIA wanted to use an Air Force plane to attract your attention to something or distract your attention from something. But the State Department in Washington did not want the CIA Warhawks to use a real bacterial spray that would force you toward retaliation. So, distilled water? Does that make Peking feel safer?"

"Number three," Dr. West laughed in confusion. "This is the possibility to worry you tonight. You'll never sweat it out of me because I don't know what it is—except to say that those sons of bitches in the Harvard Circle get up very very early in the morning, and when they go to this much trouble to deliver a man to China, they must have one hell of a reason."

The Interrogator made a sad sighing sound. "Please, but you must tell us the truth, Dr. West. You are a brilliant man, a scientist who searches for Truth. Many years ago when you made your decision to eliminate the Dream Persons, you acted freely because you believed it was an act of Truth. In China you would never have been considered a criminal because you believed in Truth, even mistaken Truth, because mistakes can be so freely confessed. You could—you still can live here freely to work and study. In the Chinese Federation of Nations we give honor and assistance to all searchers after Truth. As our Grandfather Mao once said: 'May a thousand flowers bloom, a thousand schools of thought contend.' Only in China are you free to speak the Truth. What virus did your Central Intelligence Agency force you to spray upon the peace-loving people of the world?"

This soothing flow of words continued until Dr. West began to drowse. He was physically exhausted. The third party to the trilogue, the Harvard Circle, refused to feed new answers into his mouth.

It was as if the start of the interrogation had cued from his skull his oral self-identification as Dr. Joseph West, famous genocide expert on Esks. Now the Harvard Circle wanted to say no more at this time. Or he had forgotten what he was supposed——.

"You can sleep as soon as you tell the future symptoms of the virus, Dr. West. When do they begin?" The Interrogator resorted to flashing lights and buzzers and, after an indeterminate period of time, to small electric shocks.

Once or twice Dr. West tried to argue, vaguely aware that his voice was incoherent. Suddenly he screamed, his breath squawled, God what were they doing to him?

"Message for Mao III," he heard his voice squawk. Torture had cued the next communication from the Harvard Circle.

"I must be taken to Mao III," his hoarse voice repeated over and over. No matter what they did to him, try as he could, he was unable to tell the Interrogator what the message was. "Stop them, stop them. I don't know."

"Of course we cannot actually take him to our beloved Chairman," the Interrogator's voice agreed with someone equally invisible. "Apologies that so much time has been spent; a little more time will be needed; electrocranial accupuncture is required if we are to free the core of truth in this man——. It seems that rigid blockades have been placed in his memory, perhaps hypnotically."

Oblivion.

There were black silk slippers on his feet at the other end of him. He lay in a different room. He was wearing a coarse gray cloth uniform. His head ached. When he raised his fingers to his head, he found his hair had been shaved off and there were a number of bumps, little knobs, on his scalp. He could find no evidence of torture on his body. His legs ached and appeared swollen, but this probably was due to—he knew but couldn't remember what had caused his swollen legs. Perhaps the unaccustomed exercise of struggling up and down mountain rice terraces?

An intense-faced Chinese hurried into the white room. The man inhaled, standing very straight in his gleaming black dacron robe which was the traditionally Chinese costume Maoist officials had reassumed in recent years. Dr. West recalled that the color black symbolized virtue, and the embroidered dragons: good luck and power.

Evidently, coarse blue cotton uniforms were only for the troops.

"Time is flowing past." The man's familiar voice suggested with a typical interrogator's ploy: "Everything is known."

In remembrance of the pain with the Interrogator's voice, Dr. West's body winced, and it was with a drying mouth that he tried to answer back like a punished adolescent. "If you know everything—you are too prescient to be the—Interrogator. You should be God—or Mao III."

"That is a sacrilegious statement to your God and to Mao III, who sits in judgment here at the center of the world."

"Then I have been flown to Peking?"

"You have been disinfected both externally and internally," the Interrogator replied. "You have the honor——."

But a man in a thick leaden apron with goggles on his

forehead resembling a second set of eyes interrupted. "Ah—we need him for an hour now."

Dr. West recognized the man's profession as X-ray technician. Very funny. Did they intend to X-ray his internal organs for bombs?

"Later! It is too late. The time has been set." In the Interrogator's voice there was irritation and strain, and he turned back to Dr. West and managed a conspiratorial smile.

"You are the first foreigner in three years to be so honored. This you will remember and cherish. You can drink your tea later." The Interrogator stiffened, straight as a bamboo.

"Ta-tung!" the Interrogator shouted.

> The eastern sky reddens,
> The sun rises
> And in China the line of Maos has come!
> They strive for the welfare of the people.
> They are the great saviors of the people!

Two men dressed in black silk who appeared to be minor officials trundled in on a low vehicle with four padded seats. Dr. West thought it resembled an electric cart for a golf foursome. The golf cart was followed by half a dozen bored soldiers. They stood scratching inside their padded blue uniforms while the two men in black bowed unenthusiastically toward the Interrogator. "Ready? We only have the office for ten minutes."

"He can understand everything you say," the Interrogator snapped.

One official glanced at his wristwatch, then wearily rolled his gaze to the ceiling. "You should have notified me of that fact in writing."

It was plain that the Interrogator had much less influence here in Peking.

As the electric cart trundled along endless concrete corridors the soldiers lagged further and further behind, and Dr. West realized the building must cover acres of ground, a veritable Pentagon.

Even seated in the cart he was in pain from his swollen

legs. The electric cart whirred on and on. His head felt as if a fist were tightening inside. Apparently the Interrogator's electric needles had failed to discharge any messages intended for Mao III. The Harvard Circle must have planned one sight, one reaction which would cue a synapse in the recesses of his brain, releasing the message to his conscious mind. It seemed obvious whom he was being taken to see, face to face.

His pulse was racing as if his body expected to be cued to violent action. If there was a message in his skull, Dr. West thought it must be a dandy to justify the maneuvers of the Harvard Circle.

Again, he remembered the blue eyes of the Major widening. *Good God,* the Major's voice cried. *What was intended for me?* And Dr. West thought: *What is intended for me?*

Those callous sons of bitches! Dr. West began to shiver uncontrollably. He wanted to jump off the cart. The smiling faces closed in on him: Dr. George Bruning, Deputy Director of the CIA; Dr. Sammy Wynoski, chemopsychiatrist; Dr. Fred Gatson, bacteriologist; Dr. Einar Johansen, neurosurgeon. But there had been another member of the Harvard Circle, a disembodied voice.

Tom Randolph, a narrow-eyed man who chain-smoked cigarettes as if he had a death wish, had become a full professor of parapsychology at Duke University at age twenty-six. In the basement of CIA headquarters, Dr. West had recognized Tom's off-kilter face. While Joe West had been a graduate medical student at Harvard, Tom Randolph had been the undergrad who led the protest march which culminated in the dynamiting of the Quad.

The crazy kid should have ended in jail instead of as a Ph.D. with his hands on millions of dollars of Defense Department money for extrasensory research. Surprisingly, Tom Randolph had resigned to take a seemingly less important position. This was with the Central Intelligence Agency when the President of the United States appointed fellow Harvardman George Bruning as Deputy Director.

To Dr. West, the memory of Tom Randolph's narrow eyes inspecting him as if he were as expendable as a bomb was terrifying. After the injections, it had been Tom Randolph's

disembodied voice which rasped: "Mao III has a faith healer. Remember that, Joe. He needs his faith healer. Remember, Joe, when we were young wise guys at Harvard and you
scared the hell out of me at a drinking party. That was a
pretty good parlor trick. That's what turned me on extrasensory research, and we are turning you on———."

Remembering the undergrad Tom Randolph gaily swerving
his sports car to run over a cat, Dr. West felt like the cat. He
felt claustrophobia even tighter than when he had been
trapped in the aircraft capsule. Now he tried to climb off the
electric cart.

But they were too strong for him. The carved dragon
doors opened, and the dwarfed man behind the huge desk
glanced up. He wore a simple agricultural commune costume.

"You are not Mao III," Dr. West's mouth immediately
announced. "You are a double."

The man blinked and glanced at the Interrogator's shocked
face. The Interrogator whirled, screaming at Dr. West that
he was insulting the Chairman of the World, the Father of
the Chinese Federation of Nations———.

For a moment Dr. West experienced the weird feeling that
he had been about to explode. The faces of the Harvard
Circle, electric eels, biopower, heavy legs, for those sons of
bitches was he a bomb that walked like a man with plastic
sacks of nitroglycerine in his leg muscles, and was cued when
he saw Mao III———?

Another official appeared from a side door. "Quiet please.
Clear the room. Your scheduled time is over. The room is
needed."

The man behind the desk rose obediently and departed.

Even before the Interrogator was able to stop screaming, a
third official appeared with soldiers. "Lieutenant, investigate
this foreign prisoner's document-locator number. Update his
Sparrow Folder and file in Pending."

Some afternoons Dr. West was taken from his cell to a
waiting room. Through the swinging door to the main waiting room he glimpsed nervous men in Pakistani garb with
briefcases and weary men in Western suits who sat on benches
day after day. Sometimes he recognized the Australian

Premier. When janitors began sweeping the floor, the men with briefcases would file out and Dr. West would be taken back to his cell.

Once a Lieutenant peered through the bars: "Ah, I hoped I'd locate you eventually. According to records transferred from Szechwan Province, the twenty-one-day incubation period for unknown infectious virus is over. Now you can be shot."

"No Esks were sick or died?" Dr. West demanded.

"No reports of illness," the smiling Lieutenant replied and left.

One sleeping period Dr. West was awakened and a barber shaved him. Drowsily, he protested this disturbance of his routine. "This is the wrong time to go to the waiting room." After a month of regular hours between cell and waiting room, Dr. West tended to become irritable whenever routine was disturbed from the outside. An electric cart transported him at this wrong hour to his empty outer waiting room and to his surprise carried him on into the main waiting room where the janitors were emptying ash trays and on into the empty office with the large desk where he had last seen the Interrogator and on along a hall and into an elevator. It plunged endlessly into the earth, stopped. The attendants were replaced by other attendants who smiled and smiled. Dr. West was led into a large-roomed apartment which was dim because the hunched shape of a man was watching a television screen beneath a bas-relief golden dragon.

At the end of the news program, the man switched off the TV set by remote control. "Is this Dr. Joseph West?"

"Yes, Chairman. His file has been placed on the tea table at your left hand."

"Some years ago when I still believed there was a purpose to be served by personally making speeches, I announced to the world that I wanted to meet you eye to eye, Dr. West. The implication then was that I would righteously tear you limb from limb. The occasion was my address to the United Nations General Assembly on the subject of the attempted genocide of the Eskimos by you and persons unknown, such as the United States Government."

Dr. West made no attempt to answer. No message to Mao

III from the Harvard Circle emerged from his mouth, but now Dr. George Bruning's voice was echoing in his memory: "Listen and observe, when Mao III or any man speaks of his strengths and beliefs, soon his contradictions and weaknesses will stick out like handles—by which you can seize him."

Mao III stirred clumsily in his padded chair. Dr. West saw that Mao III was not wearing a simple commune costume. He was engulfed in an ornate black silk robe embroidered with a traditional dragon.

"Tonight while I was watching television coverage of the latest CIA intruder aircraft to crash I was reminded of an intelligence brief on my desk some months ago. This extrapolated a minimum of facts into a theory that a Dr. West had been delivered to China because I once had expressed a desire to meet him. This amused me at the time. It would be better for your President to communicate with me directly. I am a busy man and cannot deal with minor intermediaries."

Dr. West observed the awkward position of Mao III's right wrist and left leg. Although Mao III was a comparatively young man evidently he had suffered a paralytic stroke. Probably about three years ago when he vanished from the public eye.

"The intruder aircraft which crashed tonight was a converted passenger transport painted black," Mao III continued in his precise voice. "It contained an estimated dozen Eskimos confined in three large parachute ejection capsules, which did not eject. After the crash of the aircraft, one of the capsules preserved its four corpses from burning."

Dr. West straightened mentally, glimpsing the unknowable faces of the Harvard Circle. What was going on? Twelve Esks murdered.

Mao III was saying: "——were to be parachuted into the mountainous region of Szechwan Province where our Dream Persons now comprise more than 90% of the population. The bodies of these Eskimos or American Dream Persons were dressed in commune costumes. They were equipped with machine pistols, plastic explosives, miniature radios and related equipment as if the CIA intended that they organize guerrilla warfare. As my grandfather, Mao Tse-tung, often said: 'The guerrilla is the fish who swims among the people.' But to swim among our Dream Persons would be more frustrating."

Mao III laughed as if he liked to hear his own voice. "Times have changed since my grandfather was Chairman. He had no Dream Persons to perplex him. Surely you CIA assassins do not really believe that American Eskimos or even a sentient strain of American Dream Persons could arouse our Dream Persons."

This was a statement rather than a question. Like other leaders, Mao III swept into a monologue. "It is not psychologically possible for Dream Persons to take the aggressive initiative necessary for revolution. Your Eskimos cannot arouse our Dream Persons because there is nothing to arouse. If your heavily armed corpses are not Eskimos, if they are American Dream Persons the joke is even stranger. This is like sending the blind to teach the blind how to see."

Dr. West felt physically ill, suspecting the black aircraft had been purposely crashed by the Harvard Circle. The planeload of Esks might be simply to remind the Chinese that the CIA's Esk expert was filed away somewhere in a Peking prison. Had those Harvard sons of bitches in effect murdered twelve Esks as another little move in the attempt to place an American face to face with Mao III? His distance to Mao III was about fifteen feet. What did the Harvard Circle expect him to do, explode—or strangle Mao III with his bare hands?

"——Marxist-Maoists are anti-Malthusian," Mao III was saying, "because we have faith in mankind's ability to find new food supplies, new living space beneath the sea, new planets. There cannot be too many Chinese when there is so much work to be done. For the present, there cannot be too many Dream Persons. It is strange that the CIA would send you to China. From the beginning you have had a closed mind concerning the Esks. Dr. West, what rational message could you possibly bring?"

Dr. West stood there swaying. He did not know. If the Harvard Circle had given him a message for Mao III, it was lost or buried too deep in his skull. He stood face to face with Mao III and no message had been cued.

"——Marxist-Maoist position regarding the origin of the Dream Person," Mao III was orating, "is that the renewed thermonuclear testing by Russia in the Arctic during the 1970s caused the mutation. No other nation would have both the vicious deviationist disregard for human life and the technological clumsiness to explode weapons so unexpectedly filthy with radioactive cesium."

This cued the one track in Dr. West's mind. "The mutation theory has no basis in fa——."

"The lichens, the little plants on Arctic rocks were contaminated with radioactive cesium." Mao III's voice swept on emotionally, drowning Dr. West's voice. "The lichens were like rice to the herds of caribou, and radioactive cesium concentrated in certain organs of these extinct beasts who were eaten by the Eskimos who are an Oriental people. Don't tell me there was no mutation!"

Mao III gasped for breath, evidently emotionally involved with his interpretation of the Esks. "The most important mutation in the world took place on the Boothia Peninsula in the Canadian Northwest Territories. An Oriental child was born."

"Even though there were not Three Wise Men in attendance, even though no angels sang," Mao III laughed breathlessly, "the metabolism of this child was at least three times as efficient and he matured in one-sixth as many years as other children. Whenever this precocious Eskimo mated, from each conception to the time of birth was only a month."

Near Mao III's right hand gleamed a glass of water. He looked at it longingly. "The rapid multiplication of these Dream Persons has proved vital to the rightful growth of the Chinese Federation of Nations. My original decision to rescue the Eskimos from imperialist genocide has been proven correct."

Mao III's right hand jerked and he stared at Dr. West. "——I recall from the United Nations discussions of seventeen years ago, your own theory of the origin of that first Dream Person was more unlikely and—sinister."

"I was the first——. I was encamped on the Boothia Peninsula within twenty years after the event took place." Dr. West spoke quickly. "I tried to interview the Eskimos who——."

"There is no need for you to defend your theory," Mao III interrupted. "You have attempted to justify your mass murder on many occasions. I, for one, would be equally disturbed if I believed your theory."

Mao III's right hand made a tentative movement toward the glass of water. "At the present time it is to the advantage of the Chinese Federation of Nations to breed several billion more Dream Persons at the very least."

"And drown the world!"

"Are you worried about the disappearance of hairy, Anglo-Saxon man? ——Because the Dream Person's traits invariably are dominant?" Mao III laughed. "Perhaps the world would be a happier and more peaceful place if all peoples were absorbed by the Dream Persons?"

Mao III's eyes narrowed. "Perhaps you are a member of an extremist group in the United States. In angry disagreement with your own Government, you are plotting the violent elimination of Esks everywhere. Are you sure there is not already a political splinter group in the United States which has decided that I am a Dream Person, that even your President hides an Esk in his ancestry. It cannot be true. Dream Persons are remarkably unqualified for the violent leadership that is necessary in the world today."

Awkwardly, Mao III's paralyzed right hand attempted to reach the glass. "The Chinese people and all the peace-loving peoples of the world—know that the vicious racist American propaganda campaign claiming Chinese maltreatment of the Esks is a hypocritical attempt to pressure the Chinese Federation of Nations into unilaterally limiting our greatest source of agricultural growth, our Dream Persons!"

Dr. West watched the shivering hand. Instinctively because he was a fellow human being his eyes wanted Mao III's hand to be able to reach, to grasp the glass of water.

"Ah!" Mao III proudly clutched the glass in his hand. Shuddering, he raised it to his lips and drank deeply.

When he had finished, an attendant stepped from the

shadows to take the glass. "No, no," Mao III coughed. "This time, this time I will not drop it———."

Dr. West's eyes concentrated on the cautiously moving hand on its long journey with the empty glass down toward the table. The glass clunked on the table.

"Ah! You see I am making great improvement. Until tonight I always broke the glass. I am informed you originally were a medical doctor who attempted to save lives rather than destroy them? If so, you will understand the importance in my condition of such a sudden improvement. It was as if a voice in my head was telling my hand to move downward. Amazingly, my hand obeyed. No doubt new nerve wires have been growing as my doctors promised, growing past the dead spot in my brain, and tonight contact is made! Look at this. I am going to raise my arm. Soon, you will see, soon I will stand before the people again. I will astound the world with my words. This is the greatest moment in the history of the world!"

While Dr. West's eyes watched, Mao III tried to stand up.

"I am standing!"

Fall, you bigmouthed little tyrant! Dr. West thought.

Mao III pitched forward, upsetting the table and glass. Attendants sprang from the shadows to assist Mao III. An attendant's hand closed on Dr. West's elbow to lead him from the room.

Tell them to leave me alone! Dr. West thought.

"Leave him alone," Mao III gasped.

Tell them to bring me a chair!

"Bring him a chair." Mao III collapsed on his couch.

Dr. West sat down. His heavy legs were twitching, and he was reminded of Galvani's early experiments with electricity and a frog's legs. His legs tingled. His face felt numb with shock.

Those incredible Harvard sons of bitches! Heavy legs, electric eels, biopower, parapsychology, this was why they had connived to maneuver an American into close proximity with the Chairman of the Chinese Federation of Nations, the ruler of four-fifths of the population of the world. Within how many feet of Mao III did he have to remain?

Dr. West was afraid he was a poor choice for this kind of power. Had the Harvard Circle selected him because Mao III once said he wanted to meet Dr. West eye to eye? Selected him because they thought he could control a paralyzed dictator?

He remembered when he was a med student at Harvard, startling Tom Randolph, who tried to laugh it off. "That's only a parlor trick."

But perhaps he did have a certain empathy and power of suggestion. Sometimes it had extended its corona to startle imaginative persons such as undergrad Tom Randolph. And Tom had grown. Professor Tom Randolph's experiments at Duke University in which one soldier attempted to control another hadn't satisfied the Defense Department. But Dr. West remembered Tom Randolph's excuse. "A human's bio-power to broadcast his thoughts through his neuron-electrical system is simply too weak."

But a man with biological booster batteries as powerful as electric eels' installed in his swollen legs, Dr. West thought, such a man close enough——. *Tell them to bring me a glass of water.*

"Bring him a glass of water," Mao III murmured hollowly from his couch.

Because there were no peculiar reactions from the attendants in the room, Dr. West concluded that he had been neatly conditioned to focus his control at only one man, Mao III.

Tell them to prepare a couch for me. Tell them you believe I have a healing power. When I am near you, your paralysis is cured.

When the water was brought, Dr. West was afraid to drink. It might be poisoned. He knew he would have to suppress such fears. Now every move would be into the unknown.

When the couch was brought, Dr. West was afraid to sleep. What was going on in Mao III's head? The man had not spoken or moved since——.

"I move. I speak," Mao III said. "What do you wish to speak about?"

Sleep until I awaken you. Dr. West lay there staring up at the triumphantly grinning faces of the Harvard Circle.

Dr. George Bruning, boy wonder, geophysicist, astronaut, political climber, and buddy of the President.

Dr. Sam Wynoski, chemopsychiatrist.

Dr. Fred Gatson, bacteriologist and ladder climber.

Dr. Einar Johansen, neurosurgeon and electric eel fancier.

Dr. Tom Randolph, parapsychologist.

You CIA sons of bitches, Dr. West thought so gently that Mao III did not awaken, you've succeeded in planting your man in Peking.

But am I your man? You may have implanted general guide-lines in my skull such as "love America." But you could never prepare me for all the quick and unexpected decisions a new dictator must make. I have a feeling I am free now—to do what I want.

Within a few days we'll find out.

9.

UNDERGROUND
DYNASTY

DEEP WITHIN THE ASSASSIN-PROOF VAULT, A TRADITIONAL dragon symbolizing good fortune flaunted his gold-painted tail above the most important telescreen.

Across this surveillance screen moved *Chiu Hsing* (Saving Star) electric fuel cell powered sedans rolling off an assembly line in distant Shanghai. Click, televised from even further south, in Canton well-fed students in traditional dacron robes sprang erect to face an antique blackboard of chemical formulas.

Click, televised erect as if disdaining underground silos and contemptuous of strategic dispersal, protruding enormously above the pink-walled courtyard of Peking's ancient Winter Palace, threatening nose cone symbolizing——.

"Now show what's really important," Dr. West challenged. "We both know what feeds all this——."

Tapeworm, you force me too much pain, the protesting thought flickered faintly within Dr. West's brain.

Beside Dr. West, the thin fingers on the control console remained obstinately motionless. Dr. West could feel the other man's resistance like sparks within his own skull. Authoritatively, Dr. West withdrew his support. Beside him, the opposing face sagged while paralysis again spread from the stroke-damaged brain. Dr. West returned his mental support, and those narrowing eyes widened.

The two men were alone in the Command Vault beneath Peking, but they were not alone.

"Now!" Dr. West commanded aloud, and beside him the unparalyzed fingers moved more obediently across the numbered push buttons on the control console.

Click, on the surveillance screen, shimmering across a

290

thousand miles, appeared the contorted mountains of Szechwan Province, laboriously terraced. Up new tiers of glittering
mountain rice paddies, swarming shapes with hoes clambered
into graying rain.

Closer, Dr. West thought. *Signal for a closer view.*

Beside him the man's fingers which had been paralyzed
moved. Click-click across the thousand miles, and in Szechwan Province a telelens panned along the rain-gray mountain. Across tiny rice paddies, beaded along a precipice,
swept the rain. Dissolving mudlips slipped. Whiskered rice
paddies smaller than bathtubs burst down the terraces. Scurrying Esks struggled to repair dissolving edges with dissolving
mud.

The whole cliff's about to slide, Dr. West thought as the
telelens zoomed at a random rain-drenched face. In this
moment of peril, the surveillance screen was flooded by the
Esk's infuriatingly senseless grin.

"Dammit, even now, that one's looking north!" Dr. West
shouted, his body tightening in another of his uncontrollable
agonies of rage and frustration. "Every day. More and more
Esks looking north at the sky." His voice choked as his
breathing squeezed tight. His rage or fear was making his
heart muscle wince.

Beside him at the console the thin hand contracted like a
dying spider. Dr. West felt his own pain reflected through
Mao III as they both grasped for breath. He blinked at Mao
III's loud-gasping face, now waxen above the luxurious black
dacron robe.

Instinctively, Dr. West's hand slid another tiny white pill
under his own tongue. The tightening was in his heart, not
Mao III's. The stinging sensation beneath his tongue helped
him relax even before the .32 mg trinitroglycerine tablet
dissolved, diffused, reopened the constricted arteries within
the cramped muscle which was his heart. He relaxed,
sheathed with sweat.

Beside him the partially paralyzed Mao III regained his
breathing rhythm, emitting rhythmic hissing sounds in the
Command Vault 4000 feet beneath Peking.

On the telescreen the random Esk still stood grinning at

the sky as if symbolizing a billion, two billion Esks spreading over the world, all smiling into space.

"There is nothing up there but sky," Dr. West muttered.

Unconscious of the surveillance lens, the Esk bent his rain-washed back once more, and his obedient hands scooped mud upon the dissolving rim of the rice terrace. Beside him worked a child, and another child, dozens of Esk children working rhythmically in the rain.

So much more quickly maturing than Chinese children, they appeared to be twelve-year-olds. Dr. West estimated this swarm of children had been born two years ago. In another year they would be reproducing babies of their own.

"You fool!" Dr. West shouted at Mao III. "You still insist they are human. But such unhumanly quick mothers and embryos! A one-month gestation period——." Dr. West closed his eyes. "Human?"

Up there on the mountainside, Dr. West thought, *even a man's hardest labor could not produce the equivalent of 1800 calories of rice energy each day he needs to keep him working and alive. But these Esks are producing a rice surplus.*

"You fool!" Dr. West glared at Mao III. "Do you still think you are leaping fifty years of Marxist-Maoist agricultural frustration? Yes, you have a rice surplus this year. Yes, you are elbowing into world trade. With surplus rice, you are filling the bellies of Chinese industrial workers and troops all over Southeast Asia and spreading west——. You are increasing the Esks to produce an even bigger agricultural surplus next year, but the Principle of Diminishing Returns is not an economist's myth. And the ghost breathing on your neck is Malthus."

That discredited eighteenth-century English pessimist, Mao III's thoughts taunted, *who did not foresee that the scientific improvements of Maoist agriculture can race ahead of hunger.*

"How can *you* talk about scientific agriculture," Dr. West shouted, "while depending on Esks? Even with scientific agriculture in the sea, this planet has limits! The human population is only doubling every twenty-five years. We both know the Esk population is doubling every year in China."

Dr. West stared at Mao III's lopsidedly smiling face, and

added bitingly: "Are you master or tool? The first few Esks did not appear in the Arctic because Maoist theology wished them there."

At this, Mao III's thought-projection turned as blank as Arctic ice.

If there is a purpose in life, Dr. West thought and oddly visualized a spinning globe with a Geographic North Pole set in the white Arctic Ocean and, rotating closely around it, the bare rocks of Canada's Boothia Peninsula, present locus of the Earth's magnetic lines of force, of the North Magnetic Pole. There he had discovered the first few grinning Eskimos who were not———."

"What are they?" Dr. West croaked, his thoughts circling back in the old rut. *So nonviolent, so obedient, so happily increasing as if they can feel their purpose approaching. Always smiling, no matter what we do to them, as if they feel their purpose approaching. Closer every day.* "What is their purpose? Their purpose can't be our purpose!"

He stared at Mao III.

No purpose. Mao III's thoughts derided Dr. West with startling humor for a paralytic who was gasping for breath. *No purpose anywhere. End-purpose of the universe when I die equals nothing. No ten thousand years of Maoism. Nothing. So you cannot frighten me with too many Esks.*

Mao III's throat corded with effort, and he managed to gasp aloud, "Nothing frightens me after what you did to me, my brain tapeworm. You parasite———," his voice struggled.

Dr. West's forehead wrinkling with effort, Mao III's voice gurgled to silence. But Mao III's thoughts like javelins penetrated Dr. West.

My power is nothing. Squirm, my tapeworm. So shrewd, the capitalist plan to invade me with you. But your success is nothing. Mao III's face contorted like a smile. *Squirm in my intestine of power, my tapeworm. You a new leader? I laugh. Since the beginning of time, the world has been impossible for leaders. What can you do?*

Dr. West's thoughts and body tightened defensively, and Mao III's face sagged. His transmitted thoughts were blurred by pain. Dr. West watched him gasping for breath. It would be catastrophic to let him die.

Cold with sweat, Dr. West squirmed on the console chair. *Instructions must have been given me,* his thoughts revolved, *in case I succeeded like this.*

Confused by echoes of Mao III's thoughts, Dr. West moaned with motionless effort turned inward. There was no coherent clue to his next line of action. His memory seemed torn apart.

He knew the electrointerrogation after his "capture" had contributed to his present disorganization. And this symbiotic relationship—Mao III was cursing it as parasitic—might be permanently disorganizing both of them.

His dreams—until he began giving Mao III sleeping pills, Mao III's dreams had awakened him.

The pink walls enclosing the Great Square had echoed from marching troops and awakened Dr. West, imagining it was his own dream. Then dim ranks of children wearing red bandanas around their throats had passed through Dr. West's mind even though he was awake. Endless ranks of children with red balloons, white balloons, and Dr. West felt a growing sensation of joy and pride. Mao III must be watching them from his dream. "*Mao Tse-tung wan shui! Mao Tse-tung wan shui!*" their shrill voices shouted. *May Mao Tse-tung live ten thousand years!*

In unison the balloons in the dream were released. But Mao Tse-tung had been dead for nearly forty years. Mao III must have been an unknown young man then. Dr. West realized that Mao III was dreaming of his youth before the interregnum of committees and armies which followed the death of Mao Tse-tung.

The following fatherly figure, Mao II, had been a desperation figurehead. But Mao III was here in the Command Vault, whether in command of China or subtly trapped by a coalition of generals, Dr. West still was unable to determine.

"Command into the telecom," Dr. West blurted. "Speak to your interrogators on the surface who failed to protect you from me. Order them to prepare any Esk. I—you want to ask that Esk one question."

Mao III's breath hissed out, and Dr. West allowed the paralyzed hands to move across the console.

Without Dr. West's mental concentration, Mao III's stroke-paralyzed body was useless sinew, skin and bones. Now it moved as if Mao III still were in command.

Such a small decision. Mao III's thought derided. *To question an Esk. For seventeen years we have been peeling their brains like onions—to find nothing. They are simply mutated Eskimos. Nothing more.*

As Mao III's finger stabbed a pattern of buttons, Dr. West detected no discernible treachery in Mao III's thoughts. Colossal contempt emerged from Mao III: *Tapeworm, you will learn that Esks contain no magical racial memory. What magical question can you ask? My technicians have questioned them electrically until I was ill from the smell of charring flesh. Such innocent people: Esks cannot even think of lies to confess.*

There was a humming from the communications contact with the surface interrogation clinic, and Dr. West allowed Mao III's voice to speak. What emerged were Dr. West's orders.

The distant answer: "Within fifteen minutes an Esk will be positioned, *Chiu Hsing*." Click.

Dr. West's eyebrows rose. "*Chiu Hsing*, an honorific title meaning Saving Star? That also is the name of your mass-production automobile," Dr. West laughed softly as Mao III peered questioningly at him.

With the dignity of a Mandarin, Mao III nodded. "I gave happiness." As he detected the derision in Dr. West's thoughts, Mao III scowled. "You are a monomaniac convicted of attempted Eskimo genocide," Mao III's voice rushed as if he expected Dr. West to shut him off. "You would not be here if I had not suffered my brain-stroke, parasite! You have such little plans. To question an Esk until he dies. Listen, my tapeworm, the deepest words you will excavate from a stupid Esk are their incorrect Arctic myths, a confusion of bear worship and imperialist Bible fables." Mao III smiled. "Maoist science has proved Esks are nothing but mutated Eskimos." His voice shrilled. "You fraud, perhaps you were in the Arctic when the Esks still were few. But it is I who saw the future for China, who managed the rescue of thousands of Esks from Canadian starvation."

"And you're helping them breed beyond a billion?"

"They are as human as I am, and more human than you, you genocidal maniac." Mao III gasped for breath.

As Dr. West mentally strangled his speech, Mao III's thoughts continued attacking. *Tapeworm, you are sitting in my Command Vault as if you imagine you control the greatest organized power on Earth. Yet your mind is so small, you are planning to waste time personally interrogating, yes, torturing one little Esk.*

Dr. West said nothing. Finally he nodded his head. "As you say, the questioning is a small step. A larger step will follow." Dr. West improvised, forcing his weary smile at Mao III. "You are going to reappear before the world."

That plan now elaborated so swiftly in Dr. West's mind he thought he accidentally must have cued some original hypnoinstructions. "You are going to appear before the telecamera to demonstrate that your rumored retirement, nice word, is false. You have recovered from the rumored stroke. You are going to ask for an international teleconference between you and———."

No name automatically was formed by Dr. West's voice. Dr. West blinked. Nothing flowed, no well-ordered plan from his damaged memory. If the Harvard Circle had implanted further instructions in case he reached Mao III, they were erased. He was alone. Had he always been alone?

"The subject of the teleconference will be———." Dr. West waited. Nothing. He made his own decision based on his own beliefs of thirty years———. "You will propose a split-screen teleconference with the President of the United States. Before a world audience you will negotiate for international population control."

Dr. West smiled. "This may seem even more difficult than weapons control. Because population limitation proposals invariably enrage the populace of nationalistic countries, you will negotiate only for population limits for our Esks. It seems reasonable that the U.S. and China each should agree to limit their Esks to one billion."

"Limitation of Esks?" Mao III laughed aloud. "Your monomaniac fear of Esks reappears in another new disguise.

International limitation agreement? Impossible ideal. More impossible than atomic control."

Mao III's smile became malicious. "The United States could never agree to limitation of your Esk population. You look startled, my tapeworm. Either our electrointerrogation burned holes in your memory, or those murderous plotters in the CIA neglected to correctly inform you of what has happened in the United States during the last sixteen years."

Dr. West blinked in confusion.

"Don't you remember where you—slept during the last sixteen years?" Mao III persisted. "At least I have seen your dossier. Do I know more than you? The New China News Agency knows where you were. Seventeen years ago, in Canada you had been convicted of genocide as the whole outraged world remembers. You should have been executed. You were coddled in the New Ottawa Reformation Center. For some reason, which I do not know, soon you were moved to what Canadians euphemistically refer to as the Cold Room. So you can't remember what's truly happened. You've been asleep for sixteen years. Were you startled to awaken in the United States? You confessed to my own interrogators that you regained consciousness in a large basement room in a large building across the river from Washington."

Mao III laughed. "The imperialists finally had a use for you—you mass murderer. You were stolen from an indeterminate sentence in Canada, rescued because the United States Government finally concocted a filthy use for you."

Dr. West blinked. A circle of memory faces peered down at him. He had been startled by how old Fred Gatson looked. Beside him a man with a hypo also appeared vaguely familiar.

After a few weeks of "therapeutic adjustment" they had taken him upstairs to the Assistant Director, who was——.

Dr. West tensed. "I know all that, I know all that, the Harvard Circle!" he shouted as if in guilt. "Shut up or I'll stop your breathing."

But I have said so little, Mao thought, and shrugged. "Now you have negative feelings because the CIA has used you like a blind tapeworm. I am going to show you what truly is happening in the United States." His skeletal hand crept across the console toward the television buttons. "The U.S. no longer is what they described to you. Those imperialist warmongers never let you out of Central Intelligence Agency Building to see——."

With a frightened thought, Dr. West stopped Mao III's hand.

The worst sin is ignorance. Mao III's thought slashed.

"——your attempt is—to confuse me," Dr. West gasped. "Trying to disorient me, so I'll lose my—need to take action, lose my desire to control you."

My motive is exactly that, Mao III thought calmly, *but facts are true regardless of the motive of the one who brings them to your attention. Let your eyes witness truth, see telebroadcasts relayed from our satellites stationed above America, see films made by enlightened tourists.*

Dr. West's throat tightened. "I reject your attack. I don't want——." He closed his eyes. "Give orders through your foreign office," Dr. West shouted. "Now! Transmit to your so-called ambassador in Warsaw, to make an offer, an ultimatum for a teleconference within one week with the President of the United States."

"What a beautiful flower," Mao III exhaled after Dr. West had released his voice, "is each moment of life. Particularly beautiful is the last flower seen by a mountain climber whose grip is weakening on the precipice of life. I am that climber, and you are roped to me, Tapeworm. My military could not allow such a conference."

"I don't give a damn what your generals want."

"But the art of government is quite complex. During the three years since my first brain-stroke, the generals have been watching each other while waiting for me to die." Mao III's face contorted. "Already there must be rumors of your presence in this hole, my faith healer, but each general has hesitated to take action because this would arouse the suspicions of the others as to his real purpose."

Mao III smiled. "My pure-hearted generals! Each man dreams of the power to save the world. Each desires the empty thing which he thinks is down here in this Command Vault."

Dr. West said nothing.

"Is it power or the ghost of power?" Mao III laughed. "Now if I disappoint my generals and tell them that my health has been regained, that I plan to embark on a revisionist foreign policy without their guidance, that I intend to recognize and dignify the existence of the United States by engaging in a teleconference with that Barbarian Assassin whose capital is Hollywood, or Toledo or Washington, my generals will conclude I have gone mad. ——Or I have been captured by a rumored non-Chinese faith healer. My generals will be forced to unite and rescue me."

Dr. West glanced at the ceiling. Supposedly, it was 4000 feet to the surface.

"This hole, this coffin is not inviolable," Mao III taunted. "Perhaps today someone is drilling down through the concrete slab beneath the Winter Palace. Twenty-five years ago when my power was democratically confirmed, I ordered construction of this vault as a patriotic base against an imperialist or Russian revisionist preemptive nuclear attack. It was designed so that revisionist assassins would have difficulty fighting their way down to this vault. Under the concrete surface cap is entombed the device. Since then the architects of my vault's defense have died. But shrewd drilling might locate and disconnect this small device. An overimaginative general once intimated that I hold the whole city of Peking a hostage against my assassination. But truly it is a very small device only intended to seal off entry to this vault. Not even the Inner City would be obliterated."

Where is the detonation control? Dr. West thought.

Mao III shrugged. "If the generals and my loyal surface guard, and the civil police, and my Party police all could agree to trust each other, it would become a simple matter to drill down a series of exploratory holes and eventually disconnect the device."

Dr. West found himself listening for the elevator.

"Careful technicians with small loss of life should be able to locate the alarms and gas jets in the long elevator shaft even though all plans were burned twenty years ago when the architects were liquidated." Mao III laughed like a pleased young boy. "Then soldiers can be lowered on long cables. It would be fatal to use the elevator as long as I——." Mao III inadvertently visualized a switch on the control console. "Pull it and immobilize the elevator if you panic. But the soldiers will come down on ropes. They will push my servants aside because my servants are nonviolent, even too innocent to poison me."

"Then all of your servants down here are Esks," Dr. West said.

"The soldiers will push my servants aside and rescue me— from you."

"Then—welcome them," Dr. West retorted. "If this is what will happen, you should be happy to start the flow of events. Simply give orders to prepare for the teleconference. Now give the orders!"

Mao III sighed. "You still lack the subtle understanding necessary for a leader who desires to continue his long reign. Let me explain to you——."

Dr. West's brow wrinkles deepened, and Mao III cried out as his terrible cranial pain echoed dizzily into Dr. West, who relaxed the pain. If he killed Mao III he would be left with—nothing.

"——with nothing," Mao III gasped, "for either of us. The generals will come down to rescue something from you, my tapeworm. Not me, my power. For them, my living body will be an embarrassment like a mangy dog." He laughed bitterly. "But a dead leader can be used as a political martyr, you— CIA assassin."

"Goddammit, give the orders for the teleconference!" Dr. West repeated.

Mao III bleated in pain, and Dr. West had to wait for the grayness to clear from Mao III's brain.

"Consider," Mao III whispered and managed a twisted smile. "What is the simplest way to rid an old dog of his tapeworm? It is to smash his skull and give him a glorious funeral through the Great Square of Peking. This is the way I would like to die, but consider—is either of us ready?"

Dr. West's rage whirled Mao III's thoughts into gray confusion.

Unexpectedly, Dr. West glimpsed Mao III's visualization of an inconspicuous keyhole, a locked panel in the console.

Now Mao III was imagining an earthquake rumbling from the surface as he twisted in pain, and Dr. West felt the childhood clutch of claustrophobia. Mao III really would turn the key, detonating the nuclear device, erupting the Winter Palace, sealing them 4000 feet beneath Peking. Where was the key?

Dr. West knelt beside Mao III's contorted body on the floor and lifted the silver snakechain from Mao III's neck, drawing out of the black dacron robe the skin-tarnished key. *My control isn't as all-encompassing as I thought. I never detected the existence of the key, but perhaps you never thought of the detonator key until now—I hope——.*

Dr. West hung the key around his own neck.

When Dr. West helped Mao III's limp body back onto the chair in front of the console, he could detect no more mental resistance. Mao III's surprisingly determined resistance to a teleconference seemed at an end. His thin fingers depressed the proper buttons on the console. His sagging lips mouthed Dr. West's orders to the Chinese Foreign Office, and Dr. West warmed with excitement as he heard his orders being transmitted into action.

Although the Chinese Federation of Nations now held three seats in the United Nations General Assembly, and their dacron red-and-black robes no longer attracted tourist attention within the glass-walled U.N. sanctuary on Manhattan Island, all diplomatic contact with the United States still was carried on via the Catholic Capitalist Principality of Warsaw. Thus, the U.S. Ambassador in Warsaw was invited to sit in secret session with his Chinese counterpart. Negotiations leading toward the international teleconfrontation had begun.

"Tapeworm, you are uselessly sacrificing your life and mine because your President will not agree to face me in a television debate."

"Wishful thinking on your part. Signal your interrogators on the surface. What has happened to that Esk who was supposed to be readied for me to question——?"

"Let me show you telecasts of the situation of the Esks throughout the United States."

"No!" Dr. West shouted with unexplainable rage and pain. "Show me the Esk in the interrogation room."

A shuffling sound caused Dr. West to whirl. False alarm. An Esk servant had wandered into the Control Room carrying the afternoon tea tray. Dr. West ignored this Esk.

On the telescreen appeared the frightened face of a Chinese interrogation technician, confessing there had been minor technical difficulties in wiring the Esk's frontal lobes. There would be another short hold.

Dry-mouthed, Dr. West waited for his tea to cool, waited for Mao III to drink first, noisily.

"Tapeworm, I am alive because my Esks prepare my meals. Do you consider Esks inhuman because they not only eschew violence, they are too innocent to poison———?"

"Why should they bother to poison you? They're poisoning the whole world with sheer numbers."

"You're hysterical and stupid," Mao III replied. "Your Esk strapped on the table up there will be as unable to explain the purpose or lack of purpose of the Esks as you or I would be if we were tortured to explain the purpose of man on this Earth."

"Is your strategy," Dr. West retorted, "to argue against anything I try to do? By deriding me are you trying to erode my self-confidence? Are you trying to wear me down? I'm so much stronger than you, you won't escape that way!"

"Your President cannot agree to confront me in a teleconference if the agenda includes the international problem of population limitation of the Esks. He is a practical man, as practical as I am, and he will create an excuse, an incident to avoid facing me in a teleconference if the subject is to be population control of the Esks. Tapeworm, let me show you the United States. I will show you why your President cannot agree to———."

"Shut up!" Dr. West turned away and closed his eyes. *The President would welcome another international teleconfrontation.* His thoughts had the sound of another man's voice.

Now he remembered George Bruning's calmly intelligent face. Dr. Bruning was not a medical doctor; he was the Assistant Director of the Central Intelligence Agency. "——— my idea but the President took it up," George Bruning had

said. "A fresh innovation in international diplomacy——."
Dr. West blinked. George Bruning had been briefing him for
this purpose.

To his memory, George smiled expansively. "Everyone has
a use. Ages ago when Paul and I—the President and I were
in the Hasty Pudding Club—that's at Harvard, I said *Paul
you ought to enter politics. At nineteen you're already a
greater actor than Lincoln*——." George Bruning had leaned
toward Dr. West. "——both our previous international
teleconfrontations have made use of our U.S. Information
Service relay satellites blanketing the Earth—split screen,
each leader in his own country, almost face-to-face—instant
audio translations from a hundred satellites covering the
world. They saw it all. The BIG audience! And both times the
President scored!

"——the first time he was a little nervous, even though we
had dug one pitfall for the Premier." George Bruning had
smiled shyly. "——before accepting, the Premier was cautious. Maybe he'd read U.S. history, the Kennedy-Nixon
debates, little pitfalls of television. The Premier agreed to
discuss only three of our suggested subjects. These safe subjects were coffee prices, weather control and the international student exchange program.

"Unimportant agenda," Dr. Bruning said, "but at least the
personalities of both men were to be exposed to the world.
To our dismay the Premier projected surprisingly great dignity for an assassin. He appeared to be an upstanding man,
which he was not." Dr. Bruning's frown gradually spread into
a smile of remembrance. "Our President—what a warm
personality! As a former motion picture actor, Paul really
knows how to come across. But it would have been a stand-
off." George Bruning grinned. "I crawled underneath his
teleprompter and handed him the pics.

"——since they were on the final subject for discussion,
the international student exchange, the President could use
those enlarged pics." George smugly smiled. "Of course, I'm
only Deputy Director of the Agency. But one of my agents
actually helped the Premier's other policemen set up that
machinegun. My man was wearing one of our 4mm cameras.
This happened three months before the teleconfrontation."

"The Premier had assured their relatives that the student leaders merely had been exiled because of the march. The Premier had said the troublemakers were benevolently sent to China as part of the student exchange program. Already their relatives had been receiving enthusiastic but typed postcards from China. They liked China so well they might never return, the postcards said."

"——until our President held up the pics to the TV camera, clearly revealing to the world the students' bodies lying at the foot of the wall. In the background was the Premier's easily recognizable Capitol Building." George Bruning sighed. "The mob dug up the bodies of the students while the Premier was trying to escape out the other side of his Capitol Building. The new government is much more acceptable to the CIA." He spread his arms.

"——after that another teleconfrontation with another head of State was difficult to arrange. Necessarily, its arrangement had to be more subtle. The President lost, as promised. Like billiards—pool, you know, like a hustler. We're looking ahead to the big one——."

There was a buzzing sound, and Dr. West blinked. A yellow communications light was flashing on the control console.

"Do you still desire to attempt your useless interrogation of an Esk?" The thin voice beside him was Mao III's.

On the telescreen gleamed a white room with white-gowned figures bending over a surgical table. Dr. West winced at the similarity. It could have been the same room in which he had been interrogated.

Now the viewpoint from the closed-circuit TV system shifted to a high lens looking down from the ceiling. Dr. West remembered staring up from the table at the ceiling grill with a camera lens glinting behind it while cold hands forced wired needles into his skull and consciousness faded.

On the table, the Esk's eyelids were creeping closed. His shaven head glittered like a pincushion with a tangle of wires leading to the electrosensitizer and the reaction dials. As the electric current increased, the Esk lolled his head from side to side. Wide-cheeked, with a massive lower jaw, barrel chest and short legs, physically this Esk resembled an Eskimo.

One of the white-capped figures twisted a knob, and the Esk's eyes snapped open. Dr. West recognized the humming sound and the distant voice questioning. In Chinese, the Esk mumbled his name, a Chinese name, and the name of the Esk segrecommune where he labored.

A technician glanced up meaningfully at the camera lens.

Dr. West swallowed convulsively.

Tapeworm, Chinese electrocranial occupuncture is at your service, Mao's thoughts derided him. *You have only to think, and my mouth is happy to question this Esk or a hundred Esks. Every conceivable question already has been asked.*

Mao III's thoughts collapsed as Dr. West intruded strongly, and Mao III's mouth hesitantly formed a word. Mao III's voice spoke in Modern Eskimo, a language he did not know. *"Ilaga,* my friend——," Mao III spoke as Dr. West thought. *"Nanuktuakjung,* little bear, Grandfather Bear approaching——"

Dr. West's thoughts poured from Mao III's mouth while the Esk's eyes gradually closed. There was no reaction. Dr. West stopped, distressed.

He fails to understand you, Mao III thought maliciously. *He is culturally Chinese. Of course he can't understand Eskimo. He was born in China, and three years before that his father was born in China, and three years before that his grandfather was born in China, and three years before that his great-grandfather was born in China, and perhaps his great-great-grandfather was one of the first thousands of underprivileged Eskimos the Chinese Federation of Nations, at my orders, rescued from Canada some seventeen years ago.*

Dr. West concentrated, squeezing aside Mao III's thoughts, and using Mao III's mouth.

"Grandfather Bear is approaching," Mao III's voice gasped Dr. West's thoughts, this time in Chinese. "Great White Bear from the sky," Mao III's voice helplessly hissed through the microphone at the Esk, and Dr. West's memories of the original little group of Esks telling night stories of the bear in the sky poured from Mao III's mouth with increasing intensity. "He will come. Grandfather Bear coming down from the sky. He hungers for us with joy. With joy, all will be one."

The Esk's eyes widened in ecstasy, his mouth opening. "Grandfather Bear, Grandfather Be—Grandfather Dragon-Tiger!"

Dragon-tiger? Dr. West thought with disgusted surprise, and glanced at Mao III.

Dragons, tigers, Chinese symbols of spiritual power have overlaid the fading Bear symbol. Mao III's smugness enclosed Dr. West. *My tapeworm, your Polar Bear symbol is nothing more than an animistic relic of prehistoric Eskimo beliefs polluted by capitalist biblical underexposure. Nothing more. Did you think——.*

"Grandfather Bear is coming down from the sky. Prepare this world," Dr. West's voice-thoughts surged from Mao III into the microphone, and the Esk lolled his head from side to side, and Dr. West paused, trying to remember how it was out under the Arctic stars——.

No matter how deep you interrogate this lump of flesh, no matter how ridiculously you try to trigger his racial memory, Mao III's thoughts taunted, *he can tell you nothing new. How can he tell you secrets of a World Beyond when the only imprint within him is from this humble world?*

One of the white-capped technicians glanced up at the ceiling camera, and gradually the electrosensitization of the Esk's cerebrum was being increased while Dr. West's thoughts spoke through Mao III. Dr. West was reproducing the religious excitement of Edwardluk twenty-two years ago, when Edwardluk had clutched his arm.

"Grandfather Bear approaching, closer and closer as we increase. He is coming! Our bodies are preparing the world for him. His great hunger is for us. Our bodies will reward him for our birth!"

As if in answer, the Esk's voice squealed with—joy? Abruptly, the Esk's pulse rate jumped to 150 per minute as his smile opened in a shout. "Grandfather, I—we altogether in you." His face strained with joy and tears. It almost seemed as if his hair was standing on end in a static-electric effect as he relived the myth his father must have told him.

"Grandfather, come down! We prepare world for you! For you we are ripening——."

The white gowns flurried about the Esk. On the table they were giving him oxygen resuscitation. Now external heart massage——.

A lot of them die like that, Mao III thought. *Wasted, I suppose due to an electrosensitization overload.*

A white-robed technician glanced up at the camera as if in frightened apology.

Dr. West sat there sweating. He stared at Mao III. "After I rest we will question another Esk." Dr. West's voice rose with excitement. "I don't believe this Esk died from incompetent electrosensitization. If Esks could be made to die—triggered by mental suggestion of something coming down from the sky? I—he died—so happily as if——."

"He was electrocuted," Mao III taunted, and released a hail of words upon Dr. West's weariness. "Tapeworm, Pavlovian cues such as the wave of a flag can cause a soldier to leap up into machine-gun bullets. Other triggers such as the news of the death of a loved one can cause a man already subject to arteriosclerosis to fall down with a heart attack, and so a sudden gust of wind plucks an overripe fruit."

Mao III's voice rose. "Even if you triggered that Esk to die, this does not prove that your words or his belief had Marxist Materialist reality, or even that other Esks can be psychophysically conditioned to ripeness for such nonsense. All Maoist Esks know there is nothing physical Out There In The Sky which desires to eat them. Marxist-Maoists stand on scientific dialectical logic. In any case, that childishly suggestible Esk will be proved to have died of too much electricity, which is a physical force——," Mao III stammered, as Dr. West was able to shut off his physical voice.

But Mao III's thoughts swept on like an erosive river. *Tapeworm, we both should admit that Esks simply are mutated Eskimos, human beings like ourselves, merely more fecund and more obedient. Listen to me, my tapeworm, subconsciously you have been searching for excuses to murder Esks. You want proof they are not human so it will salve your conscience for the mass murder of the Eskimos you consummated more than seventeen years ago. With imperial-ist-cultured bacteria you almost succeeded in Eskimo geno-cide. Was it twenty-two Eskimos died? Before the eyes of the world you were convicted of mass murder. Even in the most reactionary capitalist news media you are, shall we say, enshrined as a homicidal genocidal maniac!*

"No! You have twisted it!" Dr. West shouted. "My in-tent——." His voice trailed off, and he felt Mao III's stream of destructive thoughts backing him into a corner so that Mao III could escape.

Tapeworm, your insane attempt to seize my power is paranoid. Admit you are God who will cure the chaos of the world. You are trembling. Little man, you can't even remem-ber what you were instructed to do. The little imperialist schemers of the CIA were able to conceal what has happened during the last sixteen years from you. You! Why else would they select you, who have been inert in a Cold Room for sixteen years, for this mission? Because you don't know what's been happening in this world.

Tapeworm, you are their last weapon for mass murder and not only of Esks! Mao III closed his eyes. *You have forgot-ten your orders because they are so horrible you cannot allow yourself to think. Once you were a good man. There still is humanity in us both. At least, we are both of the human race. Yes, we are on the same side with all of enlightened humanity. We are both human. You can rise and walk from this vault into freedom. No one will harm you. You are freed of all murder. In China there is no murder and I declare you free of all guilt. You are cleansed of the bloodstains of CIA control. Good-bye, my friend, you are free to walk to the elevator and rise into the sunshine.*

"You sly bastard!" Dr. West rose, his muscles tightening.

His head aching with concentration, he caused Mao III to slump to the floor, where he lay jerking with spastic agony.

"Don't try to attack me again." Dr. West swayed in the echoes of Mao III's smothering agony as he writhed on the floor.

"When I am ready," Dr. West gasped, "you—I will exam-ine other Esks until we——."

Murderer! Even from the floor Mao III thrust up his

javelin thoughts. *You hope you find evidence of nonhuman origin and that it will excuse your crimes. Maniac! You think you warn the world and now people listen? Seventeen years ago your lies that Esks are not human were disproved. Mutants* ARE *human! You biased expert, the joke is on you. I know more of the origin of the Esks than you.*

In his memory, Dr. West saw the bare rock ledge where the Boothia Peninsula thrust against the frozen sea. Climbing onto the huge ledge he'd looked down into the crater of the Burned Place, what Edwardluk had called the Navel of the World. No airplane crash had made that scar. There was no metal wreckage. The only odd fragments, some white, some charred, were small shards of what might have been ceramic pottery.

Erected on the bottom of the shallow Burned Place stood old Peterluk's tent. Only his wife emerged. Peterluk had fled again as if he feared the whiteman, as if he had a bad conscience, Dr. West thought. And Peterluk had returned after concealing his rifle, avidly eyeing Dr. West's rifle. Dr. West had asked him where all these young—Eskimos had come from. Peterluk had hunted on the Boothia Peninsula before the Eskimo Cultural Sanctuary was established. But Peterluk was evasive, angrily attacking the beliefs of the new people.

"There is no Grandfather Bear coming down from the sky. You and me don't believe ignorant things like that!"

But Peterluk accidentally admitted a "star" had fallen; denied it.

In inexplicable anger, Peterluk lied that the crater was made by whitemen with sticks of dynamite. "You think this person lies? Then you don't believe the Egg of God fell here. You don't believe a whitemen's ship poke up its eye on a stick. Like a whale with many whitemen but this person was stronger than—you!"

Peterluk had tried to wrest away Dr. West's rifle. Dr. West had been too young and strong in those days. The injured Peterluk had fled toward his hidden rifle, but he had not used the illegal rifle that summer to kill a whiteman.

He shot the priest-pilot when winter and Dr. West returned. So Peterluk murdered a whiteman with his rust-stained Russian military rifle, and was confined to the New Ottawa Reformation Center, never properly interrogated concerning the origin of the Esks.

And Dr. West had begun to understand that Peterluk and his old wife had been the only two Eskimos among————.

Yes, Esks, you had to count the days of your wife's pregnancy before you even realized how different they were, Mao's thoughts taunted. *Whiteman, you arrived years too late to see what the Russians saw in the Burned Place.* "Your Navel of the World," Mao III laughed from the floor where he lay like a sack. "It is amusing that even now, after another twenty-two years, you still don't understand what you saw. It is not that Maoism has so many more well-trained believers throughout the world than the CIA. It is simply that Chinese travelers collect even the most useless data, rumors, photographs. Everything is noted, filed and cross-filed. And we have more highly placed spies in Russia collecting observations. From infinite unrelated data, the computer arranges valid and reliable patterns."

Dr. West permitted—mentally helped Mao III to rise to his chair in front of the console. Mao III was leading him on for some reason.

"It is odd," Mao III laughed, "that I am the only head of state who has taken the trouble to learn how to question an Information Retrieval Computer directly. Surely direct access to infinite global data multireferenced and computer-rated for reliability should be more useful to a head of state than the filtered information which is sprinkled on the head of your President by his cabinet officers, by his Presidential staff, by his CIA advisors, by his Joint Chiefs of Staff, none of whom agree."

Mao III's fingers riffled over the index buttons. A still photograph of a rock ledge appeared on the telescreen. Separately projected across the top of the photograph was a date; and some symbols separately projected beside it appeared as a row of index numbers, presumably guides to related data. "Do you recognize this photograph?"

"I assume it is the Burned Place but————," Dr. West stared uncertainly. "There is rarely that much snow. The high Arctic is dry. The wind sweeps off————."

"It is not the Burned Place. It simply happens to be the nearest photograph to what was the location of the North Magnetic Pole thirty-eight years ago. See the date in the corner: 1971. The other numbers are keys." Mao III's fingers signaled these index numbers into the console. "The skill is in selecting the most pertinent general key number—subjects. Eskimos. Scientific searches. Perhaps meteorites. Aircraft crashes. Satellites which have fallen. I repeat the location designation: North Magnetic Pole, Boothia Peninsula, not too specific. In the computer, an immense pattern of related information has materialized. A leader's whole life would be wasted reading it. To place an electronic pinpoint in this vast matrix, I introduce the phonetic number-name Peterluk."

Mao III's fingers moved, and the photograph of a cautiously smiling young Eskimo holding out a white fox fur appeared, new index numbers materializing above his head.

Dr. West blinked. "That doesn't look like——. It must have been taken when he was a young man. What's that behind him?"

Mao III depressed one finger, and a photograph of what evidently was an official report appeared—printed in Russian characters.

"For translations from the language of imbeciles," Mao III said, "the sound vocoder is slowest but will allow us to simultaneously study the photographs. The inefficient vocoder should stammer a synopsis of those items which are pertinent to Peterluk—and to my question pattern, which still is too diffuse."

His finger moved, and the mechanical voice of the vocoder howled: "CANADIAN ESKIMO SELF-DESIGNATED PETERLUK. CANADA. NORTHWEST TERRITORIES. BOOTHIA PENINSULA. ESKIMO CULTURAL SANCTUARY EXTENDING NORTH FROM——."

Mao III's finger pressed. "Spare us these bureaucratic details." A blur of documents and index numbers swept across the screen. "Unfortunately, this computer is not capable of a direct answer to your amorphous question as to what caused the Esks. This Information Retrieval System simply flickers through molecular patterns of data, abstracting. My prod here and poke there narrows its tentative synopsis until the edge of a pattern small enough for a human mind to grasp is offered to me to guide———."

A still photograph of an old-model nuclear submarine appeared on the screen. The vocoder howled: "POLAR RE-SEARCH SUBMARINE KOLOGRIVOV. REVISED MISSION. UNDETECT-ED INVESTIGATION OF TERMINUS METEORIC OR MANMADE ATMOSPHERIC STREAK."

Mao III pressed the button corresponding to the first index number, and a jerky movie film appeared on the screen. Bundled men were clambering from the deck of the subma-rine into a rubber boat. Another Russian-made film clip, evidently photographed from the conning tower by the same hand-held camera, showed the rubber boat bunting among the ice cakes. The distant men scrambled onto the rocks and upward.

Dr. West finally recognized the promontory. "The Burned Place."

"U.S. HAD NOT SENT AIRCRAFT TO INVESTIGATE PSEUDOME-TEORIC-TYPE FLASH. THEREFORE RUSSIANS IN STATE OF READ-INESS FOR U.S. MILITARY TRAP ON CANADIAN SOIL," the vocod-er howled, and Mao III nodded. "This is as closely as the computer approaches reasoning as it abstracts the pertinent essentials from a hundred documents and offers us its synop-sis with the best internal reliability."

Film from a hand-held camera was showing bundled Rus-sians walking gingerly among large broken objects and nerv-ously glancing at the sky as if expecting the contrails of USAF jets.

Rising from his chair, Dr. West shouted: "Close-up! Is there film showing a close-up of what in hell those things are."

As if anticipating Mao III's finger, the computer projected a close-up of a Russian hammering with his rifle butt at a huge dark curve. It looked like ceramic clay. The rifle butt failed to chip it. The camera shifted to another broken curve. *The two might fit together,* Dr. West thought. The outside of each curve was roughened, darkened as if charred. The insides of the curves gleamed white. A broken edge was thicker than the Russian's hand-width. *Like a gigantic mol-lusk's shell,* Dr. West thought as a Russian walked upright under the jagged upper end of the curve and turned and grinned bashfully at the cameraman.

"RUSSIANS UNABLE TO IDENTIFY BROKEN OBJECTS," the vocoder howled. "PLANNED TO REMOVE FOR FURTHER STUDY."

"Good," said Mao III's voice, "the computer has narrowed the available data and is attempting chronological order."

The Russian film-maker must have whirled with his camera. On the screen there was a glimpse of Russians scattering, a rifle was raised, and then the camera steadied at a stocky figure clambering down over the ledges.

A closer view showed the young Eskimo holding out a white fox fur and grinning expectantly as if he imagined all whitemen who illegally entered the Eskimo Cultural Sanctuary came to trade. Dr. West blinked. "I'll be damned. It *is* Peterluk as a young man. Look at him grinning at that Russian's rifle. He wants it so bad he can taste it!"

"ESKIMO ADMITTED OBSERVATION OF METEOR FLASH," the vocoder howled. "UNABLE TO ESTIMATE DATE. CLAIMED TOOK NOTHING FROM BURNED SITE. AFTER REPEATED QUESTIONING ADMITTED HE HAD BROKEN A SMALLER SHELL."

The film showed a Russian lifting a white curve perhaps only an inch thick and large enough to shade the Russian's head and shoulders like a huge eggshell.

"FROM ITS POSITION IN WRECKAGE, RUSSIANS CONCLUDED REMNANT OF SMALLER SHELL WAS INNER SHELL. QUESTIONED ESKIMO AS TO SHELL'S CONTENTS. ESKIMO DENIED HAD BROKEN INNER SHELL."

The film showed a Russian carrying a curve of the inner shell toward the water.

A long shot showed four Russians dragging a fragment of the larger outer shell into the rubber boat. "ELEVEN TRIPS TO FERRY ALL SHELL TO SUBMARINE. WHILE QUESTIONED, ESKIMO DENIED PREVIOUS OBSERVATION OF METEOR FLASH. ON FURTHER QUESTIONING, ESKIMO ESTIMATED DATE OF METEOR FLASH AS ONE MOON BEFORE BIRTH. ON FURTHER QUESTIONING, DENIED ANY OTHER ESKIMOS ON BOOTHIA PENINSULA. WHEN QUESTIONED IF HAD OBSERVED U.S. AIRCRAFT, ESKIMO STATED HAD NEVER SEEN AN AIRCRAFT. WHEN FORCE APPLIED TO ESKIMO, ADMITTED FLOCKS OF AIRCRAFT DARKENED SKY EACH

DAY. CAPTAIN CONCLUDED SAFER TO CONTINUE QUESTIONING ON SUBMARINE THAN TO DISPOSE OF UNRELIABLE ESKIMO WHILE ON CANADIAN TERRITORY."

The film showed two towering Russians smiling, their friendly arms draped over Peterluk's shoulders. Between them the Eskimo stood like a worried dwarf, his white fox fur hanging limply from one hand.

"INVITED ESKIMO TO VISIT SUBMARINE," the vocoder howled its chronological synopsis from what must have been Russian naval reports. "ESKIMO STATED HAPPY TO VISIT INSIDE OF WHALE. SUGGESTED BEFORE GOING MUST CLIMB LEDGE TO GET OUTER PARKA. RESTRAINED BY A RUSSIAN. ESKIMO STATED MUST TELL WIFE AND NEW BABY—DESCRIBED AS QUICK BABY SINCE LAST MOON. TWO RUSSIANS RESTRAIN ESKIMO."

The screen was blank. Evidently the cameraman knew what not to film.

"SEARCH FOR REPORTED WOMAN AND CHILD INTERRUPTED," the vocoder howled. "HIGH CONTRAIL OF AIRCRAFT OBSERVED. SUBMARINE SUBMERGED. SHORE PARTY SCATTERED. ESKIMO VANISHED. LEAVING FOX FUR. HURRIED SEARCH FOR ESKIMO UNSUCCESSFUL. SHORE PARTY EVACUATED TO SUBMARINE. ALL TRACES OF LANDING ELIMINATED. CRATE OF AMMUNITION LOST. ONE RIFLE UNACCOUNTED FOR."

"Replay that part about the quick baby," Dr. West exclaimed. "Signal for more information about that——."

"——IDDEN BY RUSSIANS DETAILED QUOTE: THE TREACHEROUS ESKIMO INFORMED CAPTAIN GOGOL AND MYSELF THAT HE WOULD BE VERY PLEASED TO ACCOMPANY US INTO WHAT HE APPEARED TO ASSUME WAS A SPECIES OF WHALE BUT FIRST HE MUST BID FAREWELL TO HIS WIFE AND NEW BABY. WHEN I REMINDED HIM THAT HE PREVIOUSLY HAD INFORMED US THAT HE WAS THE ONLY ESKIMO ON THIS SIDE OF THE BOOTHIA PENINSULA, HE STATED THAT THIS WAS A QUICK BABY CONCEIVED LESS THAN A MOON AGO. NATURALLY OUR DILIGENT SEARCH PRODUCED NEITHER THE NONEXISTENT MOTHER NOR THE NONEXISTENT CHILD."

Mao III was pressing index numbers which had been projected during this quotation from the naval report, and the vocoder howled inane statistics about the Boothia Peninsula and the periods of the Moon. Mao III shrugged. "Evidently there is no additional information filed in the category: Quick Babies, Boothia Peninsula."

A still photograph showed men in white coats standing proudly in front of a darkly oval patchwork reconstruction. Seen as a whole, the outer shell had less resemblance to a huge mollusk's shell. Darkly charred, it loomed behind the white-coated men.

"LOCATION MURMANSK, MINUS THIRTY-SEVEN YEARS," the vocoder howled. "RECONSTRUCTION IN MAXIMUM SECURITY SITUATION. CHEMICAL ANALYSIS BY POLITICALLY RELIABLE SOURCE. THEORIZE LIQUID SHOCK-ABSORBING LAYER BETWEEN HEAT-DARKENED OUTER SHELL AND WHITE INNER SHELL. DUE TO HIGH LEVEL OF INTERNATIONAL COOPERATION IN ASTRONOMY IN 1970s INNER POLITBURO DECISION TO WITHHOLD ALL INFORMATION FROM RUSSIAN ASTRONOMERS. POLITBURO DEBATE SIGNIFICANCE OF NO U.S. EXPEDITION TO CRASH SITE. PENDING POLITICAL CLARIFICATION, OBJECT CLASSIFIED TOP SECRET. FOR MAXIMUM SECURITY FURTHER SCIENTIFIC RESEARCH TO BE CANCELLED. FILMS ORDERED BURNED."

"But impossible to keep a secret in Russia," Mao III's voice laughed, "especially in the 1970s when that object fell, when Maoism was again the wave of the future, and friends of China, old Stalinists, were reemerging everywhere. As you saw, even the motion picture films, which the Inner Politburo of revolving revisionists ordered burned, evidently were secretly copied by alert Stanlinists in the pay of Chinese military intelligence agents. With so much corruption in Russia, I suspect your CIA also possesses ancient copies. But those who sent you here would not confide in you, my tapeworm."

On the screen, microphotographs showed the molecular structure of the inner shell. "CARBON-OXYGEN-CALCIUM," the vocoder overly condensed a long scientific report. "MICROSCOPIC SMEAR LIFE SUBSTANCE INNER SHELL. POSSIBLE HEAT-DEGRADED PROTEINS. DNA UNIDENTIFIABLE. DISARRANGED BUT POSSIBLY HUMAN OR ANTHROPOID PATTERN. NO EVIDENCE OF CAUSE-DISAPPEARANCE OF THEORETICAL LIFE-FORM IN SHELL."

"I am more free than my computer to theorize," Mao III laughed. "That barbarian Eskimo, when he poked whatever was mashed within that inner shell, probably sucked his finger. Then hungrily smiling he ate the strange meat without a bellyache. I hope it was only the remains of a NASA chimpanzee and not an astronaut."

"INNER POLITBURO DECISION BY VOTE OF 4 TO 1," the vocoder howled, "ORIGIN OF UNKNOWN OBJECT WAS U.S. BECAUSE NO U.S. INVESTIGATION OF CRASH OBJECT MUST BE PROVOCATIVE U.S. STRATEGIC HOAX, VOTE 3 TO 2. POLITICAL RESULT UNPREDICTABLE, VOTE 5 TO 0. PROVOCATEUR SHELL TO BE DESTROYED AT ONCE AND NO FURTHER COGNIZANCE."

"Even so, a beautiful hoax," Mao III laughed. "For once you American bunglers nearly were able to keep a secret from the Russians—and even from us. In the years since then, our friends of China at Cape Kennedy and at Vandenberg never were able to collect reliable information as to just how the hoax was secretly constructed, launched and deliberately crashed. In fact, we never have found the evidence of U.S. origin. Do not look so discontented because the CIA did not inform you. After all, this CIA hoax was perpetrated about thirty-eight years ago, in 1971."

Mao III's voice was smooth as poisoned honey. "Even now, you would not be informed of its secret historical malfunction because you were to be parachuted into China where the CIA still thinks we are retarded angry children who know nothing. But I assure you that such a hoax never could have been consummated, even in those days, upon alert Maoist scientists."

Dr. West said nothing.

"You are wishful thinking it was not a hoax," Mao III taunted, "because your life—your beliefs tremble on a pinpoint hope that something which fell upon the Boothia Peninsula will confirm your monomaniac insistence that Esks are not human. Murderer, you would lunge anywhere for evidence of nonhuman origin to justify your hatred of the Esks. You would embrace any obvious U.S. hoax. Always you would clutch false evidence that Esk origin is from the sky because that is what you need to believe—that Esks are nonhuman. Otherwise you would be forced to see yourself as the rest of the world sees you, you convicted mass murderer. See yourself as you are, monomaniac murderer, leave me, tapeworm. Go! Leave this vault."

"You bastard," Dr. West gasped. "You can't wear me down with talk. You can't drive me insane. I won't have a heart attack because of you. If your spies in America could find no evidence of construction and launch in America—of a nonmetallic object of large size—I know damn well it wasn't built in America. It was no hoax built on this Earth. And I'll tell you this. The crash wasn't investigated by an American search party because sophisticated radar would have told the Air Force it was not a metallic object. It would have echoed radar pulses as if made of stone. Maybe the Russian radar of that period was not able to discriminate, and they thought one of our space experiments had fallen. Curious, like cautious vultures, they sent the sub. Undoubtedly U.S. forces had crossed off the atmospheric streak as only a stony meteorite."

"Tapeworm, don't you wonder why the fall-streak of such a large meteorite did not attract an American scientific expedition?"

"I—that was years ago, in the 1970s. I——." Even in his heart-pounding anger Dr. West realized from Mao III's quick thoughts that the orange flashing light on the telescreen indicated a high priority telesatellite transmission.

On the telescreen appeared a symbolic dove of peace, then a film clip of a peaceful wheat field dimpling in the breeze, and a peaceful baby smiling in living color, its arms outstretched to the world, then the American flag gently waving, while the audio played: "Oh, beautiful, for spacious skies——." All this was an introductory film clip, a station break via hundreds of U.S. Information Agency satellites sprinkled throughout the heavens. Shielded from the jamming of rival foreign teleinformation services, the U.S. telesatellites were relaying on all eighty-two channels down to every square foot of the Earth.

Magnificent redwood trees appeared against the sky, and dissolved into a friendly faced man standing with his hand resting on the shoulder of a smiling boy, a boy who was deeply tanned and slightly Oriental around the eyes so that he could be recognized as almost any nationality.

Smiling into the teleprompter, the friendly man was speaking, and the telesatellites over China relayed a peaceful-voiced Chinese translation: "Friends, I bring you greetings from your friend, the President of the United States. I am his good friend. My job is Secretary of State. I want to be your friend. The President and all my friends throughout the world call me Dino. My friends, don't go away from your television sets. Please tell your children to listen. This important announcement also concerns them. The President of the United States has asked me to tell you how happy he is that the Chairman of the Chinese Federation of Nations has suggested a friendly teleconference."

The Secretary of State smiled through his transparent teleprompter and took a deep breath. "The President of the United States has asked me to tell you he feels honored that the Chairman of the Chinese Federation of Nations has invited him to a split-screen teleconference. Don't go away from your television sets. This historic meeting which promises greater happiness for all peoples throughout the world will be broadcast at this very same time tomorrow. You, your children, all ages will want to witness this historic meeting. Be sure to tune in———."

Jagged static squealed off the sound and momentarily distorted the smiling face of the Secretary of State as he was dissolved into majestic redwood trees. The American flag billowed in the sunset as Mao III switched off the broadcast and the picture contracted to a little bright spot which vanished.

"Tomorrow." Dr. West felt hollow and unprepared; there had been no mention of the agenda: were the subjects for discussion still being haggled over in Warsaw?

"Now the military will be forced to face the fact that I am—insane. Insane to have suggested such a meeting," Mao III blurted. "The military will disconnect my external broadcast antenna. It stands undefended on top of the Winter Palace. They will not be sufficient fools to let me match myself against your robust President. Perhaps one of my understudies———. No, the generals are too cautious even for that. They will deny there was an agreement for a teleconference. China's prestige must be preserved. They will denounce your Secretary of State as a hoaxer. Then they will come down the elevator shaft and—rescue me—kill us both!"

Dr. West glanced at the guard lights on the console. Evidently the elevator shaft still was safely locked at the surface. If the console could be believed, the protective devices still were cocked——.

"It is a U.S. hoax!" Mao III blustered. "Your Secretary of State was afraid to mention that population limitation would be on the agenda. It won't be. Your Government already has gained a propaganda advantage. Now the CIA will create an incident. Perhaps an American ship will sink, and this will be blamed on our nuclear submarines defensively stationed off your coast. Your Government will use the television time tomorrow for a taped denunciation. Your President will not face me. How can he, when the agenda we sent to Warsaw requires a discussion of the International Esk Problem? Your Government fears I am going to suggest bilateral population limitation with quotas and international inspections of our respective populations of Esks."

Mao III ended triumphantly: "Any suggestion that the increasing number of American Esks should be limited would cause a political uproar in the United States. Any suggestion that their number should be reduced would cause revolution!"

"You're unfamiliar with the United States' way of life," Dr. West replied.

"No. You are. Admit that you haven't seen the United States for more than seventeen years."

"Dammit, let me see the United States!"

"But the ghastly collapse of Canada proves my foresight in China. From the first, I segregated our Esks in their own separate labor communes. There were two reasons for this." Mao III's hands moved on the console. "I'll show you. These are merely recent film clips from Canada, so you can deny your own eyesight. In Canada——."

No! Dr. West thought forcibly. *First show me the United States.*

And Mao III's skeletal fingers obeyed.

Across the screen jiggled an electric bus as if filmed by a tourist. The neon advertising below its windows blinked: FINE FUNERALS FOR HUMANS OR ESKS; then ASTROBOY CONVENIENT MINIMUM EXCRETABLE BREAD. The crowded bus turned toward the camera. Its destination tape read: WILSHIRE TO WESTWOOD. The film with an amateurish zoom enlarged the bus driver's calmly smiling face.

"You see," Mao III said triumphantly, "the bus driver is an American Esk. He is the capitalist solution to all the undesirable jobs for which a living wage had to be paid— until the willing Esks appeared."

"FILMED MINUS SIX MONTHS," the vocoder of the Information Retrieval Computer howled, "BY STUDENT-VISITOR LOS ANGELES."

Mao III's finger shifted on the console, and Dr. West stared at a film of a huge white truck entering a suburban driveway of a high-rise apartment. As it stopped, a great white scoop-jaw above the cab of the truck reached forward and downward like a dragonfly larva's jaw. From the cab of the truck, a hurrying man in white emerged, seized a garbage can and emptied it into the jaw. The camera zoomed at the man's happily smiling face, an Esk. "With Americans wedded to the four-hour day," Mao III laughed, "how could all these necessary services function without Esks?"

Click, on the screen appeared towering condominium apartments beside the East River near the ancient United Nations building, and this more expertly handled camera explored past the Esk doorman into the ground floor lobby of the apartment building where a short-legged but attractively uniformed and smiling maid was walking toward the escalator.

"Another Esk." Mao III restlessly pressed a button, and an unsteady film showed a large concrete-block house. "SIOUX FALLS," the vocoder howled as the lens-view zoomed into the screened window. An American Negro family were sitting down to supper, and a neatly uniformed Esk maid appeared from the kitchen carrying a steaming platter of franks and sauerkraut. "An Esk," Mao III chortled. "I am so familiar with imperialist oppressor history. What a satisfactorily capitalistic solution! Esks are happy to be at the bottom of the American peck order."

Click, a dozen small Esk boys were shown industriously polishing an autocopter while an American boy and girl played on a revolvo-swing and their father lay on a lawn dais officiously gesticulating to an obedient Esk who was laden with a lawn rake, a fertilizer injector and a dandelion extractor.

Click, along a college dormitory hall a svelte-hipped Esk maid balanced a tray of martini-shaped glasses through a Princeton-bannered door chalked FRESHMAN STUD-Y RUM, and she didn't come out.

Click, the sign on a huge new windowless warehouse read: ESK RESCUE MISSION #9. *Chicago Aid-to-the-Esks Society*. And underneath, *Healthy Canadian Imports. Also Fresh Raised Local Stock*. At the bottom a pricelist was taped to the door: AIR EXPORT TO SOUTH AMERICA AND EUROPE. *Wholesale Prices on Request*.

"Damn!" Dr. West was sweating and laughing and shivering at the same time, horrified. "God! In a few years when there's no more countries to which this surplus can be exported——."

"*You* are supposed to be the birth control expert," Mao III replied maliciously. "A scientifically humane solution such as forcible birth control injections still should be simple, if capitalist and revisionist oppressors are able to cooperate and behave rationally. But there is an unknown factor. Even rational Maoist scientists cannot explain it. In the first country to have a preponderantly Esk population, which was Canada——."

Click, across the screen moved an impenetrable barbed wire fence stretching along the Saskatchewan prairie. Filmed from the U.S. side of the border, the fence bulged with dark clots, bodies in the barbed wire, on the Canadian side. Further behind the International Boundary, indistinguishable masses who appeared to be Esks stood waiting.

"MINUS FOUR DAYS," the vocoder howled. "U.S. TROOPS IN FOREGROUND REPORTEDLY GUARDING FENCE AGAINST RENEWED CUTTING ACTIVITY. GRAY-BEARDED HUMAN PRISONER REPORTEDLY SOLE REMAINING MEMBER NEW YORK SAVE-THE-ESKIMOS LEAGUE."

A close-up through the boundary fence showed skeletons, humans or Esks? Starvation or?

"I can't stand to look at this. Let me look at Ottawa," Dr. West blurted, "where I was imprisoned."

Click, instead of the angry mob of Canadians who had reviled him seventeen years ago, the streets of Ottawa now were stagnant with starving Esks. Hordes of children were wandering in the streets. From a copter, the first film clip failed to show a single moving vehicle on the streets of downtown Ottawa. "MINUS SIX MONTHS," the vocoder howled. "NOW REPORTEDLY CITY POPULATION REDUCED. LACK OF TRANSPORT AND FOOD."

"But what happened to the Canadians?" Dr. West bleated.

Tall white towers like grain elevators appeared against the skyline of the city. "That's it, the New Ottawa Reformation Center," Dr. West said remembering his loneliness for Nona. *What's happened to her?* "Are there prison personnel close-ups on file?"

Click, Esks were wandering in and out as if the towers had become giant dormitories. "What happened to the real people? I knew some of the guards, when I was a prisoner———." *Nona,* he thought, *all I see are Esks.*

Click, Mao III's hands moved at the console, and the computer howled: "INSUFFICIENT DATA REGARDING PRISON STAFF FOR DATA RE; PRISONER DR. JOSEPH WEST REFER TO ———." Mao III switched to the next item. "FOR DATA PRISONER PETERLUK ESKIMO BOOTHIA REFERENCE 85234." Mao III's fingers moved. "85234 PETERLUK BOOTHIA DIED NEW OTTAWA REFORMATION CENTER MINUS SEVENTEEN YEARS SELF-HANG-ING."

"So Peterluk was dead before I even entered the Reformation Center and they wouldn't tell me," Dr. West muttered. "Dead, and he was perhaps the foster father of all Esks. His own lying statements must have contained evidence of their origin. Dammit, they're not human!"

Mao III laughed contemptuously. "Many in the United States agree with you on that. To relegate Esks to subhumanity justifies buying and selling." Mao III's voice softened. "The unanswered question to me is why the Canadians finally in self-defense did not massacre enough of their Esks. Because there was some confusion due to interbreeding as to who was an Esk is no explanation. Human beings have been willingly massacring each other since the beginning of our species. But so inefficiently in Canada——."

Click, a jiggling film of men with axes and shotguns showed Esks being herded like rabbits against a fence corner, the axes rising and falling. "LYNCH MOB, BRITISH COLUMBIA," the vocoder howled. "MINUS FIVE YEARS." A close-up showed a Canadian farmer retching and staggering away.

"It should have been so easy to exterminate them when there were only a few million," Mao III mused. "Nowhere have Esks put up violent resistance. When the first rumors of the failure of Canadian rioters to accomplish anything substantial reached me, I ordered my 8th Route Army here in Peking to carry out an experimental massacre of one small commune of Esks who had been planted on the dust desert west of Peking—as a scientific experiment. Using machine guns, the number of Esks had been reduced about 10% when it began to rain. Surprisingly, tough Chinese troops sought shelter from the rain. The commanding general also had other excuses. Machine guns overheated and jammed. After I removed him and ordered the massacre completed, the new commander, my former aide, General Chen Yung, had difficulty with trucks bringing replacement troops to the scene. Finally an air attack with napalm was successfully carried out and I believe a good portion of those Esks eventually were eliminated, although now there seem to be more Esks out there in the desert than ever. To superstitious troops the unexpected mental difficulties of the execution were disturbing——."

"Damn right they are disturbing!" Dr. West yelled. "Here you are letting Esks increase to a billion in China, and you don't even know if you're capable of eliminating them."

"It could be done, it could be. Mass executions become simple matters when competently organized," Mao III replied. "With historically scientific logic, Maoism can solve any problems of mankind."

"Then do it, dammit. Now!"

"Tapeworm, you forget that you are in command, not I."

Dr. West closed his eyes. *What did those bastards in the CIA instruct me to do?*

"Nothing that our interrogation could locate," Mao III taunted. "Squirm, tapeworm, squirm with all the problems of the world which wiser men than you have only made more complicated each generation until——."

"Shut up!" Dr. West visualized U.S. ramjets spraying China not with distilled water or an ineffectively safe bacteria but with a savagely virulent gynecological bacteria which would slightly infect the Esks—and of course totally sterilize the Chinese.

Dr. West smiled bemusedly. This might be carrying measured escalation too far. He thought the Chinese would strike back with more than birth control biological warfare.

Even the Pentagon wouldn't launch that preemptive spraying attack, he thought, *unless the retaliatory Chinese counterstrike against America could be disorganized from within China?* "Dammit, I can't have been sent here for that."

"Your aggressor-indoctrinated thoughts are of the type which continually disturb my military," Mao III sighed. "As long as the Asian continent must defend itself from imperialist invaders, our larger population is our main defensive weapon. My military will never agree to unilaterally massacre our Esk population while an uninspected Esk population continues to increase in the United States."

Mao III's voice rose. "The United States is using its own irresponsibly increasing Esk population as an aggressive threat to world peace. If the United States should outnumber China, and this could happen because your Esks are multiplying unchecked, then 5000 years of Chinese cultural heritage would be threatened. Tapeworm, can't you understand that my military cannot agree to any limitation of our Esks while——."

"Shut up!" Dr. West's face contracted, concentrating all his frustration against Mao III, and the paralyzed man toppled to the floor with a brain-blinding thud. Blackness!

Dr. West clawed at his own eyes, momentarily unable to see. His vision glimmering, he crawled to Mao III and shook him, then groped for his faint pulse.

As he sat there wondering if Mao III ever would regain consciousness, Dr. West remembered the smug faces, the excited faces in the Harvard Circle of the CIA. *You smart sons of bitches,* he thought, *right now you must be thinking you've almost scored your biggest one, if you're trying for birth control negotiations. You've planted a monomaniac named Dr. West in Peking. You've used me to set up a teleconfrontation with Mao III.*

The Secretary of State had reacted too quickly. *The ready response through Warsaw must have been prepared even before you parachuted me,* Dr. West thought.

But even if the teleconfrontation takes place and the President verbally destroys Mao III, you'll be falling into a new box of problems with the Chinese military—and the Esks still will be increasing—including the increasing millions of Esks in the United States.

Dr. West blinked, and then his eyebrows rose. *What if you CIA geniuses are two steps ahead of me? Could it be the President will support Mao III? Try to make him look good in the negotiations? That way the Harvard Circle hopes population control of the Esks in China will begin. After all, Mao III is supposed to be controlled by me, Dr. West, monomaniac hater of the Esks. If China limits its Esk population, then public opinion in the U.S. may permit the U.S. government to limit the number of Esks belonging to individuals and corporations in the United States.*

In realization, Dr. West began to shake with excitement. "Do you hope that I, the population expert, hopefully the controller of Mao III, will initiate China's first population limitation offer? And I did. You hope this will allow public opinion in the U.S. to follow. Are you indirectly trying to control the Esk population explosion in the U.S. which you're now politically unable to do anything about?"

Dr. West propped up Mao III's head and desperately sought his pulse. "The teleconference is tomorrow!"

A red light flashed on the telescreen. Dr. West didn't know what to do. Evidently the broadcast was of such high priority it contained a code-servo override. The screen switched itself on.

Across the television screen, gracefully stroking lines of ink converged to form a calligraphic dove of peace. A dissolve into living color showed ranks of red-neckerchiefed Chinese children marching across the Great Square. Their red balloons and golden balloons bobbed above their heads. En masse the balloons rose into the blue sky. Dr. West recognized this as the standard introductory film clip used by the New China News Agency in its worldwide telecasts. Magically all the golden balloons drifted in front of the gigantic silver rocket which protruded from the pink-walled courtyard of the Winter Palace. All the red balloons drifted over the ancient marble curve of the Jade Rainbow Bridge. "China is a bridge of peace to all people," a soft voice hummed, and Dr. West knew translations were soothing televiewers in Afghanistan, Algeria, America.

The Chinese Foreign Minister bowed to the television audience, his hands pressed together in a gesture of peace. "Friends throughout the world, our reverenced Chairman, our Saving Star, regretfully will be unable to appear in the teleconference which he proposed and the President of the United States seemed to have accepted. It is well that the Chinese Federation of Nations clings to peace in this moment of imperialist aggression. Last night a black aircraft of the warmongering United States Central Intelligence Agency made an unprovoked attack upon Szechwan Province."

The Foreign Minister smiled humbly at his teleprompter. "Of course the imperialist aircraft was shot down by our ever-vigilant civilian defense militia." He nodded his head, and a film of several girls with rifles standing beside massive wreckage strewn across mountain rice terraces was projected while his peaceful voice rose to outrage: "Unfortunately, those genocidal murderers of the Central Intelligence Agency of the United States were able to parachute a capsule loaded with a murderous virus upon peaceful Szechwan Province. The shock of this treachery has caused a relapse in the health of our beloved Chairman, and he will be unable to appear on television to confront the guilty President of the warmongering United States!"

The film showed an oddly familiar terraced mountainside. Across the stair-step rice paddies sprawled a gigantic parachute. Dr. West blinked in recognition. In the mud lay a standard aircrew ejection capsule from a U.S. Air Force ramjet bomber. Dr. West blinked. Was this the viral or bacteriological capsule?

"——until such time as the United States can show a sincere desire for peace," the Foreign Minister's voice was crooning, "the Chinese Federation of Nations democratically and unanimously believes that an international teleconference would be futile."

"You fraud," Dr. West gasped aloud at the smug face on the telescreen. "That parachute, that terraced mountain, that's my old ejection capsule. That film was taken over six months ago after I—we came down in Szechwan Province."

Dr. West moaned in frustration and banged his fist on the floor, and shouted at the telescreen. "Liar! Chinese generals invented this incident to get off the hook of a teleconference."

Beside him, Mao III's eyes had opened.

"Did you hear that, you prematurely senile-brained idiot?" Dr. West shouted, his futile rage hammering his heart. "Your Foreign Minister announced you've had a relapse. Now the generals are calling all the shots. You're finished as Chairman. You blob of dead flesh, you were nearly useless even when I took control of you. Now you're nothing! I've ended as nothing. We're both nothing!"

Mao III writhed on the floor from Dr. West's radiated anger, and Dr. West grabbed his wrist, felt for his erratically shivering pulse. Dr. West tried to calm himself, and gradually Mao III's pulse regained a semblance of a rhythm.

A brilliant stratagem. All are loyal to the line of Maos, Mao III's erratic thoughts seeped. *China is Maoism, and I am Mao, and all is well.*

Dr. West stared in frightened fascination at the Command Microphone on the console. He couldn't endure waiting. He had to know. Could he or Mao III still broadcast orders from this vault? IS THE POWER DEAD?

"Dead?" Mao III's voice chirped with startling cheerfulness. "I am nearly dead. But I have patience. Help me up, my tapeworm. I will die peacefully in my bed. No man expects more." His personality seemed altered. "My generals will have to wait. I have a headache. Perhaps they may need me tomorrow."

Dr. West dragged him to the console and ordered him to

contact any place on the surface. "The Interrogation Room."

Mao III did not respond.

In Dr. West's arms, Mao III was a frail sack of bones, smiling blissfully as if unaware of Dr. West's order.

"I have patience," Mao III sighed, "this is how I control my generals, patting one dog, then another until they snarl at each other in jealousy. Because I have patience, they will fail to negotiate their differences. Power is Mao. All will be well."

Dr. West emptied him on to his bed, and Mao III's face sagged in a smile like melting wax. *All will be well*.

Mao III's personality seemed so softened that Dr. West surmised another hair-thin vein within his cerebrum painlessly had ruptured. Another tiny area of his brain tissue was dying. Mao III had undergone another little stroke.

"I am *Chiu Hsing*, the Saving Star," Mao III sighed dreamily. "Grandfather Mao and I are history. I am the unifying symbol for China, power and love and forgiveness. When my generals bow down before me, I will ask that you be painlessly shot."

Dr. West made no comment.

Mao III closed his eyes.

While Mao III sank easily into the smiling sleep of the pure in heart, Dr. West glared at the oppressive ceiling. Sleepless, Dr. West writhed. He sat up and stared at the Control Console.

With surprisingly mnemonic power Dr. West remembered from watching Mao III the pattern of push buttons which should open a command line to the surface, in this cautious instance to the Interrogation Room. On the telescreen the white Interrogation Room appeared, empty except for the modernistic electronic interrogation table and an old Chinese on his knees, scrubbing the floor by hand as if he had remained in the seventeenth-century.

On the console in front of Dr. West glowed the light indicating the Command Microphone was *live*. It dazzled with power. Dr. West whistled into the microphone. The old man did not look up.

"Summon your superior," Dr. West commanded in impeccable Neo-Chinese, and still the old man went on scrubbing. "Stand to attention or be shot!" Dr. West snapped in Mandarin, beginning to sweat with anxiety as the old man continued wearily sloshing his big handbrush back and forth on the wet floor as if he had not heard.

"Deaf fool!" Dr. West shouted in frustration, while the old man sloshed his brush in the bucket.

Dr. West knew he didn't hear. The military already must have disconnected the vault's command transmission lines. For the moment the Command Vault still retained its exterior television eyes. The telescreen showed Chinese troops climbing into armored trucks as if——.

The military has silenced Mao III, Dr. West thought. *Mao III's—my ability to broadcast is finished. No more commands to the outside—. What do I do now?*

Numbly sitting, Dr. West felt amputated. *No more commands to the outside.* Dr. West felt himself shriveling. *My purpose is gone.*

"Gone! Got to get out." He could feel the ceiling pressing down, 4000 feet of rock and subsoil and earth crushing him into thickening claustrophobia as he walked, not ran, to the elevator.

His face twisting with pain, he turned around and ran back to his bed and covered his head.

Even if they don't shoot me when I appear at the surface, I'd be powerless. Free on the surface I'd be nothing. I would see the billions of Esks increasing while I did nothing, having lost my chance for power to stop them.

Dr. West turned over on his back.

I'm lying here in the vault of power. The power's off but my hope——. He tried to open his memory, to search through the shambles left by Chinese electrointerrogation.

He visualized the faces of the Harvard Circle bending over him in the basement of the Central Intelligence Agency building.

Bunglers, each subliminal instruction was to be cued by predicted events. But this is a terminal event. Please let an alternate plan rise to the surface of my memory. Oh God, how I need——. Have you deserted me?

As if those distant faces had become his gods, Dr. West

prayed for a vision, and felt only the endless emptiness of the universe.

What was my purpose? Dr. West lay on his back feeling waves of universal time curving back to the edge of sleep.

Suddenly he smiled. *Perhaps I am all-important. I am the seed of life in this buried vault.* He slept, and dreamed he arose with power over the world: "The Esks are to be sacrificed to me." He was huge and snow-white as a polar bear.

10.

THE PURPOSE OF LIFE

AWAKENED BY THE CAUTIOUS MOVEMENTS OF AN ESK WITH his breakfast tray, Dr. West sat up, blinking. Gradually he remembered he was trapped 4000 feet beneath Peking. He got up, wandered over like an early morning drunken bum, and stared down wonderingly at Mao III's sleeping face.

"When I wake up too soon," Dr. West muttered, "I see these Esks as something else." For breakfast he was surprisingly hungry. He ate ravenously. Rubbing his head, he thought he'd dreamed he was a polar bear. Bear or man, he was trapped. He stared at the smiling Esk servant, then walked back to Mao III's bed.

Mao III did not open his eyes. *Why your hatred of our gentle Esk comrades, they who feed us?* Mao III's dagger-sharp thought incised, *if you had been born in the closeness of a Chinese commune you would be an open man instead of a closed man. Can't you love Esks who feel only love for you?*

"I don't hate them. I have never hated them." Dr. West was wide awake now. "But as they increase, crowding me everywhere, I feel my elbows—my teeth grating. Why is that light blinking?"

"Activity outside the surface entry door," Mao III said quickly, his face blooming in a smile. "My generals have come to rescue me."

Pushing the proper combination of buttons on the console Dr. West focused a picture of workmen welding the steel frame for a new door approximately one foot outside the surface entry door. The Chinese up there were working directly under the warning lens so that Dr. West was looking down at the tops of their heads. When he shifted to a second

331

lens at an oblique angle, he saw military officers in black uniforms standing watching the work from further away within the great concrete blockhouse which he knew was encased within the ancient Winter Palace.

"Who are they?"

"They are too small for me to recognize their faces," Mao III muttered from his bed. "It seems our surface door will become a door within a door."

"Instead of simply welding our door shut——." Dr. West carried Mao III's slack body to his chair. "Why are they enclosing us with a second door?"

"Historically, Chinese are cautious because they are so intelligent," Mao III said unself-consciously. "Those who possess the key to the new outer door will be able to reach me quickly enough if events so guide them." He smiled. "Welding my door permanently shut would have seemed too irrevocable. There is more artistry in a door within a door. I may be needed tomorrow."

A fading illusion, Dr. West thought. *We are being permanently sealed down here with the Esks.* "There are too many Esks down here to be fed, and on the surface Esks are being allowed to multiply as if the nations of the world have less foresight than ants." Dr. West's voice rose. "At least ants recognize that many intruders in their nest as enemies! I've got to get out of here."

"You fear even my Esk servants?" Mao III asked and smiled. "Since I, too, once placed great value on survival when I was younger, there are freezers full of supplies in this vault for myself and for fifty Esk servants for twenty years. The vault was constructed and stocked during a period when I thought the American hawks were suicidally sincere in their talk of preventative war. Breathe this sweet air. It is a recirculating system which cannot be poisoned by surface assassins, either Chinese or American. We can wait, self-sufficient, safer and years longer than in a submarine. My vault is protected by 4000 feet of solid rock. If the United States warmongers had attacked, and won, amusing word, I could have waited down here like a seventeen-year locust and then emerged with my own personal Esks to repopulate the world."

An Esk carried away the breakfast tray.

"You were looking at one of my sons," Mao III said proudly. "Until my stroke three years ago I was extremely functional. The historical duty of a great man is to pass on his seed."

In the concrete corridors which surrounded the inner vault, neatly uniformed Esks wandered as if there was not enough work to do. Dr. West noticed a few young Esks dressed in what appeared to be bedsheets, as if there no longer were enough uniforms for the increasing number of Esks. Hordes of naked children skipped gaily ahead in the corridor.

Beside Dr. West, an Esk pushed Mao III's wheelchair.

"Already you are plotting how you can murder my children," Mao III said pleasantly, as they passed the steel door to a tunnel which led down to the atomic-electric power source.

"Speculative force of habit," Dr. West replied as calmly. "Yesterday, I showed one of your—sons or grandsons how to conduct a census by touching each Esk with a dab of red paint so he wouldn't count the same child twice. I showed him how to make counting marks on a tablet. There are twenty-eight mature males, twenty-two breeding age females and—prepare yourself—396 children and babies."

"So? ——Under normal conditions the excess children are sent to the surface," Mao III replied as if undisturbed. "It has been convenient that babies need to be breast-fed for less than a month."

"Sixty-two of the children would reach breeding age if we were down here a year," Dr. West remarked. "Of these, thirty-two are female."

"It is unlikely we will be down here a week," Mao III replied. "My generals will need me, as they always have needed the line of Maos."

"Then this is purely a theoretical problem," Dr. West shrilly laughed. "The thirty-two future breeding females added to the twenty-two females now adult, means there would be fifty-four breeding females within another year. Suppose we're optimistic and estimate two menstrual failures or miscarriages per mother during the next twelve months, each of the fifty-four women would give birth to only ten children instead of twelve, for a total of 450 more mouths to feed. And I'm forgetting to add children born to the twenty-two existing mothers this year."

"You're talking as if we could be left to stagnate down here for two years," Mao laughed. "The generals will free me and kill you within a month."

"In two years, counting existing Esks, mainly children now, plus babies who will be born, the total number of mouths to feed will be more than 1000."

"You are intimating I lacked foresight because there are only supplies for fifty Esks for twenty years."

"Supplies for fifty Esks for twenty years equals supplies for 1000 Esks for one year." Dr. West walked toward the myriad sounds of babies.

"I am as familiar with arithmetic as you are," Mao III's voice retorted triumphantly. "I also am familiar with birth control pills."

"I can see from the age distribution of your Esks and the terrible preponderance of children, that no birth control pills are being used," Dr. West said softly; as he stepped into the crowded sleeping dormitory, his nose wrinkled.

"These are my grandchildren," Mao III replied. "So there has been no reason to stifle my own ancestral line with pills. Do not panic. My generals will free me in a few days, and if the generals procrastinate and you become frightened of all these harmless Esks there is a whole closet full of birth control pills."

Dr. West blinked. He smiled fleetingly.

"It might be wise to start testing these pills," Dr. West remarked as if it were of no importance.

He had glanced into the steam-blurred kitchen where Esks were boiling rice and freeze-dried vegetables. "Unless the birth control pills are effective, their food will be gone in less than two years."

"We will not be down here three months." Mao III's tone of voice was a verbal shrug. "But you are a medical person, and it might add to your medical knowledge if you begin testing the quality of those pills. They were manufactured in the United States."

When Dr. West opened the closet, he saw the old labeled bottles of pills. They were an abortifacient put out by an American pharmaceutical company, based on research begun years ago while he was Director of Oriental Populations Problems Research. The original abortifacient pills had been intended for humans. Dr. West hoped these had been tested on Esks. Only one abortion-inducing pill a month was necessary. In Canada it had been found impractical to force Esk women to take the daily pills.

Taken only once a month, ideally before the woman had grown large from her monthly pregnancy, these abortifacients might do the job if the Esk women would swallow them.

Dr. West smiled grimly, thinking: *That brilliant mathematician, Mao III, has stocked twenty large jars of 300 pills each. That's 6000 pills. Mathematically, enough pills for twenty-five women for twenty years. Assuming the pills are 100% effective, by the time all the existing 396 children mature, even assuming no new births, in three years we will have a total of 220 females of breeding age. They will need 2640 pills each year.* "There won't be enough pills to complete the fourth year. Chemical birth control will cease. Soon we'd be jammed shoulder to shoulder except for one lucky circumstance. We already will have starved to death.

"But I'm ever the hopeful experimenter." Dr. West wondered if he would be more successful than the Canadians in inducing the Esk women to swallow monthly pills. "I can't use force. Too many Esks. I can try deception." He slipped one bottle under his coat and carefully locked the closet. He frowned. *Why did the Canadian government fail?*

He waded through naked children romping in the thermostatically heated corridor.

The abortifacient pills so strongly contradict the Esk women's instinctive purpose in life, he thought, *what insidious things can happen when we trick their instinctive urge to give birth?*

His face twisted with grief as he thought of Marthalik, his wife——.

In the crowded dormitory, he stared at an Esk woman sitting on the edge of a cot, hunching over her baby. Her strong hands were steadying her newborn baby who was hungrily suckling her breast.

Genetically formed in both of you, Dr. West thought, *is such an overwhelming urge to multiply. Even stronger than ours——.*

He knew within the uterus of this blissful woman the next fertilized ovum already was clinging, growing, already an embryo, efficiently growing without wasted energy or unnecessary gills or prehuman tail, and in less than a month it would emerge into the world. *Your whole being, all of those smiling instincts, your inoffensive survival instincts were designed by—something to help your rapid multiplication. And you help each other. Unlike men, you don't kill.* Uneasily he smiled down at the woman, who cradled her baby protectively in her arms.

Mother, he thought, *would anything you suspect of interfering with your purpose in life cause you to——. But I've never heard of Esks deliberately killing anyone,* he thought. *I should be safe enough.*

He gave twenty-two pills to the steward, who seemed unusually intelligent. Although his Esk characteristics were dominant, the steward undoubtedly was one of Mao III's sons. He listened placidly to Dr. West's instructions. "You understand," Dr. West repeated, "these twenty-two calcium pills must be given only to each woman. That is, one to each woman."

"Eh?" The Esk smiled.

"One pill for each woman in her rice," Dr. West said. "Tonight. Good calcium pills to make bones strong," he lied.

"For babies?"

"No, for the mothers! Give the pills to the mothers."

As Dr. West returned to the Control Room, Mao III was leaning toward the telescreen, his skeletal face twisting in a comedy of outrage and black humor.

"I am reported to be dying. A national year of mourning is being prepared. This same day Chu-Ti's personal aircraft has exploded in flight, accidentally, the teleannouncers say. Lin Po died last night at a banquet, of indigestion. Here in

Peking, Chen Yung's 8th Route Army has canceled all leaves."

"In the south," Mao III laughed nervously, "Peng Huai's troops have entered Canton to calm a very little disturbance caused by less than a dozen ancient reactionary revisionists who drank too much wine. To put them down, his troops temporarily have occupied all the airfields and the television station." Now Mao III laughed as faintly as the ghost of a man. "——the Cantonese dogs say they are preparing for democratic elections. No doubt the general with the most troops hopes to receive the most votes."

Dr. West wondered if this revolution would help him.

"When their armies have bloodied the streets," Mao III muttered, "and still the fighting continues, they will remember me, their Saving Star." He laughed faintly. "I can rise from the dead?"

After a silence Mao III opened his eyes and announced: "The survivors will unlock my steel door, and I will permit them to come down in my elevator, and bow down before me. Humbly the surviving generals will beg me once more to command all China——."

Dr. West made no comment. They would shoot him.

The next day many television stations transmitted only their focusing pattern, the white lotus star. From the south, a few broadcasts showed waving flags and martial music and schoolgirl poetesses with Cantonese accents reciting instant odes to the heroism and patriotism of General Peng Huai, Liberator of Canton, Savior of China.

"Southern traitor," Mao III blurted, and his quick fingers clicked through the other television broadcasts. "Why don't they praise Mao? Traitors! This Cantonese rebellion will produce loyalty in Peking—to me."

The next day none of the Peking stations was broadcasting.

In the dormitory, Dr. West stared anxiously at the Esk women. *They should be aborting by now*, he thought. None of them showed any discomfort.

As he walked back along the corridor, Dr. West noticed a scar on the doorjamb of the closet, beside the lock. Breathing hard, he unlocked the closet door. The jars still were white with pills—no, with grains of rice. "——The pills, where are the pills?"

The steward continued smiling while Dr. West violently shook him. "Pills?" the Esk gasped. "Please, sir, which pills?"

"Did you give the women the pills?"

"Eh?" the Esk giggled with embarrassment as Dr. West stopped shaking him. "This person gave away pills."

"You're lying."

"Eh-eh, this person is lying." the Esk laughed placatingly.

"Where are all the other pills?"

"Eh? Pills here? This person does not know."

"The whole closet was full of pills!" Dr. West shouted.

"Eh-eh, this person is telling the truth. No pills."

"You're lying."

"This person is lying," the Esk patiently agreed as if soothing an insane man. "It is the truth."

Dr. West hurled the unresisting Esk to the floor.

By now most of the Chinese television stations were off the air. Some of Mao III's remaining surveillance cameras, which were automatic equipment, showed circling flies or perhaps distant aircraft circling clouds of smoke beyond the horizon.

One surveillance camera suddenly blurred with the too-close face of an Esk smiling stupidly into the lens.

That night Tele-Pravda's satellite broadcast that General Peng Huai's troops from Canton were meeting only token resistance outside Nanking. A victorious Cantonese television broadcast was expected hourly.

It came with joyful music and a triumvirate of smiling Chinese physicians, the first doctor announcing that the beloved Chairman, Mao III, was showing superlogically materialistic improvement from his three-year illness. The second announced that new developments in traditional Chinese accupuncture had completely cured the paralysis from which their beloved Chairman for three years had suffered. The third announced that the Chairman, the Saving Star, now was able to speak to all of his people.

In the dim vault, Dr. West watched Mao III's expression change from surprise to rage.

On the telescreen a Mao III appeared, walking briskly forward. With sturdy peasant gestures and a confident voice, this Mao III reassured the world that: "The Maoist Party shines like a gun barrel! Your Chairman once again is able to labor for the welfare of the people. All is now peace, for I am with you."

This Mao glanced at the teleprompter and announced that he had appointed General Peng Huai of the Canton Military District to rebuild three bridges to the people, to assume three responsibilities. "The Ministries of Defense, of Dream Persons and of Internal Security." Pseudo-Mao bowed perceptibly. "General Peng Huai's heroism has saved my life, and through me the life of China.

"With Comrade Peng Huai's guidance we shall build an even larger China, worthy of our great population. Together, arm in arm, we will lead all the free peoples of the world into the future."

Beside Dr. West, Mao III gurgled with rage, and Dr. West remarked: "Is that one of your former doubles? You used so many to confuse your assassins. Now they've discovered one Mao is as good as another."

Mao III glowered at the waving flags on the screen, the rising balloons, the traditional ranks of marching children, until the Canton station abruptly signed off the air. "Air raid warning!"

"I will be rescued," Mao III blurted. "My favorite general, Chen Yung, Commander of my personal 8th Route Army here in Peking, he, too, desires power. Now he will need my aid in exposing this impostor. My General Chen Yung personally will descend the elevator and bow down before me."

There was more news about the air raid scare. False warning.

The next morning Tele-Pravda reported that General Chen Yung, Commander of the 8th Route Army based in Peking and formerly considered the most influential of the inner council of generals, and the former favorite of Mao III, had been appointed Ambassador to South Belgium. "General Chen Yung already has departed to assume his new post."

"If his aircraft does not explode in midair," Mao III

hissed, and began to sob like a little boy who has lost his last toy.

"Which leaves us with the Cantonese General Peng Huai consolidating his power." Dr. West asked, "Do you recall Peng Huai's attitude toward the future increase of the Esks?"

"That traitor first gained notoriety as Field Commander in our pacification of India." Mao III smiled crookedly at Dr. West. "Peng Huai always has maintained that China will need many more people for a still greater effort, therefore as many Esks as possible. Each Esk replaces on the homefront a peacefighter to free the world. Have I answered your question?"

That night, Mao III cried out in pain. Rising, Dr. West saw that Mao III was suffering a more massive stroke. The whole left side of Mao III's face was twisted down. Even when Dr. West's mind strained to help, Mao III was unable to move his lips as his thoughts leaked out: *Tapeworm, leave me alone. At least permit me to die.*

But Mao III's righ hand twitched in a signal for his Esk night servant to bring him a sip of water.

Finally, Dr. West walked away. When Dr. West was able to escape into sleep, in his dream he was clutched by a nightmare earthquake shaking apart the elevator shaft to the surface, filling it with rubble, squeezing the vault while the smiling Esks grew like balloons filling——.

The bed shook him awake as he sat up, his eardrums still echoing the dull thud of—an explosion?

The lights still worked. He felt as if he'd been slapped on the side of the head. He blinked at the ceiling, at new hairline cracks in the concrete here 4000 feet deep in the earth. Through the reverberations of his eardrums, he could hear the excited chattering of Esks.

He noticed an Esk standing stupidly by the locked control panel, with an oddly shocked expression for an Esk. No smile now from Mao III's night servant. Swaying from the Esk's hand hung a thin silver neck chain dangling the key.

Dr. West's hand rose to his own neck where the key had been, and he bounded across the room, seized the key from the unresisting Esk.

Dr. West stared at the lock now turned to a horizontal position above the depressed red lever. "You idiot." The dull thud must have been an explosion at the surface.

Dr. West remembered Mao III's mental slip: The vault's defensive threat was the small nuc device encased in tons of concrete beneath the Winter Palace. As Mao III's last act it could be detonated by this lock and red lever, to entomb forever this vault in which Dr. West stood breathing hoarsely.

"You suicidal fool," Dr. West blurted at the Esk, "you stole it from me while I slept. Tell me why——."

The Esk smiled with nervousness and glanced toward the dragon-curtains of Mao III's sleeping alcove.

Dr. West tore open the curtains. "You paralyzed old bastard. You communicated to this Esk to steal back your key. Wonderful! Bang! You've sealed us forever in this coffin."

Mao III's lopsided face smiled up at him. *Tapeworm, fear?* Mao III's triumphant thought filtered out of his blood-clotted brain. *With so much fear, you are unable to think. You must listen to my thoughts——.*

"Like hell I will!" Dr. West ran along the corridor to the elevator. The elevator door bulged out jaggedly due to the mass of smashed rock which had jammed down the shaft. Would the radioactivity from the nuc extend down this far?

He tried to calm his unevenly thudding heart.

He walked to the end of the farthest concrete tunnel and stared at the concrete wall. "It is not possible to dig out. We're nearly a mile beneath the earth." He trudged slowly back with his hand pressed against his breastbone and flickers of reflected pain inside his left arm. "If I'm going to drop dead—heart. Good! Now!" But he took a nitro. He searched through janitors' closets, and a small storeroom containing trays of spare modules for the computer and a vast storeroom of tiered shelves stacked with plastic-wrapped freeze-dried vegetable bricks. He wandered between mountains of sacks of rice and on into the kitchen equipment room.

By now he carried a crowbar he had found, and a handful of flimsy plactic-handled screwdrivers and a ball-peen hammer. He found a short-handled scoop-shovel intended for loading rice—not intended for digging straight upward through 4000 feet of rock formations to the surface. "Got to get out———."

When the next pain in his chest subsided, he herded eight male Esks to the end of the corridor and set them to chipping at the concrete wall. The plastic split off from the handles of the screwdrivers, and their soft iron shafts bent. The head of the ball-peen hammer popped off. The crowbar bounced back from the concrete with ringing protests.

Dr. West located an electric twist drill and enough extension cords, and the whole set of steel drill bits soon was ruined. He unbolted the hinges of the massive steel door of the Power Source room. Puzzled by his orders but smiling, eight heavily-breathing Esks carried the steel door up to the end of the corridor. The corner of the steel door made a clumsy battering ram. The noise was deafening. Wincing, Dr. West stared toward the shower room, and visualized a long hose.

The concrete within the corridor wall seemed slightly softened after a stream of hot water was hose-lengthed from the shower room. His Esks rammed the steel door against the wet wall.

"Cheap Maoist concrete," he laughed shrilly. "But who could make a profit?"

After exhausted relays of Esks, the clanging corner of the steel door smashed through concrete into darkness.

Dr. West leaped forward as if into a miraculous hidden tunnel, but his flashlight illuminated only the yellow-brown solidity of prehistoric sandstone strata, 4000 feet beneath the present surface of the Earth.

The battered point of the crowbar, hurled full force, penetrated nearly one-eighth inch into the sandstone. It left a tiny dent.

"This damned sandstone's been pressed down here so long and hard, it's not even sedimentary. For me, it's hard as metamorphic———." Sourly smiling, Dr. West set the Esks chipping upward at a 45-degree angle aiming the slanting tunnel away from the nuc explosion's ground zero. "Not too steep for you to scramble up a gopher hole barefoot, yet steep enough for the debris to slide down."

He foresaw a narrow tunnel with one Esk digging at a time. It would have ventilating problems enough without being stuffed with other Esks passing the debris down by hand. He found a draftsman's 45-degree triangle and tied a string to a bolt. He suspended the bolt from the triangle like a plumb bob. "You understand the direction? Dig upward in line with the hypotenuse of this triangle."

"Eh?"

"I mean the tunnel must line up with this longest leg of the triangle."

"Eh?" These Esks all smiling stupidly made Dr. West want to scream with rage.

Smile, Dr. West thought at the cheerfully scurrying Esks, who already were carrying away double handfuls of granulated sandstone. *Smile, at least this work gives you another purpose down here besides——.*

Their primary purpose scampered small and naked on the corridor floor, more children each day. Children's fingers traced childish symbols in the sand spilled on the corridor floor circles, circles around circles, and an amorphous blob reminding Dr. West of a bear.

In the shoulder-wide hole up into the hard sandstone Dr. West measured daily progress. "A good three feet in the last twenty-four hours. I like you, all of you. Now, dig faster!"

Dr. West exploded in irritation. "No! Don't dump the sand in the shower room! Empty it in the food storeroom."

Each day there was more space in the food storeroom to store sand, less rice——.

During the "night" shift, below the sounds of the upward tunneling Esk, Dr. West scowled at his penciled diagram on the wall. It was an inverted right triangle with its hypotenuse at a 45-degree angle to its vertical and horizontal lines.

Beside the vertical line he wrote: 4000 feet up. Beside the horizontal surface line, he also wrote 4000 feet. He scowled at the diagonal line symbolizing the tunnel. "This damn gopher-hole hypotenuse will be a lot longer than 4000 feet, you—ghost of Pythagorus. The sum of the squares of the other two sides is 16,000,000 plus 16,000,000 equals 32,000,-

000. Now what in hell is the square root of 32,000,00? It's more than 5000 feet! This slanting tunnel will be more than 5600 feet long. Digging three feet per day, that's 1866 days——."

He stared at the unhearing Esks. "God help us all, 1866 days, that's five years!"

He walked into the food storeroom where Esks were piling sand from the tunnel. "Even if these smiling fools could stop having babies as of this minute, all the food, just for the Esks alive right now, will be eaten in a couple of years. This stupid tunnel will starve to a stop not even halfway to the surface." He smiled like a starving clown. "We will have eaten ourselves to death three years below the surface."

I'm not going to murder any Esks, he thought. *I don't want to. If I kill a few, the others gently will restrain me. If the humans on the surface can't effectively control their increasing Esks, how can I? On the surface, the humans have the guns and are supposed to have the brains but the Esks still are multiplying. Down here, I'm already outnumbered 500 to 1, and—more Esks eating more each day. Could I create a poison?*

His face twisting from his heart pain, Dr. West looked across the food storeroom at the children laughing and rolling down the sandpile. At the edge, a little boy was scratching with his fingers in the sand so that the concrete floor showed through.

"What are you drawing?"

"Eh? Grandfather Bear—so he come for us."

"Down here?"

"Eh!" The little boy shaped the sand and patted the sand.

Dr. West turned away, his chest tightening with pain. He sat down against the concrete wall. A little girl ran over, threw her arms around his neck and snuggled on his lap. His breath tickled the delicate beauty of her ear, and she giggled. He closed his eyes, motionless and unbreathing as concrete. When she went away, he considered suicide.

Instead he gathered the twenty-eight adult men and twenty-two mature women together, only now there were thirty mature men and twenty-nine pregnant women. He drew

pictures on the wall showing the great distance to the surface. He drew squares of diminishing size showing there soon
would be no more food. The Esks giggled, and Dr. West saw
that one, aping him, was drawing on the floor—a bear?
"Dammit, listen to me! Something must be done."

Smiling patiently, the Esks volunteered to eat less. One
man would stand guard outside the food storage room. Dr.
West hoped so.

In the artificial night, children began to whine with hunger, disturbing Dr. West's sleep. In the artificial morning, Dr.
West read from the small footprints in the sand that children
had been allowed to enter the storeroom to gnaw the freeze-
dried vegetable bricks.

When Dr. West tried rationing the food himself, after
locking the storeroom, the Esks seemed cooperative. In the
night hungry children cried and the Esks gently took the key
away from Dr. West without hurting him and opened the
storeroom and everyone was happy again.

When Dr. West stared down at Mao III's lopsided face,
the left eye opened. *Help me*, the desperate thought rose, *to
speak.*

Concentrating to the utmost, Dr. West was unable to
control Mao III's damaged speech center, and Dr. West
thought: *Only the spark of a man remains.*

Bad poetry while you look at my living corpse? Mao III
thought with surprising strength. *Kinder to kill me.*

"Then who would I talk with?"

How many of my Esks have you murdered?

"None," Dr. West answered.

*Fraud, you thought you could solve the Esk problems of
the whole world but you can't even control this vault.* Mao
III's thoughts sparkled with laughter. *Paint a line across the
corridor, separating the men from the women.*

"You are taunting me," Dr. West replied without anger.

*Induce the mothers to sacrifice their babies to a god, either
you or me.*

"In Canada the Esks shielded their babies from the mob
with their own bodies."

*Ineffective mobs in capitalistic countries. Arrange a mirror
so I can see the telescreen.*

"Strangely ineffective mobs. Your surface explosion destroyed our TV antenna."

If you understood statesmanship, you would divide our Esks into two tribes. Paint the foreheads of one tribe white, the other tribe black.

"We both know they're not that genetically combative. They're not as self-limiting as some human populations have been. No wars."

Somewhere in the Data Retrieval computer, ancient Polynesian Island customs became effective when not enough taro patches for growing population. Polynesians solved their problems. Use the push buttons on the console.

"Not anymore. I was killing time, an hour playing the console, endless interesting data pictures from your computer. Already I can play it like a visual piano. But suddenly, only a repeating pattern of information about volcanos, avocados and phrenology appeared on the screen, as if the Data Retrieval System has suffered a stroke. I replaced what seemed to be the damaged electronic module, and now the computer doesn't work at all."

Because you have the wrong specialization, Doctor, you're not qualified to be even an electronics technician. Your specialty is population control. With minimal intelligence you should be able to lead the Esks to the one logical course— cannibalism.

"Stop taunting me. There have been no examples of Esks killing each other for food, not in Canada—have there?" Dr. West wondered if, in the last extremity of starvation and still driven by their urge to multiply, the adult Esks here might feed their own bodies to their children. "I doubt it. At least not organized——."

Not yet organized makes it easier for you. There are no troublesome congenital leaders among Esks. You should be able to organize these few Esks into any behavior pattern you decide.

"You flatter me. For me, one man, now to curb the Esks' overpowering instinct to multiply like lemmings, after all the Canadian attempts to organize birth control among the Esks failed."

My Szechwan agricultural planners easily organized millions of Esks to hand-shape mountains into rice paddies.

"Easy because it was helping Esks multiply."

For Maoist progress, yes. Esks were so much more easily controllable than Chinese within my Twenty-Year Plan. If you imagine yourself my intellectual equal, you should be able to organize the lives of these mere 500 Esks, most of them little children, so that one of their overpowering instincts will conflict with another, and they will destroy themselves. This is how I maintained control over my generals.

"And look at you now!" Dr. West immediately realized his own retort was inadequate, childish because Mao III had retained power longer than most leaders; any leader can suffer a brain-stroke, and all men sink into death.

Having nothing better to do today, I am trying to help you.

"I doubt that!" Dr. West seemed unable to restrain his childish anger. "How were you so stupid as to help Esks multiply like a billion cancer cells in China? Brilliant leader, you can't answer. Perhaps Esks have an as yet unidentified psychological advantage. Smiling with love, they are leading us."

Ridiculous! You are a defeatist born of a disorganized nation whose historical moment has passed. If my television still were operating, while you starve you could watch the triumph of Maoism throughout the world.

"Triumph? Soon, Esks will outnumber us throughout the world. Next year four billion, the next year eight billion. The next year sixteen billion Esks will——."

Statistical trickster. Any fool knows that the rate of Esk increase will be slowed down and then stopped. In America, when your relatives feel the bite of hunger in their fat bellies, they will limit their Esks. With guns and clubs if necessary. In China, rational Maoist economic planning will reveal when the total number of Chinese Esks is optimum, and further increase will be painlessly discouraged.

"Are you sure? This is not how things ended in Canada. Is it possible that the Esks have an overgroup psychological influence on our actions?"

Now you are a small boy whimpering at the darkness which conceals nothing but your teddy bears.

At this thought, Dr. West broke into laughter like dry coughing. "I've been a small boy—whimpering a warning for years. And ever since those first Canadian years, the Esks have been recognized as a population problem. But they have continued increasing. Name for me one instance in which organized human activity effectively has limited the number of Esks anywhere. The few lynchings, your experimental napalm, ineffective pinpricks! Name an effective population control action. It's been all talk, and the number of Esks keeps increasing."

..Loud prophet, emerge from your hole and take action, Mao III taunted. *There still is time. I have been told that the world can support a population of twenty billion.*

"There are ten billion humans now in 2010. Next year four billion Esks, the next year eight billion, the next year sixteen billion Esks plus ten billion humans would be twenty-six billion if chaos and starvation permitted it."

"Twenty billion——."

"The twenty billion you're thinking about is the humans the world could support if we had fifty years of gradually increasing population during which time we could prepare the world for them. Even with developing marine plankton farming and direct chemical food sources, we may not have time, even without the Esk problem. Why am I wasting my time talking to you? Up there, anarchic collapse will come before the human population plus the Esk population totals twenty billion, and after disorganization of our sensitive technology and food distribution systems the world probably won't support three billion starving survivors, less people than in the 1970s."

It would support more Esks than that, Mao III taunted. *They don't eat as much. At least Esks have faith in the future. They believe——.*

"Believe?" Dr. West whirled, staring in recognition at the gold-painted dragon which still grinned above the blinded telescreen. The dragon's jaws were painted red. His hungry jaws symbolized——.

"Malthusian nightmare!" Dr. West's voice shouted. "Or

Freudian dinosaur. Even you are not as hungry as Grandfather Bear."

Dr. West strode out into the corridor, thinking. *In its creation, an effective religion must conform to the most pressing needs,* Dr. West pondered, *of its creator.*

He stalked through corridors where the Esks meekly stepped aside. He unlocked the huge empty room Mao III's architects must have intended for———.

"Official audiences, but in these last three years since his stroke, that egomaniac was afraid—avoided being seen. I'll meet with all sixty adult Esks at one time, only I won't be here." Dr. West locked the door from the inside and set to work in the Audience Room.

As creator, he thought he knew his own needs.

When he emerged wearily, his work incomplete, he locked the door to the huge room behind him and wandered back to the Control Room to sleep. But first, in the Control Room he unlocked the Master Heating Panel and turned down the dials. "Like a god, I control my weather."

When he awoke he was shivering slightly. As he walked past Mao III's curtained bed, he detected distress, shivering, but continued to the Master Heating Panel, unlocking its little metal door again.

Inside gleamed the row of temperature control dials, one for each room in the vault plus others for the corridors.

He thought their sensor thermometers must be concealed in the individual rooms. The other elements of each thermostat were here in front of him, their wire nerves extending within the walls.

"Maoist architecture, authoritative central control of all thermostat settings." With a cold smile he turned down each thermostat another degree. "This Control Room must be equally chilled or eventually, as the Esks become painfully cold, they'll all crowd in here, squeezing around me like a demographer's nightmare of the 1000% utilized planet. At first we must have equality of coldness throughout the vault."

But Dr. West located extra blankets for Mao III.

Apparently in China, Dr. West thought with wry humor, *or at least in this Command Vault, electric blankets are banned for their softening revisionist tendencies.* He suspended a small electric radiant heater above Mao III's curtained bed.

I am shivering. My tapeworm, you who will soon be without a host. Why not painlessly smother me with a pillow instead of chilling me to pneumonia—to which I already have been susceptible. I wish to die, but, I dread the choking sensation of pneumonia fluid in the lungs. Simply use a pillow quickly.

"I'm not your assassin. I'd be lonely without you, mine host." Dr. West went away to get the paint and loudspeakers; laden with tools, he unlocked the Audience Room.

Each day he worked alone in the huge hollow-sounding Audience Room. After he had hung the black curtain at the rear wall, the echoes were muffled.

Each day he reduced the temperature throughout the vault one degree. As a side effect of the cold the Esks digging the tunnel worked faster. Dr. West soon wore overshoes with three pairs of socks. Chilled, he donned two layers of padded uniforms and wrapped a blanket around his shoulders and ate more.

Unfortunately, the Esks also ate more. Since few of the children had shoes, whenever they tired of running around they huddled, rubbing their feet, whimpering.

"But human children would have colds and pneumonia." Dr. West coughed and laughed and cleared his phlegmed throat. "Comes another Ice Age, only Esks would prosper."

With disturbing initiative the shivering Esks in the kitchen left the electric cookstoves turned on all the time. Esks smashed chairs in the dormitory and built a fire nearly overpowering the carbon dioxide-monoxide filters.

"Dammit, you nearly fumigated us all." As Dr. West kicked apart the fire, he felt a gentle hand on his shoulder. The Esks were on the verge of restraining him. He wondered, if warmth had become so vital an instinct, they would——?

"Warm today, disregard tomorrow," Dr. West muttered his conscious superiority at these people, but he worried that eventually the Esk servants might realize how the thermostatic heating system was controlled, and the Esks gently would take control of the weather in the vault.

He accelerated his plan. Unlocking the Heating Control Panel, he turned up one thermostat dial. It was the thermostat whose thermometer element was in the Audience Room. "Warmth will become like heaven."

When he unlocked the Audience Room, delicious warmth spread outward to the chilled faces of children in the corridor.

"Stay out! This is for adults." He discovered there was no way to keep the children out.

The crowding Esks were so solicitous of their children that they smilingly ignored his protests and pushed their children past him into the darkly warm Audience Room. The women carried their babies in their arms into the heavenly warmth. The room jammed with all 800 Esks. He'd intended only the eighty adults. Shoulder to shoulder, luxuriating in warmth, the Esks were smiling sleepily at the black curtain Dr. West had arranged to conceal the loudspeaker. How they were peering with recognition, with whispering excitement, at the lifesize portrait Dr. West had created on the black curtain with white paint.

Before leaving the dim room, Dr. West switched on the spotlight. Against the curtain, the spotlight's circle enshrined the immense snow whiteness of the polar bear.

Hypnotically humming behind the curtain, the electric fan made the curtain undulate, and the bear moved. In the sleepy warmth, from long staring into its centered whiteness, the gigantic polar bear seemed, even to Dr. West's eyes, to be enlarging, almost alive.

Children whimpered, gasping for breath in the thickening atmosphere. Dr. West slipped out of the overcrowded Audience Room into the cold reality of the corridor. He hurried along the concrete corridor to the Control Room.

His heart drumming with excitement, he stared at the closed-circuit image being transmitted to the telescreen from the Audience Room. He pursed his lips and blew softly against the microphone on the control panel.

On the telescreen, from the Audience Room, the thickly crowded Esks seemed to sway. He was seeing them from the camera high in the curtain above the bear. He felt himself high above the multitude, as if floating above the excitedly smiling faces of the Esks.

Are there instincts stronger than life? Dr. West thought, *stronger than this multiplying like rodents for no purpose other than more life itself? Is this the end-purpose for which the Esks were planted on this earth?*

"Look at me," Dr. West breathed in Modern Eskimo and the Esk's eyes widened. He knew they did not comprehend his Eskimo words, and he inhaled, preparing to speak to them in the simplified Chinese that their recent Esk progenitors had absorbed during these seventeen Chinese years since Esks were flown here from the Arctic winter night.

For many nights he had been planning what he would say, remembering what he had said before, remembering the prophetic excitement in the igloo so long ago. In the night, Edwardluk, who was not an Eskimo, rose on the ice, shouting with expectant joy, Edwardluk's arms reaching toward the Arctic stars, ice-bright galaxies where man could never go. "Grandfather!"

As Dr. West spoke into the microphone, his plans vanished and his voice poured out with unthinking freedom.

"——the darkness, the light from the sky, I am white bear, your Grandfather in front of you, all around you, above you, I am your Grandfather of whom you dream. Like a white bear from the sky, you see me coming for you. In joy your heartbeats are rising to the sky so that all become one with me. I in you, and you in me. We rise! We rise!"

On the telescreen the images of the Esks swayed forward toward his voice.

"You have filled the world for me and now I have come for you and we become one again," Dr. West's hoarse voice paraphrased the myth. "In joy we become one!"

Esks' faces were shrieking upward with joy or agony. Esks were rising on tiptoe. It appeared as if the hair of an Esk man was standing on end. He fell down in a convulsion like a man being electrocuted, and became motionless, concealed by the pressing multitude. As if unaware of his fall, the other adults were straining forward sobbing with joy, and a woman fell among the shrieking children who had been forgotten and were being trampled.

"Grandfather, we have prepared this world for you. Grandfather! Grandfather!" He saw another man's face ripen in an agony of joy and his hair was standing on end just before his body toppled. Beside him, a woman in joy had fallen, vanished, trampled. A slender man, barely matured, frantically was beating the walls with his hands as if trying to climb. In the turmoil, children were screaming. In joy, a woman strained upward and fell. "Grandfather——!"

Dr. West's face twisted with pain. He was crying.

He switched off the microphone which had transmitted his voice behind the black curtain to the loudspeaker. On the black curtain, the whiteness of the bear vanished as he pulled the switch that plunged the Audience Room into darkness. His trembling hand reached into the Master Heating Panel and turned down the thermostat controlling the Audience Room. He directed the icy blast of air conditioning into the Audience Room.

He stood in the corridor watching crying children flee the cold wind from the Audience Room.

Adults staggered out with faces waxy as corpses. They shuffled away along the corridor. A moaning mother carried her little girl who had been trampled.

In the Audience Room, his flashlight beam flitted like a white moth over slack faces of ten prone Esks, all adults. He knelt, feeling for a pulse. This Esk was dead. "God help us all."

Tomorrow he thought he would guide the Esks to remove the bodies. His eyes narrowed as he went out into the light of the corridor. He was afraid to drag away the bodies himself because the Esks would see this. They might see a casual connection between the dead Esks and him.

I did not murder them. They wanted to go. They were hoping to go, Dr. West rationalized. *They behaved as if they were going to the purpose of their lives.* "They were shouting with happiness."

And I should feel relief, Dr. West thought. *I can control their numbers now. It is possible to postpone starvation. It may be possible to reach the surface if we try.*

Dr. West collapsed facedown on his bed, groaning. It was many hours before he regained self-control and purpose to get out of bed, intending to send the Esks back to the tunnel. But he found they were already digging.

Much faster and more purposefully than before, the surviving adult Esks were digging upward and carrying away blue-gray rock. They were smiling.

"Smile at what? At what is happening up there, years above our heads where the world is filling with Esks." Dr. West was not smiling. "Dig faster!"

Broken blue rock rumbled out of the steep tunnel.

"We are rising through a pond," Dr. West announced as if the loudness of his voice could make the stupidly smiling Esks understand. "You are digging upward through blue silt which has become stone. Yes, giggle. Do you realize we are buried millions of years beneath the surface? Dig!"

Staring at a massive blue slab of stone which had rumbled from the tunnel, he blinked at irregular whiteness, fossil teeth too jaggedly huge to be mammalian. "Dinosaur? Oh my god, how deep are we? So deep in geological time we'll never get out."

Dayless day after nightless night, he watched alternating shifts of Esks burrowing upward. A clumsy Esk dropped a brown-stained slab and giggled. Beside Dr. West's foot, the slab had split, and on the rock's flat brown face there curved, like a tiny white necklace, a pattern of small teeth in a lower jaw.

"Specialized teeth. Extremely specialized for a little reptile." Dr. West bent over this fossil as if searching for a key to time.

Within Dr. West's eyes, the pupils like dark mushroom extensions of his brain enlarged with excitement. He was remembering himself as a sleepy premed student, a zoology lecture and diagrams so long ago. "The dental formula of this little bastard in my hand——." *Incisors 3/3. Canines 1/1. Premolars 4/4. Molars 3/3. A little shrewlike mammal?* "Beautiful! We're going to escape from those damn dinosaurs."

He laughed too loudly. "Dig. Already, I think, we're up in the late Cretaceous. Among the ultimate dinosaurs, you little shrewlike mammals seemed as unimportant as the Arctic Esks. We're burrowing up into the Paleocene, up toward the Eocene, crowded with little five-toed horses, beyond the last dinosaurs. We may be less than eighty million years from the surface," he said with irony. "We're entering the glorious Age of Mammals."

"It means nothing to you because you were not born of this planet," he told the blankly smiling faces of the Esks. "But to me! I'm part of it," he laughed. "Evolving upward, we're entering the upper layer of my planet's cake. Already we're standing on top of four billion years of life struggling up from the original hot rocks of my planet. It's my planet, not yours."

"Eh?"

"Smile. Dig! We'll reach the surface and find out whose planet it is." Dr. West stalked off toward the Control Room because he needed to talk to a human being.

"I found mammalian teeth!" Dr. West's lonely voice rose with boyish excitement. "We'll get out of here. Digging up through—life," he laughed, "From the bottom up——."

Mao III appeared dead. But in Dr. West's consciousness something writhed, *Tapeworm, kill me, fiend, please free me,* Mao III's thoughts screamed soundlessly into Dr. West's brain. *Have you no humane conception of euthanasia? Press the pillow against my face. So simple. Lean on it. Please.*

But Dr. West walked away from the agony of the man unable to die, his fingernails gouging his palms. *Why can't I kill him?* Dr. West knew he was vacillating within neurotic indecisiveness. He walked away past the Esk servant approaching to pour water into Mao III's throat tube as if tending a vegetable.

"When he dies, I'll be alone for four or five years." Dr. West walked in sweat. "Alone with more Esks every day unless I——."

New and beautiful little girls and boys scampered in the corridor, laughing and playing in their world. Stream-bed gravel rattled out of the long 45-degree tunnel for them to play with, followed by a thud of mineralized bone.

"Yes, giggle. Heavy rock for little girl. Heavy bone. I see an Oligocene beast with bones like a small tuskless elephant.

Perhaps you have a right to laugh. Perhaps this bone you are playing with is only an evolutionary dead end."

Watching the children play, more hungry children every day, he knew he had to kill more of these people. But he dreaded. "I am not God, what right have I?" He procrastinated.

One impatient day, Dr. West stared at a fanlike spread of little bones in a water-smoothed boulder. "Fragile as a monkey's hand. Dammit!" He felt anger at the prehistoric stream bed for eroding previous strata, treacherously restacking fossils and disordering time. "Protosimian fingers. But where are we? Up to the Miocene Period? No. I feel as though we're still buried at least sixty million years beneath the surface."

Dr. West procrastinated, slept poorly as he chilled the vault preparatory to luring the Esks back to the Audience Room where the white bear waited. He faced the day with the horror and fascination of an executioner, a torero, a bomber pilot. Shivering as he watched on the telescreen the closed-circuit transmission of the Esks jamming into the Audience Room, he felt his heart thudding. His face twisted in pain. Either I'm burdened with guilt feelings or my heart——.

His fingers played with the microphone switch. *If I didn't do this*——. He thought of the genocidal executioners stationed at Buchenwald and those other hundreds of camps in a long-ago world. *Was it delighted horror which squirmed within their armor of pride in their professional skill and devotion to duty?* "It is justified because there is not enough food for all. I must do it as quickly and painlessly as my skill will allow. They would all die anyway—some day."

"Look at me, I am white bear, Grandfather Bear from the sky, coming down to you, rise to me——."

Afterward he showed the surviving adults how to stack the bodies neatly in the freezing chamber which once had contained food. He tried to give first aid to children who had been crushed in the ecstatic stampede. He tried to comfort children whose mothers now were refrigerated. And he shoved a surviving male up the tunnel to dig. In loneliness he walked back to the familiar hatred of Mao III.

Dr. West laughed thinly. "The Esks say—those who—have died, have risen into happiness."

Tapeworm, you fear to kill me. It cannot be simply because I desire death that you refuse to release me. You are not that cruel? Mao III lay totally paralyzed, begging.

But the tube Dr. West had taped in the corner of Mao III's mouth implacably seeped liquid nourishment into Mao III's stomach.

Tapeworm, when your host dies do you fear everything dies? When I die, you die! I die: the universe dies. You, you billions of tapeworms who exist only in my consciousness, of course you try to keep me alive. You fear nothingness without me——.

"Taunting me won't make me kill you," Dr. West muttered.

But I need to die. Torturer! Let me die.

His face twisting with sympathetic pain, Dr. West walked away in enclosing loneliness like a clear ice cave.

He suspected at least three years stretched ahead before the Esk tunnel possibly could reach the surface. *I'll lose control of myself before then—alone with my victims,* Dr. West thought. *God help me, and up above, on the surface of the Earth, billions of smiling crowding faceless Esks!*

Dr. West walked into the bathroom and stared at the razor blade, *I'll leave now.* The razor blade gleamed between his fingertips.

"You sick bastard, you'd never find out what happens!" Dr. West threw the razor blade into the wash basin. He glimpsed his wryly thin face turning in the mirror as he walked out of the bathroom. He walked back toward the cruel little prison which was Mao III's body.

And on past it away from Mao III, he hurried into the corridor where smiling Esk children scampered away, and the handful of breeding adults carried sand and rock from the tunnel to the supply room where more heaps of sand replaced sacks of rice each day.

"Dig faster!" he shouted uselessly up the thin tunnel which had only elbow room for one Esk to dig at a time, and a rattling of descending rocks rushed down at him.

"Miocene dust, a local dry period, you stupidly smiling nongeologists. Yes, smile at the brown ridge on this rock. Smile stupidly because the little animal whose straight femur this was—who crept down to drink—may have been my ancestor. He sure as hell wasn't yours!"

Brown stone from hardened grasslands, then darker stone formed in temperate forests slid down the tunnel each day, gradually reddening to rain-leached laterite stone typical of rain forests. "The rainy sweep of the cycle, and now blue swampy clay."

In a discharge of gray slabs from the tunnel tumbled a massive thud, a giant's bone, followed by an odd-shaped white flat——. "Tooth as big as a spade! A shovel-jawed mastodon. Pliocene? Only thirty million years from the surface."

"Dig!" Dr. West laughed like a crazy man. "Dig, you smiling fools, at this rate only two more years to go. Your children will see the sun."

You won't, Dr. West thought, staring at the bent back of an Esk woman sweeping little rocks into a frying pan. His vision blurred as he almost saw Marthalik. He hurried away to the supply room. Shakily he counted sacks of rice. Always too many mouths were being born again. *He must face the hungry white bear of necessity. Grandfather Bear, if you are truly up there in the sky, accept these, your children.*

"Then what am I?" Scowling, he knew now he had the strength to reach the surface, if he clung to the belief his human world was still up there.

Dr. West walked to the Control Room to turn down the thermostats, again to prepare for the hungry bear. Something squirmed in his mind. With extra blankets, he bent over the withered remnant of Mao III. The paralyzed man's trapped thoughts frantically raced and squirmed like agonized white rats and burst out.

Dr. West stood in the squealing wind of Mao III's incoherent thoughts. A dagger appeared, as if a mind could stab itself to death with a visualized dagger. Now the dagger struck out at Dr. West and he felt a sharp stinging as if the beginning of a tiny stroke spreading within his own brain. He bowed his head in the rain of Mao III's inner sobbing.

Tapeworm, my friend, my last contact with life, please kill me.

Dr. West's hand lay gently on Mao III's throat and his

thumb and forefinger closed on the twin faint pulsations of the carotid arteries. He felt gratitude like sparks of laughter from Mao III.

Pressing in, his forefinger and opposed thumb narrowed the flow from heart to brain until the last vivid picture—armies of Chinese children with white balloons marching along the pink walls of the Great Square turned gray in Mao III's blood-starving brain. Dr. West glimpsed a single huge gray—what was it? A loud squawling seemed to emerge from within himself, and he realized he was seeing upward through the eyes of a baby instinctively loudly commanding food, warmth, love. A huge gray hand was descending.

Into his crib? Dr. West couldn't see. There was nothing. He opened his eyes at the waxen face of Mao III. Beneath Dr. West's fingertips there was no pulse in the throat arteries. From Mao III's brain, his own parasitic brain no longer could feel organized electrical activity. In fifteen minutes Dr. West confirmed irreversible clinical death.

He did not freeze Mao III's body. Somberly, he buried it under Pliocene sand in the supply room, and smiling Esks emptied soup pans full of broken rock from the tunnel face onto that growing pile of debris, and smiled and smiled.

"I'm alone with you now, you smiling Dream Persons. I just hope that others of me are alive on the surface."

"Eh?"

"So you don't understand. You see this sliver of bone from the rock. All that is left of a wolf, hyena, baboon, or undiscovered anthropoid who ran on the ground upright, I don't know. All I know, this fossilized bone and I are more closely related than you and I. The ancient imprints in my cells have been continuously reshaped by this Earth for four billion years. You—your ancestors have been part of this world less than fifty years. I belong here. Your progenitor invaded. Were you sent here for a purpose? Now you are digging upward. But where are you going?"

"Eh?"

Dr. West talked to the Esks a great deal now. It was another form of talking to himself. Thickened by fermented rice wine, Dr. West liked to shout at the ceiling. "Up there in the sky, come down here to hell, Grandfather Bear."

Into the tunnel four years had gone. "On the surface, four billion, eight billion, sixteen billion, thirty-two billion Esks?" But he knew thirty-two billion Esks was beyond the Earth's limit.

Suddenly his Esks were staring at the ceiling, and they were smiling, laughing and running about in confusion. Shouting with joy, some of the adults scrambled into the tunnel, struggling upward.

"No! No! You'll smother the man digging. We're still a thousand feet below the surface." Dr. West kept trying to pull them back, but they wriggled free, stronger and so much younger than he.

Those who couldn't force their way into the tunnel ran against the walls, climbed on chairs. As the excitement grew, shouting Esks tried to climb the walls while their children whimpered uncomprehendingly. In mounting desperation, an Esk man stretched his arms toward the ceiling, shouting unintelligibly.

Dr. West became afraid something really was happening at the surface, were the billions of Esks up there becoming frantic like this? *Marthalik!*

Dr. West grabbed an Esk woman. "Dammit, what's happening?"

"Eh? Let me go, please. All becoming one." Her excited laughter gradually muted to frustrated sobs as the adult Esks sagged down on the corridor floor. They seemed so strange staring at the ceiling without their smiles.

Esks slept in exhaustion where they lay, and their non-plussed children scampered around them whining and playing. It was Dr. West who had to drag the smothered bodies out of the tunnel. It was Dr. West who boiled the great tub of rice for the children, while the surviving adults sat stunned with disappointment. *At what———?*

Lethargic, they had to be loudly ordered to work in the tunnel. It seemed strange to see Esks who did not smile. They drooped as if they no longer had a purpose in life.

They cannot know what has happened at the surface, Dr. West thought. *But their organisms knew something was happening, and now it has stopped.* "You, there, hurry up, carry that sand to the supply room. We'll never reach the surface unless everyone works the way you used to——."

Something had happened up there. Down here the Esks ceased to mate. The last babies emerged too soon, as if cast out, spontaneous abortions, dead.

Dr. West resorted to shouts and shoves to make the Esks dig.

"Dammit, why have you lost your purpose in life?"

"Eh?"

Now the swarm of older children were better diggers than their parents, and the tunnel proceeded under Dr. West's constant direction. Their lives required so much more guidance and reassurance now from Dr. West, he began to feel like the father——.

"Dig! That's the way. We're nearer the surface every day." Pleistocene gravel less than a million years old was rattling out of the tunnel. "Dig my children and we'll see the Earth."

Sometimes Dr. West dreamed the surface was green with willow trees along a silvery brook and from his childhood he poked straight sticks deep into the water which bent them. He dipped his face in the cool water and raised his head. Behind him the surface of the Earth was barren and dry, all life obliterated.

"Which is it?" He awoke, and when he slept again the cities hummed with life as if he'd never been away, and the humming grew and spread shoulder packed against shoulder in a solid mass of Esks spreading through the streets. The surface of the Earth turned black with bobbing heads of Esks, and the humming rose while their heads drooped, and the Esks died in sagging masses melting into a golden honey, gleaming and flowing between the buildings and down the valleys. He began to run, looking for Marthalik. Like golden honey it covered the Earth, as he shouted for her. The humming grew louder coming down from the sky and Dr. West tried to look up——.

He blundered into the corridor toward the chattering voices of the Esks. They were carrying black clods from the mouth of the tunnel. He awakened fully. It was crumbling rock flecked with bone, blackened within as if containing the ashes of an ancient campfire.

His fingers picked out a glint of sharpness. "Flake of flint. Dig, my children! We've reached the Age of Man!"

He laughed. "Peking Man? True man? Who knows what man? Ancestor, we've passed you." He poked at slender humanoid femurs split for their marrow. "You Paleolithic cannibals! We're trying to pass you. By stepping on your heads, we'll get out."

Day after day the dark rock became lighter-colored, more sandy.

Out of the tunnel bumped chunks of compacted loess dust, the yellow windblown dust from the Gobi Desert, the deep soil of China. "The climate has dried. Cold dusty winds from the advancing Arctic may have driven prehistoric man away from this place. Is the ice approaching Peking?"

But the next day, in a crumbling yellow clod, which had been loess dust, gleamed a beautiful leaf-shaped javelin head with delicately pressure-flaked edges. "Sharp as the day you made it. And this sharp splinter, was it an awl? We're up among the real men now, who outsmart the cold, perhaps in intricately sewn wild reindeer skins."

Dr. West stared up the tunnel hole. "Am I the first amateur archeologist to make his dig from the bottom up?" he laughed excitedly. "Am I the first with a rear-end perspective of history, a proctologist's view of civilization?"

As the tunnel extended upward, shards of fire-burned pottery rattled down out of the hole. "We must be up into the Neolithic. Pots are used to store grain. Deliberate farmers must have produced a more assured food supply, and the rules of Malthusian starvation have eased. Because food production is increasing more rapidly, for the first time population is increasing rapidly, faster and faster. Dig!"

When Dr. West with his flashlight wormed his way up the slanting tunnel, wheezing through dust, slipping on loose rocks, squirming past Esk children who had been sent up to clear bottlenecks in debris slides, struggling upward for a mile through hot dusty air which made him gasp, his chest tightening with warning heart pains, he finally reached the buttocks of the Esk who was digging.

"Move aside. Let me look." Dr. West raised his flashlight to sun-dried yellow bricks. "Foundations. Permanent village."

But the bricks above were fire-blackened. When the Esk jabbed the crowbar up among them, crumbling bricks roared down, releasing a landslide of compacted chunks of kitchen midden against Dr. West. Struggling to free his leg, he found his fellow man.

"This green lump encloses a skull. Helmeted he was buried in the trash of *his* ancestors. The green oxide was copper, a helmet or a crown. Already we're digging up through the graves of men more sophisticated than Eskimos."

The crowbar clanged upward against masses of harder brick. "A village built upon a village."

Bricks thudded down, and Dr. West swept them between his legs, centered them rumbling down the tunnel. "More blackened brick and charcoaled wooden beams. This village has been raided, burned."

A clod of fire-darkened soil contained a triangular stain of rust. "The killers came with iron arrow points. We must be within 5000 years of the surface. Dig! We're only a heartbeat from the surface of man's long evolutionary climb."

A clod slashed his palm. It contained white shards sharp as glass. "We've broken into recorded history. Perhaps your head and shoulders are in 1100 B.C. among the descendants of the semimythical Yellow Emperor. Yes, armed with civilization these ethnic Chinese had migrated northward. They built fortifications on the future site of Peking."

The crowbar was dislodging masses of crumbling brick into the hole. "They rarely built with stone. After the roof beams burn, the protective roof tiles fall. Chinese castles dissolve in the rain," he laughed. "But in 300 B.C. the King of Yen began the Great Wall."

A charred beam slid into the hole. "North China was overwhelmed by the Hu tribes. In distant Europe were they called the Huns? Already we are past the time of Christ. Dig! Before we reach 605 A.D. the Grand Canal will reach Peking. The population is multiplying rapidly now. Dig!"

In the falling debris lay a green gourd-shaped vase unbroken, but under its surface glaze appearing spider-web cracked. Dr. West gently extricated its smooth beauty. "Already we must have reached the 1100s A.D. because this is a Kuan vase, and the crackle-lines in the porcelain are intentional."

The crowbar smashed upward, and burned wreckage fell down. "Genghis Khan has taken Peking."

Blue-and-white porcelain shards fell like rain. "Already we are through with the Mongols and you are poking your crowbar into the Ming Dynasty. We are less than 500 years from the surface."

Sand streamed down from a rodent's tunnel. Above them glowed a little round hole like a luminous eye. "It is daylight up there!"

Gently, Dr. West laid his hand on the shoulder of the Esk and took the crowbar from him. "I am your leader, your *angakok,* your Mao, and only I have the power to break through to the Present. Close your eyes. The Future is blinding."

Dr. West thrust up the crowbar through the worn brick paving of the Manchus, shouldered aside the thin new bricks of the Communists, and lifted his head into the dazzling sunlight.

The long pink walls within the Imperial City glowed with sunlight. The vast paved square lay golden with dust. Covered with motionless ripples of loess dust, the Great Square where millions had paraded before Mao's platform was shrouded with Gobi dust.

A distant chopping sound made Dr. West turn his head uncertainly, his ears confused by the echoes. His low angle of vision, with only his head above the widespread pavement of the enormous square, made the pink walls seem to lean inward. Arches appeared too close or too distant. Empty brown flower beds along the walls seemed tilted like brown stripes, as Dr. West blinked in the strange perspective of the Great Square and arches as if his head had risen in a Daliesque painting. His nervous gaze sought the sound. Chunk-echo! Chunk-echo!

So close he had not noticed in the foreground glowed clean white rib cages in the golden dust. In waves of dust floated smooth white ovals. He stared at the shadowed eyeholes of the skulls. *Esks or men?*

Thousands of skeletons lay all around him no matter which way he turned his head. The perspective made them appear to him as if they lay in concentric circles around him, as if fallen from a dance pattern. He blinked his eyes. Close to his hand a skeletal hand overlapped another's hand as if——. *Esks or men?*

Dr. West struggled up out of the hole and whirled, peering down at the smiling Esk in its darkness. "Stay back! The sun will kill you," he lied. "My command is wait. Send down this word." Already he could hear his other Esks chattering in the tunnel. "Until darkness, wait."

He stared at a fallen signboard. The withered paint still extolled Mao III's last Three-Anti's Campaign: *Anti-Imperialist. Anti-Revisionist. Anti-Intellectualist.* He dragged the flimsy signboard over the hole.

From the effort of dragging the signboard, Dr. West swayed like an old man, his heart pounding.

Chunk-echo! Chunk-echo! Turning, scanning for the chopping sound in the burning sunlight, he dizzied, the pink walls flowing past. He stopped.

On the distant pink wall, the dark shape, the shadow of the shape, bent up and down. Chunk-echo! Chunk-echo!

His throat clutching his soundless shout, Dr. West ran forward. Across golden ripples of dust, he ran toward the pink wall. He saw moving on the brown strip of the bare flower bed, shadowed upon the pink wall, up and down, the dark figure wielding a hoe.

Man or Esk?

Startled, whirling, cornered, the squat figure raised its hoe like a weapon.

It is a man, Dr. West thought as joy blurred his eyes.

He felt his face stretching. Smiling senselessly as an Esk, Dr. West staggered toward the man.

The ragged man backed against the pink wall. The sunlight glinted on his hoe's blade.

"We both are men," Dr. West blurted in Chinese.

The old man shifted his weight. On the chopped dirt, with his foot, he was trying to conceal something behind his incongruous blue tennis shoe. Dr. West extended his open hand, and the old man's eyes slitted in fright, his elbows rising, the gleaming snake's head of his hoe poised to strike.

"It is true I am an American——." Dr. West spread his open hands in a gesture of peace. "——a whiteman, but you and I—not Esks. We are men."

The old man's forehead creased vertically as if squeezed by conflicting beliefs, his foot guarding the sack. "These seeds are not to be eaten. They are for—seeds."

"May your crop be——," Dr. West fumbled into his pocket and handed the old man whatever he found there, "——be fortunate."

Hesitantly, the gnarled hand closed on the pencil stub. Dipping his head, the old man abruptly lowered his hoe and squatted down. From a grease-stained knotted rag he extricated a leathery strip. Twisting it apart, he proffered the larger part to Dr. West.

Solemnly the old man chewed.

Dr. West chewed the hard-smoked meat, salty as tears. "Where are—the people?" Dr. West's eyes burned.

"Planting." The old man seemed surprised that the question had been asked. "Outside the walls the dirt has more dampness for crops." His hand fingered the dry soil of what had been a flower bed in the Great Square. "But my wall keeps out the wind. My knees ache. Before the electricity stopped, I was a subway conductor, not a——."

"Whose skeletons?" Dr. West interrupted.

The old man's eyelids closed, wrinkling, and his forehead wrinkled as if he had begun pondering a deeper question. "You say you are an American. I never truly believed that the Americans sent the plague. Our bodies, the stench in the subway——. None of the Smiling People were sick. They cared for us as best they could."

"Then these are the skeletons of men?" Dr. West's heart contracted.

"No, Esks, of course!" The old man's face showed surprise at Dr. West's ignorance. "Their souls have flown, I think."

"The Esks are dead everywhere?"

"I do not think they are truly dead. They joined hands."

The old man glanced at the sky. "The flesh has been gone from their bones for a season."

Dr. West covertly expectorated the salty meat into his palm, and stared at the old man's leathery face.

"Who can say who is dead. In this little world———," the old man ruminated his salted meat solemnly, "———little can be understood———. Circles like dancers. Many little circles joined together like a net. But they did not dance."

"All the skeletons are in this square?"

"I think everywhere in Peking, and in other places all over the world, I am told. They did not dance, although they were smiling like bridegrooms and brides at the sky." The old man squinted upward.

Dr. West blinked from the skeletons of the Esks to the blinding sky. "What did you see—up there?"

"See? We old men know only the body dies. When men are hungry enough, meat can be salted and it makes no difference to the soul. A poor man like myself understands only how to survive on this Earth."

"What did you see?" Dr. West repeated, his voice rising.

"They are all around us, I think." The old man turned his weathered face. "Years ago when there were not so many, we called them the Smiling People. We called them the Dream Persons. Perhaps they were smiling because they were in a dream and they knew what was going to happen. Your face is angry."

"I'm not angry. I want to know!" Dr. West's chest pain was tightening.

"Nor I," the old man muttered, closing his gnarled knuckles around the handle of his hoe. "After the confusion, the lack of rations, some of us killed Dream Persons. Not enough. Pulling out a few hairs does not kill the head."

"What did you see!"

"It is too difficult to explain." The old man glanced sideways toward the pink arch. "Some day someone will repair the electricity. The subway cars will move. I will receive my ration tickets because I was—am not a peasant! In my subway car———." The old man stared past Dr. West's shoulder toward the center of the Great Square.

On the glaring sand out there was a dark movement.

Beside Dr. West, the old man raised his hoe with a hissing inhalation of fear or rage, and scurried out across the dust, running like a spider across the golden ripples of the Square toward the dark spots emerging like ants out of the pavement.

"Oh god, they're coming out of the tunnel." Dr. West saw his distant Esks wandering out into the glaring sunlight.

As the old man's diminishing silhouette reached them, his hoe's blade flashed high and struck. One small figure staggered, clutching its shoulder. The old man struck again with the hoe, and another figure slumped to its knees. Somehow the old man appeared entangled among them but his hoe struck down, and his back heaved up but his hoe did not rise. The old man's small figure lurched away.

Empty-handed, the old man ran back toward Dr. West, his face contorted. "More. Again! Returned." His breath hissing, he ran past Dr. West through the pink arch out of the Square.

Dr. West knew the old man had run for help, for other men to help slaughter his Esks. The old man could not know how many Esks were spreading out of the tunnel. *The consequences?*

Dr. West's heart pain clutched. He stared at his Esks emerging like lost children into the Great Square. Dr. West started toward them.

"Go back!" he shouted. "Go back down into the hole."

He tried to herd the spreading Esks back to the tunnel.

You are too late, he thought sadly at them. *Your purpose*——. "Go back!" he shouted in sudden anger. *You have destroyed my life,* he thought as he pushed helplessly at them. *Without malice, you have multiplied. All over the world your increasing numbers have hastened the Malthusian forms of death for man. All of my adult life, you have multiplied, confronting me with my inability to halt either your purpose or lack of purpose.* He was past anger. "Please go back."

His Esks were smiling at the empty sky. Their hands were linking. On all sides of Dr. West, they were forming little circles of Esks touching other little circles throughout the Great Square. They stood waiting.

"You are too late. Go back." Dr. West glanced from the

dark tunnel to the pink arch through which savage human men would attack.

The wind moved. The dry air crackled. Dr. West thought he heard a humming sound. It was coming from the Esks.

"My God!" All around Dr. West, the Esks—their hair was standing on end. They were smiling upward as the whip-crash of lightning blinded Dr. West. The lightning arose from them. His retinas and the visual part of his brain retained the imprint of the lightning flashing upward in static electric discharge as he lurched in the deafening boom of colliding air molecules refilling the gulf.

In the prickly scent of ozone, on his knees he groped, his hand closing on the soft back, the still-warm shoulder of an Esk woman as delicately boned as Marthalik had been so many years ago, and Dr. West cried out. His sight was returning but he was afraid to look upward.

All around him lay the fallen bodies of the Esks in their dance patterns. He thought he heard the humming sound above his head. Crouched in the dust, instinctively he clung to the Earth. His eyes closed tightly as fists. In tightening pain his heart labored.

Because he had almost seen the end, he thought he understood the beginning. Forty-two years ago the huge white shell had fallen down through the polar inbending of the Earth's magnetic lines of force, down through the weak inturning of the Earth's ionospheric radiation belts, smashing down on the Boothia Peninsula near the North Magnetic Pole. *Oh God, why couldn't it have fallen at the lifeless South Magnetic Pole?*

The humming sound seemed closer, huger.

Everywhere, he thought, *are your eggs wafting at random through the universe?*

He was afraid to look up as the humming grew inside his skull, and his evasive mind fled backward. *Forty-two years ago a young Eskimo stared at the Burned Place,* Dr. West thought frantically. *Peterluk, yes, with his grimy finger he would have poked whatever lay within the inner shell. He stood too close to———.*

Sharp heart pains reflected from Dr. West's chest down the inside of his left arm. His thoughts blurred as if something from above overlapped his brain. *From the nucleus of the cell—no, shell—a repatterning flowed—through Peterluk—to his gonads? Yes, for your purpose his genetic material was altered. His offspring would be patterned for your purpose.*

Dr. West's face twisted like a tired smile as his thoughts clung to the Boothia Peninsula. Peterluk's fanciful explanation of the first Esk emerging as a fully grown baby-man from the splitting hump of a dying monster, who was perhaps Peterluk, had been an inexplicable lie. Peterluk's wife's explanation was closer. Yes, Eevvaalik's explanation that the first Esk was born a month after a huge glass hypodermic repeatedly violated her, in artificial insemination, was only half a lie.

Yes, unknowingly Peterluk carried your purpose to Eevvaalik's uterus, Dr. West thought, *where it grew more efficiently than the babies of our purpose. Your Esks had the advantage of a one-month gestation period and more rapid maturation. In rapid generations of Esks, your purpose almost covered the Earth.*

His hand pressing his chest, his cramping heart pain, Dr. West grimaced at the golden dust. *Those unsophisticated Esks believed you were coming down for them. For them you had become the true myth of power like a huge white Grandfather Polar Bear coming down.*

Dr. West was afraid to look up. *Who are you? You, whose pattern was passed on through billions of Esks, your pattern that included such adaptability! Smiling, smiling, your Esks instinctively behaved in a nonviolent manner. Yes, nonviolence enabled their maximum survival in the peculiar environment of this particular planet at this time. How they multiplied! But your time fuse was burning in them. Cued somehow, your Esks joined hands in their billions. In vast dance patterns for—whom?*

Dr. West wanted to look up. *Joining hands,* he thought, *Esks looking upward. Upward toward your purpose, your purpose——.*

Dr. West looked up at the sky. Dazzling blue, the sky was visually empty, but Dr. West was seeing sparkling representational patterns imposed directly on his brain. With his eyes there was nothing up there with sufficient molecular density to be seen. But in the visual portion of his brain he was being communicated with——.

He understood. He was being shown a diagrammatic pattern of a brain, flowing thoughts, circling memories. Transmitting neuron cells were represented as strings of sparkling dots. Electric potentials within these cells discharged in sequence, symbolic dots blinking in succession like falling dominoes, symbolizing the flow of conscious thought. Life!

All around Dr. West in the Great Square the Esks lay dead. The vital electric flowings which had been their consciousness, the sum of their memories and experience, and their subconscious dreams, had stopped—forever?

From his memory the symbol for a single free electron was drawn, a dancing *e*. He supposed he was being shown the essence of life as the electron skipped along a neuron pathway in the brain.

Surprisingly, the electron was towing an unknown symbol. As if connected by an invisible string, the unknown symbol followed its electron along the neuron pathway, bobbing like a red balloon pulled by an erratic electron child.

A simplified pattern of a brain was outlined by billions of these moving symbols.

On the blackboard of his consciousness enlarged a more sophisticated diagram of an electron with its unknown satellite. The connecting string of force was behaving more like a rabid rubber band, so that the unknown symbol was whirling everywhere around its electron. Strangely, the electron was not near the center of this activity. All the varying orbits of the unknown symbol were distorted upward. The unknown symbol was being acted upon by another force from below.

As if rising from the center of the Earth, tiny particles were shown bombarding the unknown symbol. Illustrating gravitons? To Dr. West's surprise, the force of gravity seemed to be REPELLING the unknown symbol. Unable to break free from its electron, the unknown symbol strained upward in each distorted orbit as if trying to escape from the Earth. At the same time, all the unknown symbols were being moved along the neuron pathways of every living brain.

Dr. West cried out from the pain in his chest. He felt an abstract brain dying. Diagrammatically, he saw the vital differences in electric potential of neuron cells leaking out like water until all were level and in stasis. Unconsciousness. No directional electron flow. Random movement of free electrons up through the cell walls. If there had been an electroencephalographic machine available, it would have graphed this brain as clinically dead.

For the electrons which had outlined the brain's pattern, Dr. West saw their freed movements of "escape" were not wholly random. They were moving upward because of the repelling pressure of gravity upon their whirling satellites, the unknown symbols. And the orbits of the unknown symbols still overlapped adjoining symbols' orbits so that the whole pattern which had been in the brain still held its shape.

"This is the spirit?" Dr. West cried out in realization. Out of the diagrammatic brain, perhaps representing a dead Esk, rose the whole intricate pattern of the unknown symbols like the skeleton of the Esk's consciousness and memory. It retained its general shape even as the free electrons were skipping upward from one temporary molecular perch to another as they rose from the dead Esk's skull into the air. The overlapping orbits of the billions of unknown symbols maintained the general shape reminiscent of a brain even though the brain pattern was spreading as the electrons skipped upward through the thinning atmosphere.

Atomic perches were further apart in the stratosphere. Yet the enlarging orbit of each unknown symbol around its electron still overlapped the orbits of adjoining unknown symbols. The shape of a man's brain pattern, with all its intricate electroskeletal pathways, still was being maintained even though the diameter of his brain pattern had spread to hundreds of yards.

Continuously repelled outward by the diminishing force of gravity, the man's brain pattern was spreading over the sparse atoms in the near vacuum beyond the Moon. Now the immense brain pattern was being driven out of the solar system by the gravitational force from the sun, out into the hard vacuum between the stars where each Esk's mind pattern was expanding larger than a planet.

"Are they still alive?" Dr. West cried aloud. "Are they conscious?"

In his chest, in his mind he was given the feeling of pressure of billions of Esks' patterns like invisible balloons packing together due to the speed of their individual expansions. Their individual brain patterns could not overlap, perhaps because within each brain pattern the orbits of the unknown symbols had developed characteristics unique to that individual. Pressing outward against each other in every direction, the brain patterns pushed outward from Earth in contiguous expansion through the solar system. Except where repelled by gravity of the planets and the sun, the brain patterns filled the solar system like invisible bubble-foam. Beyond the solar system, they were pressing outward in every direction into the blackness of space.

Toward the gravitationless void between two distant stars the outermost patterns were expanding toward—Dr. West's heart hammered with excitement—toward an immense extrusion from another group of strange patterns stretching in from vast light-year dimensions of the Galaxy. This immensity was not born of Esks. Its billions of strange patterns extending had reached the brain patterns of the Esks.

Dr. West understood from whence his mind-pictures had been transmitted. Already the billions of Esks who must have died a year ago on every continent of the Earth, while his Esks clawed in frustrated rapture at their tunnel, had spread across the intervening blackness. From galactic space, contact through those Esks and through his Esks who had just died in the Great Square, still crowding from Earth into the stratosphere, had been made with Dr. West. He feared this contact would be lost forever when gravity forced away the last mind patterns of the Esks from Earth. "Wait!"

"Wait——." He did not know to whom he spoke.

His awareness was lifted through the blackness and dazzle of space. As if overwhelmed in a psychedelic journey, he soared outward toward the rim of the Galaxy. He remembered rapture. He remembered his passion of years ago when he strained with Marthalik in his arms. Again he was falling toward that Strange Sun. Again, as if he were sharing the subconscious dreams of the Esks, he was searching for the green planet.

Without Marthalik to support him, he fell past mountainous asteroids dotted with white domes. Like colossal barnacles they opened their gigantic green nets toward the strange sun below. As if trapping the sun's radiant energy, they turned their chlorophyllous green nets. And he glimpsed an opening in the whiteness of one of these rock-digesting domes. It was expelling spherical white eggs.

With unfolding purple fringes like immense curved sails, these gigantic organic-lime eggs slowly drifted away from the pressure of the strange sun's light, their purple sails diminishing into the blackness. *Its fleshy sail burned off,* he thought in recognition, *when its white shell fell through our atmosphere smashing down on the Boothia Peninsula———.*

He was falling toward the third planet. The planet was brown and dead.

For him, the picturization spun backward in time and the planet became green and densely populated. Slender and with a seemingly infinite variety of specialized organs, nevertheless they were all of one species, capable of skilled psionic electron adjustments of the genes of their unborn. He felt the frightened thoughts of a varied population. Rich in telepathic empathy, they had achieved gentle social control of themselves. But they had not achieved space flight. Their evolutionary climb was trapped on their single planet when the viral catastrophe exterminated them. All together they died. Their bodies had decomposed while their planet turned brown.

Their strange brain patterns rose across Dr. West's inner vision, expanding out through their solar system past the minimum gravity asteroids into the emptiness of space. His heart struggled with the nervous expectation of a miracle.

But death, irrevocable and complete, loomed at him. He saw that their brain patterns, like the patterns of the Esks, simply were rising in nonconscious death.

The only movement was outward expansion. He was shown a single brain pattern outlined in glowing dots. He knew each dot represented an electron surrounded by the activity of its whirling satellite, the unknown symbol whose orbit-shell still overlapped the orbits of adjoining symbols so that the dots remained in contact, the pattern retained its cohesiveness. As the pattern expanded, so did the diameters of its dot-orbits of the unknown symbols connecting its electrons. Intricate bead necklaces of dots still formed the electroskeletal pathways of what had been a brain.

But there was no flow of dots along the pathways, within the pattern no circulation of dots analogous to consciousness. Without an energy source, the dots simply retained their positions relative to the whole pattern. The only movement was expansion. Like the mental patterns of the Esks and everything that had ever died, in their billions these dead brain patterns were expanding outward through the universe in eternal death.

But we are alive! The immense thought overlapped his consciousness. *We have made death reversible. Almost——.*

Dr. West was made to feel their crowded patterns pressing against each other, each still lacking internal dot circulation and consciousness.

Due to their vast numbers, each was receiving more and more exterior pressure because the sum of their individual expansion rates was greater than the expansion of the outer surface of their whole group. Either there was a limiting velocity for brain patterns, which those on the outer surface had reached, or the faint gravitational fields of surrounding stars supplied at least a temporary caging effect. Something was maintaining a pressure within the group.

Within the vast group, he felt the individual patterns being pressed and pressing warmer and warmer against each other. Not warmth in a human sense, this pressure-energy was being released not as warmth but as movement of the symbolic dots within their brain patterns. Along familiar pathways, the bead strings of dots were flowing faster and faster throughout each brain pattern in a circulation similar to consciousness. *We are alive!*

Dr. West's erratic heart struggled with excitement. With the primitive desire of LIFE, his mind and body contorted with joy.

But then he saw that the pressure-energy was provided by the repelling gravitational forces from the stars. Between the stars in all directions the vast group continued to expand outward into the infinity of space. Another massive pain cramped his blood-starving heart muscle. As if personally defeated, he saw their diminishing pressure-energy; unconsciousness and final death were awaiting as the finite group expanded in the infinite emptiness of space.

He understood their fatal problem. Although repelled by gravity, they were spreading out between the stars along the channels of least gravitational pressure. Already the group's immense outer surface had expanded so many light-years through the Galaxy there was lessening of the vital pressure within. As they expanded, the pressure which gave them the energy of consciousness could only decline. The number in the group was finite. Space seemed infinite, he thought sadly.

To maintain and stabilize their inner pressure they would have to fill all of space. But their brain patterns could not reproduce themselves. Their own numbers could not increase. Their individual expansion rates were reaching their limits. As pressure-energy against a brain pattern lessened, the inner circulation of dots of consciousness slowed.

Even though the brain patterns of other dead creatures arisen forever from a billion planets throughout the Galaxy were being swept up and by inertia packing against the outer surface of the expanding group, the pressure within continued to decline. For all, death was returning.

Now Dr. West thought he understood the purpose for the Esks within the larger purpose which was immortality. He understood the purpose of dying in cohesive billions at one time, all over one planet, the Esks——. "Their brain patterns fill a little more of space," he whispered, "to help maintain the pressure of life for you."

But they too are alive, the immense thoughts soared. *Billions of—souls rising from your planet into immortality.*

"You gave the Esks life on my planet," Dr. West sighed, "and you have taken them away." He realized those strange patterns out there were unable because of repelling gravity to reach in and kill the life-forms on a billion planets. "To increase the pressure, to maintain your consciousness, if you were able would you have murdered all of us?" Gravity kept them away——. "You gave so little. One white shell falling toward the Boothia——."

You! Man of so little faith in life over death, see! Believe! Eternal life is triumphing for everyone. For you——.

In his mind he was shown, distant in space, an insensible white dome feeding in perpetual isolation on its rocky asteroid. As it always had, the dome emitted a white egg. As the egg unfolded its purple sail, Dr. West realized it must be drifting through the invisible brain patterns.

"You reached in," Dr. West muttered. "Against the gravity of Earth, you reached us indirectly by means of——."

He was shown the symbolic lines of dots from space overlapping the huge white egg as it drifted through the Galaxy. The overlapping mind pattern was concentrating a node of dots within the immature reproductive cells of the egg. Within an incomplete sexual cell, within one chromosome he saw the glowing dots flowing through the genes of the egg's inherited characteristics.

As his view magnified within a gene, he saw the glowing dots flowing through the gene's complex molecules of life. As if he were falling inward among vibrating atoms, he saw the glowing necklaces of symbolic dots among the molecules. He saw these controlled lines of electrons flowing, influencing the movements of other electrons among the ionized atoms of the genetic molecules. Here within the gene, within its molecules, he saw the egg's characteristics of inheritance were being altered.

Not like cosmic radiation causing a random mutation, here a whole set of interrelated characteristics had been altered purposefully for a purpose beyond the egg.

Outwardly unaffected, the egg sailed on through space. Instinctively, its sun-sails altered its course toward another drifting egg in their age-old necessity for inheritance variation by mating, for adaptive survival of their species. Mating would have been impossible for the adult white domes immobile on their scattered asteroids. Only in the drifting egg stage could they meet. In space, he was shown two stony shells on converging courses. The two impenatrable eggs bumped. Between them flashed lightning. Exchanging electrical imprints of their genetic essence, they had mated for an instant. They drifted apart into the vastness of the Galaxy. Each carried the new characteristics the strange brain patterns had designed for them to transmit throughout the universe.

Within the huge white egg, he was shown that the incomplete sex cell by mating had been doubled. Doubling itself, the new half completed the whole. One half resembled the genetic arrangement from the other egg. The completed cell replicated while the huge shell drifted, and on collision course, smashed against an unoccupied asteroid. The new dome grew, and in time it began to emit eggs with unnatural rapidity.

Opening their purple sails, the altered eggs sailed unnatural courses. In the past, sailing by light-pressure from the stars through space, eggs always had steered away from gravitational fields. For species survival this was necessary because the white domes could feed and grow only on asteroids of minimal gravity. But genetically altered eggs steered toward gravity forces, toward stars and then away from these blazing suns when radiation stabbed with unbearable intensity through the flesh within the inner shell.

Down toward a billion planets the aberrant eggs were plunging, now attracted by gravity but at the last moment repelled by the radiation belts trapped by magnetic forces around gravity planets. Readjusting their sun-sails, deflected eggs streaked on orbiting courses above the radiation belts shaped by the planets' magnetic lines of force.

Down through the polar funnel in the Earth's radiation belts, down through the inward turning of the Earth's magnetic lines of force, THE egg had plunged toward the North Magnetic Pole. Its fleshy sun-sail burning away in the atmosphere, the egg had smashed down on the Boothia Peninsula. In time turned back forty-two years, Dr. West was shown Peterluk, with a puzzled smile, poking the fleshy contents of the inner shell with his finger.

No mind pattern of the unknown symbols was waiting to invade Peterluk's genes. The Earth's repelling gravitons would have driven out any stowaway brain pattern while the egg still was above the ionosphere.

But the life-force designed by the strange brain patterns was there. Indirectly they could cause mutations in Earth's sanctuary.

Within the egg's electrogenetic material, its altered chromosomes quivered. The slippery outer mass which Peterluk's finger touched had a cellular consistency similar to the batteries of an electric eel. This egg had not mated. It had not discharged. Since the parent domes are stationary on their asteroids, it is only through the drifting eggs that genetic imprints are exchanged—with electric jolts!

Dr. West felt Peterluk's surprise and chagrin to regain consciousness lying on his back on the cold rocks of the Burned Place. "Evil jelly flesh!" Peterluk's voice echoed through time as he struggled to his feet. "May foxes devour you!" He had fled.

That night, Peterluk did not confess his mysterious fainting weakness to his wife. Boasting, he warmed himself in her smile, and in her arms. In the rhythmically gasping darkness, of the millions of his sperm the successful one to penetrate Eevvaalik's monthly ovum carried his altered chromosomes. The first Esk was conceived with the designed characteristics of adaptability, fetal growth efficiency resulting in a one-month gestation period, a rapid maturation rate with the potentiality of rapid multiplication—and an unlit fuse. This fuse was the hope of the strange brain patterns distant in space. On Earth, population maximum would ignite it. As long as the delicate psychic emanations of the Esks increased, their fuses were dormant. When their total emanation shrouding the Earth no longer increased, the Esk population would have reached its zenith; the maximum number had been achieved. The physiological fuse within each Esk on the surface of the Earth had ignited.

Instinctively joining hands for death, the Esks had fallen-risen. Their freed brain patterns had ballooned into space. Too well, Dr. West understood the purpose for which the Esks had died.

But they are alive! the great thoughts surged through Dr. West's brain. *We—they—everything which has ever lived will become alive. When we have filled the universe there will be eternal life.*

From distant space the great thoughts flowed——.

Dr. West felt their hope and excitement as he lay in the golden dust of the Great Square, his contorted body gasping for breath. From his heart the massive pain so filled his chest that he felt himself being squeezed out of himself.

The contribution of even a single life's pattern, the great thoughts surged, *increases the vital pressure of immortality for all.* He felt their sympathy. *Believe! Life can be sustained beyond physical death—for all.* The feeling was excitement, hope.

In his physical agony, he knew he should try to reach his hand into his pocket for the bottle of nitros, the trinitroglycerine pills for his heart. It might not be too late to survive a little longer. His thoughts were dimming as he felt their enveloping sympathy. He was not yet alone. Surrounding patterns of his departing Esks still were transmitting the thoughts of those beyond—to him—with sympathy. Why else, he realized, would he have been communicated with in this last possible moment as the last expanding mind patterns of the Esks crowded upward from the Great Square in continuous contact across space——.

Writhing on its side, his breathless body contracted in a fetal position. He glimpsed the blue sky so beautiful. He laughed like a naked savage with wonder and awe, but soundlessly. He laughed as his heart's terminal fibrillations stagnated the flow of blood to his brain into visual darkness, and he did not take the pill.

Freed from lifelong fear he laughed with amazement at the universe of which he was a part. *Marthalik?*

His last human thoughts rose above the bodies of the Esks in the Great Square. He imagined a sharply questioning voice in Chinese. Hard hands were attempting to lift his body. But his heart had stopped long ago.

In the dissolution of death, the electrical flowing within his brain was completed. It—he had risen outside. His upward expanding thoughts laughed with joy at the purpose of the Esks and those beyond.

Hopefully he pondered with wonder at the tiny Earth. *Now all we need to know is* OUR *purpose in life.*

BRILLIANT SCIENCE FICTION FROM THE BALLANTINE LIST

THE WANDERER
(Hugo Award)   Fritz Leiber

A CASE OF CONSCIENCE   James Blish
(Hugo Award)

MORE THAN HUMAN   Theodore Sturgeon
(International Fantasy Award)

THE WHOLE MAN   John Brunner
(Hugo Runner-up)

DAVY   Edgar Pangborn
(Hugo Runner-up)

FAHRENHEIT 451   Ray Bradbury

CHILDHOOD'S END   Arthur Clarke

In Science Fiction
Ballantine Books Brings You
the Best of the Established Authors
and the Most Exciting New Writers

THE NIGHT OF THE WOLF	Fritz Leiber	50¢
WORLD OF PTAVVS	Larry Niven	50¢
FAHRENHEIT 451	Ray Bradbury	60¢
THE LONG RESULT	John Brunner	50¢
NEEDLE IN A TIMESTACK	Robert Silverberg	50¢
TARNSMAN OF GOR	John Norman	75¢
BERSERKER	Fred Saberhagen	60¢
OUT OF MY MIND	John Brunner	60¢
B.E.A.S.T.	Charles Eric Maine	75¢
TO OPEN THE SKY	Robert Silverberg	75¢
DOLPHIN BOY	Roy E. Meyers	75¢
TREASURE OF THE BLACK FALCON	John Coleman Burroughs	75¢
THE WORM OUROBOROS	E. R. Eddison	95¢
MISTRESS OF MISTRESSES	E. R. Eddison	95¢
CHTHON	Piers Anthony	75¢
RESTOREE	Anne McCaffrey	75¢
THORNS	Robert Silverberg	75¢
THE ESKIMO INVASION	Hayden Howard	75¢
OUTLAW OF GOR	John Norman	75¢
THE SEED	Dan Thomas	75¢

MORE BALLANTINE SCIENCE FICTION

❖❖❖❖❖❖❖❖❖❖❖❖❖❖

SPECIAL RELEASE
OF EARLY CLASSICS
FROM
THE BALLANTINE LIST

U2341   **AHEAD OF TIME**   Henry Kuttner   50¢
The first collection of one of science fiction's greatest.

U2342   **BRAIN WAVE**   Poul Anderson   50¢
The novel that put Anderson on the s.f. map.

U2343   **GLADIATOR-AT-LAW**
Frederik Pohl & C. M. Kornbluth   50¢
One of the three magnificent novels by this famous team of collaborators.

U2344   **NERVES**   Lester del Rey   50¢
The book about a nuclear reactor that had minions of the Pentagon in a tizzy.

U2345   **THE GREEN ODYSSEY**
Philip José Farmer   50¢
A joyous, roistering science fantasy adventure in the grand old tradition.

U2346   **TO LIVE FOREVER**   Jack Vance   50¢
A darkly ingenious extrapolation on the theme of immortality.

———◆———

Send for our complete catalog

To order books by mail, enclose price of book plus 5¢ a copy postage and send to Dept. CS, Ballantine Books, 101 Fifth Avenue, New York, New York 10003. (On orders of 4 books or over we pay postage.)